THE PRESIDENT'S SANDBOX

A NOVEL

GARY WAYNE FOSTER

HELLGATE PRESS ASHLAND, OREGON

THE PRESIDENT'S SANDBOX

Published by Hellgate Press
(An imprint of L&R Publishing, LLC)

Hellgate Press
PO Box 3531
Ashland, OR 97520
email: sales@hellgatepress.com

Layout Design: Harley B. Patrick
Cover Design: L. Redding

Library of Congress Cataloging-in-Publication Data available from the publisher on request

ISBN: 978-1-55571-796-4

Printed and bound in the United States of America
First edition 10 9 8 7 6 5 4 3 2 1

To my sister Carol Jean Bolton

CONTENTS

1. Exhaustion and Perception 1
2. Dueling with Gifford 8
3. House on Stilts 18
4. Think Tank 24
5. Rex Hotel 30
6. Know Your Enemies 38
7. Message to Congress 44
8. The Guns of Co Roc 51
9. B5T8 57
10. The Congo Comes Calling 62
11. Xe Dap Tho and the Xe Cong Nong 68
12. Yankee Clipper 72
13. Letter to Sarah 78
14. Damned North Koreans 82
15. The Pines of Dong Loc: He Won't be Coming Back 89
16. Executive Order 95
17. Jade Spring Hills 101
18. Resolution Fourteen 107
19. A Last Visit 114
20. Canned Peaches 121
21. Memorandum for the President: The Situation at Khe Sanh 125
22. Chuc Mung Nam Moi 131
23. Cheap Smokes, Beer and Whiskey 137
24. An Even More Remote Outpost 142
25. René l'Escalier 149
26. A Solution for the President 156
27. Millennia Past: Madison, Wisconsin 159
28. The Prime Minister 164
29. Old Ebbitt Grill 173
30. Heritage of Earth 178
31. Building 213 182
32. More and More Amor 188
33. Beagles 192
34. Three Marines 196

35. The Khe Sanh Terrain Model 200
36. West Covina and Mobile, Alabama 206
37. Arrival at the North Portico 210
38. Mexican Standoff 214
39. Press Briefing 221
40. Seven Lakes Country Club 228
41. Stairway of the Dragons 235
42. Flatlander 243
43. Bob Arrotta and the Skyraider 248
44. The Fox 253
45. Playmate 261
46. Runnin' the Injuns Off 267
47. Whispers in the Wind 272
48. "Hey, Hey, LBJ..." 277
49. Star 282
50. They're All Probably VC 286
51. Lion of Khe Sanh 291
52. Sunsets...Before They End 297
53. Tanglefoot 301
54. Thanh Pho My: A Poem for Sally 304
55. Thrown Off Course 313
56. PAPA 27 0308 ZULU FEB 68 322
57. Minot, North Dakota 327
58. M-1 Thumb 336
59. Turning Point 340
60. Sermon in the Clouds 343
61. Back and Forth 348
62. Tran Quy Hai 353
63. MACV 358
64. Creation of Strike Group CT43 363
65. Medevac 366
66. Friends and Family Gather Here 370
67. Ruy Lopez Opening 379
68. Rain 384
69. Burial Ground 388

70. No Way to Start a Memorable Day 391
71. Crossing the Trail 395
72. Binh Tram Hai Moui 406
73. How's All This Going to End? 412
74. The Political Officer 418
75. Battlefield Interlude 421
76. We Will Make It to N3 426
77. Agony 429
78. Beo Nhay Tien 433
79. The TIO 437
80. Khu Tan Cong So Ba 449
81. Something's Fixin' to Happen at Khe Sanh 453
82. Hours to Come 456
83. Ocelot Cell: The B-52s Rise Up 459
84. Come and Take It 465
85. We Did Some Damage Today 467
86. True Sound of War 473
87. Intrigue Six 477
88. The Honarable William Vacanarat Shadrach Tubman 485
89. Rescue...or Relief? 489
90. A Vigilant America 497
91. FPO San Francisco 503
92. We've Got Some Difficult Days Ahead 508
93. Get the Heck Out of Dodge 513
94. Resurrection and Retaliation; Redemption and Reconciliation 518
95. Hanging Gardens 524
96. America's Finest 529
97. Dewey Beach 534
98. The President's Sandbox 539
Afterword 543
Appendices A and B 545
Acknowledgments 549
List of Historical Characters 551
About the Author 553

THE PRESIDENT'S SANDBOX

A NOVEL

GARY WAYNE FOSTER

Honoring the United States 26th Marine Regiment (Reinforced)
and other American Defenders of Khe Sanh on the
Fiftieth Anniversary of the Siege
(1968-2018)

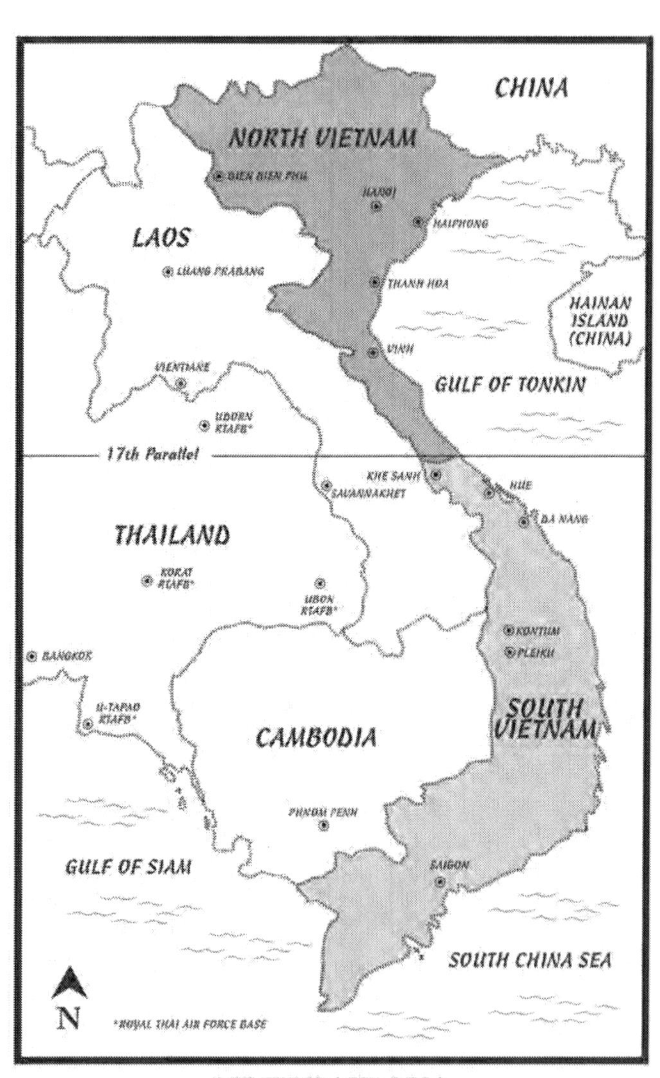

SOUTHEAST ASIA

CHAPTER ONE

EXHAUSTION AND PERCEPTION

The endless meetings in the White House since the spring and summer of 1967 consumed President Lyndon Baines Johnson. Exhausting, they stretched late into the night, often resuming before six the next morning. The subject of the meetings was always the same: the war in Vietnam.

Richard Helms, Director of the Central Intelligence Agency, attended one such gathering in the Situation Room that lasted three hours in mid-December, just days before President Johnson was to travel to Australia, and not long after his first daughter's wedding.

Concern focused on decisions made by Hanoi that would affect the conflict with the Americans. The North Vietnamese, assuming a more belligerent stance, were declaring a new military policy.

Aerial photographs from U.S. reconnaissance flights, spread out on the conference table, confirmed a sharp increase in enemy activity south of the Demilitarized Zone. Certain battle loomed in Quang Tri Province, one of five South Vietnam provinces in the northern region of the country known to the American military as the One Corps Tactical Zone. The U.S. Marines' encampment in the extreme northwest corner of the CTZ was vulnerable. That place was called Khe Sanh.

At the conclusion of the meeting, the President's senior advisors packed their briefcases and put their suit jackets back on. Some attendees slipped into a dining area called Navy Mess for coffee.

The CIA Director assembled his papers and stuffed them into a black folder.

Born in St. Davids, Pennsylvania in1913, Richard McGarrah Helms attended schools in Europe. He became fluent in French and German. After graduating in 1935 from Williams College, he secured a position as a European correspondent for United Press International. Helms covered the 1936 Summer Olympics in Berlin. He was among a group of journalists who interviewed Adolf Hitler after the so-called Rally of Honor at Nuremberg. Helms received his officer's commission in the United States Navy in 1942. A year later, his language skills in demand, the Navy transferred him to a mysterious organization: the Office of Special Services. His early assignments in the OSS were the beginnings of a lifetime of espionage.

Shortly after World War Two, the OSS was dissolved. The Central Intelligence Group took its place. It morphed into the Central Intelligence Agency. Officially recognized in 1947, the CIA's covert activities weren't employed until 1949. Richard Helms, struggling through the nascent years of the CIA, forming its unorthodox methodologies, was in the middle of it all.

A precisionist, Helms believed the CIA must provide a President finished, non-politicized intelligence based on exacting analysis of all relevant data.

The Bay of Pigs and the Cuban missile crisis, the assassination of Ngo Dinh Diem in Saigon in 1963 and, three weeks later, that of John F. Kennedy in Dallas, moved Helms steadily into the intelligence spotlight. President Lyndon Johnson appointed Richard Helms to directorship of the CIA in June 1966. A year later, the accurate predictions he made about the Arab-Israeli Six Day War propelled Helms to the pinnacle of his trade.

Now, holding his folder, Helms stood alone in contemplation just outside the Situation Room. He caught sight of Marvin Watson, the President's appointments secretary and de facto Chief of Staff, and George Christian. However, he focused mostly on Walt Rostow, the President's National

Security Advisor, and Arthur Lundahl. The two men were talking in hushed tones.

Helms crooked his index finger at both men.

"Walt, Arthur. We need to talk."

Helms adjusted his glasses. "You know, map scales leave a lot to be desired."

Rostow and Lundahl looked quizzically at the director.

"Sir?"

Helms dismissed the inflection, the word stated more as a question.

"It takes time for someone to acquire a feel for geographic information shown on maps. Understanding terrain and elevation is difficult, but distances, well, that may even be harder. For foreign visitors to the United States, traveling from Los Angeles to San Francisco by road might seem easy. A matter of only a few hundred miles between the two cities, right? But, a full day is required to make the trip. Get my drift, gentlemen? It's the scale that's difficult to perceive."

Lundahl nodded his understanding.

"Mr. Director, I..."

"No, Arthur. Let me finish my point."

Helms could be loquacious at times. "Europeans think in terms of kilometers, not miles, which are longer...miles that is. Europe is smaller in area than the U.S. Distances seem less, but the numbers indicating those distances are greater. Map scales are, let's just say, different."

Lundahl scratched his head. Kilometers, miles, scale...was this going to be a long lecture?

"Many Americans understand that China, Brazil and Canada are big countries. But, how big? Bigger than Texas? It takes forever to drive across the President's home state."

Walt Rostow was growing impatient.

"Mr. Director, the President..."

Helms held up his hand.

"Both of you have traveled abroad. From Brussels, four countries can be accessed within an hour, right? One can go to Paris, have lunch and be home easily before dark. No one in their right mind would drive from Washington D.C. to Connecticut on Thanksgiving for turkey and back on the same day."

Rostow massaged his forehead while Lundahl straightened his tie.

"Now, about Vietnam. The President's struggling to understand the geography. He has to make adjustments away from perceptions about distance, land and space. We need to help him see the entire CTZ, especially around Khe Sanh, more clearly in the context of coordinates, elevation, difficult terrain…and distances."

What was Helms going on about? Why the sermon?

Helms's pedestrian speech, bordering on tedium, changed in tempo.

"You'll recall General Westmoreland's plans for cutting the Ho Chi Minh Trail to stop North Vietnam's flow of men and materiel to the South. Khe Sanh was to blunt North Vietnam's efforts."

"Yes, Sir," Rostow responded. "The President decided against that action last April."

"Right, Walt. Even you said it could be the most damaging decision in the war."

"His decision could work against us, Mr. Director."

"Listen, North Vietnam's 325C Division, which pulled back after they were mauled around Khe Sanh last spring, has returned. They lost close to one thousand men during the fights in the hills. They're still a threat. Ever since Operation Scotland began on the first of November, the President has been acutely worried about the continued influx of NVA into the area.

"We expect the entire 304th Division to be in theater soon. The 320th Division and the 675th Artillery Regiment will completely invest in early January. Further, the North Vietnamese high command has been studying various battlefield scenarios to determine points of aggression."

Helms paused. "And, there you have it. Before the New Year starts, that's how 1968 is already shaping up. In Hanoi's eyes, its military preparations over the past ten years will have been for nothing if they don't accelerate their agenda.

"Something big is about to happen in Quang Tri Province. It could spell disaster for the Marines and determine the fate of the President's administration."

Helms fell silent for a second. "Election year is coming up, gentlemen."

Walt Rostow spoke in an aloof tone.

"Well aware, Sir."

Helms pointed his finger at Rostow's chest.

"Walt, you've been vocal about our involvement in Vietnam, that we should use our military more effectively. Did you not provide the President with an analysis of our defensive measures at Khe Sanh in the face of probable attacks?"

"Indeed, I did. I pointed out that currently the First and Third Battalions of the Twenty-sixth Marines are at Khe Sanh. The Third Battalion, mobilized the previous May, was pulled out in early September. They deployed again on the thirteenth of December. The movement was phased so as not to alert the NVA that we were augmenting our forces. Our analysis confirmed we should reinforce Khe Sanh and not Camp J. J. Carroll which we originally thought was the primary target.

"I'm still concerned that we don't have sufficient strength at Khe Sanh against an attack by two or three NVA divisions. Back in November, four NVA regiments, six thousand troops, attacked Dak To. The enemy lost about seventeen hundred men killed while we lost close to four hundred KIA. But some would argue the NVA fared better."

Richard Helms cocked a curious eye.

"Why's that, Walt?"

"The North Vietnamese know that any direct confrontation with the Americans in the coastal plains of Vietnam will be ruinous to them. They seek the rugged terrain of the highlands that do not favor our forces. They want to entice us closer to the border with Laos. This is the scenario for Quang Tri Province, possibly the prelude to Khe Sanh."

Satisfied with an explanation he already knew, Helms smiled.

"OK then. You know what I'm talking about. Look, we don't have the luxury to explain to the President every little thing that's occurring over there.

"He appreciates a good aerial photograph, but to him the ground is flat. The details gleaned from high altitude photographs are difficult for him to grasp. We need a clear visual aid to inform the President. Got me?"

Helms spoke out of context. "The manner in which the war is being managed is...well, quite frankly..."

"Mr. Director," Arthur Lundahl spoke up. "Why not an enlarged map... wallpaper size? A map free of unnecessary information. Just the key locations and main roads. Maybe the maps we use are too cluttered with details. We can enhance shading to better represent the terrain, use miles instead of kilometers, if that would make it easier for the President."

"Arthur, my boy, you may be on to something."

Walt Rostow and Arthur Lundahl looked at each other in mild surprise. It was a simple idea, really.

Richard Helms left the west wing of the White House and climbed into the waiting limousine near the southwest gate. He caught sight of Arthur Lundahl. Helms rolled down a back window.

The cold December air froze his breath, its white vapor swirling around his face.

"Lundahl, come over here for a minute, please."

"Sir...Mr. Director."

"Arthur, we're ex-Navy officers. We understand the need to manage events properly. It's incumbent on us to make sure the President has easily understood information. You analyzed thousands of photographs during World War Two. You've written a number of papers about photo interpretation. You created the National Photographic Interpretation Center, NPIC, as you call it. You're the top dog there.

"The special commendation you received from President Kennedy during the missile crisis speaks highly of your analytical skills. Your group received a Presidential Unit Citation. Here's the deal, Arthur. We've got a bad situation. Your map idea makes sense."

"I'll look into it, Sir."

Lundahl stood back from the limousine. The rear window slid up, then abruptly down.

"Oh, Arthur, your analysis in that meeting was excellent...Merry Christmas to you and your family."

The heavy iron gates swung open. The black vehicle exited the White House grounds.

"Holy cow," Lundahl said just above his breath. "I can't believe it. Helms led me by my nose and I opened my big mouth. Now, I've got a project on my hands."

The limousine made its way past President's Park and the monument commemorating the U.S. Army First Division, the Big Red One, and on to Constitution Avenue.

The easiest way back to the CIA was to turn toward the Lincoln Memorial, cross the Roosevelt Bridge to the George Washington Memorial Parkway and proceed up the Potomac River to Langley, Virginia.

Had Richard Helms made the journey a few hours later, he would have witnessed colorful Christmas lights adorning the homes on the opposite bank. Helms always enjoyed the scenic drive along the Potomac valley near Fort Marcy, especially during the holiday season, but his thoughts, now centered on a possible NVA ground attack against the Khe Sanh Combat Base, precluded such pleasure.

CHAPTER TWO

DUELING WITH GIFFORD

The jungles of western Quang Tri Province turned tranquil just before dawn—very tranquil—but not completely quiet. The only sounds heard were those of small birds, the occasional rustle of palm fronds and the low roar of the Quang Tri River as its muddy water sluiced through the cataracts below the canyon walls.

The heavy rains subsided during the night. A break in the clouds allowed some sun. Still, everything was saturated.

Captain Jason Becker led his Marine patrol on a mission to reconnoiter a section of Highway Nine far from the Khe Sanh Combat Base. Becker looked at his map. He and his men were on the north bank of the Quang Tri River just downstream of the confluence with the Da Krong and the Rao Quan Rivers. Becker confirmed his location in the eerie landscape by spotting two islands in the river that barely showed up on his map.

Lieutenant Gerry Gifford, who Captain Becker had placed at point, gasped for air as he ran back to the patrol. His M-79 grenade launcher and M-16 assault rifle, both slung over his shoulder, bounced on his back. Gifford always carried both weapons. He reached Captain Becker's position just below the cliff.

"Captain," he urgently whispered. "Something's happening on the other side of the river."

Captain Becker returned with Gifford to the river's edge to investigate. They scanned the tropical landscape from behind large boulders, looking for movement, for patterns. They heard the muffled but unmistakable commotion of personnel handling military equipment. Soon, they saw through the early morning grayness camouflaged figures toiling in the jungle.

Captain Becker strained his eyes.

"The NVA must have been on the move for a few days. What the hell are they doing, Giff? What's their strength?"

"Not sure," Gifford responded. "Maybe a couple of companies, half a battalion. Sure as hell seems to be a lot of 'em over there, Sir."

"What do you see, Gifford?"

"A couple of .30 cals, Sir. I don't see heavier machine guns...but there!"

Gifford quickly pointed. "Over there, Skipper. See 'em? Mortars."

"Eighty-two millimeters! Shit me alive, Gifford. We'd be crazy to start a firefight against that kind of firepower. Plus, we don't know what they got hidden in the jungle. There's no intelligence about NVA units operating here."

Captain Becker, assessing his men's position, looked downstream, then over his shoulder up to the steep hills toward the flat plateau on which sat the Khe Sanh Combat Base.

"Lieutenant, we don't have the advantage."

"Yeah, with Highway Nine behind us, I'll bet they're settin' up for some kind of ambush."

"Gifford, what do they know that we don't know?"

Captain Becker, low to the ground, took another quick glance at the enemy through the brush. Sweat rolled down his dirty face.

"Gifford," Becker said in a whisper. "Let's get back to the platoons. Give the arty guys some coordinates and let them take the bastards out. If we maneuver, they'll cut us down."

Captain Becker and Lieutenant Gifford moved stealthily back from the river. Becker whispered again, "Gotta find Agostino and his radio quick. Gotta call in fire missions. Go, Gifford! Stay low!"

"Got it, Skipper."

Gifford started to run for the forward observer and the radioman. But, it was too late. The distinctive metallic sound of mortar rounds being dropped down the hollow NVA mortar tubes signaled what was going to happen next.

Suddenly, the valley resonated with loud explosions. Both men hit the ground.

Mortar rounds tore up the landscape, but way short of the Marines. The pungent smell of explosives quickly pervaded the area. The NVA sprayed the nearby brush with machine gun fire. Small bullets peppered the trees and ripped the ground apart in spurts of mud. Becker and Gifford could hear the bullets as they zinged overhead. The recognizable short, staccato sounds of AK-47 assault rifles broke out. It all happened fast.

"The bastards! How the hell did they spot us so quickly? They're gonna find the range and march their mortar rounds right up our ass."

Becker yelled louder. "Gifford, run like hell. Get me the FO. Get Agostino!"

Both men, Gifford in front, ran toward the Marines who were protecting themselves where they could.

More enemy mortar rounds arced through the sky, fell to earth and exploded violently.

Captain Becker and Lieutenant Gifford made it back to the patrol.

"Return fire! Return fire!"

The Marines opened up with their M-16s and two M-60 machine guns.

The NVA answered the Marines with much larger, more potent rocket propelled grenades from shoulder-held B-40 and B-41 launchers. The flight of the warheads terminated in deafening explosions.

Both sides exchanged long torrents of machine gun and rifle fire. The firefight on the banks of the Quang Tri River, just what Captain Becker was trying to avoid, had started. The now-isolated Marines were in a serious fight for their lives.

Captain Becker called out to his radioman, cursing that he had ever left him in the first place.

"Agostino, we're facing more than a company of NVA. Get Navajo on the phone."

Little could be heard above the noise of the explosions. Becker yelled at his forward observer.

"Schuster, we got pre-assigned fire missions for this area?"

"No pre-planned fires here, Sir. Farther downstream. Toto two, Toto four and..."

"Lieutenant, no time for an explanation. We'll call in a new fire mission...new grid and azimuth. Figure it out."

Becker reached out.

"Agostino, give me that phone."

The captain talked into the radio's hand-held receiver while the FO plotted the fire mission.

"Navajo, this is Oscar Alpha."

The captain repeated.

"Navajo. Do you read me? Oscar Alpha."

No reply.

"What's wrong with those arty guys?"

"Sir, too steep in this valley."

"Navajo. Oscar Alpha. Need fire support."

The captain waited for a reply. "Come on you cannon cockers, pick up the phone, for Christ's sake."

He pressed the button. "Navajo! Do you read?"

The NVA's eighty-two millimeter mortar rounds were now coming closer. The air was thick with shrapnel.

Captain Becker turned to Gifford.

"They'll have us bracketed within seconds."

Gifford looked around. The steep cliff rising from the valley floor up to Highway Nine above him cut off any easy retreat. The only escape was moving up or down river—suicide either way.

"Navajo, Oscar Alpha. We need arty now! Repeat, immediate! Do you read me?"

Someone shouted.

"Corpsman down!"

In one quick movement, Gifford replaced the contents of his pack with four hand grenades. He put several fat, shotgun-like M-79 cartridges in his vest pockets. He grabbed his loaded grenade launcher, positioned his M-16 across his back and, with the satchel of hand grenades, ran across the islands, tripping on rocks and fallen logs, to the river's edge.

The Marines' fire coming from behind was matched by the NVA staccato fire in front of him.

North Vietnamese RPGs sizzled just above Gifford's head. They made horrendous shrieks as they left behind long smoke trails and a stench of burnt propellant. He heard the explosions behind him.

Gifford hid behind shoulder-high boulders. He eyed two NVA mortar crews to his left and the third mortar crew far to the right, all on the other side of the river. Gifford decided to hit the two outside mortars first.

He pushed the M-79's safety to the forward position and aimed the weapon. Its effective range was not much more than four hundred meters, but it was enough.

Gifford pulled the trigger.

The projectile flew on a true trajectory across the river and within seconds, exploded among the NVA mortar crewmen, killing them all.

"You dumb-shits don't know who you're messin' with."

Gifford ducked down and moved ten meters to his left to frustrate enemy snipers. He pushed the M-79's barrel locking latch to the right and opened it. He slid in another shell, closed the breech and moved the safety latch forward. He took aim through the weeds. The shot flew across the stream. Again, it met its target and exploded, disabling the second mortar and killing its crew.

Machine gun fire swept over and to his right and into the trees far behind him cutting down limbs. Bullets ripped through the thicket and zinged off rocks. A line of earth fountains marched right past him to his left as the bullets ripped up the ground.

"Have to take out the machine gun. You sonzabitches."

Gifford reloaded his M-79. "Damn single-shot weapon."

He aimed and pulled the trigger. The grenade landed way in front of the machine gun and exploded harmlessly.

A fourth shot met its target, killing the crew.

Gifford took the risk of exposure. He stood to a crouch and, partially hidden, aimed and fired the last round from his M-79 at the third mortar. The projectile struck quickly with lethal accuracy and exploded.

Some North Vietnamese soldiers, shouting and pointing, approached the river's edge on the south side.

Gifford, his M-16 at the ready, moved to conceal himself and pulled two hand grenades from his pack. He mentally measured the distance to the conjunction point of his throwing abilities and the advancing enemy. Lobbing a grenade isn't like throwing a baseball. Regardless, Gifford was going for the strike zone.

Gifford clamped the safety spoon to the round grenade casing with his left hand and pulled the arming pin with his other hand.

"Ground ball to short center with a runner on third. A straight throw to home plate from behind second base."

Gifford rose up to his full height, drew his left arm behind him and, with the strength of a Roman catapult, launched his grenade straight at the enemy. The result was deadly.

"Not bad for a southpaw."

He spotted more NVA to his left, a more difficult throw. Repeating the movement, Gifford clamped the spoon down, pulled the pin on his second grenade and stood upright. He stretched his long, lanky, sinewy left arm all the way back. Like a tightly coiled spring, his arm snapped forward in a shortened arc over and to the left of his head. The grenade sailed to its target and exploded, stopping the NVA.

Gifford threw the last two grenades in rapid succession. He retreated into the brush with bullets tearing at the leaves and waist-high grass. Gifford turned, aimed his M-16 rifle, pulled the trigger and emptied the magazine.

The North Vietnamese were now charging in force across the river. The Marines opposing them lay down an intense wall of fire.

Back with the patrol, Gifford yelled out, "Captain, I can't suppress them anymore,"

Lieutenant Schuster tried to raise the Fire Direction Center on the combat base. He had determined the grid coordinates for the new fire mission.

"Navajo, this is Oscar Alpha."

A second later, with urgent desperation. "NAVAJO, FIRE MISSION!"

"Oscar Alpha. Send your mission."

The grid would be sent in the clear. No time for shackle codes.

"Navajo, grid, x-ray delta, niner two niner four one niner, compass azimuth one four seven degrees. Request two rounds hotel echo, adjust fire, over."

"Oscar Alpha, battery engaged. Firefight near Kilo Sierra. Stand by six zero seconds."

Captain Becker grabbed the receiver from Schuster.

"NAVAJO! Oscar Alpha Actual! Negative, Negative! NVA in the open attacking our position. I repeat, NVA in the open."

"Oscar Alpha Actual, working the data. Stand by fire mission."

The Marines maintained a withering fire which stalled the NVA's advance. NVA mortar rounds fell among the Marines. Fire from the NVA machine guns ripped through the area like a scythe. RPGs punctuated the cacophony with their rocket sounds and explosions that shook everything.

The Fire Direction Center at Khe Sanh plotted the grid and azimuth, determined range and deflection and muzzle elevation. The battery responded.

"Fire!"

Two howitzers fired one round each.

The FDC spoke immediately to Captain Becker.

"Oscar Alpha. Shot."

There was a slight pause. Then the FDC gave Schuster and Captain Becker a heads-up.

"Splash."

Two 105mm shells smashed into the river bed east of the tip of the north island and short of the advancing NVA. Mud and water flew into the sky.

"Navajo, Adjust fire. Right two hundred, add one hundred."

Like before, the FDC spoke.

"Shot." Then, "Splash."

The rounds exploded in the middle of the enemy near the edge of the river.

"Navajo, good shooting. Request battery three volleys. Fire for effect. Oscar Alpha."

Within seconds, eighteen shells exploded among the NVA. The valley filled with a continuous roar of explosions. The ground beneath the charging North Vietnamese soldiers churned into brown and black geysers of dark water.

"Navajo, repeat fire for effect."

"Oscar Alpha, on its way. Will advise Romeo Papa and Charlie Charlie to provide reinforcing fire."

"Navajo, have Romeo Papa and Charlie Charlie fire spotting rounds. Will adjust. All rounds fuse quick, victor tango in effect. Danger close, repeat, danger close."

The Fire Support Coordination Center on the combat base made contact with Rockpile and Camp Carroll. Giant U.S. Army track-mounted 175mm long range guns, two from each location, fired. The projectiles arrived with a sudden impact, making the explosions of the 105mm shells look insignificant, but the large shells landed short of the target.

Schuster spoke into the receiver to correct fire.

"Add two hundred, fire for effect."

Captain Becker yelled out.

"Marines, get low. Incoming 175s!"

The big cannons at Rockpile and Camp Carroll opened up with their large shells, in two volleys. The projectiles, their shriek faint at first, screamed loudly through the air. Within seconds, round after round smashed into the area amidst the advancing NVA. The U.S. Army's King of Battle had arrived.

Suddenly stopped, the surviving enemy retreated south across the Quang Tri River and disappeared into the tall elephant grass, leaving their dead and wounded behind.

"Navajo, check fire. End of mission. Good shooting! Thanks to Romeo Papa and Charlie Charlie. I have at least three dozen enemy KIA."

Literally out of the blue, a new voice came on the radio.

"Oscar Alpha, this is White Star Two Five overhead, north your position. State status."

"White Star, ten WIAs, some serious."

"Roger that. Arranging chopper extraction. Stand by one. Changing channels."

Two minutes passed.

"Oscar Alpha, White Star. Three 46s en route. Two for extraction to Kilo

Sierra. Other will take WIAs to Da Nang direct. On ground your position in one zero minutes. Have called for Alpha Charlie support. Copy?"

"White Star, thanks for gettin' us outta here. We owe you a few drinks."

The pilot's voice was garbled by the sound of the plane's engine, but one word came out clear.

"Vodka."

Back on the combat base, Agostino and Lieutenant Schuster approached Gifford as he sat against some sandbags with a warm Black Label beer in his hand.

"The captain needs you, Lieutenant. You and Lieutenant Schuster, here. Pronto."

Gifford looked up. He shielded his eyes from the low sun with his forearm.

"Come on, Giff," Schuster said. "Get your ass in gear. The skipper wants you and me now."

Gifford grabbed his M-16 and M-79 and stood. The Marines walked to the CP and went in.

Captain Becker didn't bother to look up from a report he was preparing.

"You knocked out three mortars, eighty-two millimeters, right, Gifford? How many mortars total do you think, Lieutenant?"

There may have been five or six. They were still settin' up."

"Lieutenant, I'm thinking there may have been as many as five hundred NVA out there."

Captain Becker lit a cigarette and inhaled. He turned to his forward observer whose face still reflected the terror of the event.

"Lieutenant Schuster, that was some bad shit, but we got through it. I know you ain't been here long. If you were scared, don't worry about it. I was scared shitless."

Schuster's face brightened up.

Becker continued. "You can be my FO anytime. I appreciate what you did today. We poured some bad-ass artillery fire into the middle of those bastards."

"Chewed 'em up pretty good, Sir."

Back to Gifford. "Doesn't it strike you odd, Giff, that the NVA didn't call in their own artillery rather than risk their men?"

"I never thought of it, Sir. I was too damned busy."

"Get some rest. I'll need both of you on the next patrol. There's not many Christmas beers left. Be sure you get one."

"Had one already, Sir," Gifford said.

"Get another one while they last."

"Is that all, Sir?"

"Gifford, something tells me this crap is just gonna get worse. I think we're at Khe Sanh for the long haul."

Captain Becker drew on his cigarette as he looked at Gerry Gifford. "You done good today, Marine. Good shootin' with that blooper."

"Thank you, Sir."

"Oh, and Lieutenant…those grenades. Where'd ya learn to throw like that?"

"Phoenix, Sir."

CHAPTER THREE

HOUSE ON STILTS

Nguyen Sinh Cung, born in 1890 to a peasant family in Nghe An Province, grew up in Kim Lien Village, not far from the town of Vinh. Radicalized while still a student, and fearing arrest by the colonial government, Cung eventually quit school and hired on as a cook aboard a steamship bound for Marseille. Cung spent a few years working in Europe, Asia, North Africa, and the Americas. He read literature on philosophy and political-economic theories.

Cung, assuming many names over the years, had a number of altercations with the authorities in various countries. The Hong Kong police arrested him in 1931 and detained him for eighteen months.

During his travels, Cung observed that while poverty abounded and the poor suffered, the world was ruled by the elite. Moved by the deprivations he saw everywhere, Cung became an ardent revolutionary. He eschewed capitalism, the wayward child of democracy and the root cause of world discontent. Nguyen Sinh Cung embraced a more evenhanded dogma, or so he thought. He discovered communism.

Through a long molding process, Nguyen Sinh Cung, the young revolutionary, who also referred to himself as Nguyen Ai Quoc (Nguyen the Patriot) finally emerged with the name of Ho Chi Minh, the enlightened one.

Ho Chi Minh would apply his radical inclinations to a cause that had been seething for a long time. He became the foremost proponent of his country's independence from the French. He would liberate Vietnam from its subservience to foreign rule.

Those pre-independence days, when Ho lived in a number of locations in the far north of Vietnam, transitioned to more glorious ones. After years of fighting, Ho Chi Minh's nationalists severely beat French Union forces at a remote location west of Hanoi, near Laos in 1954. The victors were called the Viet Minh; the venue, Dien Bien Phu.

After the French Union surrender, Ho Chi Minh resided permanently in Hanoi. Finding a suitable place to live, however, was not easy. Ho Chi Minh may have been a staunch revolutionary leader, but he was also fussy.

The opulent official residence of the last French governor-general was the obvious choice. The imposing, multi-floor edifice, painted a papaya yellow, with its tall louvered windows, represented the quintessential French-Tonkin architecture. A blend of exotic Indo-China and classic French styles, the design was elegant and romantic. But, so ostentatious, the mansion wasn't suitable. Besides, on a practical level, what's an old bachelor to do with all that space?

In May 1958, Vietnam's revered leader moved into his newly-built permanent home in the botanical gardens of the formal government area. Ho's home sat immediately across the pond from House 54 where he previously dwelled.

Designed by Nguyen Van Ninh, Ho's new home was modeled after the stilt houses of the ethnic mountain people with whom he lived during the French war. While the upstairs living area consisted of two rooms with open louvers, the downstairs was open on four sides.

Ho Chi Minh, the Chairman of the *Dang Lao Dong Viet Nam* (the Central Committee of the Vietnam Workers' Party) lived simply. He fancied himself an accomplished gardener. Jasmine, bougainvillea and sprouts of larger ohmantus and sophora surrounded his house. Orchids hung from the sides of the trees. The *hoa sua* and *ylang-ylang* provided sweet fragrances year round.

Ho Chi Minh liked to stand on the arched foot bridge a short distance from his home. He would clap his hands to summon the fish which, squirming half in, half out of the water, would congregate at the stone steps.

THE PRESIDENT'S SANDBOX

Ho Chi Minh kept goldfish in a small aquarium beneath his house. He had given each one a name.

Chu tich Ho (Chairman Ho) relished the tranquility of the peaceful sunlight sprinkling through the tall trees at midday. He reveled in the nearby stands of bamboo which to him symbolized the flexible, enduring strength of his people. He was drawn to the *Sang Dao* tree and especially to a giant *Xa Cu* tree, a mahogany imported from French West Africa. The *Xa Cu* stood on the path to his house from the main gate of the palace grounds and towered over all other foliage. Vietnam will grow tall and proud, just like the *Xa Cu.*

A believer in a daily regimen of calisthenics, Ho preferred to be outdoors during the early morning hours when Hanoi was at its quietest. After vigorous workouts on a grassy area near his house, he would take walks through the lush foliage.

Now, in his senior years, his active revolutionary days behind him, Chairman Ho's daily schedule was not the toil it used to be. Wizened, a gray pointed beard sprouting from his chin, Ho Chi Minh, took time to read and write letters.

Bac Ho (Uncle Ho), the name he preferred, passed through the entrance to his garden marked by an arched flower lattice after his exercise. He walked to a large table surrounded with eleven chairs. He picked up a pack of Trung Hoa Bai cigarettes, his favorite brand, and lit one. He thought back to 1945 when he resided for a short period at No. 48 Hang Ngang Street in the Old Quarter of Hanoi. There, Ho Chi Minh penned Vietnam's proclamation of independence. In September of 1945, standing in Ba Dinh Square, not far from his future home, Ho Chi Minh read that proclamation to a large gathering of his countrymen.

He remembered the opening words: "All men are created equal...with certain unalienable rights...life, liberty and the pursuit of happiness."

His mind turned to more contemporary challenges: the honorable struggle of resistance and the reunification of the country. *Chung toi phai tien len* (We must move forward).

Ho Chi Minh's brisk morning walk along tree-lined Mango Road had done little to ease his distressed mood. Ho Chi Minh thought of his travels, especially his experience living in America. Ironically, the situation now in Quang Tri Province with the same people he lived amongst in Boston, who he found to be exciting and dynamic, but sometimes cold, was unsettling.

Ho leaned back in his chair as he looked across the pond. Equally troubling, the disharmony among his own military leaders had become nasty. He had the best generals, but they were a quarrelsome bunch.

Ho removed his glasses and smiled at the remembrance of General Vo Nguyen Giap, his old friend. Vo Nguyen Giap, however famous, had run into difficulties with high government officials and communist party members. The discord became so contentious, Giap found himself under virtual house arrest for many months. Much of his staff had been carted off. Still, Ho had absolute faith in Giap.

Ho Chi Minh also recognized the exceptional skills of General Van Tien Dung and another celebrated general named Nguyen Chi Thanh, who commanded North Vietnam's military efforts in the southern provinces through a surreptitious organization called COSVN—Central Office of South Vietnam.

Although General Giap and General Thanh made extra efforts to extend social graces to each other, their egos collided.

Vo Nguyen Giap was intellectual and polished while Thanh, though shrewd, was caught up with his self-importance, General Thanh dominated every conversation with outlandish exaggerations. He began to see his own remote command more along the lines of an effective government unto itself, and he, its glorified leader.

Nguyen Chi Thanh also liked to over-indulge. One night in early July 1967, at a major social gathering in Vo Nguyen Giap's home. Thanh consumed too much alcohol. Later, his bodyguard rushed him across town to Military Hospital 108 where he passed away soon thereafter from a myocardial infarction. Partying had done him in.

Ho's ruminations continued. Years before, during the battle of Dien Bien Phu, General Vo Nguyen Giap managed every aspect of the campaign. Now, as the country's Minister of Defense, with broader responsibilities, Giap was removed from the front. He worried that Giap's brilliant military leadership may not be felt so far away in central Vietnam.

Ho Chi Minh had another worrying concern. He was ill.

Ho's doctors emphatically warned him to refrain from smoking. He paid little attention to their reproaches. Smoking was too pleasurable. In August 1967, the Doctor's Council, reacting to their diagnosis of tuberculosis, issued a directive for Ho to seek medical attention. He went to China the next month for prolonged treatment.

On the twenty-third of December, Chu tich Ho Chi Minh slipped back into Vietnam virtually unannounced. Sadly, he would have to go back to China to continue his treatment. But, for now, being home for a week or two where he could enjoy familiar surroundings couldn't hurt anything.

His homesickness, however, belied another reason why Ho Chi Minh was anxious to return to Hanoi. He was concerned about the implementation of a controversial military-political plan. The Central Military Party Committee ordered the establishment of a major headquarters in Laos. Its mission was to isolate the Americans in western Quang Tri Province, thus creating favorable conditions for attacks farther south around Hue. The time had come to escalate the revolution to a new height.

The provisions had been hotly debated within his own government. An emergency meeting of the Politburo was convened to approve a policy that would have direct bearing on the conflict against the Americans in South Vietnam.

Ho Chi Minh was to preside over the meeting, but Le Duan, the party secretary, with his intrusive, overbearing personality, would dominate the discussions. The politburo meetings would be bitter. Sadly, Vo Nguyen Giap, whose presence would have lent moderation and sensible discourse, was not available. Ho's top general was in Hungary.

Troubled by past political and present military events, and his health, Ho Chi Minh was warmed by a special thought. He had a soft spot for Saigon and preferred it over Hanoi as the nation's capital. He worried whether the South Vietnamese, who aren't so terribly different from their northern brethren, could be persuaded to react favorably to broad interventions imposed by North Vietnam? Can he influence the southerners?

While Ho Chi Minh could posit reasonable answers to those questions, there was one question to which Ho Chi Minh did not have an answer.

Will Hanoi win the war against the Americans?

CHAPTER FOUR

THINK TANK

Having returned from his whirlwind five-day trip to Australia, President Johnson spent a restful Christmas in Washington, D.C. Two days later, the four-engine Jetstar carrying Johnson and his family landed on the long north-south airstrip at the LBJ Ranch. The plane, its engines whining, taxied to the ramp near what came to be called the Texas White House.

The President, standing outside the plane on the stair gantry, scanned the rolling countryside. The brisk Texas wind blew in his face. Lyndon Johnson was thrilled to be home in the Hill Country on the banks of the Pedernales River.

The President would enjoy quiet time with Lady Bird, his daughters Lynda and Luci, his grandson Patrick Lyndon, or more simply Lyn; and Yuki, the half-breed mutt Luci found on Thanksgiving Day in 1966.

The President glanced at the clock in the low-ceiling wing of his home that served as his Texas office. Soon, he would sit in the comfort of his living room, chit chat with Lady Bird and his daughters and watch television. He may turn the next several days welcoming in the New Year into a complete restful holiday.

The President, reacting to a soft knock at the door, looked up from his desk to see George Christian, his press secretary.

"Hi George. Come in."

Born in 1927 in Austin, Texas, George Christian joined the Marines in 1944 and was eventually shipped to the Pacific theater. Afterwards, he enrolled at the University of Texas from where he received his degree. He moved into politics, working for Governor John Connally. Later, Christian joined the White House staff of Lyndon Johnson.

"Happy New Year, Mr. President."

The President slid his ten-gallon hat to the back of his head.

"Why, the same to you, George."

Christian held up a bound volume.

"Sir, I've read this document from cover to cover. Those brain-guys know how to invent nonsensical phrases. They sure contrive the rhetoric. Just listen to this ridiculous title: 'The Systemic Politburo Structure and the Military Hierarchy of the Government of North Vietnam—Non-stochastic Decision Making Respecting the Process of the Political Strata and Interface with the Central Military Party Committee on the Conduct of the War in Vietnam: A Critical Study.'"

"Jesus Christ, George."

The President smiled. "I didn't understand what you just read. Why can't they just sum it up like that western…what was the movie's name? *How the West Was Won*…wasn't that it? They should just say, 'How North Vietnam's Gonna Win the Damn War.' I didn't really look at it. Which agency prepared the study, George?"

"It's from that analysis company in California, Sir."

"Intellectual think-tank BS by inexperienced, wet-behind-the-ears experts. Got no time for that crap. That's why I gave it to you, George."

"Mr. President, I'm your press secretary. It's more appropriate if Walt Rostow was to read this, Sir, or Helms's people…some CIA staffer. They can understand the intelligence nuances better than I can."

"Oh, George, come on. Don't short-change yourself. A Longhorn graduate is just as good as a Ph.D. from some snotty Ivy League school. I'd say even better. You're as smart as Rostow or anybody at Langley…or anyone from one of those damned schools up there in, I dunno, New England somewhere. And anyway, you happened to be the only one around. So, guess what? You got the shit detail."

"Thanks, Mr. President." Christian responded, with a prideful, yet slightly wry tone.

The President laughed.

"People give me books all the time. 'Lyndon, you need to read this,' they say. I'm trying to get through a Leon Uris novel now. Impossible. Anyway, George, what's it gonna tell me that I don't already know? The North Viet-nese are pissed at us for being in South Vietnam and we're equally pissed at them for being in the same place—pretty simple, in my mind. They're trying to kick us out and we're trying our best to do the same to them.

"We gave South Vietnam our word and by God, we're sticking to it. What kind of President would I be if I didn't defend democracy over there? Damn, I know the South Viet-nese aren't perfect. That government is standing on wobbly legs just like we did two hundred years ago."

"Mr. President, once you wade through the plodding rhetoric, the document does bring to light something interesting."

"Like what? Hey, George, wouldn't a cold beer taste good 'bout now? I don't wanna read that agricultural pricing report. It's Sunday evening. Hell, it's New Year's Eve. Almost six o'clock. Another six hours to 1968."

Christian eyed the clock.

"Mr. President, it's only 4:15, Sir."

"Close enough. Let's have a beer."

The President smiled with complicity as he picked up the phone. "Lady Bird. Hey, listen, be a doll. Have someone in the kitchen bring us two cold Lone Stars, one for Christian here and one for me, would you? What?...No. No mugs."

The President replaced the receiver. "I like a beer straight out of the bottle."

George Christian, smiling, continued.

"Well, Sir, I'm not sure how to say this exactly..."

"George, it's those damned communists, Ho Chi Minh and that Foe When Giap guy. They're the problem."

"Yes, and no, Mr. President. Here on page one ninety-two..."

"You're not serious. A hundred and ninety-two pages? And they expect me to read that thing, the President of the United States? I'm not sure my glasses will survive, much less my eyes."

"Two hundred and eighty-five pages total, Mr. President."

"Good Lord, George."

"There's another name, Sir. Le Duan. They pronounce the name *Lay Zwan.* I've never heard of this guy."

"Yeah, I've heard somethin' about Le Duan, but I don't know too much about him."

"Mr. President, he may have pushed Ho Chi Minh and Vo Nguyen Giap to the sidelines. He may have more power than we surmise…calling the shots. He's hard line, evidently pretty ruthless."

Johnson turned his head as he caught sight of Lady Bird entering the office.

"Lyndon, the kitchen staffers are gone. I got the beers for you and George myself. They're very cold, honey."

"Thank you, Bird. You're a real sweetheart. Nothing worse than warm beer. Oh, Lady Bird, do me another favor, would you, hon? Please call Juanita Roberts and tell her to take a couple of days off. Isn't her mother visiting her in Washington soon? She should take her to the Mayflower for tea."

The President turned back to Christian.

"George, I don't know where I'd be without Lady Bird and Juanita Roberts. Sometimes, I'm too hard on 'em, especially when I get grumpy. Continue on, George. Tell me about this Le Duan character."

The President placed the long-neck bottle to his mouth and tilted his head. He took a healthy swig of beer.

"Mr. President, Le Duan, who used to be called Le Van Nhuan, climbed the party ladder to decision-making prominence and, for a number of years now, has been seen as the number two man after Ho Chi Minh.

"George, those Asian commies change their names all the damned time."

Christian smiled.

"Le Duan was born in Quang Tri Province in the early 1900s and worked for…"

"Wait, George. Same province as Khe Sanh?"

"Correct, Sir. He was arrested in the thirties and spent time in prison. In the mid-fifties, Vietnam was divided at the seventeenth parallel by the

Geneva Agreement. The French and the Catholics went south. Those with communist leanings went north. Le Duan was one of them."

"The commies didn't get control of all of Vietnam, George. They're just gonna have to eat it."

Christian chuckled.

"However, Le Duan ordered that not all cadres were to go north. Instead, they went underground. They buried their weapons for another day to rise in revolt against the South Vietnam government. In effect, Le Duan founded the National Liberation Front, the Viet Cong.

"Originally, Ho Chi Minh resisted use of guerilla actions in the south. He sought a more diplomatic solution, but Le Duan, by now a strong advocate of war against the south to affect reunification, promoted much more aggressive actions. The schism that ensued revolved around whether those actions would take the form of direct military confrontation or protracted guerilla warfare."

Christian sipped his beer. "Due to his Soviet and Chinese dancing partners and their apparent jealousy over a fledgling government with pro-communist leanings, Le Duan's been careful not to offend either camp. He's been able to secure armaments without any reciprocity consideration, as they term it."

"Without reciprocity...what? Dammit, George, see what I mean? Even you can talk like some uppity east coast schoolboy. Just say it straight like we do in Texas. The cowpoke gets what he wants and there ain't no strings attached, right? He ain't gonna pay for nothing. Cheap bastards. Communists all think like that. Damn, you could teach a class on this stuff."

"Sir, the report outlines the North Vietnamese strategy. While they use the typical communist rhetoric, the report suggests they should coerce the South Vietnamese populace through intimidation."

The President tilted the beer bottle back and took another sip.

"Good beer, but later this evening, I'll have a Cutty Sark with Lady Bird. President Truman always drank bourbon and water. Can't stand the stuff."

"Mr. President, Le Duan was chosen to be first secretary of the communist party in 1959. Ho's desired choice was Vo Nguyen Giap. This may have caused a rift between Le Duan and Giap, who is now the Minister of Defense.

They've got severe differences of opinion about how to conduct the war in the south."

"Ah hell, George. Heated arguments are common in government. Look around. You got the Pentagon and the CIA over there in Virginia, on the same side of the river, not more than ten miles apart. They can't even come to agreement. I argue with my neighbor up there north of the rise over some fence he's put up. These things happen."

"Mr. President, we may be dealing more with Le Duan's war policies than those of either Ho Chi Minh or Vo Nguyen Giap."

"George, know what? I don't give a damn. He's just another blowhard in a long line of lazy-ass communists. Ho Chi Minh's still the overriding force."

"Yes, Sir. He's very popular. They call him Uncle Ho."

CHAPTER FIVE

REX HOTEL

The one thing the Rex Hotel offered that many other Saigon hotels didn't was a splendid view of the city from a bar on the roof. The sweeping vista from the top of the hotel, adorned with a huge gold crown that came to be the symbol of the hotel itself, mixed with Saigon's tropical softness at sunset, was dramatic.

Often called the "Generals' Hotel" because it hosted high ranking American military personnel, "The Rex" was a cherished icon of Saigon.

General William Childs Westmoreland, the commanding officer of American forces in Vietnam since early 1964, found the eclectic, somewhat gaudy décor of the Rex to be amusing, if not bizarre. He didn't frequent the rooftop that often, but when he did, he enjoyed the view as much as anyone.

At six feet tall, William Westmoreland was the embodiment of professional confidence and bearing. A four-star general at fifty-one, Westmoreland served as superintendent of the U.S. Military Academy. He personified West Point's motto: "Duty, Honor, Country."

Observers found, however, that Westmoreland, a decorated World War Two and Korea veteran, possessed an eccentric characteristic. To facilitate his destiny—Westmoreland's rise to military prominence had been blistering—he often contrived his own luck. If the journey to the pinnacle required him to indulge in self-promotion, so be it. Nothing would stop him.

Now standing at the rail on the rooftop of the Rex, Westy looked across the cityscape. The water hyacinth, floating languorously on the Saigon River, was captivating. In the opposite direction, the twin bell towers of the Nha Tho Duc Ba (Catholic Church), built from brick and completed in 1880, stood out clearly. At almost two hundred feet in height, the Basilica of Our Lady of the Immaculate Conception, towered over all other buildings in the city. Saigon's City Hall, on gleaming display, sat just down the side street from the Rex Hotel.

A breeze erased the steaminess of South Vietnam's capital city, which was, year round, interminably hot and humid. A few seagulls hovered lazily, directly overhead, their lonely calls echoing over the city.

By mid-afternoon, fluffy pillows of white clouds had turned gray and angry. A heavy rain would soon inundate Saigon. The city's drains would quickly overflow. The impending storm, however, accentuated the city's charm.

Below, Honda motorbikes whizzed up and down the streets. Their high-pitched sound at street level was muffled higher up on the rooftop.

General Westmoreland, with his aides not far away, sipped his Coca Cola and tried to relax. He recalled his trip back to the USA with Ambassador Ellsworth Bunker in late November 1967, to meet with President Johnson. Both he and Bunker expressed optimism to the President and to the American public on television that America was winning the war. General Westmoreland gave an upbeat view of U.S. military operations conducted in 1967. The war was going as planned. To hasten its conclusion, however, he needed to make major re-alignments of his forces to fulfill strength requirements in the northern part of South Vietnam. More soldiers were needed.

But, while Westmoreland was confident of his military's capabilities– "We will prevail in Vietnam"—he was less sure of the political environment in Saigon. The inclinations of the government and the dissensions between its rulers Nguyen Van Thieu and Nguyen Cao Ky were often hostile.

Westmoreland was also troubled by a running clash of stinging statistics. While his own MACV organization thought the enemy's strength numbered two hundred thousand men operating in South Vietnam, it seemed the CIA had put the estimate of enemy strength closer to six hundred thousand. The difference was attributed to how and what constitutes forces. If the local populace was sympathetic to the enemy, shouldn't they be counted as part of the order of battle? Had Westmoreland been fighting a force larger than he thought?

Apart from this, American policy should make the enemy realize aggressions in the south were too costly. Hanoi, however, was driving the war, not Saigon; and definitely not Washington.

But, William Westmoreland had even grander aspirations. The war of attrition thus far being conducted needed a revamp. An invasion of Laos, an operation codenamed El Paso, was essential. Khe Sanh was to be the springboard. To realize the full benefits of the operation, it had to be implemented no later than early fall 1968. Its success would be fortuitous for the American presidential elections in November.

More importantly, Westmoreland sought an alternate strategy: an invasion of the central part of North Vietnam. Such an invasion would isolate battlefields in the south.

There was only one problem: in contrast to Vo Nguyen Giap's freedom to use Laos and Cambodia, Westmoreland had no mandate beyond the boundaries of South Vietnam.

If the North Vietnamese succeeded in gaining a foothold in Quang Tri and Thua Thien, the two northern provinces of South Vietnam, the complexion of the war would change dramatically.

At the very beginning of January, five NVA soldiers were killed just outside the perimeter of the Khe Sanh Combat Base. They were investigating weak points in the Marines' defenses. Wearing American uniforms, they did not respond to verbal challenges from the Marines and were shot. Documents found on the bodies pointed to the enemy's massive infiltration culminating with a planned assault on the Khe Sanh Combat Base.

Since Vo Nguyen Giap was concentrating forces in One Corps, and if Westmoreland could entice the NVA to an all-out fight, the American commander would utilize the might of U.S. airpower to eradicate the enemy.

Westmoreland initiated Operation Niagara, a continuous bombing campaign, on the sixth of January. It gave him superior fighting muscle. A decisive blow through massive aerial bombings, coupled with acute ground actions external to South Vietnam, would surely compel Hanoi to re-think its hostile strategy south of the DMZ. Westmoreland had the weapons to assure a U.S. victory in the northern part of South Vietnam. Instead of compromising the enemy's will to fight, Westmoreland was determined to completely stop it.

Westmoreland began to sense an underlying controversy in Washington about Khe Sanh. Differences of opinions were circulating in higher offices. Should America continue her presence or should she withdraw quietly?

One influential retired general thought the Marines should not have been at Khe Sanh in the first place. He cited several factors: The Americans were too vulnerable. Weather would be unfavorable. Resupply will be difficult. American artillery may be less effective than supposed. Highway Nine, the main artery, would always be in jeopardy. North Vietnam could mobilize more forces than originally thought.

Westmoreland worried. The President had no feel for military actions or the rarefied environment attendant to a battlefield. The President didn't seem connected with the reality of Vietnam. Lyndon Johnson's speeches and exhortations came across to Westmoreland as lifeless. His words, at times vague, were uninspiring.

The general held his glass up and took another sip of his Coke. Condensation ran down the side and fell from the bottom edge of the glass.

Kate Carlson had just turned the corner from the rooftop elevator lobby. She walked beneath the awning next to the veranda bar and a small fountain. She instantly recognized Westmoreland, but then how could she not? Dressed as he was in his uniform, with tailored sleeves stitched permanently above his elbows, and with a distinctive profile, the American commander in any setting was easy to spot.

"Hello, General Westmoreland."

"Why, hello Miss Carlson. What a pleasure. How are you?"

"I'm fine, General. I didn't know you come up here. And please, call me Kate."

The general smiled and looked down in slight deference.

"OK, Kate. Kate it is. That has to be short for Katherine. That's my wife's name."

"I understand she's very beautiful, General."

"I'm a very lucky man. I met Kitsy at Fort Sill. Swept me completely off my feet. She followed me to Saigon. I had to move her away when it became unsafe. She hated to leave."

"Me, too, General."

A quizzical look crossed Westmoreland's face.

"What do you mean, Kate?"

"I'm bi-lingual in French and English. After only four months here, I'm being re-assigned to Brussels. I'll miss all this. I feel part of something important here.

"The people, the language, the clothes…I like it when the vendors, wearing conical hats, come to my apartment carrying produce in their *quang ganh.*"

"A kwan what? What's that, Kate?"

"They're everywhere, General. The women carry a flat pole over their shoulder with a basket suspended from each end."

Westmoreland nodded his appreciation that Kate had genuinely enjoyed her short experience in Vietnam.

"You can't forget the dog meat skewers."

"Oh, the *thit cho*, General. Yes, definitely not my favorite."

Westmoreland and Kate Carlson both laughed. Vietnam took a lot of getting used to.

Kate, her eyes glancing at the sudden lightning, continued. "My family wasn't exactly well off. We didn't travel much. We went to Charleston one summer in the station wagon. Dad had to fix a flat tire south of Columbia while we sweltered in the car. My folks rented a one-room house with a small kitchen near the beach for a week. My two brothers picked on me endlessly and I got a really bad sunburn."

"It can get plenty hot there, just like here, Kate."

"I earned my degree at UNC. I studied chemistry but switched to French. After my masters at Brown, I joined the Foreign Service. Oh, and I lost my North Carolina accent years ago. It can be distracting."

"What part of North Carolina?"

"Gastonia, in the Piedmont area."

"Of course, Kate. I know the area well. I was born in Saxon, near Spartanburg. Yes, you've completely lost your accent."

"I believe you attended West Point, General."

"Yeah, I really wanted to go to Annapolis, but ended up at the Citadel my first year. Then, I received an appointment to the Military Academy. Couldn't turn it down. I thought my father would be upset, but he pushed me on."

Westmoreland smiled. "Did my plebe year twice. After graduation, I ended up in a field artillery unit."

Kate Carlson smiled.

"General, I understand things are very intense around Khe Sanh."

"True enough."

"Isn't there a lot of speculation that Khe Sanh is a repeat of Dien Bien Phu? I've read a book by Jules Roy."

"Well, the speculation part is true, but it's unfounded. For some reason, the media ascribe infallible skill to the enemy. The press never give us much credit, though they like to ride in our helicopters."

Kate Carlson broadened the conversation.

"Tell me, General, if you don't mind my asking, how long is this war going to go on?"

"Kate, last April, I told the President I can win the war in thirty-six months, maybe less. No occupying force ever remains."

"Are we occupying South Vietnam, Sir?"

"No, I didn't mean it like that. To occupy, one has to invade. We didn't invade South Vietnam, Kate. We came here to help this government. By contrast, it's North Vietnam that's invading. They've invaded neighboring countries, too."

Ironically, General Westmoreland remembered his plans to invade North Vietnam, but dismissed the similarities. "They, not us, intend to occupy South Vietnam. Care for a drink, Kate?"

"Hmmm. A small glass of wine."

General Westmoreland turned to the waiter.

"Please bring the miss a glass of your best Beaujolais."

Westmoreland, consumed by his thoughts before Kate Carlson appeared on the roof, let his feelings congeal into words.

"Kate…" Westmoreland hesitated for a moment as he looked toward the spires of the Catholic Church. "It's no secret that my strategy is one of division of labor. South Vietnamese forces can provide security for the urban areas and centers of population like Saigon and Hue. This will leave U.S. forces free to confront North Vietnam's army and the stronger forces of the Viet Cong. We have to deny the sanctuaries they now enjoy and compromise their use of Laos and Cambodia."

"But, General, won't that take a lot of soldiers?"

"It's a big effort, of course, and it'll require substantially more men. But we're here either to win or not win. The President doesn't want defeat and I was sent here to assure a victory. We have to interdict the enemy everywhere. When we stop the enemy, South Vietnam can survive without an American military presence."

"I'm sure you're right, General."

Electric-white bolts of jagged lightning sliced through the dark clouds. Thunder boomed and crackled above the city. The temperature turned cool as large drops of rain splattered on the floor. General Westmoreland led Kate Carlson to the protective awning.

Bartenders, shaking chrome-colored metal vessels over their shoulders, paying no attention to the storm, mixed gin and ice.

Heavy rain suddenly fell in torrential sheets, obscuring the view of the Saigon River.

The waiter, a white serving towel draped over his arm, approached with a glass of red wine on a silver tray.

Kate smiled.

"*Le Beaujolais nouveau est arrivé.* That's what they say each year in France."

"You're fortunate, to be stationed overseas so early in your career. When I was an Eagle Scout, a long time ago, I went to England. That was an eye-opening experience. You'll learn more in one year in a foreign post than anyone back in the States can in ten."

Westmoreland would be more candid. "Kate, we make recommendations based on sound military logic that will accomplish our objectives in South Vietnam. Others are less inclined to support those recommendations.

"America's international influence is at stake over here. Politicians and bespectacled theorists, sitting in cushy leather chairs in Washington, can't possibly understand the war in South Vietnam as clearly as me and my joint staff."

"General, I've heard that the..."

"This is Vietnam, Kate, not Texas."

CHAPTER SIX

KNOW YOUR ENEMIES

The last days of 1967 gave way to January 1968, the start of the defining year of the war in Vietnam.

Ho Chi Minh stood beneath his stilt house a few feet from the large conference table with his suitcase next to him on the floor. He laid his overcoat across it.

Ho saw a military officer pass through the gate beneath the arched lattice.

"Colonel Phu, please come in and have some tea."

The colonel hung his hat on the back of a chair.

"Do you mind if I smoke, Sir?"

"Mind? Not at all, Colonel. I encourage it."

Ho Chi Minh pointed to his luggage. "I hate to leave my home again, but I must. The meeting with the Politburo was stressful, but it's over. I have no excuse for remaining here. I'm taking the plane this afternoon to China per my doctors' orders. What do you have for me?"

"Well, Ngai Chu tich—er, Mr. Chairman. You asked me to brief you about the American President."

"Yes, of course, Colonel Phu. It's best to know your enemies. However, my time at this moment is…well, I simply don't have much time. Please summarize your findings for me while we have tea. And, do enjoy your cigarettes."

"Bac Ho, if I were to choose one word to describe him, I would characterize President Johnson as an enigma."

"I would presume, Colonel."

"On the surface, he's an average person...it's, uh...well, it's hard to explain exactly."

Ho Chi Minh smiled.

"Mr. Johnson has not stumped you, has he?"

"No Sir, but to understand President Johnson, one has to understand rural America. Johnson's roots are firmly established in a remote part of the United States. Johnson was born in a small village in a region called the hill country in the middle of Texas."

"Texas has hills, Colonel? Isn't Texas flat?"

"Not totally, Sir, but the area is rocky with a special plant called a prickly pear cactus. Texas has an abundance of insects and scorpions and a type of *nhen to* [large spider] called tarantulas. Droughts have been known to last for several years."

"A desert, then."

"No, Sir, but some of the harshest land in the United States. Due to a great inaccessibility in this part of Texas—maybe the worst part—people pride themselves as being self-reliant.

"Johnson learned to face adversity fearlessly. This is how he survives. Driven to succeed, Johnson doesn't see impossibilities. Making a tractor run, fixing some irrigation scheme or persuading people to see his point of view—to him they require the same means to the solution: direct, to the point. He wants issues resolved in the most expedient manner."

"I see."

"Ngai Chu tich, Johnson may be manic-depressive. He dislikes funerals. He contrived to miss Dag Hammarskjold's funeral in Sweden in 1961, two years before he became America's leader.

"Johnson is keenly astute. He knows when to strike politically. He makes major decisions only when he must and then he does so with determination. He passes legislation when the time is right. He knows how to work the political machine.

"Johnson is a master at confrontation. He gets his way through any or a combination of compliments, manipulation, anger, even smiling. In the middle of an argument with someone, he will pick up the phone and order a gift for the birthday of the wife of the person with whom he's arguing. He grinds down those who stand in his way.

"We have a vulgar expression, *Cut*! or perhaps more colorfully, *cut bo*, but the Americans have the same expression. They call it *crap*. President Johnson sees himself as a person who does not talk in 'bullshit,' to use a crude American expression."

Ho Chi Minh laughed.

"Colonel, all politicians talk *cut bo*, some more than others."

"He lived among German immigrants and can't speak a word of German. Texas is heavily populated with Mexicans but he cannot speak Spanish. The British and French make endless fun of him, but Johnson's impervious to criticism. Everyone, as far as he is concerned, should speak like a Texan… coarse and brusque. The French would call it *sans d'elegance.*

"Johnson was elected to congress in the late 1930s and to the senate ten years later. He became the senate majority leader in 1954. Johnson rose to a man of means. He bought his property in Texas and greatly expanded it. The river was dammed up on one side of his home. A two thousand meter runway was built on the other side. He doesn't do anything small, Sir.

"He demands complete loyalty from his staff."

"Quite a character."

"He exhibits compassion to those less fortunate than he. He sees himself as a progressive who sprung from common roots. Johnson has two daughters. Both are married. His wife is…"

"Please, Colonel. I'm sure his family is very dear to him."

"Sorry, Sir. I'll just continue. Johnson's a big man. His physical stature is intimidating."

Ho Chi Minh laughed.

"All Americans are big."

"True. But combine that with his rural hardness…from where he came… and you can see his personae. Presidential elections are scheduled to occur within months. Johnson will fight to win. He will crush his opponents through his overbearing personality and political prowess.

"Ngai Chu tich, Lyndon Johnson will not let anyone keep him from achieving his goals. He is convinced America is right to support the Saigon regime."

"Colonel, stop!"

Ho Chi Minh's demeanor changed. "The false government that sits wrongly in Saigon is nothing but puppets propped up by America. Had the elections been held in 1956, all the people of Vietnam would have voted for communist rule. Instead, because they knew the fake government would lose, America thwarted the elections.

"Vietnam, north and south, will be united through our actions, military or otherwise. I was against guerilla warfare in the beginning, but I saw my passivity would result in nothing beneficial to our cause."

"Yes, Bac Ho, I understand. All I am saying is that President Johnson hates to lose. He shoves aside anyone who believes that losing is an option."

"Colonel Phu, Johnson's in the back pocket of the rich capitalists. He receives his support from the American military-industrial base. He cares little for the peasants."

The colonel blew smoke out his mouth while he stubbed out the cigarette in a wood ashtray.

"Mr. Chairman, maybe. President Johnson has initiated a number of economic and social reforms in America designed to help the poor, so I'm not sure one can say that."

"Colonel, Mr. Johnson and I exchanged letters in February 1967. The American president said he feels we should talk face-to-face. He stated in a frank manner that he cannot accept an unconditional stoppage of America's bombing campaign against us because we would exploit that cessation. He says he has tried to convey America's desire for a peaceful settlement. The key issue is to end a conflict that has brought hardships to Vietnam and the USA. He's warned that if we fail to find a peaceful solution, history will judge us harshly."

Colonel Phu sipped some tea.

"Bac Ho, President Johnson cannot accept defeat in Vietnam."

"So, all right, then," Ho Chi Minh said with impatience. "We're in a long war with the Americans because of President Johnson's character. He's intractable...stubborn."

"Sir. We're dealing with a very strong individual."

"I only know what you tell me and what little I've heard about President Johnson and...well...what I've read in his correspondence. He was being frank with me. I was equally frank with him in my return communiqué."

Ho Chi Minh stared across the large pond toward House 54. "America is many thousands of miles from Vietnam. We have never harmed the United States. On the contrary, the United States has continuously intervened in our affairs, even during Dien Bien Phu. The USA desires to turn South Vietnam into a neo-colony. In the President's letter, he deplored the destruction in Vietnam. I asked him, however, to consider who perpetrated these monstrous crimes. Colonel, if the United States wants peace talks, President Johnson must stop bombing the Democratic Republic of Vietnam. He must completely remove his military from South Vietnam. Only when these conditions are satisfied, will we consider talks with the Americans."

"Ngai Chu tich, I'm afraid President Johnson will consider those actions a prelude to failure."

Ho Chi Minh reached across the table to retrieve the teapot from the red and black lacquered insulating basket. As he sat back down, he picked up a cigarette pack. It was empty.

"My doctors tell me to quit smoking, but please give me a cigarette, Colonel. I don't have anymore."

"Pleasure, Sir."

"Colonel, I recall when we shot down an American plane in 1964 and captured the pilot. We became very aware of President Johnson's cavalier actions."

"Yes, Sir. The naval incident with the Americans off our coast in 1964 gave rise to their Gulf of Tonkin Resolution, a short, but far-reaching document... basically, an unmitigated license to conduct open warfare in Southeast Asia. Johnson slammed it through congress almost overnight. His ego was probably the driving force."

"Well, Colonel, Mr. Johnson may have an ego the size of the world, but he will not defeat us in our own country.

"Vietnam is small. Everyone knows that—just look at any map—but America cannot block our glorious reunification efforts. We are going to reunify *mien bac va mien nam* [northern region with the southern region]. I will take to my grave this conviction and this promise.

"We did not quit fighting the French until our glorious *co do sao vang* [red flag yellow star] flew over de Castries' headquarters at Dien Bien Phu and we will never quit fighting the Americans until the *co do sao vang* flies from the rooftop of every building in Saigon.

"Colonel Phu, President Johnson may be rough as a Texas cactus, and given to bombastic swearing, but he didn't get where he is today through ignorance. A person does not rise to a position of power without shrewdness...and, most important of all, support."

Ho Chi Minh lit his cigarette. "We cannot afford to underestimate the American president."

Ho inhaled on his cigarette and exhaled the smoke. "But, I assure you, Colonel Phu, President Johnson has met his first impossibility. The Vietnamese people will *never* accept talks under the threat of bombs."

CHAPTER SEVEN

MESSAGE TO CONGRESS

President Johnson retired to his bedroom about 2:00 a.m. at the very beginning of the seventeenth day of January 1968. The previous day had been excruciatingly long. He thought of having a scotch, but simply went to bed.

Some twenty hours hence, still on the seventeenth and still in the throes of yet another grueling day, the President would stand before both houses of congress, in joint session, and fulfill his obligation to the people of the United States. He would follow in the footsteps of thirty-five presidents before him. At the end of the day of the seventeenth, well after the sun had slid beneath the horizon, President Johnson would deliver his annual message to congress.

Commonly called the State of the Union address ever since President Roosevelt's administration, a president's message to congress does not have to be a speech. The annual address, however, had reached such institutional prestige that no modern president would consider shunning it. What better opportunity to give an auspicious speech that would resound throughout the grand edifice of the nation's capital and be beamed nationwide from the seat of power directly into every American's home?

President Johnson worked for weeks on his speech. He met with cabinet members, appointees and key senators and congressmen; and with his writers. Only after endless revisions until the evening of the sixteenth did the tenor of his speech finally emerge. More revisions would occur throughout the following day.

After he awoke from a few hours of sleep, the President ate little for breakfast. By 7:30 a.m., he was already meeting George Christian, Walt Rostow, Marvin Watson and others. Lady Bird and Juanita Roberts were in continuous demand. The telephone never stopped ringing.

The President's doctor gave him a quick checkup. At eleven o'clock, Johnson met with his entire cabinet. The President, working afterwards from his personal office in the executive mansion, jotted off short memos and ordered flowers for the Prime Minister of Guyana who was a patient at Bethesda Naval Hospital. Johnson ate a late lunch of veal chop, turnip greens and a tomato-lettuce salad.

Lynda, the older of his daughters, interrupted her father's meal with something he may be interested to hear. She received a letter from a young girl in Texas. Her Marine husband had been killed just before he was to come home from Vietnam. Sullen, Lynda said she could not bear such a tragedy.

Lady Bird suggested to the President that he rest after lunch. He deflected her idea with instructions for her to wear bright colors for the evening.

At 4:30 p.m., the President met with the democratic leadership—more meetings, more phone calls and more discussion with the writers. The intensity of the day continued past dusk but allowed, at least, for a haircut.

After hosting an evening reception, the First Lady left for the Capitol Building. Not much later, at 8:30 p.m., President Johnson also departed the White House for Capitol Hill.

The President's mind was pre-occupied with his speech. The address would reference many issues, but the war in Vietnam, a touchy subject, would be foremost. The assurances he received from his advisors that the war could be won came at great risk. General William Westmoreland and General Earle G. Wheeler, Chairman of the Joint Chiefs of Staff, spoke of a new strategy. They would want more military assets; an unpleasant thought.

The speech Johnson would give very shortly must reflect only victory. It had to allay any doubt or worry, especially his own.

At precisely one minute past nine, President Johnson stood at the main door to the House of Representatives. Another Johnson, this time a Zeake W. Johnson, Jr., the Sergeant at Arms, crisply heralded the President's entrance.

"Mister Speaker, the President of the United States."

The President, smiling from ear to ear, entered the House of Representatives.

A true politician, President Johnson was anybody's match. His upbringing in a hard-scrabble part of the country prepared him for the roller coaster dirtiness of Washington politics. Often characterized as a tyrannical dictator, when it came time to get things done, no one could beat Lyndon Baines Johnson.

But now, as he made his way down the aisle, shaking hands with everyone, his outward countenance was one of amiable pride. Reinforced by significant legislative accomplishments, more than any president before him, Johnson strode through the well to the rostrum with confidence.

At this exact moment, Lyndon Johnson would rather be no place else. The President stood below and in front of Hubert Humphrey, his vice president, and John W. McCormack, the Speaker of the House, both of whom were seated on a raised dais. The President acknowledged the applause from the historic chamber as he prepared to speak to the American public.

Famous for being a profane individual, Lyndon Johnson would add spice to his comments that could be distasteful, even venomous. To emphasize his disdain for someone, Johnson would refer to him as a pissant, a favorite expression.

His oration, however, would not contain the colorful rhetoric for which he was known. President Johnson, reading from his speech, would comment warmly on America's situation: past, present and future.

Down to earth, Lyndon Johnson's address and the tone with which he would deliver it came direct from the Hill Country. Johnson used straightforward words. After a short preamble where he reminded the audience that the President of the United States always receives a warm welcome when he visits the Capitol, and the rejoining ovation that followed, he began.

"I report to you that our country is challenged."

The address commented on the strength of America, that Americans have the moral rectitude to support the cause of peace in the world.

"I believe, with abiding conviction, that this people—nurtured by their deep faith, tutored by their hard lessons, moved by their high aspirations—have the will to meet the trials that these times impose."

President Johnson swung immediately into the issue of the conflict in Southeast Asia. The President reviewed the progress that had been made in Vietnam, free elections not being the least. But, he observed: "The enemy still pours men and material south. The enemy continues to hope America's will to persevere can be broken."

The President paused for a split second. "Well, he is wrong. Our patience and our perseverance will match our power."

Consumed by Vietnam, President Johnson fretted daily about the conflict. The Commander-in-Chief oversaw the largest armada of ships and aircraft and the most effective, well-trained army in the world. How could such a puny, raggedy-assed country like Vietnam cause him so many headaches?

Johnson was not without detractors. Critics felt that Johnson was miscast as a war president, that his tendency to micro-manage a war ten thousand miles away hampered American military forces.

The President gave General Westmoreland public accolades, but privately wondered whether Westmoreland might become as controversial in Vietnam as was MacArthur in Korea.

That trifling issue wasn't reflected in his address to Congress and the American people. His speech was filled with admiration for the U.S. military and its stalwartness as well as his confidence of a favorable outcome to the conflict.

President Johnson supplemented his comments about Vietnam with reference to his earlier pledge to Pope Paul VI that America will do her part to bring an end to the war.

His speech went on to cover many topics such as exploring ocean depths, strengthening the Asian Development Bank and initiating various overtures with Russia.

Building from those things that were dear to him, President Johnson turned to issues involving the nation at home.

Lyndon Johnson's words, though neither sophisticated nor stylish, revealed a kind-heartedness that balanced his sometimes vituperative character. However much he relished his family, his ranch and his state, Johnson was of the unswerving opinion that things could be better for everyone. It all began in Johnson City, Texas, many years before.

Clean water, treated sewage, paved roads, dependable bridges, medicine, heating and general household amenities were virtually non-existent for rural Texans. Education, libraries and cultural exposure were nil. Gainful employment did not extend much beyond the farm gate. Lyndon Johnson saw these shortcomings as an obstacle to the development of his community and his state. The overriding answer was electricity, something Lyndon Johnson was instrumental in bringing to the Pedernales River Valley.

He extended his efforts to the whole of the United States. Johnson wanted to reverse the adversity that affected every American.

The President learned to use whatever means he could find to accomplish positive results. But, while in pursuit of these goals, Lyndon Baines Johnson was sometimes less than nice.

The speech continued with words about drug abuse, law enforcement and violence in the cities, higher education and poverty. He encouraged congress to act.

"When a great ship cuts through the sea..."

The President drew a curious analogy. "The waters are always stirred and troubled. And our ship is moving. It is moving toward new and better shores."

Near the conclusion of his speech, President Johnson asked one question.

"Can we achieve these goals?"

Then he answered it. "Of course we can—if we will."

As the President spoke within the warmth of the House Chambers of America's capitol building, the weather outside remained blustery. The streets of the nation's capital were vacant. Thomas Crawford's Statue of Freedom, atop the Capitol Building since the 1860s, stood watchful over the city; indeed over all America. Just beneath it, in the cupola, a bright light shone. All across the United States, Americans listened to what was being said under Crawford's statue and that beacon of light.

While President Johnson was speaking, astrologers noted that Capricorn was the zodiac sign for a person born on the seventeenth of January. The Beatles' *Magical Mystery Tour* album continued its dominance as *Billboard's* number one LP. Sicily was recovering from an earthquake that occurred just days before. Two Russian spaceships docked high above earth. Economists grappled with a rejuvenated Japan whose exports to the United States were shaking the underpinnings of America's industrial output.

In Vietnam, search and destroy missions were being launched near Saigon. America lost three aircraft on the seventeenth of January. Next day, on the eighteenth, still the seventeenth in Washington, D.C., an American A-6 Intruder was shot down.

As President Johnson stood before both houses of congress, exuding his confidence in the American people, extolling a successful conclusion to the war and asking how future goals for America could be achieved, the drama at Khe Sanh continued to unfold.

An O-2 spotter plane crashed at Khe Sanh killing two crew members. A recon team of Marines was ambushed near a hill designated as 881North. The Second Battalion Twenty-sixth Marine Regiment had joined the First and Third Battalions and was assigned to Hill 558 northwest of the combat base. The arrival of the Second Battalion marked the first time all three battalions of the Twenty-sixth Marine Regiment were operating together since Iwo Jima in 1945.

While the U.S. Marines consolidated their position at Khe Sanh, and while the supporting U.S. firebases to the east were being strengthened, the People's Army of Vietnam, the PAVN, or NVA, were also building up and strengthening their forces. Farther to the west, the NVA 675th Artillery Regiment was placing its artillery in the hills of eastern Laos.

By the time the President spoke to the nation, leaders of the North Vietnamese Army concluded their discussions about revamped military operations. They advanced the launch date of combat initiatives in Quang

Tri Province. Orders were given to the 304th Division to attack Ban Houei Sane in Laos and, farther east in Vietnam, to liberate Huong Hoa District with attacks on Khe Sanh village.

The President concluded his fifty-minute speech.

"So this, my friends, is the state of our union: seeking, building, tested many times in this past year—and always equal to the test."

At 2:00 a.m. on the eighteenth of January, the President collapsed into bed. He'd been up for twenty-four hours.

The floor of the House of Representatives still bustled. Not all the lights in the ornate chamber had been turned out. The words of Daniel Webster's oration at Bunker Hill in 1825, engraved in marble over an entrance to the visitor's gallery, high above the rostrum, remained illuminated. The words spoke subtly to the nation:

> *Let us develop the resources of our land, call forth its powers, build up its institutions, promote all its great interests and see whether we also in our day and generation may not perform something worthy to be remembered.*

CHAPTER EIGHT

THE GUNS OF CO ROC

Three 122mm Soviet-made guns and their North Vietnamese crews, under the command of Lieutenant Nguyen Van Canh, arrived on the battlefield in eastern Laos before the middle of January 1968. The partial battery belonged to the First Battalion of the 675th Artillery Regiment. The guns would be strategically positioned at Co Roc Mountain and would comprise the southern battery in primary support of the parent NVA 325C Division.

Co Roc Mountain lay just west of the narrowest section of either North or South Vietnam and south of the demilitarized zone. Contained within a much larger complex of hills and deep valleys of the Truong Son Range, Co Roc offered an unobstructed view of American-occupied western Quang Tri Province, the northern-most province of the Republic of Vietnam.

Lieutenant Canh was ebullient. He met the required arrival schedule at Co Roc as dictated by the Central Party Political Bureau. However, due to a mysterious timetable advance, Canh was surprised to learn his and the other artillery crews in his regiment had actually arrived late.

Nguyen Van Canh grew up around welding and mechanical equipment in Thai Nguyen, a city due north of Hanoi. At age eighteen, following in the footsteps of his two brothers, Nguyen Van Canh joined the *Quan Doi Nhan Dan* (People's Army). Canh first enlisted in the infantry, but he quickly convinced his superiors that due to his understanding of machinery, an assignment to artillery made more sense.

Lieutenant Canh was sent to the mountainous interior of Hoa Binh Province for training with the 675th Regiment. Through a prolonged period of live fire practice, he learned the rudimentary procedures for laying the battery, how to use the *may tinh duong dan phao mat dat* (aiming circle) and a gunner's quadrant.

By early October 1967, Canh's artillery regiment received orders to make its way south.

One week after his arrival in Thanh Hoa, his regiment moved again farther south. It arrived on the outskirts of Vinh, just short of the start of the hazardous Truong Son Trail that would lead even farther south into the unknown.

Now that Canh was going to the war zone, to the B Fronts or, more simply to "the B," as the *bo doi* (soldiers) casually called it, Canh was rewarded with a promotion in rank. He now wore two stars and a bar on his yellow epaulettes signifying his new rank of Full (First) Lieutenant. He was more proud, however, of the insignia for his field uniform. His collar tabs showed two stars and a single line beneath them next to which were placed two crossed cannons on a field of red.

The grueling march south along the Truong Son Trail could take one to two months for an infantryman, depending on one's final destination, but required more time for transporting cumbersome artillery pieces. Due to the urgent need of the large 122mm cannons, Canh's artillery regiment had been given trans-shipment priority.

After each day's travel, the cannons were checked, completely covered anew and hidden several kilometers away from the road network of the Truong Son Trail. American aerial surveillance was a constant reminder that if the regiment did not take every precaution, the trucks and artillery would be discovered and destroyed from the air by enemy aircraft.

Headlights were darkened, the trucks and artillery heavily camouflaged. Fuel was pumped out of the tanks of each vehicle when they stopped at the *binh tram* (waypoint) so there would be no secondary explosion if hit by American bombs.

Artillery and the bulk of ammunition did not travel together. Ammunition for the artillery followed a more circuitous route to converge with the guns at Co Roc. To lose either the big guns or the ammunition was one thing. To lose them both at the same time would be too great a loss.

The 675th Regiment, called *trung doan khong may man* (hard luck regiment) never seemed to have anything it needed. It incurred many losses. Canh and his comrades spent hours burying bodies on the sides of hills or alongside river banks. To avoid making unnecessary noise, the men carved out graves in the earth with their bare hands.

After so many river crossings, through switchback A, the ford at Ta Le, and the passes at Phu La Nich and Mu Gia, the regiment, with its long-barreled artillery, finally reached its destination: the Co Roc Massif.

Canh had no comprehension of the effort it takes to tug artillery up steep hills, but that's what his predecessors did at Dien Bien Phu many years before.

Nguyen Van Canh remembered the story of To Vinh Dien who had thrown his body beneath the carriage of a large artillery piece to keep it from rolling downhill when the ropes broke. He saved the cannon, but died from internal injuries.

Canh and his men worked tirelessly. The three artillery pieces, the first in the regiment, were positioned in their natural lair offered by shallow limestone caves on the east side of the high mountain ridge in eastern Laos. Canh lay his partial battery using his Russian-made aiming circle. Shots from his artillery would easily clear the tallest obstruction.

Worn out from so many long days of arduous work and sleepless nights, Canh barked out orders to the other gun crews to move faster.

"Men, we can't stop now. We're the vanguard of the offensive to kill the imperialists. We can rest when we're dead."

The guns would be aimed east at the Americans who occupied a large, flat area in Huong Hoa District, Quang Tri Province, South Vietnam. The Americans referred to the base as Khe Sanh.

The forward observers had already acquired geographical and targeting details. They relayed ranging information back to the guns of Co Roc.

Canh's understanding of the layout of the targets required two days. He had only to correlate gun azimuth with coordinates and firing angles, load the big guns, fire; and repeat.

Almost one hundred artillery rounds had been brought up the steep jungle trail from the staging area, one at a time, by sweating Laotian peasants who were pressed into service. Canh positioned twenty OF530 projectiles near the guns. The fuses were set for sudden detonation upon impact. The breech at the back of each artillery piece was left open in anticipation of the first round. Canh's crew swabbed the barrel of each cannon and oiled the moving parts.

Now, well after dark, Canh and members of his gun crew squatted on their haunches around a solitary flame that was concealed at the back of the damp cave. They boiled rice and cooked a large cobra they killed and skinned that day. They sipped yellow tea from porcelain cups. For dessert, the men ate bananas and licked the palms of their hands into which they had sprinkled some salt. They smoked hand-rolled cigarettes.

A runner arrived just after midnight carrying orders in a leather shoulder bag. Communication by runners would foil any attempt by the Americans to intercept radio messages. Lieutenant Canh guessed the contents of the message. He was not disappointed.

The barrage aimed against the enemy would begin before sunrise, a few hours hence.

Canh saw flashes on the horizon to the northeast and heard muffled explosions. A strategic hill occupied by the Americans was under attack. A few hours later, the flashes subsided.

Canh looked at his watch. Irrespective of the other guns awaiting their emplacement, the time for unleashing the destructive power of his artillery was near. The emphasis of combat action, manifested by the North Vietnamese ground offensive against the Americans on a distant hill, shifted to that of Canh's more strategic artillery.

Canh took one last sip of tea from the porcelain cup. He lit a cigarette with a twig he had picked up from the perimeter of the small fire. He gave the signal to load the ordnance.

The first of many projectiles that weighed about forty kilograms, was shoved into the empty chamber at the back of the heavy cannon. The solid square breech block was slammed shut and secured. Canh checked the gun barrel elevation angle and azimuth. The round was ready to fire.

Canh spoke in a laughing but derisive manner, his smoking cigarette dangling from between his lips.

"I understand *bon My ngu ngoc* [stupid Americans] drink too much beer and whiskey at night. They have trouble waking up in the mornings without their foul coffee."

His body covered in sweat, Lieutenant Canh grabbed the lanyard and stood back. He drew on the cigarette and exhaled its white smoke. "This should help. *Do lay, lu luoi bieng* [Catch this, you lazy bastards]."

At exactly 5:30 a.m., First Lieutenant Nguyen Van Canh yanked on the lanyard of the artillery piece activating the spring-loaded firing hammer. The heavy 122mm gun jumped with a bone rattling sound that shook everything.

The spinning projectile spat out the cannon's muzzle faster than the eye could see. Shadowy silhouettes created by bright red-orange flames were instantaneously frozen on the walls of the cave. Thick, acrid smoke filled the damp, pre-dawn morning.

The shell traveled its eastward trajectory, piercing the dark sky. Its throbbing-rushing noise was the only evidence of the projectile's nocturnal flight.

The shell's velocity could not overcome the tug of gravity and, from its apogee, began its parabolic descent to earth.

Twenty-three seconds after having been fired, the shell slammed unerringly into the middle of the American encampment. The projectile exploded with a loud report creating a cloud of smoke and causing an eruption of red dirt from the crater it had created. The shell, precisely machined, uniformly shaped with features described by sophisticated terms such as ogive, bourrelet and obturating band, instantly transformed into an ugly, wild spray of hot, jagged shrapnel that spread immediately in all directions. Each razor-sharp, searing fragment sang its deadly song as it whizzed through the air.

The destructive mission of the artillery shell fired from Nguyen Van Canh's gun at Co Roc was accomplished. Many more shells from Co Roc hit targets on the American base.

At the receiving end, men of the U.S. Twenty-sixth Marine Regiment and elements of the Thirteenth Marines found themselves in frightful circumstances.

The date was 21 January 1968. The siege of Khe Sanh had begun.

CHAPTER NINE

B5T8

The U.S. military divided South Vietnam into four Corps Tactical Zones, or CTZs, more conveniently called Corps. Bounded by rivers, each Corps was designated with a Roman numeral. I Corps (One or First Corps) was located in the northern part of the country with II Corps, III Corps and IV Corps below that.

I Corps, sat immediately below the demilitarized zone, or DMZ, that separated North and South Vietnam. The seventeenth parallel identified the separation, but the Ben Hai River marked it. While II Corps was the largest of the four corps, I Corps was the most active.

Located close to the DMZ in Quang Tri Province, the northern most province in I Corps, and closer yet to Laos, the lonely village of Khe Sanh dominated a place of unspoiled beauty.

Inviting but foreboding, peaceful yet menacing, pristine and at once primitive, Khe Sanh wrests a primordial feeling of the unknown, something undefined, a fateful occurrence that happened or is about to happen. Valleys and precipitous hills, covered in a soft patina of velveteen green, provide a surreal backdrop, an allure of natural splendor. White fog, a spirit sliding up the sides of mountains only to disappear, exudes an aura of mysticism.

The translation of Khe Sanh into English is not exact. *Khe* by itself means mountain stream or mountain creek. The word can also mean "valley." When used in conjunction with another word, the meaning becomes complex. *Khe cua* means the opening between the door and the door sill. *Khe bo tho* means "mail slot" while *khe nui*, a redundancy, also means "mountain stream."

The translation of *Sanh* is more complicated. *Sanh* may have come from *Xanh*, meaning green or blue, with the same pronunciation. But, the precise word *Sanh* refers to a species of tree that belongs to the genus *Ficus*. Less common, *Sanh* can also mean a tree whose bark is used as a dye.

Khe is pronounced as it appears, like "kay," but is slightly aspirated at the back of the throat. *Sanh* is pronounced by the southern populace like "schaun," and by northern people, more like "sand" without the hard D sound.

While understandable to assume Khe Sanh is a corruption or literary progression of *Khe Xanh*, some translate it to mean "Green River." But, the more precise meaning of Khe Sanh is either "Weeping Fig Stream," or "Ficus Tree Valley."

A sleepy place, Khe Sanh Ville, the government seat of Huong Hoa District, consisted of a few huts and small buildings. The area was sparsely populated by Montagnards, a name derived from the French language, meaning mountain people. These ethnic people of slight build were called Bru. Isolated for many generations, the Bru, who elevated their homes several feet above ground, spoke in a special dialect.

Early French settlers cultivated coffee plants in abundance. Nurtured by the rich red soil, the plants required ten tedious years before producing beans.

The only road that serviced Khe Sanh originally was not much more than a path. The pathetic route allowed various forces to invade from east to west and vice-a-versa. The narrow passes also afforded defensive measures from those marauding armies.

Serious construction work on what would later become Colonial Highway Nine, eventually becoming Quoc Luong Chin (QL9), began in 1904 by the French, but it wasn't until 1918 that the rutted trail began to have the semblance of a useable road.

During the French colonial period, Highway Nine continued to play a pivotal role for infiltration and communication. In one battle near Lao Bao, the French were all but slaughtered by the Viet Minh. In the early 1960s, communist forces used Highway Nine to push eastward from Laos toward Hue. This did not go unnoticed by the Americans.

Just to the north of Khe Sanh Ville and Highway Nine sat an old establishment originally called Xom Cham. Its name was derived from the Cham people who originated from southern India and migrated to Vietnam a thousand years before. This became known as the Khe Sanh Combat Base.

Although Americans had been in and out of the region for several years, the Green Berets were the first to inhabit the area on a permanent basis in 1962. Through a progression of U.S. Special Forces, other units of the U.S. Army and finally the U.S. Marines, the Khe Sanh area of operations expanded in size and in importance. The Khe Sanh Combat Base, a cornerstone of "leatherneck square," was one of a few American outposts that dotted Quang Tri Province in the mid-1960s. Known as Ta Con by the enemy, Khe Sanh was to act as a barrier to the North Vietnamese army as the *bo doi* filtered south.

The Khe Sanh Combat Base, slightly rectangular in shape, a little less than a mile long by about a half mile wide, sat on a flat plain. The combat base had amenities attendant to its survival—sort of. Those conveniences were inadequate and unreliable. Homes were carved out of the earth and covered with rough-hewn beams and dirt and sandbags, or anything that could be found. Dwellings were drab, depressing and shanty. The unpaved streets were deep in mud when rain fell and dusty when it didn't. Light at night was a scarcity.

Water, other than rain, was rare. Drilling for water had been studied, but abandoned. A small stream at the very base of the plateau on the steep north side was the only practical source of water. A pump, strained to its limits, continuously pushed water more than two hundred feet up the side of the ravine to the base.

Fixed-wing cargo aircraft, landing on a single runway less than four thousand feet in length, serviced the base and its inhabitants. The narrow airstrip, which ran east-west, actually extended outside the perimeter wire at the east end. The metal planking beneath the plane's tires rumbled as if being ground up by some machine. The strip, a place to avoid, was a natural target for the NVA's big guns.

Revetments for six helicopters were constructed on the north side of the airstrip. Air traffic was controlled from a short tower, a sign attached to the side of which read "Welcome to Khe Sanh."

Two main ammunition storage points, ASP1 and ASP2, were located at opposite ends of the base with mini-depots elsewhere. Two batteries of 105mm artillery were positioned roughly at the east end of the base while batteries of 105mm and 155mm artillery were positioned toward the west end. Mortars, machine guns, 106mm recoilless rifles and some M-48 tanks were placed at other locations. The underground Combat Operations Center (COC) was located in the middle of the base on the south side of the runway, but dangerously close to the southern perimeter. The main gate to the base was found on the southwest to west side. The entire area was ringed with concertina wire, tanglefoot patterns, zig-zag trenches and by men of the Twenty-sixth Marines.

As a result of bloody fighting in the rough terrain around the base in the spring of 1967, U.S. Marines occupied a few nearby hills that formed a loose line north of the base.

American Forces at Khe Sanh were commanded by four successive Marine colonels. The first was J.P. Lanigan, then John Padley. The last was Bruce Meyers. But, it was David Edward Lownds, Meyers' predecessor, who commanded the base through its most perilous period.

The Khe Sanh Combat Base, home to six thousand Marines, was in a dangerous neighborhood. As the Americans compounded their efforts and increased their presence, so, too, did the army of North Vietnam.

The North Vietnamese mobilized a formidable array of military assets under the command of General Tran Quy Hai: the 304th Division, 325C Division, 320A Division, elements of the 324th Division and the Vinh Linh Infantry Regiment. To support the forces, the enemy brought south five regiments, four battalions and two companies of artillery with over two hundred cannons, two regiments and three battalions of rocket artillery and six hundred machine guns of various calibers. The North Vietnamese army mobilized one regiment and one battalion of engineers, a battalion and a company of tanks, and various reconnaissance, signal, chemical and transportation units. The Quan Doi Nhan Dan had close to sixty thousand combatants and one hundred thousand support personnel, all lined up against the Americans.

But, the North Vietnamese lacked one thing: effective defense against the United States Air Force.

By the end of 1967, Khe Sanh was beneath the spotlight at center stage of the Vietnam conflict. Colonel Lownds expected Khe Sanh would be attacked early in 1968. He issued chilling instructions to his men to wear their helmets and flak jackets. They were to carry their rifles at all times. Khe Sanh was about to get messy.

The Americans called the defense of Khe Sanh Operation Scotland. The North Vietnamese gave Khe Sanh a different code name. They called it B5T8.

CHAPTER TEN

THE CONGO COMES CALLING

The Christmas holidays, now several weeks passed, became a memory for the Johnson family. The state of the union address slid into history. Again in the Oval Office, President Johnson was reading a diplomatic letter from the Republic of the Congo. He took a deep breath and, with a sign of agitation, breathed out heavily. He looked up from his desk at Richard Helms, the CIA Director, who had come for a meeting.

"Dick, we will inform the High Honorable Mobutu Sese Seko Nkuku Ngbendu Wa Za Banga that the U.S. will send limited humanitarian supplies to the Congo, but no troops and no military airplanes. I don't give a damn what his request is. We're not gonna get embroiled in central Africa—talk about an endless quagmire."

"Understood, Mr. President."

"Please prepare a formal communiqué in French—you're good at that, Dick—from me to him and tell him to get lost—in a nice way, of course."

"Will do, Mr. President. You'll have the draft response by end of the day."

"Send it through Rostow. He'll handle it for me."

The President looked at Helms quizzically. "What's his name mean, anyway, this wa za banga stuff? I can hardly pronounce it."

"The cock that left no hen standing. Something like that, Sir."

The President laughed.

"Well, whatever…Poor hens. I don't have time to worry about central Africa right now."

"Mr. President, Jordan is requesting one hundred million dollars in military aid. They want F-4 Phantoms…twelve squadrons in fact, and tanks, anti-aircraft guns and howitzers. Israel will be very upset if we give the Jordanians tanks or artillery, or any F-4s. But, if we don't do something, Jordan may turn to Russia."

"A delicate request, Helms. The world is still feeling the repercussions of the Six Day War. The Arab-Israeli thing is so damn volatile. You know this first-hand."

"Yes, Sir."

"We'll look at that later. Let's move on. What about the B-52 crash in Greenland?"

"Sir, the aircraft crashed in the sea ice about seven and a half miles short of the runway. It was carrying four devices…"

"Devices? You're referring to bombs, right? Not just bombs, H-Bombs, I believe."

"The B-52 was on a Chrome Dome mission. The pilot reported fire on board and declared an emergency over Thule Airbase. Smoke filled the cockpit. The crew ejected."

"Damn cold up there."

"As far as we now know, Sir, the B-52 rests on the bottom of the Arctic Ocean. The ocean depth there is about three hundred feet. Disaster teams are on their way to the scene, Sir."

"Richard, the real reason why you're here. What's this crap about attacks on some hill around Khe Sanh, and NVA artillery action that set off a large explosion? Damn, if it's not one thing over there, it's another."

"Sir, the hill to which you make reference is Hill 861…"

"What's with the 861?"

"It's just a number, Mr. President, the elevation designation seen on topographic maps. Hill 861 is eight hundred sixty-one meters above sea level."

"Oh, OK." The President smiled. "I should have been able to guess that."

"It's defended by Kilo Company Third Battalion Twenty-sixth Marines. On the evening of the twentieth of January, Sir—Vietnam time—the hill sustained hits by rocket propelled grenades and from heavy mortar fire. The NVA attacked after midnight on the twenty-first. The Marines used star shell rounds for illumination. Hundreds of NVA were seen coming up the hill. The Marines on Hill 881 South supported the Marines on 861 with mortar fire. We lost a number of Marines but the NVA lost far more men, maybe as many as two hundred. Kilo Company pushed them off the hill."

"I can't keep the locations straight in my mind. What else?"

"Sir, some bad news. Khe Sanh Ville was attacked. It seems a helicopter relief force was trying to reach the village and ran into fierce opposition. The effort went disastrously wrong and we lost a number of pilots and several helicopters. Reports indicate about eighty men were killed, Sir...Americans and South Vietnamese."

"God almighty, Helms."

"Sir, the NVA are picking off easy targets in an effort to squeeze us. We evacuated the town of Khe Sanh and brought those Marines back to the combat base from their listening post."

Helms looked at the report. "Says we got Mutter out on the last chopper... the codename of the radio operator, Sir. He was on the radio for thirty-six straight hours while the NVA surrounded the town."

The President tapped his knee as he looked to his right through the doors to the Rose Garden.

"Helms, I hope we're not exceeding our capabilities. The number of Marines we lost at Con Thien last summer...well, Khe Sanh may be worse. I get so damned many conflicting reports, all official of course. I can tell you, the American people will raise hell if something goes awry. Westmoreland wants more troops, but for what? To build more forts? Rostow is a strong supporter of Westy's request. Bunker, too. The Joint Chiefs are pushing me into a corner. They're concerned about contingencies that may occur around the world. I understand their point, but I also know Westmoreland's itchin' to invade Laos."

"Sir, our presence in One Corps is essential to our mission in South Vietnam."

The President noticed that Helms's reference was One Corps, not Khe Sanh directly, but he let it pass.

"Helms, what the hell have the Viet-nese ever accomplished? They live in huts and eat rice and fish. So what? On the other hand, the loss of one American boy, a boy from any city or from some farm in New Mexico or Nebraska or anywhere, is a disaster as far as I'm concerned. Someday, they'll build some monument to this war. I would want it to be a memorial to our moral resolve and victory, to the Americans who lost their lives for the cause of freedom. I want to win this damned war. If we don't, that monument will be for nothing. The sacrifice will be too bitter. We gotta win, Helms."

The President was clearly speaking his mind. Helms appreciated the genuine candidness, but still, a palpable discomfort arose. He looked down at his shoes.

The President continued.

"Texas won its independence from Mexico. The Mexicans left Texas alone. South Vietnam and North Vietnam became independent, too. Why, in God's name, can't Ho Chi Minh just leave South Vietnam the hell alone? Why can't the two countries co-exist peacefully? There's nothing there anyway. West Texas is more productive than either country or both combined. It's because...dammit...I swear, it's because of those greedy, communist bastards."

"Sir, ancestry and ancestral home are everything in the Vietnamese culture...to the Buddhists. Even if they wanted to, they can't leave Vietnam. The people are attached to the land. They'll abandon their departed family."

The President drummed his fingers on the desk, an irritating habit, then pointed to Richard Helms.

"I'm not suggesting they leave their country, Dick. Ho Chi Minh is not the Pied Piper, he isn't George Washington and he sure as hell ain't no Jesus Christ."

Richard Helms tried to speak, but the President continued.

"How in hell can a Buddhist become a communist? I dunno."

"Sir, I talked with..."

"Helms, my correspondence last year with Ho Chi Minh didn't yield a damn thing. In Texas, we iron out our differences face-to-face. I'll wager odds if I could get Ho Chi Minh to visit the ranch—why hell, he can bring his whole damn government, I don't care if they're a bunch of communists—Ho Chi Minh and I could sit beneath the live oaks next to the Perd'naliss after a Walter Jetton barbecue dinner—God, he can cook some barbecue, now..."

The President smiled. "I swear...and talk through our differences. I'd probably end up likin' the guy, beard and all. I'd give him a ten-gallon hat, a gray one to match his beard. He'd probably give me one of them conical hats. Anyway, I just know we could come to agreement. They can have North Vietnam. They can have their silly communist government. Just stay the hell out of South Vietnam."

"Sir, not to argue a point, a hundred years ago, our country was split ideologically, too."

"Yeah, I'm well aware of that fact, Dick, but there were no communists back then trying to dominate the world through their Bolshevik revolutionary crap."

"Sir, as far as Ho Chi Minh is concerned, they're all Vietnamese and the entire country should be under a communist flag."

"Dick, why Ho Chi Minh sided with the communists is beyond my understanding. What claim do they have over South Vietnam? The South Vietnamese don't want communism. Ho Chi Minh used parts of our Declaration of Independence for his own. Why did he choose to follow Lenin or Marx? That Marx. What a charlatan...a Russian communist revolutionary, but where did he choose to live? He was no fool. He lived in London."

Helms chuckled.

"Marx was German, Mr. President. But, you're right, he lived in London for a number of years and wrote articles for the *New York Tribune*."

"German, Russian, I don't give a shit. What's Marx or communism done for the world? Why didn't Ho Chi Minh follow Hancock or Jefferson? I just don't understand these people. Communism ain't gonna do a damn thing except prolong misery."

Helms cleared his throat.

"Mr. President, William Colby visited Vietnam in 1960 when he was Director of the CIA. He was even in the Khe Sanh and Lao Bao areas. And, a point of interest, Sir. A handful of Americans led by a Major Allison Thomas parachuted into the Bac Viet region of northern Vietnam behind Japanese lines in 1945 and worked with Ho Chi Minh and General Giap for a number of months. I believe they became good friends."

"Really? Well, perhaps we should have tried to work something out with that bony Ho Chi Minh years ago. If I could get him to the Perd'naliss, I'm satisfied we could resolve this thing."

President Johnson sighed. "We're stuck with it, Helms. It is what it is."

"I'm afraid so, Mr. President."

CHAPTER ELEVEN

XE DAP THO AND THE XE CONG NONG

The Truong Son Trail, a series of interwoven paths, wound its way south through eastern Laos along the west edge of Vietnam. The supply corridor linked North Vietnam to the battlefields of South Vietnam. Beginning in Ha Tinh Province, south of Kim Lien Village, the birthplace of Ho Chi Minh, the Truong Son Trail terminated at various points on the northern, western and southern provinces of South Vietnam.

The responsibility for the trail's complex transportation network fell to North Vietnam's Army Group 559 under the command of an imposing general named Dong Sy Nguyen.

Faceless and nameless, tens of thousands of volunteers maintained the roadways, foot paths, bridges, river crossings, underground storage and accommodation bunkers, and intermediate way stations. They built the complete support infrastructure including medical facilities, repair shops and communication systems.

Armed with picks and shovels, men and women gouged out the famous trail and the connecting spurs. They created rudimentary roads and paths across swamps and along hillsides by hand. Workers concealed the routes from view by tying together overhead canopies of trees and bamboo stands.

Floating bridge sections were made from bamboo. Pieced together at night, the sections were untied and hidden along the river banks during the day.

Millions of interminable hours of human labor pushed the supply trail south. Workers never had enough to eat. Skinny, their arms were like toothpicks. Their bare legs and feet bled continuously. Still, they worked round the clock.

Generals Vo Nguyen Giap and Dong Sy Nguyen made an inspection of progress in mid-1967 and handed out commendations. The generals warned the assembled crowd of workers that sacrifices were necessary, that losses would be many until the invaders were pressed forever into the East Sea.

After the awards and speeches, *bia hoi* (beer) was distributed. Young women sang songs while men played tunes on roughly crafted guitars.

At many places along the route, workers had placed impromptu signs. One sign read "Because of the trail, we will have our glorious victory." Another sign admonished "An idle shovel is no help!"

Construction work on the Truong Son Trail was often disrupted by American air attacks. *Phao phong khong* (air defense artillery) provided some protection, but the American warplanes were never deterred. Many workers were killed. They were buried where they fell.

Beginning in late summer of 1967 and into early 1968, a continuous stream of soldiers and war materiel flowed from North Vietnam down the trail to locations south of the Ben Hai River.

Old men pushed *xe dap tho* (pack bicycles) each loaded with two hundred kilograms of ordnance. Inner tubes were so worn out that straw was compacted inside the tire to give it strength. Often the tire itself was missing, leaving only the rim. The pedals and drive chains had long ago disappeared. To overcome the lack of locomotion, long, sturdy sticks, attached to the handlebar frames, protruded to one side. Two men would push a xe dap tho along the path using the side sticks as they steadied the bicycle with another stick attached upright to the frame next to or just behind the seat. Like a train, the xe dap tho continued endlessly down the serpentine trail.

Small, one-cylinder *xe cong nong* (small tractor trucks) bringing supplies, driven by men wearing only shorts and sandals, arrived constantly. The annoying, pounding drone of un-muffled, one-cylinder diesel engines, with their pervasive staccato rhythm and singular puffs of exhaust smoke, marked the steady progress of the mini-cargo trucks as they clambered along the rutted jungle trails. The width of the wheelbase was much less than the wheelbase of the larger Chinese and Russian trucks. The *xe cong nong* was only as long as the Russian trucks were wide.

Large trucks carrying heavier artillery shells and rockets continuously rumbled through the mud. Some of the tires were blown out. The other tires, still inflated but with gashes in their sidewalls, carried the heavy loads. Workers threw green bamboo in front of vehicles struggling through swampy areas. The cracking sound as the tires rolled over the stalks echoed throughout the jungle.

Bundles of bamboo hung from the truck doors to serve as armor against shrapnel.

Women, two or three in a bunch, transported ammunition in baskets suspended from the ends of long poles. They would appear like stick figures on some rise and disappear in the distance down the trail.

On side hills, workers excavated dirt and rocks with picks, long pointed poles and small, square-bladed shovels hammered out in iron shops in Nam Dinh. The same shovels were used to excavate cavernous chambers deep below the surface, and by soldiers for entrenching operations as they crept closer to the American lines.

Workers pushed large stones down the hillside. Foremen, shouting orders, urged the laborers to work harder and faster. They yelled, "Vietnam's freedom is more important than your safety." Another message directed at the less productive workers was shouted, "A sleeping worker is a worthless cockroach."

Logicians directed forces, military supplies and ordnance into Laos and around the area just south of the DMZ, to various depots and to H1 and H2 artillery zones.

Ordnance was the priority. The war effort against the American invaders couldn't be bothered with food and clean water. Workers and soldiers could eat off the land and boil river water.

At the end of each fourteen hour shift, some workers picked up a *dieu cay* (bamboo pipe). They would clean the pipe's bowl, fill it with tobacco and light it. The taste wasn't as good as that of opium.

Construction efforts, imprecise as they were, never stopped. Through the labors of so many people, Group 559, building a rudimentary transportation conduit from the jungles and mountains, prepared the way south.

The network that defined the Ho Chi Minh Trail, beginning at a remote place in Ha Tinh Province, was a confusing knot of roads and interconnecting paths, but they all led toward one objective: the destruction of the American imperialists.

CHAPTER TWELVE

YANKEE CLIPPER

Juanita Roberts answered the phone."Yes, Mr. President, may I help you?"

"Juanita..."

Lyndon Johnson pulled impatiently on one of his big ears. "Is the commissioner here yet?"

"He just arrived, Sir."

"Well, whadaya waitin' fer? Show him in. I've looked forward to this for days."

President Johnson stood from the executive chair and walked around the wood desk. The President would greet his famous guest in the middle of the Oval Office. He straightened his suit jacket and tie.

Lyndon Johnson had always been a dapper dresser. One never gets a second chance to make a first impression. Smart dress was the mark of a successful man.

President Johnson preferred dark suits, but for this occasion, he chose a lighter color. Spring was still far away. Perhaps the President could speed it along with a pale blue shirt and a bright tie.

He was wearing a new pair of brown shoes that his daughters had given him. How the President relished receiving spontaneous gifts from either of his two daughters. That's the Texas way; the Hill Country way. Damn, it's the Johnson way.

One detail irritated the hell out of Lyndon Johnson. Shouldn't a President of the United States of America be able to dictate the timing and duration of meetings, especially when such a famous person shows up in the White House?

The special guest entered the Oval Office. The President's grin revealed the pleasure of the acquaintance.

"Well, if it isn't Commissioner Joe DiMaggio in the flesh. I can't believe my sad, ole Texas eyes. The Yankee Clipper right here in the Oval Office."

"Mr. President, you know I'm not the Commissioner of Baseball."

"Well, dammit, you oughta be."

The President shook the famous baseball player's hand vigorously. "Come in, Joe, come in."

DiMaggio surveyed the place where the President of the United States works.

"So, this is the Oval Office. I've always imagined it to be much bigger."

Johnson chuckled.

"It's pretty damned small."

The President's office, painted white, was decorated with white drapes and imitation gas lamps on the wall. A dark green carpet covered most of the floor. Paintings of George Washington and Andrew Jackson hung on the walls to either side of the President's desk. Another painting of Franklin Delano Roosevelt hung over the fireplace on the opposite side of the oval-shaped room. Two opposing white couches and a round marble-top coffee table were positioned in the middle of the room in front of the fireplace. A telephone console had been installed in a sliding drawer that could be concealed in the coffee table. A rocking chair—obviously the President's—and an odd foot stool and a small end table beside it were positioned next to the round coffee table. Behind the ensemble, flags of the armed services framed the three doors to the Rose Garden. The flag of the United States Marine Corps stood proudly to the far left of the four flags. The American flag and the blue flag of the office of the President stood behind President Johnson's desk. A globe sat next to the presidential flag. A low cabinet, positioned a few feet to the left side of the President's desk, contained three TVs, one for each network: CBS, NBC and ABC. A photograph of the President and Mrs. Johnson sat in its frame on top.

Left of the TVs, a larger console contained teletype machines for the wire services. So impatient, Johnson would sometimes kneel down on the carpet to read the printout the second it emerged from the teletype rather than wait for it to appear beneath the viewing glass on top.

DiMaggio pointed to the President's desk.

"That's one hell of a phone, Mr. President."

"Ah, Joe, I'm on the phone all the time. I've got 'em everywhere. I tell my staff if I can't get you by the third ring, your ass is fired. Every call from any member of congress better be returned that day. No excuses. If a visitor bores me, why hell, I'll pick up the phone and call someone for no reason. That won't happen today. Not with you."

"Mr. President, I know all about boring people."

"That phone has seventy-two lines. Hell, I get calls from Europe, South America, Africa...even from Russia."

The President laughed. "Don't get me wrong, though, I don't particularly like to receive calls at night."

"Mr. President, it's a great honor to be here."

"Oh, come on," the President laughed. "What would you like to drink? A whiskey, perhaps?"

"Just water."

"When I learned that the baseball delegation was coming to the White House, I told Juanita to arrange my schedule so I could meet the great center fielder, the three-time MVP."

DiMaggio laughed pretentiously.

"I usually get paid for public appearances."

The President smiled.

"I've always been a big fan of yours. I played first base in Johnson City—never was the athlete I wanted to be. Got punched out once in Fredericksburg, Texas by some German kid."

The President shook his head. "I'll never forget that night."

President Johnson stooped and reached for the phone beneath the round marble table as he continued to talk. "We need a photo."

Then, speaking into the receiver; "Juanita, get the photographer in here...

what do you mean you don't where Okamoto is? Go find him. And bring a glass of ice water for my honored guest."

The President winked at DiMaggio.

"Yeah, Juanita, we need a picture of the commissioner and me in the Oval Office."

DiMaggio shook his head at the President's reference to him being something he was not.

Johnson put the phone down.

"I think President Polk was the first president to be photographed."

"When was that, Mr. President?"

"Polk? Oh, hell. I don't know. Eighteen forty-eight, forty nine...something like that. I'm the first president to put a photographer on the White House payroll. And please..."

President Johnson waved one hand in a dismissive gesture. "My name's Lyndon."

DiMaggio laughed.

"Are you sure, Mr. President?"

"Oh crap, I hear it all the time. Mr. President this...Mr. President that... Some coffee, Mr. President? Are you OK, Mr. President? People come in here and they sit in awe of the almighty President. That's all I hear around this high-falootin' homestead...Mr. President, Mr. President. Lyndon's my name...not as famous as yours."

The two men laughed.

"This old place. I swear. The floors creak like the place was filled with ghosts. Ventilation is terrible. Can't open the windows. When I moved in here, the shower was horrible. I told them to install a new one."

Yoichi Okamoto entered the Oval Office carrying a camera and a glass of ice water.

"Come on, Joe, let's stand next to the fireplace for a photo."

The flash brightened the room for a split second.

"Thanks, Mr. President."

The conversation turned to many baseball topics—Bob Feller's fastball, Babe Ruth, Mickey Mantle, Roger Maris and his homerun record, the ease with which the ball could be knocked out of Fenway Park and the historic rivalry between the Yankees and the Red Sox.

But, the discourse assumed a different tone as a more disconcerting topic was broached.

"So, Joe, tell me. I've heard you just returned from a visit to Vietnam. You were there in late sixty-seven—last month, in fact—December."

The President looked at his watch. "Damn. Where does the time go? Quick, tell me what you saw."

"Lyndon, I'm a ball player, not an expert on Vietnam, but I think things will get really bad over there unless we take additional steps."

The President raised his eyebrows.

DiMaggio took a sip of water and continued. "North Vietnam, South Vietnam, Russia, China, the U.S., it's a five-way ball game and nobody's playin' by the same rules."

"Yeah, I want to negotiate, but I can't agree to Hanoi's terms. Did you go to Khe Sanh, by any chance?"

"No, why do you ask?"

"Just curious. The Marines have come under attack in the northern most province in Eye Corps."

"I'm sorry, Mr. President, you mean capital I? I thought it was One Corps or First Corps."

"Yeah, I had the same problem. It's One Corps, or I suppose, First Corps—they use Roman numerals—but Roman numeral one looks like a capital I and so they sometimes call it Eye Corps and even spell it E-Y-E Corps... just like eyeball, or, you know, I Street...E-Y- E. Anyway, whatever...I was just wondering what you saw if you went there."

"No, Lyndon, I didn't go there. All I ever knew when I was in Vietnam was that I needed a shower all the damned time. Man, was it ever hot and sweaty over there."

The President chuckled as he held his right hand up to his chin.

"The Pentagon tells me if we disengage from Khe Sanh, we'll lose the initiative. If we leave, the communist propaganda machine will kick into high gear touting a commie victory. Many feel Khe Sanh is our anchor in

Quang Tri Province. The NVA have been building up just south of the DMZ for weeks now. It ain't lookin' good.

"Westmoreland says we gotta cut the Ho Chi Minh Trail. Hell, McNamara's advocated building a wall that stretches the length of the DMZ, like, I dunno, the Berlin Wall. They called it McNamara's Line."

"A wall, Mr. President? That'll take a bunch of money. Wouldn't it have to extend all the way to Thailand?"

"Probably."

The President raised both his hands in a gesture of exasperation. "I dunno. The right and left wings are on my ass. Congress is on everybody's ass. Westy wants to invade Laos. I'm on his ass."

"Lyndon, I can tell a batter to be careful of a three-two count with a pitcher who throws a mean curve ball. With two runners on base and a line drive to right field, I can tell you where the play is. But I know little about military tactics."

"Yeah, I have to believe my generals are right. They have the Twenty-sixth Marines, all three battalions, and a battalion of the Thirteenth Marines up there. A battalion of the Ninth Marines is deploying there now."

The President looked at his watch nervously.

"I understand Carl Yastrzemski's with you...last year's MVP."

"You bet. American League. Yas has only played with the Red Sox."

"Just like you. You only ever played with the Yankees...nine times world series champions."

"As the quote goes. 'I'd like to thank the good Lord for making me a Yankee.' Sadly, team loyalty will soon be a thing of the past. It's all about money now."

"Joe, so sorry, I have another meeting I can't delay."

The President motioned the way out. "It's been terrific seeing you. Listen, some of the staff want your autograph, so if you'll indulge them in the hallway, I'd 'preciate it."

CHAPTER THIRTEEN

LETTER TO SARAH

The letter to Sarah began: *You cannot believe how my heart misses you. I haven't heard from you for so long.*

Ben Bradford, from Fullerton, California, and now a rifleman with Lima Company Third Battalion Twenty-sixth Marines, had to compose the remainder of his letter to his girlfriend quickly on an aerogram another Marine had given him. Hunched over a splintered, shrapnel-torn plank laying across his lap, Bradford scribbled out sentences that would convey his truest feelings to his girlfriend. He made an attempt at some humor, but it didn't work. He thought he might tell Sarah he'd like to take her fishing in Yosemite, but she wouldn't be interested.

The gash in Ben's right thigh bled through the medical gauze field dressing. The blood soaked the torn pant leg of his muddy utilities. He also suffered a nasty cut in the back of his head. Blood ran freely through his matted hair and caked on his neck. His face was crisscrossed with scratches and his lower lip and gum continued to bleed from the fall he took when he dove for cover during the NVA shelling the day before.

Bradford wrote several paragraphs, paused for a few minutes, then continued to write.

Sweetheart, I'm doing all right, here. Khe Sanh came under a severe artillery attack. One ammo dump was destroyed. We get shelled each day and often at night. We're expecting an NVA attack any day, but we'll beat them back.

Ben absentmindedly bit the end of the ball point pen as he struggled to express his deepest affection. He looked across the expanse of the base hoping to see something that would inspire intimate words, but all he saw was desolation, chaos and misery.

Finally, the last of the words came to him. He ended his letter to Sarah, the only girl he ever cared about.

Ben signed his name in his usual manner; with bold, block letters.

Just as he did, beads of sweat from his eyebrows fell to the aerogram and soaked round spots through it. The blue ink dissolved and spread out on the flimsy paper.

"Dammit! Just when I finish."

Although smeared, the writing was still recognizable. A red hue from the dust appeared in the dampness on the paper. He folded and sealed the aerogram, his fingers leaving red smudge marks on the crease. He hurriedly addressed it to Sarah's parents' home.

"This'll have to do."

Ben put the letter in his shirt pocket and grabbed his rifle and helmet. Desperate to send his letter to Sarah, he intended to give it to a buddy who was to be medevaced out that day. He hobbled through the mud as fast as he could from his position at the west end of the base, to the Charlie Med LZ. His leg hurt like hell from his wound, but he paid no attention to the pain. Light headed, Ben moved with a heavy limp that got worse with every step. He kept low to the ground, his heart pumping. Sweat rolled down his face in rivulets.

Ben saw the helicopters arriving from the east.

"Marine pilots are the best," he said out loud. "They ain't scared of nothing."

The helicopters would land in less than five minutes and, within one minute, lift off again with the wounded.

Ben spotted Howard Cornelius, the Marine to whom he wanted to give the letter. The two men always played cards together each night in their bunker. They became amiable buddies.

"Corney, man, you're so ugly, you'll frighten the hell outta the gooks," Ben would say. "When you get back to the world, they'll give you a medal because you scared them off and we didn't have to fire a shot."

Not hesitating to respond but always keeping his cool, Cornelius would counter.

"Listen, you pansie-ass howdy doodie. I gotta scare them off 'cause you can't shoot for crap."

The humorously insulting, but friendly banter helped pass the time. Howard's laughter congealed a friendship. His bright white teeth shone when he smiled. His face came alive with the affability of a gentle giant.

Howard Cornelius, born outside Birmingham, Alabama in 1949, moved with his family at age seven to Mobile. He joined the Marines at eighteen and had been at Khe Sanh for a number of weeks.

Cornelius was seriously wounded by shrapnel, his entire left side cut to ribbons. He would probably lose his left arm and leg. Morphine had kicked in relieving the pain, but it caused some deliriousness.

Ben Bradford knelt next to his friend and touched his shoulder slightly.

"Corny, it's me, Ben...Corny! Look at me! It's Ben!"

Bradford took his helmet off and held it over Cornelius' face to shield him from the sun.

Cornelius opened his eyes and turned his head. Barely alert, he smiled slightly at Ben Bradford.

"Hi, Bro."

"Corny, you're goin' home, man."

Ben shook Howard's right hand by his fingers. Howard's grip was weak.

"Hey, Marine." Ben shouted, "You're bound for the USA, man, the big PX. You're too short now."

Bradford tucked the letter he had just written in the pocket of Cornelius's blood stained utilities. "Corny, please try to mail this letter to Sarah for me. It's important. I don't know who else I can give it to. It'll be a favor I'll never forget."

Cornelius touched the pocket with the letter and feebly gestured thumbs up. Then, in a raspy whisper.

"I'll mail your letter."

Howard Cornelius's voice trailed off. "Good luck, Ben."

Not a minute later, the Marine chopper with Howard Cornelius onboard, lying in a stretcher and carrying the letter to Sarah, lifted off the Khe Sanh plateau. It made its rotational dip and then sped east the length of the runway, all the while gaining altitude.

Ben heard enemy machine gun fire.

"Bastards, they better not shoot that chopper down."

The dark green helicopter lifted higher and higher, out of rifle range and flew east. Ben watched as the chopper increased its distance high above the hills. Its sound faded to nothing before Ben's eyes lost sight of it.

Ben could only hope Howard Cornelius, whose life would never be the same, would arrive home safely and the letter on which he had labored so hard would reach its destination.

"You're gonna live, Corny. You've got to make it, man."

Ben gazed at the eastern horizon, wishing he could fade with that chopper straight back to Sarah. He removed his helmet, wiped the sweat from his head. His ears were ringing. He felt dizzy. Ben surveyed the pervasive wretchedness around him. Alone in the midst of this sinister bloodshed, forsaken by all time, bereft of a joyfulness that once was, and a dark, terrifying realness that took its place, Ben Bradford, seeking comfort, extolling his true feelings, mumbled.

"Sarah, you mean more to me than you can ever know."

Ben's leg hurt badly. The throbbing became worse. The wound began to bleed profusely again as he limped back to his fighting position at the Red Sector, at the west end of the Khe Sanh Combat Base.

The acute physical discomfort, however, was nothing compared to the pain in Ben Bradford's heart.

CHAPTER FOURTEEN

DAMNED NORTH KOREANS

Late at night, at the beginning of the last full week of January 1968, well after everyone had retired, the quietude of the residential quarters of the White House was shattered. The telephone next to President Johnson's canopy bed on the second floor punctured the silence. The incessant, loud ring seemed unusually urgent.

Lyndon Johnson rolled onto his side as he fumbled for the phone. He placed the receiver next to his right ear.

"Yeah. What is it?"

"Mr. President…"

"Good lord, it's dark as a damn cave."

"I'm sorry to disturb your sleep, Sir. We've received startling news. The Situation Room just called me…just now, Sir."

President Johnson, collecting his thoughts after being abruptly awakened from a remarkably deep sleep, still holding the phone to his ear, threw the covers back. He placed his feet on the carpet.

"Mr. President. Are you there, Sir? It's Rostow."

The President massaged his face.

"I know who the hell it is. What news?"

Walt Rostow, efficient and organized, was the best. The President could always count on him. Born to Jewish parents of Russian ancestry, Rostow was raised on the streets of New York City. His parents stressed loyalty to faith, family and friends. So imbued with a boundless sense of achievement, he entered university at fifteen and graduated at nineteen. In addition to having received a Ph.D. at the age of twenty-four, Rostow was also a Rhodes Scholar.

Rostow served in the OSS selecting bombing targets in Germany during World War Two. Later, he helped with the development of the Marshall Plan. He lectured at Cambridge and MIT and wrote a book about how countries evolve through stages of economic growth. Articulate, Rostow wrote Johnson's first state of the union address. Pleased with the speech, Johnson promoted him to National Security Advisor.

Walt Rostow was positive about America's involvement in Vietnam. He had advised President Kennedy to send troops to South Vietnam early on. Rostow advocated bombing targets in the north to stop the flow of arms to the south. He urged President Johnson not to compromise negotiations with North Vietnam. America is right to help South Vietnam. The United States can win the war and stop the domino effect of communism in Southeast Asia.

The President took a deep breath as he looked at the clock next to the bedside reading lamp.

"Mr. President, there's an emergency that..."

"Rostow, it's three-thirty in the morning. What kind of emergency? Vietnam? Are the Viet-nese attacking Khe Sanh?"

President Johnson, falling into the lazy trap of the southern-drawl habit of shortening unfamiliar sounding words, often pronounced Vietnamese incorrectly. He didn't care.

"No, Mr. President. North Korea. They've seized one of our ships, Sir."

"The North Koreans seized a U.S. ship? At 3:30 a.m? What the hell are you talking about, Rostow? Where? What ship?"

"Sir, the USS *Pueblo*."

"What kind of ship is that...what's the name again?"

Lyndon Johnson could hardly sit through a movie, but not too many weeks before, he watched a Robert Wise film. Starring Steve McQueen and Candice Bergen, *The Sand Pebbles* traced a U.S. Navy ship's involvement in China in the 1920s. The name of the ship was the *San Pablo*. Although *pablo* and *pueblo* mean two different things in Spanish, the phonetic pronunciation was too coincidental.

"*Pueblo*, Mr. President, the USS *Pueblo*. I've been in touch with the Secretary of the Navy and Wheeler and McNamara."

"Be sure you make contact with Helms, too. Surely he already knows."

"Yes, Mr. President. Helms knows, Sir."

The President put down the receiver and picked up the clock. He had read the time wrong.

"For cryin' out loud, it's only two-thirty in the damned morning."

The First Lady, in her own bedroom, heard the disturbance in the President's suite. She hated the nightly interruptions which seemed to occur all too often. She put on her night robe and walked to the President's chambers.

"Lyndon, what is it?"

Lyndon Johnson, still disheveled, hugged his wife.

"Lady Bird, honey..."

He looked around aloofly.

"Lyndon, talk to me."

"First, it's those shit-for-brains North Viet-nese and now it's North Korea."

The President scratched his head. "This twelve hour time zone difference is killing me. I can't get a damned bit of sleep in this place. Those blockheads pull their shenanigans in midday over there to interrupt my sleep at midnight over here. They can just go to hell, all of 'em."

"Lyndon, honestly...your language. Cursing won't help. Tell me what's going on."

"I'll tell you all about it later, Bird."

"Lyndon, tell me now."

The President was dressing, tucking his shirttail in and combing his hair. He was known sometimes to visit the Situation Room late at night wearing his robe and slippers. He sat on the edge of the bed and bent over to tie his shoelaces. He broke one when he pulled on it too abruptly.

"Dammit."

Lady Bird picked up another pair of shoes and handed them to her husband.

"Here, honey. Put these on. I'll have those laces replaced today."

"Where're my glasses?"

"Lyndon, you would do better to turn a brighter light on."

Lady Bird switched on a floor lamp as she pointed with her other hand. "They're right over there on the table where you left them."

"Lady Bird, you go back to bed. I'll be back in no time."

The President softened his tone. "I'll have toast with my oatmeal at breakfast at about six. Any chance I can get a stack of blueberry pancakes with some hot maple syrup and Canadian bacon?"

Lady Bird, her hair a mess, looked squarely at her husband.

"Lyndon, look at me. You tell me what's going on."

"Ah, Lady Bird...now look..."

"Lyndon. No!"

"Oh, all right, honey. The North Koreans have seized the *San Pablo*... Dammit, I didn't mean that. The *Pueblo*, the USS *Pueblo*...some kind of ship. They've seized one of our ships on the high seas."

The First Lady's eyes widened. She was as shocked as was her husband.

"My God, Lyndon. Are our sailors OK?"

Clearly agitated, the President was gesturing excitedly, while he talked with his wife.

"Lady Bird, there's nothing you can do. I'll be back within an hour. I have to see what's going on, OK?"

At well over six feet tall, the President leaned down and kissed Lady Bird on her forehead. "Please don't forget the pancakes, puddin."

The President left his bedroom. Walt Rostow, who emerged from the elevator, met him in the hall.

"Mr. President, I came straight over after I called you. I knew you'd be up."

"Well, I am now. Let's get down to the Situation Room."

The two men talked as they walked along the carpet.

"What do we know, Walt?"

"Sir, North Korea isn't saying very much."

"I can imagine. Any Americans hurt?"

"Sir, complete facts are not known just now."

"What do our commands in Japan and Hawaii say?"

"The same thing I'm telling you, Sir."

President Johnson and Walt Rostow entered the Situation Room.

"Do we have maps of North Korea? I wanna see the area where the boat was seized."

A few general-area maps were thrown up on the wall.

"I don't believe this. A friggin' war with North Korea. Jesus H. Christ, we're already over-extended in Vietnam...and Khe Sanh..."

The President paused, then continued. "Things aren't very good up there on the thirty-eighth parallel. The plot to kill the South Korean president ain't helpin' matters one damn bit. And now this crap. Let's get this thing sorted out. I don't want a war with those idiot North Koreans. What's next, Berlin?"

The President looked around the room. "OK, I need details: how, where and for what reason? What are the options, military and political scenarios and ramifications...solutions?"

The President took off his glasses, put them back on and took them off again—a nervous tic.

"Walt, got a cigarette?"

Because of a heart attack in 1955, when he was Senate Majority Leader, Lyndon Johnson had quit smoking. He'd still sneak a cigarette once in a while. If Rostow or some aide in the Situation Room had offered him one, he damn well would have accepted it, but neither Rostow nor anyone else had any cigarettes.

"OK, give me the scoop about the seizure. Start from the beginning, Walt."

"Mr. President, at about oh five hundred Zulu..."

"Walt, please, in east coast time, if you don't mind. I have a lot to digest and I can't be bothered with this Zulu time crap."

"At midnight our time, Sir, the USS *Pueblo* was attacked and seized by the North Koreans."

Walt Rostow pointed to an area on a map. "About here, Sir. A patrol boat approached the ship. The *Pueblo* indicated to the patrol boat's crew that it was a hydrographic ship."

"We surrendered a U.S. ship?"

"Sir, I doubt surrendered is the right word. Anyway, the ship was boarded by North Korean navy personnel."

"Rostow, for Christ's sake, is this the USS *Maddox*, the Gulf of Tonkin incident, all over again?"

"There are similarities, Sir, but the North Vietnamese never boarded the *Maddox*."

"I know that," the President said curtly. "Did the *Pueblo* open fire?"

"Not that we know of, Mr. President."

The President's eyes widened.

"An American ship that didn't try to thwart an enemy threat?"

"Mr. President, the *Pueblo* is not really a warship. It's an intelligence gathering ship. It has small weapons, fifty caliber machine guns, maybe only two, in fact."

"Did they try to get away?"

"The *Pueblo* can't make much more than thirteen knots. I can almost run that fast...or, anyway, thirty years ago I could."

"They call for air support? Where's the nearest carrier?"

"That would have been the USS *Enterprise*, Sir, CVN65, but it was about five to six hundred miles away. Mr. President, it would have been impossible for *Enterprise's* air wing to have reacted swiftly to disrupt any action by the North Koreans."

The President reflected on events in Vietnam two days earlier, on the twenty-first of January, when the North Vietnamese began shelling Khe Sanh. His anxiety and anger were evident from the expressions that crossed his face.

"Walt," the President said, while fixing his glasses. "The Tuesday luncheon is today. The National Security Council meeting is scheduled for 1:00 p.m. on the twenty-fourth—that's tomorrow. You make damn sure we have all the details about this stupid little incident and place it at the top of the agenda. I expect a complete up-to-the-minute briefing. I repeat what I said twenty minutes ago. I don't want no war with North Korea. We got enough problems at Khe Sanh. We don't need another shit-hole Asian crisis on our hands. Got me?"

"I completely understand, Mr. President."

"Good, I'm going back to the mansion and try to grab a couple of hours of sleep. I could sleep for a damn month."

The President turned for the door mumbling. "Commie pissants, I swear."

CORPS TACTICAL ZONES IN SOUTH VIETNAM
(U.S. MILITARY)

CHAPTER FIFTEEN

THE PINES OF DONG LOC: HE WON'T BE COMING BACK

One hundred North Vietnamese soldiers had traveled from Hanoi three hundred kilometers south to the coastal village of Vinh. Some arrived throughout the day, others at or well after midnight.

Originally known as Ke Van hundreds of years ago, the town's name changed several times before being called Vinh. Noted for the Hong Son Temple and Quyet Mountain, and void of the bustle that once characterized Hanoi, Vinh had a special holiday appeal.

But, the men didn't stop at Vinh. A day later, they arrived at a place nestled between mountains just south of Ha Tinh. Located at the remote intersection of three roads, the spectral area, dotted with pine trees on the sides of the mountains, held special meaning.

From that point, the soldiers were soon to embark on a historic trek that would take them to Laos and to stranger parts of Vietnam, to places none of them had ever seen. The brown-skinned, dark-haired teenagers sat on their butts with their legs bent at the knee in a cathedral-like clearing of trees that was concealed from the sky above by higher limbs. They wore an array of pith helmets, floppy canvas bush hats, even *cai non* (peasant hats) made from bamboo. Some men quietly exchanged stories about their trip from Hanoi. Others openly discussed their melancholy to the point they would break down.

Nguyen Tran Quoc, a native of Saigon who had fled north with his parents in support of Ho Chi Minh in 1954, stood beside a table facing the men. A large piece of cloth on which a map had been drawn hung behind him. Quoc was wearing the red lapel insignia of a colonel. He lit a Tam Thanh cigarette, then tapped the table lightly with a pointer stick to quiet the assembly.

"Gentlemen, you are at Dong Loc, the very origin of the Ho Chi Minh Trail, Farther south is the DMZ, supposedly a neutral area."

Quoc paused for a second. "To hell with neutrality. We care only about winning this war. We're about to launch an offensive throughout South Vietnam with a major effort in Quang Tri Province."

Quoc's pointer fell on a small location on the map. "B5T8 or Ta Con to us, but known as Khe Sanh to the Americans. We're engaged with the Twenty-sixth Marine Regiment here."

Quoc paused to let his words sink in. "The success of the Quan Doi Nhan Dan is dependent on soldiers like you. Within two days, when you are south, but still not far enough south, I will be standing in front of another group of men making the same speech; and two days after that, the same thing, and on and on, until we have triumphed over the criminal invaders. The imperialist Americans are here senselessly to be killed and we will kill them."

The colonel removed his hat and laid it on the small table to his side. Sweat dripped off his graying hair. "You will proceed south in four main clusters, A, B, C and D, each divided into subsets formed from this assemblage. Subsets will depart every thirty minutes and make their way south through Laos to Quang Tri Province. Three people make the optimum size of a subset for travel, but we have no time now. We have increased the subset size to between five and ten. Jumping off time starts at eighteen hundred."

Colonel Quoc moved his hand in front of the map. "Each subset will cover about twenty to twenty-five kilometers per day. At strategic points, further apart, there will be larger *binh tram*. The waypoint numbering increases sequentially as you proceed south. You will be led from each binh tram by a guide for the first thirty minutes. After that, you're on your own. About two kilometers before the next binh tram, you will be met by the *giam doc* [superintendent] who will escort you to the waypoint. The giam doc will not come searching for you.

"As far as *your* destination is concerned, there are twenty waypoints. You won't find much at the intermediate rest stations, but at each waypoint you will receive medical treatment and something to eat. You'll get four hours rest, then you'll continue on, again in the same subset. You will not cook on open fires or smoke in the open. You will not talk excessively…and no musical instruments. You will maintain distance from the other subsets at all times."

Quoc pointed to the alignment of the Ho Chi Minh Trail. "Now, here, the trail splits into five branches. Each branch continues south. Vehicles and those of you on foot will not travel on the same roads.

"You'll be given a coded slip of paper. The last number in the double parentheses identifies the number of men in your subset. That number of men must arrive at the destination.

"You must not lose the paper. It will be relinquished to the giam doc at Waypoint Twenty, south of the Ben Hai River. Your final destination will be given to you at that time. You will wear no rank and carry no identification. Burn your personal letters now."

Quoc sipped water from his canteen. "The minimum weight of material and equipment each man is to carry has been increased from thirty-six to forty-one kilograms."

Colonel Quoc picked up items from the top of a table situated to his right. "Each man: Two pair of trousers, shorts, a belt, two shirts, sandals made from tires, a toothbrush, small medicated bandages, three-day ration of rice in bags you wear around your neck, dried meat to get you started, some vitamin B pills and tea and salt. You will forage for food."

The news got worse.

"You are soldiers but you're also porters. In addition to your assault weapon, each of you in Cluster A will carry two to three hundred rounds of

7.62 mm ammunition and five to ten hand grenades. Each of you in Cluster B will carry two rocket propelled grenade launchers and one hundred rounds of rifle ammunition. Those in Cluster C will each carry two mortar shells or two rockets or a clip of five 37mm anti-aircraft shells in satchels, and a bandolier of rifle ammunition. Cluster D will transport small caliber mortar tubes and baseplates.

"You must press on as fast as you can. The landscape will be alien, the trip hazardous. You should arrive in theater within thirty-five days.

"The survival of our country rests on your shoulders and on your legs. Yours is an honorable march to glory. It starts here and ends hundreds of kilometers south of here."

Each man, faced with a stark reality, was going off to war. There was no talk of return.

"Now, line up over there."

Colonel Quoc instructed his assistant to count the men off one by one.

"*Mot. Hai. Ba. Bon. Nam. San. Bay.* That's the first subset of Cluster A. One. Two. Three. Four. Five. Six. Seven—second subset."

The count continued until all the men had been assigned into their respective clusters and sub-sets.

The men made their way to a deep, well-guarded tunnel. When each man emerged, he was encumbered with his share of provisions and armaments.

Afternoon turned to dusk. The stars appeared.

The first subset moved out from Dong Loc onto the Ho Chi Minh Trail. The burdened men passed through a moonscape of craters. A crew was busy excavating a bomb which had not exploded. The soldiers disappeared into the darkness. The thirty-five day trek south to Quang Tri Province had begun.

After sunrise the next morning, Quoc, his work done for the moment, drank tea and lit a cigarette. He walked casually around the assembly area where he had processed thousands of young men in the same manner.

Quoc opened a notebook he found lying on the ground. Even though he warned each person never to carry documents, many paid no attention. On the inside of the front cover, Quoc read: "The Diary of Bui Van Que."

Quoc flipped through the pages of the diary. The writing was precise, the words uniformly spaced. He read an entry:

> *My Dearest Hang, I can only pretend to write to you in my diary. Vinh has been completely destroyed. We camped on the south side of the Lam River before coming down to Dong Loc. Bomb craters cover the valley. Oh, Hang, I think of your beautiful eyes...*

Quoc looked at a slightly-wrinkled photograph of a young, smiling girl. He unfolded a letter inserted in the diary.

> *My charming, most tender Que, Please come back to me...*

Quoc skipped to the second page and read that Hang was soon to turn sixteen—her birthday was in March. The letter ended with "*I will forever wait for you.*"

Quoc reflected briefly on his life and the girlfriend he once had, also named Hang, as he slid the sheet of paper back into the diary.

Quoc never allowed the young soldiers to know that half his stomach and intestines had been ripped away by shrapnel from an American bomb one year before near Ninh Binh. His convalescence at Bac Mai Hospital had been tenuous. Quoc was told he would die, but he survived. A career military man—his only life being the army—Quoc was still serving his country, but he could no longer fight. The hideous scars that he now bore were hidden beneath his uniform.

A hard, knowing truth swept over the colonel. He had sent so many young men like Bui Van Que to the south into the *coi xay thit* (the meat grinder). They'll not be as lucky as he had been.

Colonel Quoc lit another cigarette. While the smoke swirled around his face, he thumbed through Bui Van Que's diary again. He looked at the photograph of the smiling face and sharp, bright eyes of a beautiful girl named Hang.

Quoc walked over and tossed Bui Van Que's diary and the letters on a fire.

"Born in the North to die in the South. He won't be coming back."

Quoc laid the photograph of the young woman on top of the embers. The edges of the photograph turned brown and curled up. The smiling image of Bui Van Que's girlfriend faded. Suddenly, the image was consumed by flames and disappeared. The blackened pieces of flimsy ash disintegrated and flew across the assembly area, into the pines of Dong Loc.

CHAPTER SIXTEEN

EXECUTIVE ORDER

President Johnson slid his glasses to the top of his head. He eased back in his chair as his eyes scanned the official document in front of him.

The President's signature at the bottom would trigger a desperate act. With the stroke of a pen, families would be distressed, people's existence thrown into turmoil and some lives placed at great risk. His forehead furrowed, Lyndon Johnson leaned forward on his left elbow and rested his cheek in his hand. He gazed across the executive office toward the fireplace.

"How many men is it going to take to win over there in that damned Vietnam? They keep wanting more and more."

Johnson called the residence.

"Lady Bird, would you tell Art Krim to come down to the Oval Office, please? I really need to see him...uh huh...see you at the luncheon, hon... Yeah, I know. In the Treaty Room."

Art Krim held no official position. Nor did he hold any political appointment. A man of keen intellect, he possessed one advantage about which others in the White House were envious. He had full access to the President in a capacity that wielded influence but was not constricted by protocol. He was like an indispensable butler who goes about his duties without fanfare. Often present at the White House, few paying much attention to his sway, Arthur B. Krim was, however, no butler.

Krim graduated at the top of his class at Columbia University Law School. He became the chairman of United Artists. Krim turned to fund raising at the request of John Kennedy, but he was not completely comfortable in that role.

Art Krim met Lyndon Johnson in 1962 when he was Kennedy's Vice President. They met again sometime later at Krim's home in New York City, at a party for President Kennedy. That evening, Krim observed first-hand what the inner-circle knows. In the immediate presence of a president, any president, the number two man is relegated almost to irrelevancy.

At another party in Washington, D.C., this time hosted by Lyndon and Lady Bird Johnson at The Elms, the vice presidential residence, Krim observed Johnson's inclination for dancing.

Later, Lyndon Johnson, as president, asked Krim to join his staff, again as a fund raiser. During the 1965 inaugural parade, the new president surprised Art Krim by inviting him and his wife Mathilde to sit with the Johnsons in their reviewing stand. The friendship grew.

Krim enjoyed working for Lyndon Johnson. When in D.C., he would often sleep overnight at the White House.

Krim came to understand the compassion the President had for others. Crotchety though the President may be, Krim recognized Lyndon Johnson genuinely cared about people.

President Johnson placed the phone down and shuffled some papers. He tried to think of something that would forestall the inevitable, but he knew it would still be waiting..

A few minutes later, Juanita Roberts stepped into the Oval Office.

"Mr. President, Mr. Krim is here, Sir."

The President looked up from his desk.

"Beautiful dress, Juanita. Very bright."

"Thank you, Mr. President."

Krim stood behind Juanita.

"Hi, Art, come on in…sit down over there on the couch."

Johnson pointed at the painting of Franklin Roosevelt over the fireplace. "FDR will keep you company. I'll be with you in a minute. Coffee?"

"No thanks, Lyndon. Mathilde and I just finished a pot while we chatted with Lady Bird."

"Art..."

The President walked from his desk to the couches that faced each other on the opposite side of the Oval Office. His face was anguished, his tone serious. "I'm about to do something that is bothersome. I'm hesitating. The Pentagon says it's the right thing to do for this country, it's a national security issue."

"Lyndon, maybe I'll have some coffee after all...black...uh, with a little cream."

"Art, sometimes being the President is a real pain in the ass. I've made decisions that cost hundreds of millions of dollars, decisions that affect state and local governments. Nothing about the great society was easy. I've supported many federally-sponsored programs. Education is my favorite."

The President became sullen. "My ratings have fallen to an all-time low. People used to think the world of me. Now the same people hate me."

"What can I do to help, Lyndon?"

"Not a thing, Art. It's my burden and mine alone."

"I can see you're upset, Lyndon. I'm here to listen."

"Art, I haven't had any sleep in months. The underlying problem is that Vietnam is eroding what I have tried to accomplish in this country. This war thing is eating me from the inside. Rostow is becoming more assertive. He feels we should be applying more pressure on Hanoi. He supports landing troops on the coast in North Vietnam in an effort to cut the southern supply trail. If it were up to him, he'd lay mines in Haiphong harbor. Why, he'd even invade Haiphong."

The President looked up at the ceiling. "Krim, we have six thousand Marines at Khe Sanh. They're very vulnerable. The NVA attacked Khe Sanh Ville about four days ago. Had to evacuate our Marines out of the village. There's a lot happening in this so-called Eye Corps."

"I understand. Aside from the *Pueblo*, the topic is never far from your mind. It's in the press more and more every day and, yes, the press is anti-war and increasingly anti-President Johnson."

"Art, even during the AFL playoff game between Oakland and Houston or the NFL game between the Dallas Cowboys and the Green Bay Packers four weeks ago. I couldn't enjoy either game. Not for one damn minute."

Krim smiled.

"Oh, yeah, Dallas-Green Bay, the ice bowl, that's what they called it. Coldest football game in history. Right on New Year's eve in Green Bay. Fifteen to twenty degrees below zero, they said—my God."

"Well, Krim, Green Bay. Whadja expect?"

"The world championship game that followed in Miami between Oakland and Green Bay, well, that was a good game...and a lot warmer. Those Packers are amazing and Bart Starr—most valuable player, too."

"Criminy, Art, the choice for MVP would have been tough. Starr passed for two hundred yards and one touchdown, but Don Chandler's field goals and that interception by Herb Adderley had to count for something, too. How far did Adderley run, anyway?"

"Not sure, Lyndon. Sixty, seventy yards? Oakland never had a chance."

President Johnson smiled slightly.

"Dallas should have won the NFL playoffs in Green Bay and gone on to Miami, not the damn Packers."

Krim laughed.

"You wouldn't be partial to a Texas team now would you, Mr. President?"

A broader smile swept over the President's face. His eyes came alive through his glasses.

"God, I will say, I made myself enjoy the championship game on TV."

The President changed the subject matter. "Art, I nominated Clark Clifford to replace Bob McNamara at Defense. McNamara's going to the World Bank."

"Yeah, I know. The *Financial Times* ran a piece about it. How do you feel about that, Lyndon, About McNamara, I mean?"

"Well, McNamara...Berkeley grad and all...he may be the most intelligent man on my staff...he and Rostow. Lectured at Harvard, President of Ford Motor Company, then Kennedy tagged him to be Secretary of Defense. He favored blockade during the Cuban missile crisis. About a year ago, maybe less, I..."

Art Krim's coffee was brought into the Oval Office. Johnson pointed at the round marble coffee table. "Put it down here between us."

"McNamara's the most powerful member of your cabinet, Lyndon."

"How do I put this, Krim? Bob McNamara's lost his verve. He's becoming vague about our efforts in Vietnam. Last May, he wrote a memo about Vietnam. Man, did that ever stir up some shit. The numbers are not working in McNamara's favor, and we all know he's a numbers guy. Last November, at the beginning of the month, McNamara wrote another memo to me stating that our present course would not bring us closer to victory in 1968. I wasn't too pleased with what I read. You can imagine."

"Lyndon, why don't you…"

The President, his mannerisms showing a level of irritability, cut Krim off.

"McNamara's actions and his thinking are contradictory. He's sending conflicting messages."

The President adjusted his glasses. "He's lost confidence in our policies. He's unsteady in his decisions. I need someone confident in their conviction that we can win."

Arthur Krim looked at his host.

"Mr. President, did you create that opportunity at the World Bank for Bob? I heard that to be the case."

The President maintained his stare.

"Krim, McNamara's been a forthright public servant…and he's been faithful to this administration. Let's just leave it at that."

Johnson sighed. "I believe Clark Clifford will be a more suitable war chief. General Maxwell Taylor's also advising me. Kennedy appointed him Chairman of the Joint Chiefs, but he's retired, of course. He's got independent views."

"Well…Lyndon, I guess I didn't know the extent…"

Art Krim stopped talking abruptly. He sipped his coffee. "Lyndon, something other than McNamara is bothering you. You didn't request my presence for coffee and football talk."

The President hesitated for a second.

"Art, Westmoreland and Ambassador Bunker have informed me over the last many weeks that North Vietnam has been sending division after division of infantry and artillery south of the DMZ. We've experienced a lot of fighting around the Khe Sanh base."

Krim re-filled his coffee cup from the silver pot. Johnson continued.

"Westmoreland says we need to increase troop levels. He's sure Laos will become the real battlefield.

"The Joint Chiefs have asked for additional men a number of times. They worry we can't respond to crises such as North Korea. The Pentagon has requested me in the strongest of ways to increase military assets globally. The JCS raise the topic with me at the smallest mention of security. But, an augmentation can only happen if I sign the document that's sitting over there on my desk."

"An Executive Order, Mr. President?"

"Precisely, Krim."

"My God, Lyndon. Are you going to call up the reserves?"

"Art, it's the first time since the Berlin crisis that America has called up the reserves."

"In an election year? Lyndon, are you sure about this?"

"I'm the unlucky bastard who's gotta do it, election year or no election year."

"Lyndon…"

Johnson held up his hand.

"Today is the twenty-fifth of January. We're not even through the first month of the New Year, I got two major contingencies on my hands. Not even two weeks after my state of the union address, I have to go and do this."

The President, frustrated, pointed over his shoulder to his desk. "Executive Order 11392 will become law before dinner."

CHAPTER SEVENTEEN

JADE SPRING HILLS

Chairman Ho Chi Minh, in deep contemplation, held a black pen in one hand and a cigarette in the fingers of his other. He turned quickly from the table, removed his reading glasses and smiled. He stood to clasp the hands of an old friend.

"General Vo Nguyen Giap, it's so nice to see a familiar face. How good of you to take time to visit me here in Beijing. I assume your trip from Hungary was comfortable."

"A long trip, Bac Ho. And you, Sir, how are you?"

"Well, Giap, I'm making progress with my health."

"You're looking quite well, but I see you're still smoking."

"This retreat has been beneficial, Giap. The lake and the pagodas are pleasant. The Garden of Light and Tranquility is bigger than our botanical gardens in Hanoi. I'm free to walk all day. Around every turn there is something to discover, but there is little to do otherwise, so, yes, I smoke. It's the only vice I have."

Ho Chi Minh changed the subject. "Did the treatment go well in Budapest?"

"Thank you, Bac Ho. I never realized how painful kidney stones could be. I was virtually paralyzed."

"These medical issues at our age…they are such a bother."

Giap smiled.

"My father warned me never to get old."

"Sit down, Giap. This place isn't as comfortable as my home in Hanoi, but it'll do."

Ho Chi Minh gazed skyward out the window of his guest house located at the communist government rest home of Ngoc Tuyen Son (Jade Spring Hills) thirteen kilometers northwest of Beijing.

"See, Giap? At least the sun does shine in winter. Beijing is so uncomfortable this time of year."

Vo Nguyen Giap, smartly dressed but looking a bit plump, laid his briefcase on the conference table. He placed his overcoat on a couch and laid his Russian-made Cossack hat on top.

Ho Chi Minh poured tea into his cup. He stroked his beard. It seemed perfectly suited to his face, but it made him look old.

"Giap, do you recall the many discussions we've had about Resolution Fourteen."

"Chu tich, it's a bold policy but it does not provide for..."

"Comrade Giap, please."

Ho Chi Minh held up his hand. "The central committee affirmed the strategic direction through the resolution."

Ho Chi Minh paused, then spoke again from a different angle. "Giap, a Colonel Phu enlightened me about President Johnson some time ago.

"Yes, Sir, I would like to have heard that myself. Colonel Phu is an excellent officer and a thorough researcher."

"What I was struck with, Giap, is the tenacity with which the American president solves problems. His character is tough as steel."

"Bac Ho, I'm sure this may be the case in America, but his character will have no effect on the situation he faces in Vietnam. We are tough as steel, too, Sir."

"True, Giap, but listen, America will vote for a president in November of this year. Surely, President Johnson is seeking re-election. The Americans will undertake whatever is necessary to secure a major war victory in South Vietnam in 1968. This scares me. They have a couple of options: increase bombing or augment their forces in the south by bringing more soldiers from the U.S. Or, both.

"A clear military victory for the Americans will be to Johnson's benefit. His political strategists will leverage that to re-elect him, and force negotiations...but on their terms. This is unacceptable, Giap.

"Although I was not as vocal in my opposition to some of its provisions as you were, I'm aware of the shortcomings of Resolution Fourteen. Due to the gravity of the military situation, the Politburo had no option but to approve an aggressive direction.

"Resolution Fourteen was concocted by party first secretary Le Duan and some of your staff, and, before he passed away, the ever-pretentious Nguyen Chi Thanh. I know it doesn't comport with your theory of warfare, but that's the plan."

"I don't think anyone cares to listen to me, Bac Ho."

"Giap, I take it we have inflicted losses on the American armed forces, even more than they are prepared to admit, but we have been unable to keep pace with them. We must regain the initiative. You have said so yourself, from the Marxist belief...constant militancy to achieve goals."

Ho Chi Minh sipped his tea. "I understand an artillery bombardment of U.S. forces in Quang Tri Province has started. Please tell me about our battle efforts there."

"Bac Ho, yes, we began actions against the Americans on the twenty-first of January."

Giap looked at a Swissair calendar hanging on the wall. A picture of the Alps dominated the top sheet. He eyed the date, 26 January. "After months of preparation, our military interventions south of the DMZ are now just underway, but in very early stages. Forces have moved to within striking distance of the provincial capitals. Hue will be a major target. It will serve as our provisional revolutionary capital. It is too soon to assess the likelihood of an outcome. We are..."

"No. I'm sorry to interrupt."

Ho lit another cigarette and tossed the smoking match into the ashtray. "Giap, you're a believer in protracted war but you're also a proponent of large, well-defined battles where you have clear advantage. I'll come straight to the question. Are you developing plans for a major set-piece engagement with the Americans and, if so, can we win?"

"Bac Ho, Westmoreland told the American people when he spoke to congress in April of 1967 that the United States was winning the war. In what could have been construed as admonishment toward his government, Westmoreland said that if backed at home by resolve, determination and continued support, America will prevail in Vietnam. Later, in November, Westmoreland again delivered a similar message. He stated that the end was coming into view."

"Yes, Giap, Westmoreland's visit to the United States was contrived for propaganda purposes. It seems Johnson prefers to speak to the American public through his general."

"True, Chu tich. President Johnson declared in his national address, not even two weeks ago, that America was close to victory. But, counter to that, American troop levels are increasing, now approaching a half million soldiers. The question must be asked. How can the United States claim to be close to victory while at the same time infusing additional troops?"

"Good question, Giap. It seems the American military doesn't know in which direction to turn. President Johnson's rhetoric is slanted toward the elections. The anti-war demonstrations in America provide an interesting backdrop. They reveal a crack in public support. The war against us is becoming less popular. The Americans are stalemated…here and in America. A continuation of the war will cause a schism in Johnson's political sphere. The support about which Westmoreland has spoken will evaporate. As a result, I fear America will be overly aggressive. The President's party needs a victory this year."

"Bac Ho, we must be prepared for a long war. I still think …"

"Giap, it's incumbent upon President Johnson to be victorious to maintain his presidency and his party's political influence. Johnson has proved to be more a warmonger than was Kennedy who I never trusted in the first place.

"I said many months ago, early drafts of Resolution Fourteen presented a good plan, but the provisions needed work. We must understand our own logistics issues. We need to husband our resources while arming the NLF.

And lastly, we must grow stronger on the battlefield. Argue as we did, the final version of Resolution Fourteen is seen as the foundation of our glorious victory."

Ho Chi Minh, reaching for another cigarette, looked out the window of his apartment at the gray clouds now hanging just above the horizon. Snow would fall that night.

Giap sipped his tea.

"Chu tich Ho, if we were to ameliorate the strategy, Khe Sanh may become ripe for the..."

Giap suddenly stopped. When he least intended, he mentioned Khe Sanh outright. A ground attack at Khe Sanh was not a component of Resolution Fourteen. Any mention of such a ground attack would receive scornful criticism. Giap had to retreat from what he had just said—he'd implied enough about Khe Sanh—but he was now obliged to continue with his thought.

"If our efforts succeed throughout the provinces, then the *coup de grace* could be an attack on a big American encampment. Their defeat will result in the complete undoing of General Westmoreland's military adventure in Vietnam. America's involvement will crumble."

Ho Chi Minh sighed as he poured tea into his cup. He became distracted by pleasant memories.

Ho missed his strolls in Hanoi through the dark shade along Mango Road. He longed to see his goldfish in the aquarium beneath his home. Ho Chi Minh remembered the many times he walked along Hoang Van Thu Street to visit Vo Nguyen Giap's home. Giap's children, full of noisy mischievousness, would sit on his lap on the porch and pull on his beard.

Ho removed his glasses and looked straight at Vo Nguyen Giap. Sadness crossed his face, but did not diminish the burning intensity of his stare. His reverie interrupted, Ho Chi Minh spoke softly.

"The Chinese tolerate me, but they have little regard for me. I've been dismissed by our Soviet and Chinese comrades as nothing more than a skinny, old nationalist from an unimportant part of the world who wears shabby clothes, whose teeth are stained black from tobacco. I may be old and scrawny, and maybe I don't have the best taste with my attire, and I may not be the communist revolutionary they think I should be, but Giap, reunification of the entire Fatherland is my only priority. The Chinese, French, Japanese, the British, the Americans…it's all the same war."

Ho drew on his cigarette. "Giap, I don't question your military prowess. Attacks against the provinces is one thing. But attacking the Americans outright at the same time, if I'm guessing you correctly, may be quite another. Would we not be a bunch of ants trying to eat an elephant? Do we have the resources for such a dual undertaking?"

Vo Nguyen Giap remained quiet.

"Giap, your actions were often beyond our understanding. We escaped so many brushes with the *Phap* [French] as a result of your cleverness. Had we been caught, the *Phap* would not have waited for the guillotine to arrive from Hanoi for the execution like they used to do. The bloody basket from which our bleeding heads would have been held up by the strands of our hair wouldn't be needed. We would have been shot, our corpses thrown in a duck pond."

"I recall our history very well, Bac Ho. Our time in Bac Viet solidified our cause."

Ho Chi Minh looked at the threatening clouds. Sullen, he lit another cigarette.

"Giap, I'm not sure when I'll return to Hanoi. The doctors say I must continue my convalescence here…perhaps a few more months."

Giap put on his hat and gloves.

"Ngai Chu tich, with all respect, I must leave you now. Please take care of yourself."

CHAPTER EIGHTEEN

RESOLUTION FOURTEEN

Foreign and domestic policies, generated by the Hanoi government and ratified by the politburo, are forwarded to the central committee for final approval at which point they are elevated to the highest priority and transformed into formal resolutions that carry the full backing of the government and the party.

The roots of Resolution Fourteen, numbered sequentially with other resolutions, were found in a predecessor, Resolution Nine, approved in 1963.

Vietnam was officially divided in July 1954 into the Democratic Republic of Vietnam—hardly a democracy—under communist rule in the north; and what was then called the State of Vietnam, later the Republic of Vietnam, a fledgling democracy, in the south. While the communist-dominated coalition of Vietnamese nationalists—the Viet Minh—became the government of North Vietnam, their presence in rural South Vietnam never subsided. The Viet Minh controlled much of the area south of the dividing line.

Not long after the division was mandated, the National Liberation Front, or the NLF, principally those dissidents who lived in South Vietnam, emerged. The NLF wanted to overthrow the South Vietnamese government. They became the new Viet Minh in the south. Eventually called the Viet Cong, their numbers increased.

THE PRESIDENT'S SANDBOX

The time had come for the North Vietnamese communists to bolster the Viet Cong. Together they would conquer the phony southern government. Resolution Nine was the key.

Proponents of Resolution Nine saw that while the U.S. military floundered with indecision, the NVA could mount a series of simultaneous strikes at key locations. The ultimate objective was the collapse of Saigon, the capital of South Vietnam. Through increased militancy, the war would turn in the North's favor.

The results of Resolution Nine, if nothing else, would send a message: the local population south of the Demilitarized Zone was not a hindrance to the movements of the People's Army of Vietnam. NVA soldiers could go anywhere they wanted.

Ultimately, their victory over the dummy southern army would facilitate immediate implementation of communist political and social reforms.

By the end of 1964 and early in 1965, with South Vietnam's army worn out and demoralized, and with the North Vietnamese and the Viet Cong controlling many key areas of the country, Saigon should have been forced to the negotiating table on North Vietnam's terms. But, when victory was almost in General Vo Nguyen Giap's grasp, the launching of military offensives as promulgated by Resolution Nine was in jeopardy. Giap had waited too long. America reacted.

To support the southern government, now in a desperate predicament, President Johnson announced that the United States would no longer be a spectator. The U.S. and its military would be active partners with the government of South Vietnam.

History witnessed the quickest mobilization of armed forces ever to a theater of combat. Over one hundred thousand U.S. troops went to Vietnam within a few months. It seemed overnight.

Five thousand Marines of the Ninth Marine Expeditionary Brigade landed in Da Nang in early March 1965 at a place codenamed Red Beach 2. They were met by fishermen drying their nets just feet from the shoreline. Sightseers carried welcome signs. Young women gave out garlands of flowers.

The brigade eventually transformed into the Third Marine Amphibious Force (III MAF).

Vo Nguyen Giap was bewildered by America's sudden direct involvement, but was confident it would not obstruct North Vietnam's goal of reunification. That is until he bumped head-long into the U.S. Army's First and Second Battalion of the Seventh Cavalry Regiment and the Second Battalion of the Fifth Cavalry Regiment in mid-November 1965, thirty-five miles southwest of Pleiku in the Two Corps Tactical Zone. The armies of North Vietnam and the United States of America confronted one another for the first time in a major battle and slugged it out. The confrontation occurred in a remote part of the central highlands called the Chu Pong Massif, but more specifically, in the Ia Drang Valley.

The celerity with which the Americans conducted combat caught Vo Nguyen Giap and his front commander Chu Huy Man by surprise. Neither Giap nor Man was prepared for the style of warfare imported by the Americans. With the use of helicopters, the Americans were many times more mobile. They could skip from battlefield to battlefield and, as Giap soon learned, leapfrog their artillery with ease.

Tran Ia Drang, the battle of the Ia Drang Valley, lasted five days. While less than three hundred Americans had been killed, albeit more than half in a sixteen hour fight, Giap's losses, many times greater, were shocking. Ho Chi Minh declared victory, but the battle shook the North Vietnamese to the core. Giap's army, severely beaten, could not continue the fight and withdrew. American cow soldiers, as the North Vietnamese called them, were much tougher than either Giap or Man thought. The two commanders had underestimated their foe.

Vo Nguyen Giap never forgave himself for his naiveté. But, he learned how to fight his new enemy with their advanced technology. He would exploit those lessons in the future.

By the start of 1966, the ranks of the Third Marine Amphibious Force, farther north in One Corps Tactical Zone, had swollen to almost forty thousand Marines. In total, General William Westmoreland had two hundred thousand combatants under his command. More were on their way. The window of opportunity Giap could have exploited to achieve victory slammed shut. South Vietnam's army was not routed. Vo Nguyen Giap, watched the invaders' continued mobilization in utter disbelief. He had never seen such resources.

Resolution Nine didn't work. It was shelved. But, Hanoi wouldn't give up. If the Americans were now in the hunt and, further, if they were there to stay, Giap's Quan Doi Nhan Dan, though bloodied, was there to stay as well. The communists would build on their experience and devise new plans.

Le Duan, in reality the most powerful person within the government of North Vietnam, never forgot Resolution Nine. Still the first secretary of the central committee of the communist party, he felt the final struggle must include a broad military offensive that would bring forth from its incubation a general insurrection among the people. He aggressively advocated again the rebirth of the theory contained in Resolution Nine.

Hanoi was of the continued opinion that the false Saigon government must be broken and destroyed. In early 1967, circumstances in the war with the Americans seemed to turn in favor of the North Vietnamese and their reunification goals. The government of North Vietnam observed that the Americans were in disarray. They were at a crossroads in Vietnam with no map.

As celebrated as he was, Vo Nguyen Giap had lost a few heated arguments with Le Duan and the Politburo over tactics against the Americans. Outspoken and volatile, sometimes to the point that Ho Chi Minh had to calm him down, Vo Nguyen Giap, was marginalized by Le Duan, who solidified the plan counter to what General Giap would have preferred.

Drawing on his own inclinations, Le Duan believed the people would support a country-wide offensive. *Rise to your destiny and join us against the criminal government.*

General Nguyen Chi Thanh, a constant irritant to Vo Nguyen Giap, had been even more aggressive calling for multiple engagements and major wide-sweeping campaigns. The cities must be the focal point of any offensive. 'Attack everywhere,' Thanh would say. He never expanded his thoughts beyond that. Nguyen Chi Thanh died in early July 1967 taking any such elaboration to his grave.

Seizing upon gratuitous opportunities, key government leaders promoted an unprecedented military initiative in South Vietnam, grander than what Resolution Nine promised.

The concept of massive military attacks in the south was refined and broadened.

However, a component that was essential, using the Marxist-Leninist style of mass revolt, was still in question.

So ambitious the draft policy, a special meeting of the politburo was convened in December 1967 to extract consensus from its thirteen high-ranking party members. This would propel the plan from informal discussions to prominence within the government.

The component that had been missing was now made an indispensable part of the new policy. Any thrust must have greater emphasis on and include the people in the south. The oppressed population must be shown the way forward through overwhelming intervention. The policy provided a step-by-step formula for a major country-wide offensive that would lead, more importantly, to an equally-wide uprising of the people.

The policy, subjected to close scrutiny, experienced birthing problems. Liberating all of South Vietnam followed by the reunification of the north and the south under a single communist government were inter-connected objectives. But, the means by which to attain those objectives were undermined by egos and power plays. The schism between the more militant officials who hailed from the central areas of Vietnam, and those less inclined toward confrontation who came from farther north became pronounced. The dispute turned implacable.

Although the plan was daring, General Vo Nguyen Giap was not convinced the new thrust throughout the country was the right thing to do. Giap did not disagree with the general idea, but he questioned whether it was the best way to expend military assets. When discussing early drafts, Giap countered that the provisions could work but only if there was a big battle resulting in debilitating damage to the enemy sufficient to cause him to lose his will to fight. Although a departure from his general theory of protracted warfare, Giap also believed in focused engagements that would make an impact. This would be the key ingredient to incite the populace.

To some in the communist government, Vo Nguyen Giap's conservative military strategies were no longer valid, nor satisfactorily aggressive. Giap's opinions were largely ignored as being archaic; the folly of an old man who was out of touch. But, Giap was only fifty-six; and he was hardly out of touch.

However tarnished by rancorous debate and bitterness, the Politburo enthusiastically approved the plan. It was given a name: *Tong cong kich-Tong khoi nghia* (The General Offensive-General Uprising).

In mid-to-late January 1968, one month after the special Politburo meeting, the general offensive-general uprising policy was introduced to the Fourteenth Plenum of the central committee for high government approval. The road to victory had been clearly carved out. After three years since the debacle with Resolution Nine, its provisions rose from the ashes. As was the custom, the policy was now given an insipid name: Resolution Fourteen.

What came to be called the *Nghi Quyet Quang Trung* (the Quang Trung Resolution), Resolution Fourteen put into motion the scheme the North Vietnamese would use to gain military and political advantages south of the Demilitarized Zone; south of the Ben Hai River.

The historical significance of the Quang Trung Resolution and the derivation of its name would not have been lost on any scholar. Vietnam had gained its independence from China in 980 A.D., but China continued to invade and pillage Vietnam. Fed up with this pugnacious northern neighbor, Vietnam's Emperor Quang Trung, also known as Nguyen Hue, led a surprise attack in 1789 against Chinese forces that occupied Hanoi. The Chinese were routed.

Emperor Quang Trung's attack occurred at an auspicious time: the annual lunar holiday. Almost two hundred years later in 1968, the newly planned general offensive-general uprising, embodied in the Quang Trung Resolution, would be a similar devastating stroke.

The planned offensive would be launched against the provincial capitals and the major cities including Saigon, Hue and Da Nang. America's lifeline was derived from aircraft. Hence, airbases would be a major target and, of those, Tan Son Nhut airport and Bien Hoa air base would be plums. The general assault would be bloody, savage and destructive. It would confront the abilities of the forces of the South Vietnamese and test the Americans. It would also challenge the determination of the North Vietnamese and the doggedness of the Viet Cong.

Following in the historical footsteps of Emperor Quang Trung two centuries before, enhanced belligerence would be launched at the end of January 1968, specifically at the start of *Tet Mau Than* (Vietnam's Lunar New Year).

Resolution Nine, and its descendant, Resolution Fourteen, mixed with an interim Resolution Thirteen, constituted, in fact, a continuum. But, it was Resolution Fourteen that defined the penultimate policy leading the way to a North Vietnamese victory in 1968. It was the only way.

President Johnson extruded his Gulf of Tonkin Resolution through the halls of the American congress in 1964. Four years later, in 1968, Resolution Fourteen would be North Vietnam's response. In the year of the monkey, the North Vietnamese were taking their revolution full speed to the south. The Americans and the world would soon give the country-wide assault another name.

They would call it the Tet Offensive.

CHAPTER NINETEEN

A LAST VISIT

"Giap, I apologize for the inconvenience, but I had to ask you to see me once more."

"My pleasure, Ngai Chu tich, but I must leave for Hanoi later today."

Ho Chi Minh glanced through the window at the bright white snow that covered the grounds of Jade Springs Hills. The temperature had fallen dramatically.

"Giap, what I heard you imply from our conversation two days ago has me worried."

Vo Nguyen Giap pondered Ho's vague comment.

"Uncle Ho, we need demonstrative results to show our determination. We have yet to win a single engagement in the south. We have caused damage, but without gaining anything significant against the Americans."

"Giap, do we fully appreciate the magnitude of the operation? Does the terrain suit us?"

Operation? Terrain? Ho Chi Minh had not forgotten his previous slip-up. Without mentioning it, the Chairman was making reference to that which Giap tried to skirt.

"Bac Ho," Giap said, stoically. "I can assure you the terrain favors our operations better than it does those of our enemy."

"Yes, Giap, but around Dien Bien Phu, the terrain was challenging, too."

"To an extent, Mr. Chairman. We had difficulty going to Dien Bien Phu and moving our artillery up the mountain passes."

Ho Chi Minh leaned forward.

"I know, Giap, but I wonder if the same geographical situation exists at Khe Sanh. You are referring to Khe Sanh, right? You mentioned the name in our last conversation."

The cat was out of the bag, the nuance revealed.

Ho Chi Minh continued to draw Giap in.

"All right, Giap, let's compare. After our victory at Dien Bien Phu, even though the French took revenge on a small town, we marched the French prisoners to Hanoi. Paris conceded defeat. Will the Americans? Dien Bien Phu sat in a broad valley. Khe Sanh occupies a corner of a plateau. The Dien Bien Phu area was populated to the extent that we relied on the locals for support. Can we say the same thing about the sparse population at Khe Sanh? We had provisions for our soldiers at Dien Bien Phu. Rice was plentiful. There is no food at Khe Sanh. Dien Bien Phu was three hundred kilometers from Hanoi, Khe Sanh is over twice that distance. Our supply lines to Dien Bien Phu did not cross country boundaries. They were not interdicted to an appreciable degree, not like the Americans are doing to us down the trail. The French outposts were relatively close-in to the French base, unlike those of the Americans. Am I correct, Giap?"

Giap's eyes narrowed as he looked at his country's leader.

"Bac Ho, the situation in the last regard is not the same. We attacked the American redoubts at Khe Sanh a week ago. Granted, we weren't successful. However, the Americans on their hilltop positions at Khe Sanh need the base, but they cannot support the base.

"At Dien Bien Phu, I was willing to lose five soldiers for every *bo doi Phap.* I was prepared for one hundred percent casualties. While the French lost two thousand men, our casualties exceeded six thousand.

"I've been called cold and reckless, but we were victorious and gained our independence."

Ho Chi Minh used a longtime nickname to emphasize an enduring friendship.

"Van, you are the Minister of Defense, the supreme commander of the Armed Forces, the formidable Vo Nguyen Giap. You have an adroit mind, but I'm not tricked."

Giap saw the genuine concern in Ho Chi Minh's sagging face. Ho's color looked good, but Giap detected a decline in his health.

"Honorable Chairman, the initial strategy at Khe Sanh, like it was at Dien Bien Phu, would be to render the main base helpless, the enemy immobile. At Dien Bien Phu, we cut the French off from the world, totally isolated them. There, we reduced each strongpoint and captured each hill. After the supporting hillocks of Anne-Marie, Gabrielle and Beatrice—*les points d'appui*—fell, we controlled the valley. Afterwards, we postponed further action for a couple of weeks until we reconstituted our assets. The French could not do the same, they could not resupply.

"Unlike Him Lam Hill and Highpoints A-1 and D-1 at Dien Bien Phu which were close to the French base, the hilltops occupied by the Americans are too far away. The small hills at Dien Bien Phu were crucial to our effort. The highpoints around Khe Sanh are not.

"One by one, Dominique, Huguette and Claudine were reduced. We destroyed Isabelle, east of the main base, with the 304th Division. Then, we focused all our efforts on the last objective, the main encampment. We tightened the ring of trenches every day like manacles. There was no escape for Christian de Castries. Within a short time, we overran his headquarters and took him prisoner.

"The French chose the location for their demise. They created an immobile base camp in a remote, untenable place. They misjudged its vulnerability. We naturally chose that place, too. But more importantly, we chose the time. Having the Katyusha rocket launchers didn't hurt our efforts either."

Giap became strident. "Bac Ho, *la Légion Étrangère française*, suffered a big loss. I have respect for the Legionnaires, but I absolutely detested the Moroccan and Algerian mercenaries. They were nothing but animals."

Ho Chi Minh lightened up the conversation.

"I recall that with limited resources, your concept of warfare seemed logical. You modified Mao Tse-Tung's steps for guerilla warfare. It resulted in great success for our armed struggle."

Giap laughed.

"My fighting principals are still relevant. When the enemy advances, we retreat. When he avoids battle, we attack. We harass him when he stops. If he withdraws, we follow in his tracks. We never let up."

Ho Chi Minh smiled at his general.

"Giap, I have always trusted your competence. Remind me what you once wrote. To annihilate the enemy, it is necessary to concentrate one's forces, or something like that."

"But, Bac Ho, only at the most propitious moment. The general offensive has several objectives, but destruction of a large amount of our enemy's strength must be a priority. The overriding pursuit is to kill as many Americans as we can."

"And your theory of protracted war, Giap?"

"I am not forsaking that tactic. Protracted war is the way forward. At this exact moment, however, irrespective of the general offensive, we need favorable actions on the battlefield. Subsequent protracted war will exacerbate the Americans' continued dilemma and exhaust their army.

"The impracticability of America prolonging such silliness in Vietnam will be costly. They will not be able to pursue further military operations. The people in the south will then show clear support for rightful, re-unified rule by Hanoi.

"Mr. Chairman, as for Khe Sanh, Highway Nine has been completely cut. Resupply by road is impossible. The 675th Artillery Regiment is in a superior position at Co Roc. Our artillery can compromise the surrounding enemy hill fortresses at any time and the American base and take out the airstrip with ease.

"Flights of large cargo planes will be disrupted. The Americans will be forced to rely on their helicopters for resupply. However, helicopters will never play a factor in the Americans' ability to provision Khe Sanh. They intimidated us at Ia Drang, but not now.

"The Americans at Khe Sanh, like the French before them at Dien Bien Phu, are in an untenable position. We can close the pincers."

It was not lost on Ho Chi Minh that his general stopped short of saying he was going to attack the American combat base. Ho looked squarely at General Giap.

"The Americans have artillery supporting the base. American planes control the skies, do they not? The French did not have those advantages."

"The American fighter-bombers are like mosquitoes, Sir. They cannot stop us."

"And the B-52s, Giap?"

Giap raised his tea cup to his lips.

"Yes, Bac Ho, America's big bombers present a threat."

Ho Chi Minh held up his hand. He didn't want to discuss the B-52s.

"Giap, Tell me the truth. Are you going to attack the Americans the same way you attacked the French at Dien Bien Phu? Are you planning an all-out assault at Khe Sanh?"

Giap reflected on Vietnam's history of eternal struggle. He looked at Ho Chi Minh's tired eyes. If his response matched Ho's question, Giap would deviate from a Vietnamese characteristic of never revealing one's plans directly. Chances of success are inversely proportional to how much one enlightens others. The earnest question required a symmetrically earnest answer; but not at this moment.

"America's arrogance is working in our favor. They can't afford to lose Khe Sanh—they will lose face—and we don't need…well..."

Giap paused. "A lot of Americans are concentrated in one place. If the scenario is advantageous and if other options prove less viable, yes, an issuance of orders to attack Khe Sanh is not out of the question and, like any military action, will be carefully assessed. But, only if the condition can be exploited would any attack receive consideration."

Ho Chi Minh sat immobile. He wasn't going to obtain a definitive answer from Vo Nguyen Giap.

"I see."

Giap changed the slant of his comments.

"Bac Ho, it's conceivable that the Americans will learn of our broad assaults across South Vietnam before the Tet New Year. Action against Khe Sanh will confuse them. A feint on Tan Lam, or what the Americans call Camp Carroll, with its large artillery would be a good diversion. It sits on Doi 241 [Hill 241]."

"A feint? A diversion? Giap, while you have left some questions unanswered, other questions are now raised. If I understand correctly, you are going to follow through with the general offensive component of Resolution Fourteen, while leaving your options open for an assault on an American base, ostensibly, I believe, at Khe Sanh—two independent actions. I'll ask the question directly. Can you support concurrent operations in disparate locations?"

"Bac Ho..."

Giap spoke peripherally. "Irrespective of the efforts of the *quan doi* [army], the general offensive must be seen as being primarily the work of the National Liberation Front. The subsequent insurrection will be the result of the will of the local people. Unfortunately, the Viet Cong are incapable of the level of planning required for such a comprehensive operation."

Ho Chi Minh, a blanket over his shoulders, looked at the snow covered trees. His demeanor changed.

"Comrade Giap, I try to maintain a façade but even I can't fool myself. I don't have many days left. A re-unified Vietnam will be the fulfillment of an old man's heart."

Vo Nguyen Giap desisted from further mention of Khe Sanh. He began putting his overcoat on.

"Bac Ho, the *Tet Mau Than* campaign will begin within a few days. I've stopped over in Beijing on my return trip to Hanoi to check on you. I would also respectfully ask for any final instructions you may have prior to the launch of the general offensive."

"Giap, I can only paraphrase the subtitle of Resolution Fourteen. Courageously rise and achieve a decisive victory against the Americans for national salvation."

"Mr. Chairman," Giap said, gathering his hat, "The cause for reunification cannot be accomplished without your inspiration. We need you in Hanoi."

Ho Chi Minh smiled at his old friend. Often garrulous, Ho's impromptu metaphor was a stretch.

"One day, the red constrained by the edges of the three stripes that cut across South Vietnam's illegal flag will overflow. Like a blood river cresting its banks, the red will inundate the empty meadow of yellow. It will transform into a field flooded in the glorious blood of our victorious soldiers. Our *sao vang* [yellow star] will shine brightly from the center of that crimson field."

Ho Chi Minh massaged his face. "Giap, *vous m'avez toujours été fidèle* [you have always been loyal to me]."

Ho paused. "You recall in 1954, I told you not to attack Dien Bien Phu if you thought you could not win. I am repeating those words to you now. Don't attack Khe Sanh unless you can prevail in this battle. Too much is at risk."

Ho Chi Minh reached out to shake Vo Nguyen Giap's hand. "*Au revoir, mon bon ami.*"

CHAPTER TWENTY

CANNED PEACHES

Captain Raymond Dwight was sitting on a sandbag embankment protecting a 105mm towed howitzer. He was eating peaches from a can with his knife. Tall and lanky, Dwight's arms, face and torso were sunburned to a deep red. He wore no shirt, only his flak jacket. He had written "Skipper" on his vest with a black marking pen.

Located at the eastern end of the Khe Sanh Combat Base, the battery had to be temporarily vacated the first night of the siege after the nearby primary ammo dump was hit by an NVA artillery round. ASP1 detonated like a volcano. Exploding ordnance showered the area causing heavy damage. Over the next several days, Marines spent hours policing the area, collecting unexploded rounds. Shell casings, pallets, square metal ammo containers and other ordnance lay strewn about.

"Captain Dwight, Sir?"

"Yeah, I'm Dwight."

"Sir, I'm told you studied history."

The captain looked up at the Marine as he chewed.

"Sir, Colonel Lownds sent me to talk to you."

"And you would be?"

"Lieutenant Sondheim, Sir."

"No, Lieutenant, I got my degree in political science."

"Skipper, I never understood the connection between politics and science. But, you must have taken some history courses."

"Why the questions, Lieutenant? What does the colonel want from me?"

"Captain, Colonel Lownds is asking what we know about Vo Nguyen Giap. We've received reports that he's here in Eye Corps."

"Really? Giap's ass is here?"

"That's the rumor, Sir. The colonel sent me to talk to you because you might know something about Giap that would be helpful to him and the S2."

"Not a lot, but yeah, I read a book about military engagements. The battle of Dien Bien Phu was one of them."

The captain stabbed two peach halves with his knife at the bottom of the can. He raised the knife to his mouth and slipped the halves in between his teeth. His mouth full, he continued to talk. "Giap's led a complicated life. It's hard to follow. He studied all those commie guys."

Dwight wiped his mouth with his forearm. "He was born in 1911, in a small town not too far north of here in Quang Binh Province, just above the DMZ."

The captain poured the syrupy liquid from the can down his throat. "The name of his home town is spelled An Xa, but I have no idea how to pronounce it—*Ann Zaa*, I suppose."

"Captain, I can't say any of these words over here, it's all gobbledygook to me."

"He has two sisters and a brother, but one sister was executed by the French; or maybe it was his sister-in-law. Can't remember exactly. He went to high school in Hue and Hanoi, then the University of Hanoi. Got an economics degree and a law degree."

"What's a friggin' lawyer know about military stuff?"

"Exactly. And why would a communist study economics? They don't practice any of it. Anyway, Giap had no formal military training, but he was a student of military history, especially the battles of the Chinese under Mao-Tse-Tung and the campaigns of Napoleon."

"He speaks French, then."

"To survive under the Frogs in Tonkin you had to speak the language. The French gave the brighter ones a chance to get an education. As much as he was antagonistic toward the French colonialists, Giap became perfectly fluent in French. Ironically he enjoys French literature and art and the language itself. He was well regarded by many French people as an articulate person. But I read where Giap has one hell of a temper."

Dwight stood up at the back of the 105. Six months were written on his helmet, ending with June '68. The next month was spelled G-O-N-E.

"Giap married a young girl from Vinh, named Nguyen Thi Quang Thai in 1938 or 1939. I remember the name because of the ring of the phonetics. She died some time later in Hoa Lo Prison...the Hanoi Hilton."

The captain held out a pack of Marlboros. "Cigarette, Sondheim?"

The lieutenant held up his hand.

Dwight continued. "I can't recall how, exactly, but Giap became acquainted with Pham Van Dong, the Prime Minister. They exiled themselves to China in the late thirties. Somewhere in all this, Giap's father was executed and his home in An Xa burned to the ground. Even Giap was imprisoned at some point in his life. I heard he may have been incarcerated in Lao Bao prison not far from here, right near Laos, on Highway Nine."

The captain inhaled on his cigarette. "Giap and Pham Van Dong were in China where they met up with Ho Chi Minh in about 1940. They're the backbone of the Vietnamese communist movement.

"Giap returned to Vietnam and lived in caves near Pac Bo, in the north, where the Viet Minh army got its start. They attacked the French at small outposts here and there. Eventually Giap led the Viet Minh to victory. The communists came to power and now, Giap's the Minister of Defense. That's all I know."

"Captain, do you think Giap's here, running this shootin' match?"

"Doubt it. He's the top dog, the equivalent of McNamara. SECDEF's got Wheeler and Westmoreland. Giap has Van Tien Dung and Tran Quy Hai. I'm sure he's providing overall strategy, but tactical activities are probably being orchestrated by Tran Quy Hai."

"Captain, surely he..."

"Lieutenant, how would he get down here? They don't have transport planes and the jungle trails are too dangerous for him to risk it. Look, I don't know much more than what I just told you. I'll help the CO all I can, but I really shouldn't leave my post unless it's essential."

"I'll let the colonel know I talked to you, Sir."

"Oh, Lieutenant Sondheim, there is one other thing about Giap."

"Sir?"

"Vo Nguyen Giap's entire military endeavors and the manner in which he molds his military strategy are based on the fact that in the past—and even now—his enemy had everything while he had nothing. His army was never mechanized. His soldiers moved from battlefield to battlefield on foot, very seldom by truck and never by helicopter. They stole rifles, artillery and ammunition. They ambushed French patrols and made off with their military equipment—whatever Giap's fledgling army could use—including clothing.

"We would ridicule them as being a backward, peasant army. We see this as a weakness, but in Giap's mind, it's a key strength. If one of our trucks is blown up, we expect we can get another one. Giap has learned not to be dependent on a constant source of supply.

"Giap knows this part of Asia like the back of his hand. Boundaries mean nothing here. Oh, and don't forget. They are master tunnelers. At Dien Bien Phu, they tunneled right under the French at Eliane, packed the tunnel with TNT and blew the hill sky high.

"At Dien Bien Phu, they never stopped trenching. My guess is Giap is using those same techniques here at Khe Sanh. I think the NVA intend to advance on us."

The captain tossed the empty tin can over the sandbag embankment, grabbed his canteen and took a big swallow of water. "The damned rats ain't gettin' none of that fruit."

Dwight wiped the knife-blade on his utilities and re-sheathed his knife. "Canned peaches. That was my birthday meal, Lieutenant. Today's the twenty-eighth, right?"

"Happy birthday, Skipper."

CHAPTER TWENTY-ONE

MEMORANDUM FOR THE PRESIDENT: THE SITUATION AT KHE SANH

The American President was convening a meeting in the cabinet room at one o'clock in the afternoon on the twenty-ninth of January 1968. The Secretary of Defense and the Joint Chiefs of Staff would be present.

While other attendees converged on the White House, in like fashion, General Earle Wheeler's limousine crossed the Potomac River on Memorial Bridge at about a quarter past noon.

The black vehicle took the scenic route around the Lincoln Memorial to Constitution Avenue. The limousine turned north on Seventeenth Street and, after one more turn, entered the White House grounds through the southwest gate.

Clearly marked with a large diagonal red stripe across it, the envelope General Wheeler was couriering contained an important communiqué for "Eyes Only."

The President, talking on the telephone when General Wheeler and Walt Rostow entered the Oval Office, raised a finger signaling he would be free in a moment. He motioned to Wheeler to hand him the envelope. He put his hand over the mouthpiece of the phone.

"Give me one second, Gentlemen. I'll be right with you. Good to see you, General."

And then back into the phone.

"Dammit all, now you listen to me. The budget's gonna get approved by both houses and I don't wanna hear no excuses that it can't. There is no such thing as no… Zwick? Yes, of course, Charles Zwick was sworn in as Budget Director just an hour ago."

Walt Rostow, thinking he may be able to slip out and use another telephone, turned to leave.

The President looked up as he spoke into the receiver.

"Hold on a minute..."

His hand covered the mouthpiece.

"Rostow, don't leave. I think I know what this envelope's about. Let me finish this call."

The President resumed his telephone conversation.

"Yeah, I'm back. Anyway, listen..." The President scratched the side of his face. "I don't give a crap what the senate thinks, this budget's gonna pass by God, or I'm not the President of the United States."

The President put the receiver down brusquely and mumbled.

"Damn senate."

He looked up quickly. "How you doin', Earle?"

The President opened the envelope and began to read the enclosed document. It was in response to the President's request for the Joint Chiefs of Staff to make in writing an unprecedented declaration.

The two-page MEMORANDUM FOR THE PRESIDENT, the subject of which was "The Situation at Khe Sanh, JCSM-63-68, dated 29 January 1968," began:

> *You will recall that on 12 January 1968 General Westmoreland informed me that the Khe Sanh position is important to us for the following reasons: it is the western anchor of our defense of the DMZ area against enemy incursions into the northern portion of South Vietnam; its abandonment would bring enemy forces into areas*

contiguous to the heavily populated and important coastal area; and its abandonment would constitute a major propaganda victory for the enemy which would seriously affect Vietnamese and U.S. morale...

The President read the last sentence of the first paragraph out loud.

"In summary, General Westmoreland declared that withdrawal from Khe Sanh would be a tremendous step backwards."

The President adjusted his glasses on the bridge of his nose. One hand held the memorandum while the other hung to his side. He continued to read the next two paragraphs which ended the first page.

At 0910 hours this morning I discussed the Khe Sanh situation by telephone with General Westmoreland. He had just returned from a visit to northern I Corps Area during which he conferred with senior commanders, personally surveyed the situation, and finalized contingency plans. General Westmoreland made the following points:

The Khe Sanh garrison now consists of 5,000 U.S. and ARVN troops. They have more than a battalion of U.S. artillery supporting them, and 16 175mm guns which can fire from easterly positions in support of the Khe Sanh force.'

The President turned to the second page, so denoted with a number "2" in the center at the bottom of the sheet. He learned from paragraphs "b" through "e" that Westmoreland had moved a full U.S. Army division into northern Eye Corps; General Abrams was commanding a field army headquarters in Hue/Phu Bai to control all forces in northern Eye Corps; General Momyer, Commander Seventh Air Force, was coordinating all supporting airstrikes in the NIAGARA area; and secondary explosions have been observed as a result of remunerative B-52 sorties, some forty per day.

The memorandum went on to quote General Westmoreland.

We can hold Khe Sanh and we should hold Khe Sanh. This is an opportunity to inflict a severe defeat upon the enemy. All preparatory and pre-cautionary measures have been taken...to conduct a successful defense in the Khe Sanh area.

The ending paragraph read:

The Joints Chiefs of Staff have reviewed the situation at Khe Sanh and concur with General Westmoreland's assessment of the situation. They recommend that we maintain our position at Khe Sanh.

The Memorandum for the President closed with "For the Joint Chiefs of Staff" and was signed by the Chairman, General Earle G. Wheeler, the same man now standing in the Oval Office in front of the President.

Lyndon Johnson, framed by the United States flag and the blue flag of the President behind him, leaned back in his high-backed leather chair. He held the memorandum level with his eyes. It was stamped TOP SECRET at the top and bottom of each page, The President, his face immobile, raised his glasses above his forehead. He mumbled the words he had just read:

"Everyone is confident...all preparatory measures...in his judgment."

The President, shaking his head, placed his left hand to his eyebrow while holding the memorandum in his right. He recited certain words louder.

"Can hold...should hold... maintain our position."

Juanita Roberts entered the Oval Office.

"Mr. President, General Wheeler, Mr. Rostow, I'm sorry to disturb you gentlemen. Secretary McNamara and the Chiefs have arrived, Sir."

Juanita handed the President the list of names with a check mark next to each one.

"Juanita, tell everyone I'll be with them shortly."

Then, to General Wheeler.

"Earle, this memorandum seems to sum up the Joint Chief's opinions."

"Thank you, Mr. President."

"But, I guess I was hoping your letter would convey a more...I'll be candid. I guess I was wanting to read something else."

General Wheeler and Walt Rostow looked at each other in puzzlement.

"Anyway," the President went on. "We have the meeting in the cabinet room in about ten minutes and we can discuss it in there. Now, if you please, General, I would like to have a word with my security advisor."

"Gladly, Mr. President. I'll join the others in the Cabinet Room. Thank you, Sir."

Walt Rostow saw a sudden scowl cross the President's face. Rostow had seen this before.

The President spoke in a scurrilous tone as he pointed at the memorandum.

"Walt, what's this crap? The North Vietnamese have sent the entire 304th Division down that damn Santa Fe Trail to Quang Tri Province. Helms told me they went into action immediately against us. We've lost the district headquarters of Huong Hoa. Do you realize that's the first government of any size to be overrun in South Vietnam?"

"Sir, that may be, but the NVA's position is tenuous. They need upwards of forty tons of supplies every day to support major combat actions. It's almost impossible to..."

"Hell, Walt. Forty, fifty, sixty tons, so what? They're there. The Viet-nese are screwin' with us. Quang Tri Province is their playground."

The President's eyes shifted to the last sentence on the second page. He read out loud. "They recommend that we maintain our position at Khe Sanh."

"Sir, Khe Sanh's important."

"Walt, after the twenty-first of January, when the siege began, some advisors felt Khe Sanh should be abandoned. They've even said the Marines are there because the North Vietnamese allow them to be there. They can cancel that invitation at any time. Contrary to what you just said, they base their argument on the theory that Khe Sanh holds no importance to the NVA since they could just walk around it."

"Sir..."

"Rostow, Wheeler's memorandum reads more like the minutes of the conversation he must have had with Westmoreland. He's invested Khe Sanh. I am aware of this fact. Is Wheeler now going to recommend that he leave? I don't think so. We're at Khe Sanh. I already know that. We should hold Khe Sanh, that it commands the area. They have said as much."

"Sir, just to add, the 37th ARVN Ranger Battalion arrived at Khe Sanh on the twenty-seventh and are positioned at the east end of the base. That's the fifth maneuver battalion, Sir, and we…"

"Rostow, I don't care how many battalions have arrived."

Johnson looked again at the letter and uttered. "Steadfastness…maintain our position…dammit, I want to know that we will not be defeated. Wheeler's memorandum doesn't give me much confidence. I wanted to receive confirmation from Wheeler and Westmoreland and from each member of the Chiefs of Staff collectively, individually and all together that Khe Sanh unequivocally will not fall to the NVA, or any other communist crap organization. Period."

The President stood up from his chair and, placing his hands on the desk, leaned forward on his arms. Irritated, his voice grew strident. He looked straight at his security advisor.

"Now, I'm going into that cabinet room and have a talk with the JCS Chairman. I'll get to a better understanding. Afterwards, we'll have a friendly little lunch together. But, Rostow, listen to me. I do not want this country, or our military…or this Presidency to be embarrassed by a silly, stupid-ass defeat in some raggedy-assed, backwater country at some insignificant, defunct, little rat-hole corner of the earth called Khe Sanh…not by the same pissant army that kicked the sissy French poofters outta Din Bin Phu. Am I clear?"

"Perfectly clear, Mr. President. Everyone is waiting, Sir."

CHAPTER TWENTY-TWO

CHUC MUNG NAM MOI

Born in 1894, in Yonkers, New York, Ellsworth Bunker enjoyed a lifetime of achievement. He received a degree in law from Yale University in 1916. He joined his father and became the president of the family's sugar enterprise. Bunker retired from private business in 1951 and bought property in Vermont. Not satisfied, Bunker eventually moved into the diplomatic arena.

He served as ambassador to Argentina, Italy and India. He was appointed ambassador to the Organization of American States in 1964.

Three years later, while attending a conference in Buenos Aires, Ellsworth Bunker received a cable from President Johnson. He flew to Washington.

The President explained that he needed Bunker's help with the most important foreign affairs issue facing the United States. Impressed with the manner in which Bunker handled the crisis in the Dominican Republic, President Johnson told Bunker he wanted him immediately to replace Henry Cabot Lodge, Jr. as ambassador in Saigon.

Ellsworth Bunker was overwhelmed. So much was happening. Only recently, he'd married an American woman while he was in Nepal. She was an emissary like he was. Theirs was the first American marriage involving two United States ambassadors.

Bunker was not thrilled with the prospect of leaving his wife and his comfortable home in Kathmandu, but the President's offer comes once in a lifetime. Each post in his brilliant career had been unique and highly interesting, but none would hold the same challenge or drama he would experience in South Vietnam.

Bunker arrived in Saigon on an April afternoon in 1967, on the same day that his predecessor departed.

Ambassador Bunker found South Vietnam to have the energy of a freight train mixed with political volatility. The military predicament with North Vietnam, the antagonism of South Vietnam's rival factions and the diplomatic situation he'd inherited were vastly different from anything he experienced in his professional life. Not accustomed to such heightened attention, he also found the number of U.S. government visitors to Saigon annoying.

Awarded the Presidential Medal of Freedom by John F. Kennedy in 1963, Elsworth Bunker would be a faithful servant to the United States and promote its policy toward the new republic. A believer in the struggle for South Vietnam's right to exist, Bunker was a strong proponent of U.S. military support and intervention to assuage North Vietnam's attempts to disrupt South Vietnam's independence and derail its fledgling democracy. He would also be a stalwart against the transgressions of North Vietnam. He would thwart the spread of communism.

Bunker felt that his ambassadorial-ship was providently placed upon him. He was the right man in the right place, who'd come along at the right time.

After a long day, Elsworth Bunker would often relax at Le Cercle Sportif Saigonnais, the CSS.

Established in 1896, Le Cercle Sportif Saigonnais was quintessentially colonial French and catered to the easy idleness of higher French society. Located at No. 55 Chasseloup-Laubat Street, just behind the Presidential Palace, the club covered many acres of prime real estate in downtown Saigon. CSS maintained tennis courts, a pétanque pitch, a large swimming pool with a concrete diving platform and an outside restaurant and bar. The color of the water in the pool was tinted green by the jade tiles that lined the sides and bottom. Bougainvillea and the clusters of *Bang-Bang*, nestled in the deep shade of lush trees, created a soothing, French-Cochin atmosphere.

Elegant balls and festive parties were thrown in the main hall famous for its parquet floor. Drinks were served each evening on its spacious second-floor veranda by Vietnamese waiters wearing starched white uniforms, or by young Vietnamese women dressed in traditional, elegantly-straight, white *ao dai*. The grace of the young women added to the sophisticated culture of the Cercle Sportif Saigonnais and enhanced the mystique of Saigon.

French children would try to catch mosquito-eating gecko lizards as they squirreled up the walls or slithered across the parquet floor of the ballroom. The CSS, a tropical haven of peace, was the hub of *haute-couture*, the center of the French social scene in Saigon.

When the *My on ao* (noisy Americans) arrived, they also enjoyed the grace of the CSS. But the newcomers, in such splendid colonial surroundings, corrupting the name simply to Circle Sportive, were *très gauche*—awkward, out of place.

Ambassador Bunker, wearing white Converse low-top tennis shoes and white sport shirt and shorts, was often seen playing tennis at the CSS. He was good at the net, but he preferred hard volleys where he would stand several feet behind the baseline and smash the ball with all his strength, sending it in a flat trajectory across the net.

Sometimes, the Ambassador would come to the club simply to practice his serve on the red clay court for an hour or so in the evenings before dinner. His wind-up was effortless, resulting in a blinding shot to the outside corner of his opponent's serve area. Age seventy-four, the American Ambassador held his own against anyone.

Marie-Dominique, a French girl of fifteen, watched as he practiced his serve. A native of Aix-en-Provence, she had creamy olive-tan skin, light brown hair and bright brown eyes accentuated by elegant eyebrows.

Not shy, Marie-Dominique asked if she could practice returning his serve. With her beguiling accent and an engaging smile that revealed pearl white teeth, how could the Ambassador refuse? She proved a skillful opponent. Quite the challenge for the Ambassador, her return shots were powerful. The exercise was soothing, the competition and the atmosphere of the CSS cathartic.

Ellsworth Bunker came to relish the lifestyle of Saigon and the tropical evenings on the languorous Saigon River.

But on the warm evening of the thirtieth of January, with the soft overhead incandescent lights illuminating the red clay of the tennis court, the white boundary lines and the translucent wings of tropical insects that flew above, Ellsworth Bunker's game was not quite on.

Bunker's baseline shots were long. His flat, forehand shots didn't hit the corners just right. His serve, still fast and straight, was a bit wide of the mark. Frustrated with his game, the American Ambassador retired for the evening after only one set.

He slipped the trapezoidal wood frame over the head of the racquet and, tightening the thumb screws, clamped it into place. He gathered his belongings and made his way to the limousine parked in the round driveway of Le Cercle Sportif Saigonnais.

"*Monsieur l'Ambassadeur, est-ce que vous partez*? Are you leaving, Sir? I was hoping to return a few serves."

Ambassador Bunker, recognizing the accent, turned around.

"Marie-Dominique, you came here to play tennis tonight? On the eve of Tet?"

"I thought I could play before the celebration starts. The CSS may even let me sit on the veranda and watch the party."

The American Ambassador smiled.

"I'm very sorry. I'm not playing well and I have an urgent matter that I must take care of. Also, I have two obligatory embassy parties I promised I would attend. *Peut-être demain soir*—perhaps tomorrow night—or maybe one night next week."

Now in the back seat of the limousine, Bunker sat silently, in deep thought. The frustration he experienced with his tennis game was underscored by something more troubling.

Bunker had received continuous queries from the State Department and directly from the President himself. What about the situation at Khe Sanh? Enemy actions in the mountains of Quang Tri Province were not promising.

The Ambassador was worried about intelligence reports that the Hanoi regime was planning something throughout South Vietnam. The extent of the operations and the timing were not known, but it was clear the North Vietnamese had ambitious ideas.

Military leaves for South Vietnamese soldiers had been cancelled and many units, American and South Vietnamese alike, were put on alert.

The Tet holidays, the first for the American Ambassador, were at hand. Tet, meaning the first morning of the first day of the New Year, a traditional time in Vietnam, lasts for seven days. Homes are cleaned, debts paid and differences among family members are resolved. The bright yellow *Hoa Mai* flower, prominent everywhere, encourages the arrival of spring. Bright red envelopes containing "lucky" money are exchanged.

The next day, the thirty-first of January, Bunker thought, would be a pleasant distraction. He could enjoy the giant street party, perhaps with a glass of champagne.

Bunker's limousine passed beneath Saigon's towering star-burst trees, through the city's boulevards festively decorated in preparation for the first day of the Lunar New Year.

The streets were packed with people crowding around lanterns and cooking fires while eating on the sidewalk with chopsticks. Giant colorful *papier-mâché* characters bounced along the streets. Staccato fireworks exploded and sparks flew from spiraling pinwheels. The air, filled with sulfurous firecracker smoke, was redolent of peanut cooking oil.

Gongs, large bells, drums and puppets welcoming the Asian New Year, were in abundance throughout Saigon, indeed throughout South Vietnam.

Overhead banners, cutting across Saigon's crowded streets, tethered to trees on either side read *Chuc Mung Nam Moi* (Happy New Year). The popping sound of firecrackers and the flash of roman candles increased in tempo.

But, later that night, what sounded like muffled shots coming from Independence Palace and from as far away as Tan Son Nhut Airport would be portentous. Even closer to his residence, the loud pyrotechnics that Ellsworth Bunker would hear coming from the U.S. embassy on Thong Nhut Boulevard, well after midnight, would shake him abruptly out of bed. The cacophony of explosions would not be those of holiday fireworks.

The President and citizens of the United States of America would wake up the next day to a shocking new reality. The perceptions of the war in Vietnam in early 1968, at the start of Vietnam's Lunar New Year, would change forever. The light at the end of the tunnel had disappeared. Elsworth Bunker would be caught in the center of the storm.

The Tet Offensive was about to unfold.

CHAPTER TWENTY-THREE

CHEAP SMOKES, BEER AND WHISKEY

"Man, there's some bad shit going on in Saigon. The city's friggin' exploding. They got guts, the VC, to attack the U.S. embassy. Old man Giap was supposed to attack us here, not in Saigon."

Gene Bouchet, reacting to what he heard about the sudden enemy attacks across the country, sat sharpening his KA-BAR knife using an Arkansas whetstone. His father, an ex-Marine, had given both to Bouchet before he left the U.S. for Vietnam, too many months ago now to remember. Bouchet's black M-16, with a full magazine of twenty 5.56mm rounds inserted into the well in front of the trigger guard, was leaning, within easy reach, against empty ammunition crates.

The sound of the knife sliding across the sharpening stone made a sandy, metallic-grinding sound. It had a mesmerizing effect that allowed Bouchet to escape for a moment from the craziness of Khe Sanh. He diligently slid the knife, held at a precise angle, across the flat surface of the small gray rectangular slab.

"Fiston," his father would say to him when he was a young boy, "you'll have more luck when you slide the edge forward, not backward. *Comme ca, c'est mieux*—like this, it's better."

THE PRESIDENT'S SANDBOX

A real Cajun, his father cooked a mean meal of smoked andouille sausage with red beans and rice. He knew the bayous better than anyone and when to head for home from fishing before a storm, even though the skies were clear. Above all—and what Gene Bouchet liked most about his father—he was fearless.

A miniature Louisiana state flag placed atop a short stick fluttered in the breeze. He received the flag about three weeks earlier. Emblazoned with a circle of seven stars on a vertical blue stripe, it wasn't the official state flag, not the pelican flag, but it was like the one his father flew from a flagpole in front of his cabin.

Bouchet looked at his friend Anthony Knowlton, with whom he had gone through boot camp at Parris Island. They'd both ended up in the Third Battalion Twenty-sixth Marines.

"Vietnam's blowing up in our face. Pleiku, Kontum, Tan Son Nhut, Bien Hoa…all over the damn place. The NVA and VC are friggin' all over the place. They gotta be gettin' ready to attack us…can't believe they haven't attacked the combat base.

"The real fight is here, not in some podunk provincial capital. The gooks turned friggin' yellow and targeted softer targets. Jesus Christ, man, all hell is breaking loose in Hue. They're fightin' across the Perfume River, blowin' things up. Da Nang is under attack…Pleiku, Can Tho."

"But, man," Knowlton said. "The U.S. embassy in Saigon…that's some serious shit. Hard to imagine how they could do that."

"The VC attacked the embassy sometime after midnight, right on the Tet New Year."

Bouchet spit out a long slug of chewing tobacco and wiped his mouth. "Assholes. I'll bet the whole damned town, police included, is crawlin' with VC.

"Hey, Tony, that gook that surrendered down at the combat base about two weeks ago…on the twentieth of January or so. Remember?"

"Yeah, a Lieutenant Tonc, or Tonka, I dunno, some stupid name. I heard he just walked inside the wire, an AK in one hand and some kind of white flag, and gave himself up. Must have had something good to reveal."

"Know what I think? That guy was a plant. He didn't have squat. Or, he was scared shitless of being blown to bits by our airstrikes. Just another NVA coward. Should've shot his stinking commie ass on the spot...would have cost us a two-cent bullet."

"Naw, Bouchet, come on. Can't friggin' do that, man. We needed to interrogate him."

"Shit, the bastards have been killing us for months. Remember that last patrol?"

"Bloody shit, for sure, man."

"Damn slope heads, we seen them one-by-one, but we never seen a bunch of 'em. They hide in their caves. Remember that gook who stood up from his fighting hole? He was covered with grass and banana leaves as camouflage. He leveled his AK at us. Killed two Marines on that patrol. I shot the son-of-a-bitch six times, damned near cut him in half. He had an RPG strapped on his back. The rocket was still in the tube."

Bouchet spit again. "Aren't we here to kill the bastards? You've shot more than a few. I'll bet you and I have killed a dozen. The government identifies the enemy, points us in that direction and, bingo, we take care of 'em. Job done. I was gonna take a piss on his putrid body, but Sarge pulled me back. Told me to settle down. The only good gook is a dead gook, I say."

"Ah, Geno, come on, man. You read that in some Mark Twain book. The only good injun is a dead injun..."

"Never read Mark Twain."

"This Khe Sanh siege...it's horseshit. We sit up here day after day in these shitholes and eat NVA artillery and mortar rounds, then we go on patrol and we lose three or four Marines. Next day, same damn thing. What's that Tonka gook gonna do for us, huh? And now, look. There's fightin' goin' on all over South Vietnam, and here we are with our heads in the clouds and our feet in the damn mud."

Anthony Knowlton looked down the valley toward the combat base in the hazy distance. He let Gene Bouchet rant on. Knowlton had many of the same feelings. Better for Bouchet to get it out of his system.

"Knowlton? I'll tell you what that Tonc bastard did. He gave us a little shit piece of information. Like, what could I give 'em if I went to the other side? I'd say there are three hundred Marines on that hill, but that's all I know. Beyond that, what information could I provide? I ain't no S2. I don't know squat."

Tony Knowlton nodded his head. Bouchet continued.

"That gook don't know nothin' at all. He's a stooge. I wouldn't be surprised if he didn't say he had something to do with what's happening in Saigon and Hue."

"Bouchet, you're letting your imagination get the best of you. Our intelligence ain't that bad. I'm sure the interrogators got all the facts. Come on, man, he didn't have anything to do with Saigon."

Bouchet spit again.

"Knowlton, I'm not in Saigon and I'm not down there on the base. Neither are you. We're way up here on this God-forsaken hill sittin' in our own shit. Our clothes are so rotten they fall off us. They smell like shit. We smell like shit, even eat shit out of these shit rations and the water tastes like gasoline and chlorine shit mixed. Here we are. *Ca y est.* That's it."

"Geno, give me a break, man. We're here just like everyone else. That tobacco's gettin' to you...chewin' all that stuff...I dunno...maybe some marijuana, too."

"I don't know creamola about these hills. Ain't never seen mountains until I went to Asheville just after boot camp, up there in them App-lap-chins...can't even say the damn word. I don't know nothin' about this Vietnam shit, about communist pukes. But, I do know one thing."

Tony Knowlton looked at Bouchet blankly, then turned his eyes away. He really didn't have time for this conversation, but he knew it wouldn't end.

"What would that be, Bouchet?"

"That gook's fed phony information to our people and it ain't gonna turn out no damn good, just like the embassy in Saigon."

"Hey, Geno. Take it easy, man."

"If I could, Knowlton, I'd go home to Loosiana, kick back and drink beer. I garan-friggin'-tee it...and I'd go fishin' and huntin' alligators every damned day. I hate this Khe Sanh place. I hate these spooked-up hills, the fog and rain and the shit-head NVA."

"Bouchet, get a hold of yourself, man.

Gene Bouchet breathed hard as he slid the knife along the stone several times. He looked out over the valley.

"Loosiana gators don't scare me none, Knowlton. I wrestle with 'em just like dad, and I catch giant catfish barehanded, too. I let 'em grab on my arm with that big mouth of theirs, all the way up to my elbow, and I lift them up and throw them in the boat. The swamps don't bother me none.

"If I'd seen that Tonc asshole coming toward me in the wire, I would have pulled the trigger and blown him straight to hell.

"I'll bet we're gonna level Hue. It'll just be a pile of rocks with a thousand VC buried beneath it."

"Gene, here, man. Drink some water."

Bouchet slurped water from Knowlton's canteen.

"What I'd give to have some bayou food. Cheap smokes, beer, whiskey… the evening sun low on the horizon, gold light through the cypress trees in the swamps, fireflies coming out. God, that's Loosiana. You tell me what's wrong with that, Knowlton? That's all I want. All that and a Cajun woman."

CHAPTER TWENTY-FOUR

AN EVEN MORE REMOTE OUTPOST

On Monday, the start of the first full week in February, at a little past 3:00 a.m. at Khe Sanh, a battalion of the NVA 325C Division attacked Echo Company Second Battalion Twenty-sixth Marines and breached the perimeter of Hill 861-Alpha, a spur of Hill 861. Ironically, after a brief lull in the fighting, the enemy inside the perimeter seemed more interested in collecting souvenirs, reading magazines and rummaging through the belongings the Marines left behind.

After the Marines threw a storm of grenades, they counter-attacked with knives, bayonets and fists. They completely mauled the terrified NVA. Later, NVA forces tried to attack again, but so weakened, they were easily repulsed. The Marines suffered seven KIA while the NVA lost well over one hundred men.

Two days after the fighting on Hill 861-Alpha and one week after the start of the Tet Offensive, the President received disturbing news about another savage battle at a small American encampment in Eye Corps.

President Johnson pushed open the door to the Situation Room. Walt Rostow, behind him with the usual folder of papers in his hand, was trying to catch up.

"Christ almighty, Rostow," the President said. "Communist bastards. First, it's Saigon, then Hue. Almost every provincial capital in the country is under attack…all over South Vietnam, Show me this place…whatever the hell it's called."

"Lang Vei, Sir."

Walt Rostow pulled out the map and unfolded it on the table. The words at the top of the map indicated the district: Huong Hoa.

"The Special Forces camp, Mr. President, isn't far to the southwest of the Khe Sanh Combat Base."

"Special Forces camp? That's Army. Not Marines."

"Yes, Sir. Only Army."

"This map is too small. I can't see a damn thing on it. Who was the commanding officer?"

"Captain Frank Willoughby, Sir."

The President picked up the phone.

"Juanita, I'm with Rostow. Tell Governor Hulett and the Ohio bridge delegates to just wait for me. Give 'em some coffee or…I dunno…maybe some of them leftover cinnamon rolls. I'll be with 'em shortly."

The President turned to Walt Rostow.

"OK, I wanna hear the details."

"The Special Forces camp was overrun by NVA infantry on the seventh of February."

"That's today, Rostow. Jesus Christ."

"Well, yes, Sir, but really yesterday there, Sir…uh, in a sense the same day, but in Vietnam…twelve hours ahead of us, Sir."

"Get on with it, Walt. How many Viet-nese?"

"About four hundred. The NVA used tanks and they had rocket and mortar fire support. We think they had artillery support, too, from Co Roc. Their infantry came from…"

"Whoa, whoa, whoa…just a damn minute. Back up."

The President leveled his eyes at his security advisor. "What did you just say?"

Rostow continued as if he heard nothing.

"Mr. President, the NVA struck from here…"

"Rostow, talk to me, dammit."

Rostow looked quizzically at the President.

"I'm sorry, Sir?"

"Walt, did I hear you say the NVA used tanks?"

"Mr. President, that's what I was told. I don't know everything, but..."

"What do you mean you don't know everything?"

President Johnson closed the gap between him and Walt Rostow and looked down into his face. His breath was hot. "Rostow, you're either my security advisor or you're not."

"Mr. President..."

"You're not shittin' me, are you? They've got tanks. It's not a rumor."

"No, Sir...I mean, yes, Sir. It's not a rumor, Sir. They have tanks. The NVA brought them down the trail and hid them in Laos."

President Johnson held up both hands while he shook his head from side to side.

"Well, I'll be snake bit. Out of the blue, an American camp is overrun and I learn the NVA pissants have tanks. Shit, and you tell me they hid the damned things in Laos? I never knew those commie Viets could drive a farm truck, much less a damn tank."

"Sir, on about the twenty-third of January, Air Force planes spotted some tanks near Ban Houei Sane in Laos, thirteen miles west of Khe Sanh. Then, on the first of February, last week, tanks were spotted again, but we had no idea..."

The President's voice boomed.

"You saw tanks a week ago? As early as fifteen days ago? And you had no idea? Dammit, Rostow."

"Sir, last night—early morning here—the 24th Infantry Regiment of the 304th NVA Division and the 198th NVA Tank Battalion..."

"A battalion! Holy Jesus Christ, Rostow, not one or two tanks. Now you're tellin' me there's a whole damn NVA tank battalion?"

"Yes, Sir."

"Show me again on the map."

"Here, Sir. There are two villages named Lang Vei, Lang Vei One, up this trail from Highway Nine, and Lang Vei Two, right here on the highway. It's this one on the highway, Sir, roughly halfway to Laos from Khe Sanh. The

Special Forces camp straddles Highway Nine and sits on a ridge overlooking valleys to each side.

"Lang Vei has a bit of a history, Sir. Our planes bombed the original site some distance away from its present location by accident in early March of sixty-seven. Then, in May, two months later, NVA agents posing as CIDG..."

"What the hell is CIDG?"

"Civilian Irregular Defense Group...indigenous forces, Sir. Anyway, the NVA sabotaged the camp while other enemy forces attacked. The camp was hit hard. The commanding officer and his executive officer were killed. The camp was moved to its current location farther along the highway. The Seabees rebuilt it and provided hardened concrete bunkers."

Walt Rostow pointed to the map again for the benefit of the President. "Here's the Khe Sanh Combat Base."

"Yeah, I see that, Walt," the President said, with a terse tone in his voice.

"Anyway, Sir, as for this attack, Lang Vei was manned by a group of thirteen American operatives. Fifth Special Forces, Detachment A, Company 101 and three or four hundred South Vietnamese and Montagnards.

"Evidently, in the middle of the fight...or maybe it was at the beginning... the Special Forces outpost was overrun by PT-76 tanks. One tank made it inside the wire and parked right on top of the command bunker. I think a few were destroyed by recoilless rifles, Sir. We didn't have heavy anti-tank weapons because we never thought they had tanks."

"Rostow, you just said you saw tanks in aerial photographs."

"I never saw the photographs, Sir. We didn't think they would be used at Lang Vei. We had light weapons though...LAWS, Sir."

"LAWS? Damn these acronyms"

"Something like a...I dunno, a bazooka."

"Rostow, for Christ's sake. I can't believe this crap."

The President was still reeling. "That make-believe, two-bit, peasant army actually has tanks."

"They crossed the Xe Pone River into South Vietnam, Sir, about here, we think, and attacked the outpost."

"Dammit, I thought Khe Sanh was the outpost."

"Sir, as you can see, Lang Vei is a more remote outpost and much smaller. It's primarily an observation and listening post near the Laotian border, Sir."

"What kind of tanks, again?"

"PT-76 tanks, Sir. Russian-made. They're light tanks. Not heavy like our M-48s. They're amphibious, Mr. President. That's how they crossed the river."

Walt Rostow scratched his forehead. "Anyway, Mr. President, they attacked at about midnight, Sir. Lang Vei..."

"Listen to me, Rostow. The international press is calling North Vietnam's attacks across the country a victory for Hanoi. I get one story from Saigon that things are OK, but the press presents a different picture to the public. It's damned embarrassing. The nightly news isn't helping at all. Some guy in New York City can read the news on TV—shit, he doesn't make the news. I read the Pentagon reports and the daily reports direct from Westmoreland. I don't know if I can trust either. And now, I get this crap about Lang Vei.

"Dammit, are we winning or losing? Westmoreland tells me that five days after Tet started, the enemy was routed in some of the cities. Westy cabled Wheeler that the enemy is not able to sustain his momentum. This is all good and fine, Rostow, but the CIA presents a completely different scenario. Helms says the enemy has a capability far greater than what MACV is telling me. How in the name of..."

"Sir, Hanoi has defied the Maoist doctrine that revolution begins in the countryside. The cities will be the last to fall. In reverse, Hanoi went after the cities first and..."

"Walt, dammit, I don't give a hoot about Mao Tse Tung and all that communist class-struggle crap. That fat man can swim in that, whatever the name of that river is, all he wants. But, what with attacks on Khe Sanh Ville, and on that hill...861-Alpha, or whatever the hell they call it..."

"Yes, Sir, next to Hill 861."

"And now, this Lang Vei bullshit..."

"Mr. President, Westmoreland says Khe Sanh is next."

"Christ, the enemy ain't lost no momentum. Walt, Lang Vei may have fallen and Khe Sanh may be attacked, but I don't wanna hear any talk about losing over there in that sweat tank of a country. Not one person on my staff is gonna think like that. The NVA is not gonna roll us up. No. Sir."

"I understand, Mr. President. Unfortunately, Sir, Highway Nine, from Lao Bao toward Khe Sanh, is now entirely open to the NVA."

Walt Rostow traced the curving alignment of Highway Nine with his finger. "There's nothing stopping enemy troops flowing into Quang Tri Province from Laos."

"Walt, dammit, that's what I'm saying. They've got more capabilities than we think."

The President scratched his head. "Man, Lang Vei must have taken it in the shorts."

"It's on Highway Nine, Sir…"

"Did Colonel Lownds send help from Khe Sanh?"

"Sir, with all respect, a relief column would have been cut to shreds…an impossible mission. That's what the NVA were hoping for, so they could ambush them outside the base.

"Lownds sent a patrol to Lang Vei months before to investigate how best to relieve the camp. As you can see, the straight distance is only eight kilometers, but it took nearly twenty hours for Alpha Company First Battalion to arrive there, so that wasn't a viable option."

"Yeah, probably suicidal."

"The Marines were able to support the Special Forces with their artillery. They were permitted to employ COFRAM rounds."

"You mean the secret ordnance I authorized for use awhile back?"

"Correct, Sir. During the fight, there was dispute as to whether Firecracker—codename for COFRAM—should be used. General Tompkins granted permission to use the munitions. I guess it cut the NVA up pretty bad."

"What about casualties? How many American KIAs?"

"I believe seven Americans were killed."

"Any MIAs?"

"Yes, Sir. I happen to have a list of the MIAs, Sir. It may not be complete."

Walt Rostow opened his folder and thumbed a piece of teletype paper.

"A James Holt, Kenneth Hanna, Charles Lindewald, James Moreland and a Daniel Phillips, Sir. And of course, a Private first class Jerry Elliott, but Elliott was lost about two weeks before near Khe Sanh ville—not related to Lang Vei. The others I just mentioned went MIA during the firefight at Lang Vei."

"What became of Captain Willoughby?"

"Willoughby was extracted by Huey, Sir. He's safe, but wounded."

"Why can't we just bomb that Highway Nine area since there're no American boys there now and stop the bastards?"

"We are, Sir."

CHAPTER TWENTY-FIVE

RENÉ L'ESCALIER

René l'Escalier's ride from Saigon to Da Nang in a Hercules turbo-prop in late January was uneventful. He felt he entered a giant whale when he walked up the back ramp into the C-130's cavernous insides. So new to the scene in Vietnam, René had no idea he would be allowed to board a U.S. military plane, but it was easy as catching the Metro at La Motte Picquet in Paris.

On the plane, René met a correspondent from Nice who worked for *Agence France Presse.* They hitched a ride on a Marine jeep into town. The reporter said he could sleep in a bunk in the French hotel on the riverfront which III MAF had turned into their headquarters. The cot had been allocated to *Newsweek.* At night, René could watch American movies at the press headquarters while eating popcorn.

René bumped into a wide assortment of expat civilians, the likes of which Hollywood could not invent. Each person was a journalist; or pretended to be one. The poseurs were the worst. He met an American woman with wild, bleached-blond hair who, living life on the edge, would catch rides by helicopter to Hue and Dong Ha. She had even visited Camp J. J. Carroll, the artillery base west of Dong Ha. A chain smoker, wearing garish lipstick, she could not stop boasting about the men, mostly officers, with whom she had so many liaisons.

Ever since the initial bombardment, Khe Sanh had garnished much of the news. Patrols beyond five hundred meters outside the perimeter were forbidden. Fighting took place around a hill designated as 471. The First Battalion Ninth Marines arrived at Khe Sanh on the twenty-second of January. The Ninth Marines were called the Walking Dead, a description he could not comprehend. An A-4 fighter-bomber was shot down on the twenty-third of January. The pilot ejected safely. Lang Vei had fallen and Hill 861-Alpha was attacked.

René continued his trip to Phu Bai in a C-123 to catch a ride to Khe Sanh. He immediately caught a CH-46. He had never seen anything so peculiar. The logo on the aft part of the fuselage sported a likeness of a fox inside a white circle.

"*Merde, J'ai oublié mes pellicules photos.*"

René l'Escalier forgot the bag of Tri-X he had placed on his bed in Saigon while packing. Off to a bad start, René was still determined to make a name for himself and to prove he was a competent combat photographer. But, he didn't have enough film.

"*Merde,*" he said again out loud as the helicopter took off.

But, of course, his expletive couldn't be heard. The continuous whop, whop sound of the six giant rotor blades that churned overhead and the whine of the twin turbines at the back of the Chinook drowned out all other sound.

The view through the cockpit from seven thousand feet was spectacular. The valleys and hills, however, all looked the same. Landmarks were indistinguishable.

Finally, the helicopter began a slow descent. The drone of the big blades became more thunderous as their pitch changed.

René looked nervously around at his fellow passengers. What a strange collection of Americans. Young Marines sat with their rifles and packs, helmets and canteens. Two men in white shirts, each carrying a pistol on his belt, looked at maps. What appeared to be officers of various ranks sat next to them. Like the younger Marines, they, too, carried rifles.

The shanty settlement of the Khe Sanh Combat Base, with a long airstrip as the only recognizable feature, came into view through the cockpit.

Steep mountains, deep crags and dense green foliage appeared through the round window opposite him. His traveling companions shifted and looked all around. The journey would soon end.

The giant helicopter banked hard on its left side. René could look straight down through the porthole-like window. He had a clear view of the ground.

"*Mon Dieu, regarde le terrain. Merde, c'est ça Khe Sanh.*"

The scarred and torn up earth and the multiple, large swaths, burned black by napalm, shocked the young Frenchman. Western Quang Tri Province was a very different world for the neophyte photo-journalist.

René was native to the prestigious surroundings of the 7ème arrondissement in Paris, famous for Napoleon's Tomb. He grew up in an elegant home at No. 19 Avenue de Tourville, not far from where the famous author Antoine de St. Exupery had lived. Constructed in 1892, the stone residence was designed by Eugène Dutarque, whose name was engraved on the front façade of the building. Each day when René returned from school, he would greet the two lions carved in stone above the porte cochère.

Later, but still in his early life, René discovered a name embossed on a marble plaque near Les Invalides. The plaque commemorating Pierre Lassalla, a French resistance fighter in World War Two, *tombé le 25 Août 1944 pour la libération de Paris,* indicated he was twenty-one years old when he died, the same age now as René. He never forgot that plaque, or the bouquet of flowers someone had placed in a ring attached to the wall beneath the small memorial.

René's family often took picnics in the shade of la Tour Eiffel sur le Champs de Mars. He was allowed to sip some Bordeaux, sometimes straight from the bottle, while he ate *saucisson et fromage.* With such grand history and refined sophistication, René could not imagine living anywhere else, but he was restless. The conflict in Southeast Asia stirred his imagination.

Unknown to his family, René had written to Francois Sully, a famous French reporter in Vietnam. Although Sully didn't encouraged him to come to Vietnam, he didn't discourage him either. René felt the pull of adventure. He wanted to experience Vietnam. Khe Sanh was the place to be.

René departed Paris late one evening, much to the chagrin of his aristocratic family who had learned of the shocking news only twelve hours before.

René didn't tell his girlfriend Sophie until he kissed her goodbye at the top of the stairs leading to Ecole Militaire Metro station.

René flew first to Bangkok, where he stayed for five days in a dump of a hotel on King Rama IV. He shared a room with an obnoxious American from New York. Together, they visited the reclining Buddha and other sites. Bars along Pat Pong Road, a Mecca for U.S. servicemen on R and R from Vietnam, proved too enticing. Unabashed Thai girls were literally everywhere. Place Pigalle in Paris or Blanche could not have been livelier; or more sordid.

Now, weeks later, after he arrived in Vietnam, not completely sober, René was about to step onto the red clay of the most famous, most dangerous patch of ground in the world.

René felt his pockets. He had eight rolls of film on him, and one in each Nikon camera.

René mentally calculated. Maybe three hundred fifty frames of photos. That's all he had.

"*Merde*!"

The helicopter crew chief, sitting just behind the cockpit, looking toward the passengers on each side of the fuselage, screamed out loud.

"The LZ's hot. We'll be on the ground in zero five minutes. Keep your shit tight. Get off to each side as soon as the back ramp opens. Keep your head down and move away from the chopper. Do not block the ramp. I repeat, do not block the ramp. We're gonna land fast and be gone in four zero seconds."

The motley bunch of passengers prepared for the landing.

The helicopter descended quickly; the ground rushed up to meet it. Images that seemed far away, as if placed on a stage, were all of a sudden close.

The heavy chopper flared and settled to the ground in a thick, churning cloud of red dust. Debris whipped around in the hurricane-force winds. The pilot pushed all the way down on the collective to his left side. The pitch of the giant rotor blades flattened, but they cut the air loudly. The turbines, with their screaming ear-splitting whine, continued at full RPM. The door at the rear of the helicopter clanged open and was suddenly transformed into a ramp that fell to the ground with a thud.

The crew chief cupped his hands to his mouth.

"Get out! Move away from the ramp! Away from the chopper!"

He yelled out again slowly. "Move...Away...From...The chopper! Go!"

René l'Escalier was the fourth person out the back. The man in front of him, one of the two men incongruously dressed in white shirts, stumbled and fell down the ramp. His glasses flew from his face. René jumped over him to his left. He hit the ground hard, dropping one camera. The hot exhaust of the engines smothered him with their oily, acrid-smelling fumes that seared his throat.

In the chaos, five other people jumped from the back of the chopper while litters of wounded Marines were being carried up its ramp.

The two opposite streams of hapless travelers, some heading straight into the teeth of danger with others fleeing to safety, collided on the ramp.

René picked up his camera and moved ten feet away from the helicopter.

The pilot lifted the collective and steadied the chopper with the controls. The triple blades of each rotor head tilted to bite into the air for lift. Swirls of dust were sucked down into the blades and blasted out beneath them. René raised his camera as the helicopter lifted off. He was knocked down by the pounding rotor wash. René lay there, shocked, while thick dust engulfed him.

"*Mon Dieu!*"

Amid all this chaos, shells exploded everywhere. René felt the overpowering explosions as red dirt, mixed with pervasive, choking smoke, suddenly flew up in angry fountains not far away.

The helicopter, picking up speed, flew the length of the runway. Shells exploded beneath it. The chopper rose and banked slightly to the northeast.

René, now on the ground for less than five minutes, was totally exposed to the incoming fire. Reality was right here, right now, right in René's terrified face. If this is what he wanted, he got it. This was Khe Sanh.

René recited the prayer of communion

"*Mon Père, mon Père, je m'abandonne à toi.*"

"You asshole! You can't stay here!"

A Marine lying on his stomach pulled René across the ground. René pushed and crawled with his feet and hands until he slid in between some sandbags.

"You son-of-a-bitch idiot! Don't ever do that again! Don't ever get off a Marine chopper and just stay there. You'll get blown to friggin' bloody bits, you dumb ass."

René couldn't make out the verbal broadside, but he got the message.

The Marine, white with anger, breathing hard, stared at René.

"Christ, almighty. You're new. You're still shittin' Stateside food."

"*Je ne suis pas Américain, Je suis Français.*"

René pointed to his chest. "I am France. *Je viens de la France. Je suis Français.*"

"A friggin' frog! What the hell you doin' here at the Khe Sanh crap shoot?"

"*Un petit peu Anglais. Je parle un peu Anglais. Pas beaucoup*. I not speak Ang-lesh."

"You ain't gonna live through this shit, man. You'll be going home in a box, now. I'm tellin' ya."

"*Je ne comprend pas. Je suis un peu bouché, mais...J'ai peur.*"

René's eyes, reflecting fear, were big as eggs. He pointed to himself, then to the Marine.

"I you not unnerstan."

The Marine gave him some water from his canteen. He pointed across the runway to a low embankment.

"Go there, you idiot. Stay low."

"*Faire quoi*?"

The Marine pointed.

"There, you stupid ass! Go there! Get the hell away from the strip!"

René could only nod.

"Do what you want, Frenchie, but I'm tellin' ya, the strip's target number one...bad news, man. I ain't saving your sorry ass next time."

The Marine carried his M-16 by the handle. "I'm gettin' outta here. Sayonara."

He moved quickly away at a low crouch.

René, surviving his baptism of fire at Khe Sanh, checked his cameras. He wiped the sweat from his face as he spoke out loud, "*Ces cons d'américains sont absolument fous. Ils sont idiots d'être ici dans cet enfer. Ecoute, c'est*

Dien Bien Phu qui recommence. C'est un peu plus que ce que je voulais expérimenter, mais merde, j'y suis maintenant. Paris en hiver est de plus en plus beau chaque jour. Bien mieux qu'à Khe Sanh [Crazy Americans. It's Dien Bien Phu again]."

CHAPTER TWENTY-SIX

A SOLUTION FOR THE PRESIDENT

After an early-morning coffee meeting, Richard Helms immediately called Arthur Lundahl at the National Photographic Interpretation Center.

"Lundahl here."

"Arthur, do you recall the discussion we had some weeks ago, before Christmas?"

Lundahl's eyes widened by the surprise call from Helms.

"Oh, hello, Mr. Director. How are…"

"Arthur…about distances and terrain?"

"You mean when we discussed the problem the President was having with geographic perceptions?"

"Exactly."

"Sure. I mentioned the President could use a large map."

"Right to the point, Lundahl."

"Mr. Director…"

"Arthur, planners are determined that Khe Sanh must be defended. It's too valuable to lose. On a psychological level, the loss of Khe Sanh will be sensationalized around the world."

Richard Helms leaned forward, his elbows on his desk. “Understand the implications?”

“Yes, Sir. I get the picture.”

“The Commander-in-Chief is not schooled in map reading or topographical comprehension. He’s frustrated.”

“As we discussed before, Sir. But I thought…”

“Arthur, recent Spotlight reports provide evidence of large NVA movements in Eye Corps. It’s compelling. With the skirmish on 881 North and the fighting on Hill 861, Hill 861-Alpha—forget the Tet offensive—Quang Tri Province is a time bomb.

“The fall of Lang Vei yesterday and the evacuation of Khe Sanh ville before that, and now, the NVA attack on some small hill they call Sixty-four, or Alpha-1, something like that, near the base…damned near a disaster for the First Battalion Ninth Marines—we lost twenty-one Marines in that fight. Things are moving quicker than we imagined. Maps on the dead NVA showed every detail about the combat base.”

“Yes, Sir, this could be bad,” Lundahl said.

“Hanoi is moving toward a more robust strategy. We don’t believe Lang Vei or Alpha-1 was part of Tet. We surmise it’s the spearhead of a different initiative that will be carried out against the Marines in Eye Corp. Westmoreland is certain the enemy will launch a definitive campaign. The National Military Command Center is of the same opinion. We can expect the battle for Khe Sanh to begin soon. Things could come unhinged.

“We don’t know exactly what Giap’s up to. I doubt he can re-attack Da Nang and Saigon, or Bien Hoa. The element of surprise is gone, but Giap’s still hungry for a big win.”

“Sir, a geographer has three tools at his disposal: one, contour maps, two, stereoscopes that allow for seeing geographic relief through the side-by-side juxtaposition…”

“Arthur, not now. I don’t have time for a lecture. And yes, I’m familiar with stereoscopes.”

“But Sir, the third tool…”

Helms, with impatient indifference, laughed slightly. Lundahl didn’t catch on.

"And the third tool, Lundahl? Come on."

"A three-dimensional, physical model, Sir."

"Thanks very much, Arthur. That's exactly what I want to hear. The special map you made was not good enough. Get your brain around this model idea and let's do this thing."

Lundahl had learned over the years that when someone said to him 'let's do this thing,' it always meant 'you do it.'

"Lundahl, I need it in the White House by...let's see, today's the eighth...by Tuesday, the thirteenth of February."

"The Production Services Group, Sir. They're in the National Photographic Interpretation Center in Building 213 over here in the Navy Yard. They've made models before."

Helms laughed.

"Don't they call that building the Lundahl Hilton, or something like that? You moved there from the Steuart Building. You must have a thousand people in there."

Helms shifted the receiver to his other ear. "Listen, Arthur, not to belabor the issue, we have an emergency on our hands of profound importance. A model won't stop what may happen, but it will provide the President with a better sense of the area. If the President continues to micro-manage this little war over there, then he needs to be equipped with the right tools. The war is hanging in the balance and, at this five minutes, it ain't looking too promising for the good guys. We can't be screwin' around."

"Mr. Director, the guy who runs the shop, Steve Cooper; he's a bit quirky, but he's brilliant, kinda independent. He might build the model real quick and then again, he might just go camping. I know the person to call who..."

"I don't care who you call. Kick him in the butt, Lundahl. Get the lead out and get on this thing."

"Yes, Sir."

Helms started to hang up, but a friendly quip wouldn't hurt.

"Arthur, you won't be at NPIC forever. You should think about going back into academics, be an instructor at a junior college out there in...I dunno, Idaho someplace."

"Sir, my academic days..."

"Talk to you later, Lundahl. The model...not later than Tuesday."

CHAPTER TWENTY-SEVEN

MILLENNIA PAST: MADISON, WISCONSIN

"Class, please read chapters sixteen and seventeen for Monday. We're in early February, the ninth of February, to be exact. You know how I like precision. The semester's rolling right along. We've got a lot of ground to cover...got to stay on schedule. The chapters set the foundation for our study on volcanism, after we wrap up the discussion on tectonics next week."

The students, churning to leave the classroom, barely heard the professor's words.

"Now, look. It's Friday afternoon. Because of the basketball game at the Field House tomorrow night, you get off easy. Other than the two chapters, no other assignments over the weekend. And, I promise, no quiz on Monday. You may consider my leniency to be a reprieve, but don't expect this to be the norm. Read those two chapters."

Professor Herman Tanner, one of the more trying University of Wisconsin professors with the reputation of being a tough grader, had just finished his fourth lecture on continental drift.

A loud clamor rose as the students packed their notes, slammed their books shut, put their coats on and scrambled for the door.

Professor Tanner's voice rose a half octave.

"I hope you've started your term papers. The semester will end sooner than you think. You may pick up last week's assignment at the door. Many of the reports were good, some were excellent...but, others...well...De-plor-able."

Professor Tanner, gesturing to no one in particular, his voice now strident, delivered his parting shot. "Unacceptable papers—you know who you are!"

No one was listening.

The University of Wisconsin was noted for parties. Regardless of the bitter cold of the extreme northern part of the Midwest, partying and beer drinking were exactly what the students intended to do that Friday evening—most likely all weekend. The bars were open and waiting. The Pub, The Red Shed, and Rusty's would be packed with young, rowdy patrons who, with mugs in hand, placed school and text books and everything else except beer and sex at a low priority.

The Indiana University basketball team was in Madison. Competition between the two Big Ten rivals was hot. If Wisconsin won Saturday night, the bars would be full, the beer flowing in copious amounts. If Wisconsin lost, the bars would be as full, the beer flowing just as freely. It didn't matter.

The frenzied, hormone-driven congregation of students scurried for the exit and emptied through the funnel of the classroom door, the desks were thrown in disarray.

Professor Tanner shouted.

"Have a good weekend."

Susan Wienecke buttoned her overcoat and gathered her books in her arms.

"Oh, Miss Wienecke, may I talk with you for just one moment, please."

Susan Wienecke turned.

"Yes, professor."

"I know you want to leave as soon as you can, Susan...but...well, I read your last paper on the geologic formation in Southeast Asia."

Professor Tanner handed her report to her. "It's excellent, I must say. Your paper has the makings of a more comprehensive master's thesis."

"Really? That's great. Thank you, Professor Tanner."

"But, please tell me, I'm curious. Why did you choose to write on such a remote place? I would have expected the typical report on Africa and South America splitting apart a bazillion years ago or the subterranean strain of the Red Sea basin. Why Southeast Asia? Geologically speaking, it offers little significance—not nearly as important as, say, the closing of the Straits of Gibraltar and the evaporation of the Mediterranean Sea…the so-called Messinian Salinity Crisis."

"Well, I…"

"Susan, I sense you like geology, but I believe you don't care for the dry jargon in textbooks. Although a tad long—'Millennia Past: Landmass Formation and Tectonic Displacement of the Truong Son Mountain Range in Vietnam and Laos,'—I liked the title."

"I didn't realize how long the title was until after I turned the paper in."

"It must have taken you days to research this in the library. When I was an undergraduate, I also downed my share of beer. The library wasn't exactly a magnet."

Susan's opening paragraphs were indeed descriptive:

> *Long before the dawn of man, more than one hundred million years ago, when the earth was still hot and forming, a clash of large formations of rock occurred—tectonic movement—that shaped the land masses of the planet. What geologists call the Kontum Massif collided with the South China Plate and created the Truong Son Mountain Range (or, more technically, the Annamite Cordillera), in what would come to be called Vietnam and Laos.*
>
> *This gargantuan collision, occurring over many hundreds of thousands of years, caused an ancient seabed, solidified into limestone, to lift up to form the Co Roc ridge. Over the next hundreds of thousands of years, rainwater, reacting with the calcium, melted the limestone, leaving caves and sinkholes. During the intervening millennia, mountains shifted, rose and fell. Fault lines created the area's river basins.*

"Sir, my younger brother's a lance corporal in the Twenty-sixth Marines at Khe Sanh, so I thought I'd write about the Truong Son range."

"My God, Susan, I had no idea. Have you been following the news?"

"Yeah, I watch the news each evening."

"Have you heard from him?"

"Nobody in the family has heard from him in weeks, Sir. The Tet Offensive is very troubling…all the fighting over there."

Safeguarding her thoughts, Susan scanned what she had written in her paper.

> *The area today is characterized by mountains and valleys and irregularly sloping plateaus—in general, an inhospitable, complicated landscape. The terrain around Khe Sanh is confusing. One must take time to gain a perspective of the region.*
>
> *Hills surround the Khe Sanh Plateau. Hill 1015 is the most easily recognizable feature of the terrain in the Khe Sanh area as it connects to its cousin, Hill 950. Not far east, the rugged terrain begins a long downward slope to the fault line of the Quang Tri River.*

Susan had no idea of the significance of Hills 950 and 1015, but she decided to plagiarize and include those descriptions from her brother's letters in her report. What's the harm?

> *Many visitors have traveled to Khe Sanh by road—Highway Nine to be exact. Proceeding west from Dong Ha, one passes Camp J.J. Carroll, an artillery base. The Hieu River is on the right, but after the road twists and turns and heads abruptly south at a large rock outcropping near another artillery base called the Rockpile, only later to turn again west, the Quang Tri River is found to the left. While the Hieu River empties at Cua Viet Port and the Quang Tri River spills into estuaries further south, both rivers eventually flow into the South China Sea. The highway never crosses either river. As the road begins its curving, long ascent to the Khe Sanh Plateau, it crosses the*

Rao Quan River which snakes up a long valley parallel to the Khe Sanh Combat Base.

"Anyway, Susan, your report was well written. You deserve the 'A' it received, if for no other reason, it was enjoyable to read."

"Thanks for the compliment, Professor."

"You're in your fourth year here at Madison. You should consider a graduate program in geology. I know your grades are high. You would make an outstanding Ph.D. candidate. Oh, and don't forget the two chapters for Monday. They're very important. I didn't tell the others, but I'll tell you. There will be a pop quiz on Wednesday of next week."

CHAPTER TWENTY-EIGHT

THE PRIME MINISTER

Pham Van Dong, the Prime Minister of the Democratic Republic of Vietnam, had just read the latest report from the southern front. He picked up the telephone sitting on a table next to his desk and dialed his secretary.

"Miss Mai, please instruct the Minister of Defense to come immediately to my office. I know he is resting at home today, but I require General Giap's presence on an urgent matter."

Pham Van Dong was born in Duc Tan village near the coast in Quang Ngai Province in 1906. He turned to communism at a very early age. Known for his pragmatic approach to solving problems, Dong proved himself a capable Prime Minister, but he could be curt, even rude.

Pham Van Dong looked across the quiet courtyard from the louvered window of the colonial French-designed government building. He reflected on his country's past and the big battles that culminated in victory at Dien Bien Phu very near the Laotian border in Lai Chau Province. He had heard comparisons between Giap's famous victory over the French and what the North Vietnamese *quan doi* may now be trying to accomplish against the Americans farther south in Quang Tri Province.

Pham Van Dong suspected battles in B5T8 might be focused in a direction other than what had been planned. If the Americans are cornered and begin to suffer intolerable losses, they will stop at nothing to reverse their predicament.

The Prime Minister clinched his fists at the end of his straightened arms as he leaned on the windowsill to peer at the street beyond the courtyard. There was hardly any traffic. Vehicles were scarce in downtown Hanoi.

The weather had recently improved, but turned dismal again. The air was thick with depressing fog and mist. Rain fell, stopped and fell again. The water-clogged streets, lined with trees, moisture dripping from their overhanging leaves, were messy. Hanoi's government buildings, painted once in bright mango-yellow, now faded and dirty, were gloomy like the weather.

The Prime Minister's mind shifted to Vo Nguyen Giap, a dedicated compatriot who, like he, had followed Ho Chi Minh, but a person with whom he had disagreements in the past. The competitive nature of both men and the clash of egos sometimes boiled into heated disputes.

At one o'clock, a black Russian-made limousine, on loan from Ho Chi Minh, bearing registration number HN481 on the front bumper, passed through the gate. General Vo Nguyen Giap exited the limousine. He was escorted to the foyer of the Prime Minister's office.

"Thank you for coming on such short notice, General Giap."

The two men sat facing each other in low, ornate chairs with a hand-carved tea table separating them.

"General, please tell me about our efforts in the south. I will be on the telephone to China tonight to discuss events with Chu tich Ho Chi Minh in Beijing. I will be giving Bac Ho an update."

Vo Nguyen Giap maintained an aloof demeanor that conveyed a slight outward annoyance at having been summoned for such a sudden meeting. He also resented the inference that only Pham Van Dong knew the whereabouts of the country's leader and had the only access to him when he himself had equal access to the chairman. There was no reason for Pham Van Dong to be high-handed with his spontaneous demands and arrogant presumptions.

Giap, not sure of the tone of the meeting, opened with a general comment.

"We are continuing to construct a maze of very narrow roads by hand from an area southwest of Ha Tinh through Laos and finally into Quang Tri Province."

Pham Van Dong interjected tersely.

"You are referring, of course, to Group 559 and the famous Ho Chi Minh Trail."

"Very correct, Mr. Prime Minister. Under the superb command of General Dong Sy Nguyen, Group 559 is dedicated to the task of maintaining the supply trail. Men and equipment are steadily arriving at the fronts even though we are suffering some losses from American air attacks."

"General Giap..." The Prime Minister's voice indicated his impatience. "Thank you for this enlightenment, Sir."

Vo Nguyen Giap looked squarely at Pham Van Dong, but remained quiet. What exactly did the Prime Minister want?

"General Giap, our attacks across the country caused damage, but perhaps it wasn't enough. The heroic sappers at the America embassy in Saigon were all killed inside the embassy grounds, but to what benefit?

"Overall, are the provisions of Resolution Fourteen being carried out? Is the general offensive-general uprising which began on the Tet New Year succeeding?"

"Mr. Prime Minister, I consider the attack on the embassy in Saigon a success for reasons that may not be apparent."

Pham Van Dong placed the palms of his hands together and touched his fingers to his chin. He eyed the Minister of Defense.

Giap, trying to defuse a tense moment, played along with the Prime Minister with comments about the general offensive-general uprising.

"Aside from Saigon, the general offensive in the provinces, though with some setbacks, is ongoing, but we are still in the early stages of the campaign."

Giap made no comment on the second part of the strategy, the general uprising.

"We are also taking advantage of Laos and…"

"Yes, I'm well aware."

Pham Van Dong raised his hand in a rotational movement, urging Giap, who sometimes was too effusive, to move on.

"For your information, Mr. Prime Minister, our artillery is suppressing

American activities in western Quang Tri Province. Highway Nine is cut off. We have damaged a number of American aircraft. America's technological advances are without question, but in the jungles, their effectiveness is limited. Therein lies the weakness."

Pham Van Dong sipped his tea.

"General, I know the Americans are superior in the air, yet I believe American forces are not having the success they desire."

General Giap picked up his teacup.

"The Americans cannot use the general terrain to their advantage like we can. We are mobile by foot, they are not. They must rely on helicopters."

"But, Giap, you saw how effective the Americans were in the Ia Drang Valley with their helicopters."

"Mr. Prime Minister, unlike the manner in which the Americans have isolated themselves in their encampments, the Ia Drang Valley was a maneuver battle. Both sides moved constantly. The Americans used their helicopters advantageously. But, the benefits of the terrain in Quang Tri Province and our circumvallation of the American encampment accrue to us…just as at Dien Bien Phu. It seems…"

"Giap..."

Pham Van Dong sipped his tea. "You say just like Dien Bien Phu. That was a great triumph, but what am I to understand, here? I thought our objective was not the destruction or surrender of the Americans at some base, as at Dien Bien Phu. I thought the provisions of Resolution Fourteen were clear. They allowed for the general offensive and, more importantly, the general uprising."

Giap had to be careful. Pham Van Dong was a literalist and a master of the language. There was more to his statement, than met the eye. He removed and folded his glasses. In a composed manner, he placed them in his vest pocket.

"Mr. Prime Minister, I am not prepared on impromptu notice to present a comprehensive plan in reaction to what is developing in the theater of operations north of Thua Thien. The situation is changing by the hour, even by the minute. Suffice it to say for now, we will continue to send troops and equipment south while—and this is important—we continue to open other fronts across South Vietnam that have been weakened by the transfer of Americans and their puppets to Quang Tri Province. Fighting in Hue has been difficult, but we will continue to drain the Americans away from their main supply bases and we will…"

Pham Van Dong held up both hands. The conversation was providing no meaningful information. He moved to another line of thought.

"General Giap, I have been giving a lot of consideration to other issues that may become important. Thus, I have two questions."

"Please, Mr. Prime Minister."

"My first question. Do you think the Americans may be planning an invasion of North Vietnam? I have received intelligence reports that indicate this is possible. Vinh or even Dong Hoi could be likely landing spots."

An invasion of North Vietnam? Vo Nguyen Giap was aware of the same intelligence, but he was caught off-guard by its sudden mention.

"Mr. Prime Minister, we've looked at this contingency. The Americans may be evaluating such an option, but its execution will be extremely complex, its success in doubt. Too many obstacles. We have spotters all along the coast. If the Americans were to invade, it would have to be with a sizeable force.

"First, where would they invade? If Vinh is the place, the invasion would be easily contained. Second, to what extent would they continue the invasion? Until Hanoi is captured? All the way to China? And, is Westmoreland prepared for two major fronts that are easily cut off? Such arrogance is beyond my comprehension. No, Mr. Prime Minister, I don't think this is a real threat."

"I see," the Prime Minister said.

Giap sensed that Pham Van Dong's question was not asked with any real sincerity. He was probing.

In a combative manner, Pham Van Dong continued.

"Our real goal is the destruction of the puppet government in Saigon, now, isn't it, Giap?"

The belittling tone of Pham Van Dong's statement, asked tritely as a devious question, got under Giap's skin. Pham Van Dong shifted into French.

"*Nous ne pouvons pas perdre cela de vue, n'est-ce pas Monsieur Giap* [We cannot lose sight of that now, can we]?"

Giap, now even more annoyed at the mocking insinuation that perhaps he was too short-sighted, responded in a polite but equally contemptuous manner.

"*Bien sûr* [of course] Monsieur le Premier Ministre. *Pensiez-vous que j'aurais pu oublier cela* [Did you think I would forget that]?"

Giap continued with a lecture of his own. "Re-unification of the Fatherland is our primary objective. We must not be distracted from that ultimate end."

Pham Van Dong didn't smile.

Giap tapped the table harder while he continued talking.

"Party Secretary Le Duan and others want to go for the jugular and continue with a campaign that is too broad. They are overly confident. Parts of the strategy are fine on paper, but the implementation falls short in actuality. It can't be sustained over time. Mr. Prime Minister, you must understand, invasion of the North notwithstanding, American military might is more potent than we think. Although they seem to be in disarray, the Americans have proved they can be adaptable."

Giap leaned forward. "We must win however long the war takes, Mr. Prime Minister. We need to keep coming back and back. I have always said, protracted war is the way forward. Protracted war means protracted planning, not reckless conduct. That is the best way of winning against the power of the Americans.

"Rest assured, Mr. Prime Minister, there is a lot of fight in me. I will not hesitate to exploit a good opportunity when I see one. Inflicting irrecoverable damage through a major engagement at the appropriate time, regardless of location, will be beneficial. But, aside from my desire for the bright star of victory, we cannot lose sight of something splendidly simple."

"What's that, Giap?"

"We don't have to defeat the Americans or, for that matter, even win a battle."

Pham Van Dong placed his teacup on the table.

"My apologies, Giap. I'm not clear as to what you are saying. I thought..."

"Mr. Prime Minister, we don't have to win. We just can't lose."

Pham Van Dong had tried to trip Giap up, but it didn't work. He became more direct.

"And so, Giap, you're interested in Khe Sanh, I believe."

There was a pause in the conversation.

"Your second question, Mr. Prime Minister."

Pham Van Dong poured himself more tea. He held the teapot toward Giap as a conciliatory gesture of goodwill before pouring tea into the general's porcelain cup. The two men were, after all, on the same side, *contre les Américains.*

Pham Van Dong placed a cigarette between his lips and slid the blue Les Gauloises cigarette pack across the low table to Vo Nguyen Giap, the Tiger of Dien Bien Phu, as the western press called him.

"Care for a French cigarette, Giap? These are fresh. Arrived from Paris yesterday."

"Mr. Prime Minister, you know I don't smoke."

Dong inhaled as he smiled.

"General Giap, Vietnam makes nothing. I don't have to tell you. We have never had, nor do we now have an industrial base, really. We are not technologically advanced. American planes are built in America twenty thousand kilometers away and fly over our country almost with impunity. The Americans can destroy us from the air if they so choose. We must resort to Russian artillery and a limited number of airplanes, and other weapons from China. I loathe that we are orbiting around the political spheres of those countries, that we are victims of the schism that exists between them. Right now, we must resort to any means to fight the Americans and reunify all of Vietnam. We will deal with Russia and China later."

Giap looked sideways in mild surprise.

"Your close relationship with communist officials in China is no secret."

"And neither are your pro-soviet leanings, Giap."

"Dong, China may one day be a more formidable enemy than America."

Pham Van Dong ran his hand through his thick shock of hair and stroked his chin in contemplation.

"General, I have the sense, even if we were to capitulate, America would have little compassion for us. Our leader, Chu tich Ho Chi Minh shares this belief."

Pham Van Dong looked out the window. "It may not be that we are communists. After all, the United States does maintain diplomatic relations with the Soviet Union."

"Mr. Prime Minister, Sir…"

"Giap, beyond our own reunification, communism, not capitalism, is the only way forward for us. World capitalism will crumble."

Giap looked askance. How did Pham Van Dong draw a connection between reunification and the collapse of world capitalism?

"Our goals, Giap, will not be realized overnight but rather over time. We can take communism to the next level to contribute to the benefit of all the world's people as we continue our struggle."

Giap sipped tea as he listened. Communists? World movement? Next level? Benefit of all the world's people? What the hell was the Prime Minister talking about? Didn't he want an update? Wasn't he going to talk to Ho Chi Minh that evening? Surely Ho Chi Minh didn't want to hear about a discussion that revolved around communism. The lecture was bordering on irrelevant tedium.

Pham Van Dong continued.

"Giap, you recall, we overtly asked for America's support in the past, before the American soldiers came here. The American presidents ignored our pleas. Neither Roosevelt, Truman nor Eisenhower ever assisted us. Kennedy's reluctance to help us was based on his own religion. He supported the southern Catholics. America dismissed us as a dirty, backward country with little strategic importance on the world stage. Our history, thousands of years old, means nothing. America and maybe other developed countries have little regard for who we are as a people because we have not advanced to the same extent. The western world won't accept us."

Giap thought for a moment. He was more comfortable talking about fighting the Americans than he was talking about communism and the world's disregard for Vietnam.

"Well, Mr. Prime Minister..."

"Look at you, Giap, you wear stylish French clothes from time to time, but Westerners don't accept that."

What prompted Pham Van Dong to make such an awkward statement? The conversation had taken a condescending twist—*très méprisant.* Giap shifted in his seat. Evidently, he made the wrong decision to visit the Prime Minister from home while wearing his white civilian suit and fedora hat instead of his uniform. What seemed casual may have come across as offensive to the Prime Minister.

"Giap, I've been a communist since I was fifteen. But communist or not, advanced or not, our people's cultural make-up is different from that of western society. The Americans may put us in the same category as the Japanese in World War Two—a different, let's just say, less valuable culture, an unworthy, primitive people. Since this could be their attitude, my second question, which may be more pertinent than the first, is this. Do you think President Johnson may become so desperate about winning the war against us that he will resort to alternative means without regard for the consequences?"

"Alternative means, Sir?"

"Giap..."

Pham Van Dong hesitated for a second. "Is it possible the Americans will use atomic weapons against us?"

Giap looked down at the floor and then to the ceiling. He had mistakenly thought the meeting was about the general offensive. How could he have anticipated topics on invasions, geo-political strategy or any reference to use of nuclear weapons?

Giap, ameliorating his earlier tone, reverting to his friendship with the Prime Minister, used his first name.

"Dong..."

Then he spoke again more formally. "Mr. Prime Minister, I don't think so. The world community would not tolerate it. Closer to our Fatherland, China would react strongly. Indonesia, Thailand or Singapore would feel vulnerable, Australia and New Zealand betrayed. They would object strongly to such escalation in this hemisphere. They would see America's careless use of such extreme weapons as a flagrant threat to themselves."

Pham Van Dong stared out to the empty courtyard.

Light from the sun, shining through a sliver of clear sky below the clouds, slanted through the louvered windows into the Prime Minister's Office.

"*J'espère que tu as raison, Général* [I hope you are right]."

CHAPTER TWENTY-NINE

OLD EBBITT GRILL

Days in the White House were very long for Blake Warren and Jake Ansell, two analysts who specialized in the conflict in Southeast Asia. Not many minutes after ten p.m. on Thursday night, they made their way to the northwest gate of the White House grounds. The elegant chandelier suspended from the ceiling of the North Portico, stabilized with big chains, cast shadows across the famous semi-circular driveway. The two men exited the gate and walked past a giant red ash tree behind the iron fence on their right. They strode directly in front of a public square, and, farther along to their left, a statue of that park's namesake, Marquis de Lafayette.

The two men, walking at a brisk pace, passed the Treasury Department until they reached the welcoming warmth of Old Ebbitt Grill.

One hundred twelve years after its founding, the famous restaurant-bar was still the favorite hangout of White House aides. Often noisy, Old Ebbitt was popular among the city's young and not-so-young people, and a favorite hangout of a few presidents. A visit to the more formal Round Bar at the nearby Willard Hotel invariably ended with an inebriated migration to Ebbitt's for a night cap.

The bartender placed two frosty mugs of beer on the wood bar. White froth ran down the side of each mug. Jake, having removed his topcoat and loosening his tie, threw some money on the bar.

"Man, this thing in Vietnam...Rostow, Watson and Christian, their nerves are about shot. Even Juanita's not her bubbly self lately. "

Blake swallowed some beer, licked his upper lip and turned to Jake.

"Tell me about it. The fighting in Hue and the attack on the embassy in Saigon still pisses the President off. Man, can he ever snap."

Jake shook his head.

"He's having a hard time now consolidating public support for the war."

"Yeah, bombing North Vietnam may seem a logical strategy to stem the flow of NVA arms, but many don't agree. Seems he's trying to satisfy the hawks in the senate."

"McNamara said last fall that we could not win the war by bombing North Vietnam."

"He also said bombing the north was no substitute for ground troops in the south, but then, last august, he gave three good reasons why the bombing was beneficial."

"It's confusing. The voters will not tolerate the bombing much longer. I was at the Pentagon back in October, on the day of the big protest march. Man, I wouldn't want to be in the President's shoes."

"Hanoi says the bombing must stop without condition before they'll talk to us."

Both men took large gulps of their beer.

Jake strained his eyes to look at a framed letter from Buffalo Bill on Ebbitt stationary dated May 27, 1886 to an Arkansas judge. He turned back and spoke to Blake.

"We see our military involvement from the advantage of being far removed, rich with material goods, and I suppose, a sense of happiness. The Vietnamese see the war in a different context. They don't have material goods to the same extent we do. They're basically poverty-stricken."

Blake put his mug on the bar.

"And, for all we know, they may not even be happy."

Jake continued.

"Destroying is counterproductive to our values. But the North Vietnamese may see destruction as an inevitable price they must pay. If we bomb North

Vietnam to total destruction, what else would be left to bomb? The more we destroy, the less they have to worry about, so…they don't care anymore. I don't see how we can win the war by bombing the north."

Blake picked his mug back up.

"What if we lose? Then who wins?"

"The Viet Cong, that's who wins. They keep saying they must be part of the negotiations. If we acquiesce, then the Viet Cong will have legitimacy when all along we've been saying they represent no one. If they're allowed to come to the conference table, they'll have gained credibility. South Vietnam has to prevail and maintain the victory."

Blake chugged his beer.

"Man, this tastes good. Just what I need."

Jake's gaze rested briefly on the large paintings of voluptuous women in luxurious Victorian-type settings, part of the *beaux-art* motif of the interior of the restaurant. He turned and faced the big mirror behind the bar.

"Did you see the pictures of those dead VC lying around the planters in the embassy compound?"

"Yeah, I'll bet ole Bunker was shook up."

"Blake, do you think the Tet Offensive is part of an international communist plot? I mean, the *Pueblo,* South Korea, Berlin, Tet and the Middle East. It's all so coincidental."

"That's for Sloane's brain people to figure out over there in Langley. Khe Sanh's the urgent problem now. Like you say, the situation with the Tet Offensive, the embassy and now the surprise loss of the Special Forces Camp at Lang Vei sure have the President upset.

"Khe Sanh…man, I hope Westmoreland's gamble is right. He's chosen to stay and reinforce. But, Jesus, the Twenty-sixth Marines can't constantly occupy the base, man the hills, and conduct sweeps. They don't have the resources. Plus, the enemy could just ignore the base altogether. I'm not sure anyone has a clear idea of what to do next."

"Invade North Vietnam. There's talk of that."

"If South Korea demobilizes its forces from South Vietnam which they are threatening to do, Westmoreland will have no option but to ask for more troops. I'm sure this will be a big topic when General Wheeler visits Saigon. But, invade North Vietnam? That's crazy."

"The President's fixated on Khe Sanh. If it falls, there'll be a blood bath on the other side of the Potomac. He'll clean house."

"The NVA may attack and then again, they may not. Maybe Giap is thinking if we commit to holding Khe Sanh, we preserve his options."

"And forfeit our own."

Jake, standing perpendicular to the wood bar, turned his head.

"Bartender, two more beers, please."

He turned back to Blake. "How in God's name do the North Vietnamese get all the equipment and men down the Ho Chi Minh trail when we interdict it continuously? You've seen the recon photos of eastern Laos. It looks like the moon."

"General Taylor is asking what Westmoreland may face if the NVA attack the cities again and open up other fronts?"

"Yeah, he questions our stance at Khe Sanh. Plus, he's asking whether we need to rethink the Gulf of Tonkin Resolution, maybe seek a declaration of war."

"Heady stuff."

"Taylor's got the President's ear...fourth in his class at West Point, fought with the 101st Airborne Division, ambassador to South Vietnam in '64."

New mugs of ice-cold beer arrived in front of the two men. This time, Blake tossed a ten dollar bill on the bar.

"No one knows whether Khe Sanh is a major objective or a diversion for Tet. But, if Tet is really the push and if Khe Sanh is also a target, hasn't Giap spread his forces around too much? Why would Giap expend so many resources on a ruse that cut across all of South Vietnam? How can Giap attack Khe Sanh at the same time? He couldn't possibly resupply *all* his troops fast enough."

"We can analyze Khe Sanh to death, but I'll tell you what I think, Blake. If the Marines could re-group somewhere else, vacate Khe Sanh, they wouldn't be allowed to."

"Why's that?"

"Because Westy wants a real toe-to-toe fight and not this stupid hit-and-run jungle crap. Westmoreland sees an opportunity to destroy Giap's forces. What commander wouldn't relish something like that? And of course, Westmoreland wants to let Giap know his pissant army ain't shit."

Both men chuckled at the use of the President's favorite expression.

"NVA pissants," Jake repeated as he and Blake tapped their mugs together.

"This Khe Sanh stuff is sure a complicated problem."

"I heard they're making a model of Khe Sanh for the President."

"What's he gonna do with it?"

"I dunno, just look at it a couple of times, I suppose."

Blake buttoned his overcoat.

"Hey, you won't believe this. Devin, my younger brother, was accepted into OCS."

"You gotta be kiddin' me. Didn't he play football in high school?"

"Yeah, left tackle; broke his arm. He graduated from college last spring. He reports to Quantico next month."

"My God, Blake, that's incredible."

"He'll be an excellent officer," Blake said with obvious pride as he drank the last of his beer. "I think I'll go to Langley tomorrow and talk to Sloane. He's got the latest information on NVA movements."

Jake nodded his head in agreement as he quickly collected his change from the bar top. He threw three dollars back on the bar as a tip.

"Let's go. God, I wish summer would hurry up. Can't wait to go to the Jersey shore."

CHAPTER THIRTY

HERITAGE OF EARTH

General Vo Nguyen Giap contracted a virus and was running a temperature. He called out through the open door.

"Miss Ngan, please bring me some hot tea."

Ngan, dressed in a white *ao dai*, a red sweater and a French scarf her sister had given her, was collating administrative folders on the large conference table.

Thuy Ngan's father was killed in Hon Gai in 1964 during an air raid. Her mother moved to Hanoi and tended to a humble household that overlooked Tay Ho (West Lake) near the giant pagoda.

Ngan had taken a security job at the Metropole, now called the Reunification Hotel on Ngo Quyen Street. Each day, Ngan, wearing a uniform and a pith helmet, stood guard proudly with an old carbine over her shoulder outside the hotel's entrance. Once, she was secretly given a United States two-dollar bill which she cherished. It was her lucky money.

Ngan eventually accepted a position as a junior clerical assistant in the Ministry of Defense. She would be helping a very important person who had little time for mindless chores. She knew of Vo Nguyen Giap, but never thought she would actually work for him.

After two weeks, Giap recognized Ngan's diligence. He made arrangements for her to work permanently as part of his staff. Although never allowed access to war discussions or strategic meetings, she ran small errands and performed menial tasks for the Minister and Van Tien Dung, his Chief of Staff. She became comfortable with her surroundings and the demands of high-ranking military men.

The general's office at the Ministry of Defense was cooled by a large ceiling fan during the searing heat of summer. But, during the winter months, Hanoi, one thousand miles north of tropical Saigon, was unpleasant. The offices, with only French shutters over the windows, were as cold as the outdoors.

Ngan entered the general's office carrying a lacquered basket. Beneath its lid, a porcelain pot sat nestled within thick insulation material.

"Shall I pour some tea for you, General?"

"No, thank you, Miss Ngan. I'll pour it myself."

Ngan stooped at the waist and placed the lacquered basket on the low tea table positioned between heavy wood chairs.

"Miss Ngan. I didn't mean to be rude. Won't you join me?"

"Sir?"

"Please. It would be a pleasant distraction, if only for a few minutes."

Giap, with simple red tabs on each collar signifying the rank of general, poured tea into a cup. He emptied it into a second cup and, finally, from that cup, into a receptacle sitting on the floor. Following a long tradition, a show of respect for a guest, he was washing the tea cup before use. Giap poured tea into the same cup for his young assistant.

"Miss Ngan, once, you told me your husband was in an air defense unit, a captain, I believe you said."

"Yes, Sir, but he's only a lieutenant."

"Oh, the mistake is mine."

"He was stationed around Hanoi, I think near Gia Lam, and then, just after we were married, his unit was transferred south to Phu Ly."

"That's what I thought. I do recall you telling me."

"He wants to study architecture at the university and maybe study in Europe, too."

"You're fortunate to have such a husband."

Giap poured tea into his cup. He sipped the hot, bitter-tasting liquid that soothed and burned the back of his throat at the same time.

"Miss Ngan, as part of a country-wide military effort, the *quan doi* has entered a crucial phase of the war in the south against the *de quoc My* [imperialist Americans]. The general assault, or what is now called the Tet Offensive, is underway. We are also heavily engaged in Quang Tri Province.

"Do you know which anti-aircraft unit your husband is in?"

"No, Sir, not allowed."

"True." Giap smiled.

"Sir, I know is he's in a thirty-seven millimeter anti-aircraft unit, but that's all I know."

"Miss Ngan, we don't have enough air defenses to cover our units fighting in Quang Tri Province. I'm sorry to break this to you. We're expediting thirty-seven millimeter units to the south to augment our air defense measures."

Ngan's eyes widened.

"I see. Then he's going south, down the trail."

"Miss Ngan, we can't afford to transfer the heavy anti-aircraft guns south. They are needed here to protect Hanoi. But, we need the thirty-seven millimeter units."

"General, Sir, may I ask? Why are we fighting at Khe Sanh?"

The direct question caught General Giap by surprise. There had been no mention of Khe Sanh directly.

"Miss Ngan, I am not at liberty to divulge details about any campaign, but let me just say that invading or occupying armies have never succeeded. Alexander's eastern conquest stalled at the Indus River. He died in Babylon on his return to Macedonia. Napoleon was defeated in Russia and later routed at Waterloo."

Giap smiled. "I'm a student of Napoleon. I like to study his tactics."

"Yes, Sir. I know that."

"Hitler lost his bid for Russia and all of Europe. We beat the Japanese and the French. We will defeat the American invaders, too. The imperialist's occupation of our land, south of the DMZ, will be crushed.

"Regardless of the partitions imposed on us by outsiders, Vietnam will be reunited. This is our land, from Cao Bang and Ha Giang in the far north to Ca Mau in the south. No one has the right to divide our country."

Giap pointed to his right front, toward a tall wood and glass case in the corner of his office. "Look at all the books over there. Every book speaks about a unified Vietnam."

Giap paused, then spoke just above his breath. "Miss Ngan, we have a historic mandate to re-unite all of Vietnam. Unfortunately, in so doing, we will lose a lot of lives in this war with the Americans, more than we have lost to date. In the larger scheme of life, however, the deaths we incur to realize our goal are nothing when compared to the deaths all around the world every day, year after year."

The talk was visceral.

Ngan, in an awkward moment, looked across Giap's office to the garden just outside the steel-armored door. She had no idea about military movements except it meant that people were going to be killed.

"Miss Ngan, our primary aim is the eradication of foreign forces from our soil forever. We cannot win an all-out war with the Americans. They can devastate us with superior technology and equipment. We know this.

"Our ancestors who faced similar adversity for the cause of independence are watching us in our struggle. Their fight has become our fight.

"The illegal creation of South Vietnam means we must fight a longer-distance war. It's not easy, but that's the way it is...we know the land and the people. Our heritage is derived from the earth."

"I don't know much about military or political strategy," Ngan responded. "I just want my husband to come home safely."

Tears streamed down Ngan's cheeks.

"Miss Ngan. We may not win the war this year, or the next, but we will win. Your husband will come home a celebrated hero."

Giap sipped his tea. "In the meantime, we are going to make the Americans miserable. Their unfounded aggression and their imperialist policies do not work here. Their support for the illegal government they prop up in Saigon is for nothing.

"The struggle in Quang Tri Province will be instrumental to the liberation of all of South Vietnam. We shall pursue our reunification destiny to its rightful conclusion."

Giap sipped his tea. "We will deal with the American imperialists on our terms, not theirs."

CHAPTER THIRTY-ONE

BUILDING 213

“You’re Cooper, correct?”

Startled by the stranger who came from nowhere, Steve Cooper looked up.

“Who wants to know?”

Cooper was sitting at a large table covered with maps and photographs related to a modeling project his team had just finished. A few days off were in the offing. But, the words he’d just heard from the unsmiling visitor who entered his office moments before, now standing in front of his table, portended otherwise. He twirled a pen in his hand as he looked warily up at the man.

“I’ll dispense with the politeness, Cooper. I need a three-D terrain model of the area around Khe Sanh. I understand you’re the person who can make it happen.”

“Khe Sanh?”

“Cooper, you undertake assignments for the CIA and DOD, right? You do know about Khe Sanh?”

“In Vietnam, Sir?”

“Now, listen. We’ve been following the NVA’s movements for many weeks, certainly since the beginning of the Tet Offensive. Quang Tri Province is hot. Things are changing by the hour. Khe Sanh Ville was abandoned, Lang

Vei has fallen. Dong Ha, the Rockpile and Camp Carroll are in jeopardy. The hill emplacements around Khe Sanh have been attacked. We've lost a lot of Marines. Much of Highway Nine is in the hands of the North Vietnamese. There is nothing stopping the NVA from attacking the Khe Sanh Combat Base. Got it?"

Steve Cooper responded tersely.

"Yes, Sir."

"Good. We understand each other."

A puzzled look crossed Steve's face.

"How big do you want this so-called terrain model to be, Sir?" Cooper asked, the word "sir" dripping with a hint of sarcasm. "I mean, do you want it really, really big?"

Cooper's hands widened and narrowed as he gesticulated size. "Or really, really small?"

"Don't be cute, Cooper."

The stranger unfolded a piece of paper on which a crude map had been drawn. Some words and numbers were scribbled near the edges of the paper.

"It must show these locations."

The man held up his hands to count the place names off on his fingers. "Highway Nine, Co Roc Mountain, Khe Sanh Ville, the combat base, the Quang Tri River, Hill 861, Hill 881—there's two of them—as well as the other more prominent hills, maybe some of the DMZ, too. It must show terrain features and provide enough relief and geographic information about the Khe Sanh area to orient the head honcho so he understands the scene on the ground…but don't make it overly complicated."

"I take it you don't want a really, really small model."

The stranger paid no attention to Cooper's cynical remark. He smoothed the drawing flat on the table.

"What's important is to be able to show the deployment of NVA units."

Steve Cooper hadn't shaved in three days. He wore faded jeans and a plaid shirt that was as rumpled as his hair was uncombed. Affable in social settings, but characterized as a gregarious loner, Steve liked to visit with anyone over prolonged cups of coffee while at work.

Steve preferred to be at an old cabin he recently purchased in Chincoteague, on a reclusive stretch of the Virginia coast. A lot had to be done to the place: removal of the overgrown vegetation, a roof in bad need of repair and replacement of a retaining wall. The refrigerator would be stocked with plenty of cold beer.

A year earlier, Steve Cooper inherited the management role of a small group of artisans within the National Photographic Interpretation Center. Steve eventually found it to be a burden. He wasn't suited to management, really. Artistic inclinations take precedence. Model building is an exacting craft, but it's also art.

Even though annoyed by the sudden request for a new model, Steve was already developing some ideas in his mind. He was wrestling with the size. The model could be made to any scale. It was just a question of logistics.

Steve's skill combined with those of the other three in his group were a match for any challenge.

"OK, we'll start on it Wednesday of next week, Sir, and have it to you… say within three weeks."

"Three weeks! You're messin' with me, right?"

"No, Sir. Models this complicated take time."

"Cooper, I thought you understood me. I just explained to you what we are facing in Quang Tri Province. I need this thing not in three weeks, but within three days."

Steve was not to be pushed around that easily. The weekend as planned was a badly needed break.

"I'm sorry, Sir, we've just finished a big project and I gave everyone a few days off. Today is Friday and it's past two o'clock. I promised my team a few beers at Sonny's in about an hour and then I'm driving to Chincoteague. I won't be back in the office until Wednesday. My leave was approved a month ago."

The look of surprise on the guest's face clearly indicated there was no such thing as no. He pushed right back.

"Your leave is hereby cancelled! You can forget about your weekend."

The stranger held up his hand with three fingers extended.

"Saturday, Sunday, Monday. One, two, three." He counted on his fingers. "You have three working days to build it. I need the model by Tuesday morning. Got it?"

"Sir, the first two days are not working days and..."

"I don't give a crap, Cooper. I've been instructed by Director Lundahl to tell you what to do."

"Lundahl, Sir?"

"You got the name, Cooper. Building 213 is a big building. Ugly, I know."

The stranger gestured around him. "And with a lot of people. Lundahl's the boss. He created your department in this place. He made your job and he can unmake it."

The visitor wrote brusquely on a sheet of paper.

"Here's my direct line. Call me Tuesday morning early. I need it by then. No bullshit. You have three days."

The visitor, who never removed or even unbuttoned his black topcoat, turned to leave the room.

"Tuesday, that would be the thirteenth of February," Steve said. "The day before Valentine's day."

The visitor turned back to Cooper.

"Yeah, send a Valentine's card with it. Listen, our forces at Khe Sanh are in an extremely dangerous position just now. I need that model. It's for the President, if you must know. He's briefed hourly. The model will be valuable to CINC's understanding of the area."

"The President, Sir? I had no idea this was for..."

"Cooper, get on this now."

This was more serious than Steve Cooper thought.

"Oh, and one other thing, Cooper. Don't think yours is the only weekend ruined."

The stranger left the office as quickly as he entered it.

Even if this was for the President, Steve's ire was rising. These mid-level government bureaucrats are all the same—self-important and pushy. Resigned to the fact that his trip to Chincoteague was ruined, Steve called his contractor on an outside line to postpone the roof repairs. Then, he walked to the main workshop to gather his team.

"Matt, I just got word. The President needs a model of Khe Sanh in three days. I have the details. Let's get started."

"But Steve, after that big project, we were promised time off. I've made plans and…"

Steve held up his hand to quiet Matt.

"I know all about everyone's plans, and my plans, too, but we gotta make this model."

Steve turned to the team and, amidst groans, informed them that their weekend was shattered.

"Sorry guys, an urgent assignment. Another model…this time, in a box."

Lora blurted out, "Urgent? No way. I've got tickets to a Broadway play tomorrow. Catching the train in three hours…and I'm not a guy."

Steve paid no attention.

"A flat box with sides, Khe Sanh in the middle. We'll need enough latitudinal space to show the surrounding hills and valleys, the highway and any other geographic features. The model has to be transportable in the back of a pickup."

Steve raised his eyebrows. "Or, in the trunk of Matt's meticulously maintained fifty-seven Ford."

Everyone laughed. The trunk of Matt's car, hardly maintained, was full of empty beer cans.

Steve scratched his head and looked at his assembled team. Three artisans, including Lora, sat on chairs next to the big layout table while they listened to Steve.

Steve faked some ignorance of his knowledge of Vietnam to the stranger, but he knew exactly the location of Khe Sanh. He was also aware this would be a huge challenge.

"We can do this, guys. Lora—relax, I know you're not a guy—I need political as well as physical maps of Quang Tri Province. You know where to go; but don't forget the French maps. You only have tomorrow to get these, so get started first thing in the morning. Sorry about Broadway, Lora. Nothing I can do about it."

Lora lightened up.

"I'll start making calls now to let everyone know I'll be visiting them in the morning. It'll be Saturday, but if I contact them now, they can have everything ready by then. I'll try."

Steve turned to Derek sitting next to Lora.

"Let's pull out reconnaissance photos and check incoming cables for new ones. It would be good to use the stereoscope so we need any mosaics of the area. I know there are photos from SR-71 flyovers. Let's make sure we have the most up-to-date information available."

Then, to Matt again.

"We can use plywood or masonite, or some kind of flat pressed wood for the base and lid. We should have some left over from the DOD project. We need clay, plaster of Paris and whatever green colors we have on hand. We'll use the same grid as shown on the military maps. It'll be convenient. We need to figure out how to show the grid on the model.

"Start cutting the wood to size and fabricating the sides of the box. You have to determine the best vertical scale. The terrain features can't be more than one or two inches deep. The sides of the box have to be higher than the tallest hill. Don't forget handles and a way to secure the lid."

Steve Cooper ran his hand through his hair. He looked out the large windows to the Potomac River that flowed to the Atlantic coast. The weather forecast was for cold, but clear skies.

"Geez. Chincoteague, the cabin. Another weekend shot."

CHAPTER THIRTY-TWO

MORE AND MORE AMOR

On some nights, stars would peek through thin clouds. The pinpricks of light, trillions of miles away, illuminating nothing, offered a dazzling show of brilliance and mystery. They represented places that man can only imagine, but can never visit.

Collectively, some stars formed constellations that could be picked out easily. Under this kaleidoscope of imagery containing the mighty hunter Orion, and a celestial collection of fish, lions, bulls and scorpions, men of Kilo Company Third Battalion Twenty-sixth Marine Regiment occupied an infinitesimally small nook of earth on a hill far from home and insignificant to the infinite universe. The Marines tried to catch some much needed rest, but so weary with fatigue, sleep proved more elusive than the stars above them.

The scarred earth around the mountain was quiet, suggesting that the North Vietnamese were probably resting, too, in preparation of another offensive to rout the Americans and capture the hilltop.

Two Marines removed their fifty caliber machine gun to clean it. It was the only chance they had—do it now, make quick work of it, reposition the machine gun on its tripod, load it and be ready. Surely gunfire would erupt across the hill the next morning, more than likely before the sun came up.

Crouched deep in his excavated home, Jeremy Wagner, a young Marine of twenty, fidgeted with a transistor radio.

"Come on. I know I have the right channel."

The radio usually worked at this time of night, picking up frequencies from the troposphere, but the Marine was not hearing anything except garbled noise.

Corporal Frank Fopler leaned into the dirt hootch. "Get anything, Wagner?"

"Hell, no. Just this static crap. They gotta play the tune, Flops. With all these stars, this is perfect. Come on, dammit, find the station."

Frank Fopler swung his M-16 around and leaned it against the sandbags. He lit a Camel cigarette as he concealed the flame of the lighter inside the dug-out. He exhaled the smoke.

"We're lucky to get one chopper a day on this hilltop. How can we fight like this?"

"Ah, don't worry about it, Flops. There's nothing you can do," Wagner said, as he looked at his transistor radio. "Music, come on, I want music."

"Wagner, how long we gonna be up here, man? We've been doing this bullshit for a long time now. Look how many Marines we've replaced."

Frank Fopler pushed his helmet back. "Maybe you can't get the station tonight."

"Dammit, I wanna hear that tune again."

"Ever think about all those stars up there, Wagner? Do you know any of their names? I can pick out the Big Dipper. And there's the North Star. And I can see Orion's belt, but that's it for me."

"Bet you can't find Ophiuchus. It's not part of the Zodiac. Some call it the thirteenth sign. Come on radio. Work, dammit."

"Do you think we'll really make it to the moon? Actually walk around?"

"Damn if I know, Floppo. Apollo Five was launched in late January. Unmanned...but it seemed to work. I guess they can do it, but what do I know? I don't even know if I'm gonna make it home. The moon? That was JFK's idea. Anyway, I'm just a college dropout and now a jarhead stuck on this stupid hilltop just like you. I don't know squat."

Wagner raised the radio over his head. "Why won't this thing pick up the damn station?"

"What made you leave Ohio State, Jeremy? You had it all. How come you left?"

"I didn't leave, I flunked out. I didn't know how to study. There were too many distractions...you know coeds, bars, pool halls... God, I could shoot some pool.

"Biggest damned mistake in the world to put ten thousand young people together and expect them to study. I regret what happened, but I was having too much fun. Didn't know what to do, so, you know, I joined the Marines, went to Parris Island and here I am, Floppo. I thought it'd be a big picnic."

"Never been to Parris Island. I did boot camp at San Diego."

"Fopler, you son-of-a-bitch. You're a Hollywood Marine. All I recall about Parris Island were the yellow footprints, endless push-ups, mosquitoes, bugs, the toilets all lined up, sleepless nights, humidity, mud, sweat and that son-of-a-bitch DI screamin' in my ears. He was one mean mother...Wait! I got it. I got the station."

"Wagner, what's the tune you wanna hear?"

"I don't know the name. They never say. I heard only part of it two weeks ago. Then, last week, I heard the full song but the disc jockey never said its name."

Fopler inhaled on his cigarette and flipped it to his feet.

"Damned sissy cigarettes."

He reached into his pocket and pulled out a small round tin. He opened it. He pushed chewing tobacco in between his right cheek and gum.

"I wish those guys would hurry up and clean that fifty cal. I'd feel a lot better if they'd get it back into position. How many grenades we got?"

"I think maybe six."

"What time is it?"

"About two. Only four hours to sunrise."

"You mean fog rise. Every day, the fog comes up that valley over by Hill 950 and comes right up this damned mountain. Can't see shit. Best friend the gooks ever had."

The first of several enemy mortar rounds slammed into the hilltop, acutely ending the peacefulness of the darkness and the mystery of the Milky Way.

The Marines dove for cover and crept quickly to their fighting positions. In the melee of the deafening explosions, the radio contained in a plastic box was forgotten. A voice sounded on the radio in the now-empty, hand-dug cave that served as home.

This is Armed Forces Radio Saigon. Best radio station in Southeast Asia. Time is two-oh-six a.m. by the clock on my wall. I'm Rockin' Ronnie and I'm with you from two to six every morning. Hottest Dee Jay in town. I'm outta here on R and R to Bangkok in exactly seven days. But, right now, I'm here to spin records. Got a bunch of great sounds. Platters, Marvelettes, Fifth Dimension.

Let's see what else I got. Louie, Louie...dig it... Lou-I, Lou-I-A, oh baby...I got Glenn Campbell, Martha and the Vandellas... so come on, every guy grab a girl...ah man, that's me. News and sports in about twenty minutes. Weather after the news, but it's the same. Humid.

Hey, this is a touch dreamy. I like the melody. Played it a couple of times already. For you Marines in Eye Corps vacationing in sunny Khe Sanh, here's Herb Alpert and the Tijuana Brass...More and More Amor.

CHAPTER THIRTY-THREE

BEAGLES

Marvin Watson, his hand over the mouthpiece of the phone, turned to look at George Christian, standing nearby.

"Hey, George, take this call. Juanita says the President can't be disturbed from his meeting with Rostow and the Speaker. I'm on another line."

Christian was often asked to take calls on behalf of the President of the United States. He enjoyed the trust the President placed in him.

"Who is it?"

"CIA. That's all I know."

"Helms?"

"Take the call, George. I can't talk now."

"Transfer the call into the Situation Room. I'm headed down there for the pre-briefing."

By the time George Christian entered the Situation Room, an Army major was holding the phone. He handed it to Christian.

"Thanks, Garnet," then into the phone, "Christian here."

"Mr. President?"

"This is not the President. This is George Christian speaking. May I help you with something?"

"Mr. Christian, I need to speak to the President."

"And…you are mister…?"

"Wheatley, Sir, at CIA, Langley."

George Christian paid little attention to the name.

"I'm afraid the President's unavailable. Perhaps I can be of assistance."

"Mr. Christian, I have disturbing news from Hanoi that may affect our operations in Eye Corps…in Vietnam, Sir."

"I know where Eye Corps is. What news?"

"Sir, it may also have an impact on our carrier operations in the Gulf of Tonkin."

"OK, so tell me. I don't have all day."

"We aren't sure of the implications yet, but we wanted to alert the White House."

"Understood."

"I've been instructed to deliver the message directly to the President. The Joint Chiefs already know. They've been informed."

George Christian, now agitated, scratched his forehead. This should be coming from Director Helms, he thought.

"Dammit, I'm listening. Now tell me the news."

"Beagles have landed in North Vietnam, Sir."

George Christian remained silent for a moment.

"Sir? Mr. Christian…Sir…are you there, Sir?"

Christian, asked in a sterner voice.

"Who is this again?"

"Wheatley, Sir. Wilson Wheatley at the CIA, a GS Fifteen, if that helps."

George Christian, an amiable sort of guy, was tolerant of innocent pranks, but the image of the President's pet beagles, named "Him" and "Her," both of which had died a few years before, came to his mind, as did the furor that ensued when President Johnson was caught by a photographer lifting "Him" by his ears.

"Jesus Christ, Wheatley GS Fifteen. No, I really don't care what pay grade you are. You're playing a practical joke on the President, right?"

"No, Sir, This is not a jo…"

"OK, it's funny, but your timing is bad. I'll deliver a message to the President that Director Helms needs to talk to him. Now I have to go."

"Mr. Christian, Sir. Please hear me out. Russian bombers may evidently be stationed at Phuc Yen Airbase, north of Hanoi."

"What the hell are you talking about? What bombers?"

"Sir, Ilyushin 28, code named Beagle. There are two of them. The Beagles are sitting on the tarmac at Phuc Yen. We know North Vietnam has a few IL28s, Sir, old ones that they probably keep in China. These appear to be new. We think they're Russian."

"All right, Wheatley, you got my attention. How do you know this?"

"We have aerial photos of Phuc Yen taken not more than six hours ago."

"Are you sure they're Russian?"

"Pretty sure, Sir."

"Could be Chinese."

"No, Sir, they're Russian bombers."

"The photo is six hours old, you said. Are the planes still there?"

"We believe so, Sir."

"Have you talked with Arthur Lundahl? He's the aerial photo expert. You should call his office."

"No, Sir. I was told to call the Oval Office directly...I mean, the President, Sir."

"What exactly is a Baluchun twenty-eight bomber, anyway?"

"Ilyushin, Sir...ill, like illness, lu-shen, ill-lu-shen, Sir."

"OK, OK, so what is an ill-lu-shen 28?"

"It's a bomber, Sir."

"Thank you, Wheatley. You said that. Jesus. Now, can you please be more specific?"

"It's a high winged, twin jet-engine, medium range bomber."

"How much ordnance can it carry? No, I don't care about that. I want to know if it can carry A-bombs."

"I believe it can, Sir."

"Wheatley, either it can or it can't."

"Yes, Sir, I'm sure it can carry a large bomb, Sir."

"Are you sure of the plane type, Wheatley?"

"Yes, Sir. I know a Beagle when I see one, Sir."

"I'll bet."

"But, Sir, may I point out something?"

"Go on."

"Uh…I was instructed to notify the President's office—the reason for the call."

"Jesus, Wheatley, go ahead. I can't wait to hear more bad news. You should be talking to Lundahl. Those guys at NPIC know all about photo interpretation."

"Sir, the Beagle is not an advanced jet, not state-of-the-art, cumbersome in fact."

"Ok, Got it."

"But, Sir, from Hanoi, Beagles can reach Khe Sanh within thirty minutes."

Christian thought for a moment. Wouldn't they be shot out of the sky easily? What other surprises are there?

Christian looked at his watch. The President's briefing was due to begin in thirty minutes. The Situation Room was already filling up for the pre-briefing.

"Thanks for the call, Wheatley. I have to go. I will inform the President immediately. He'll be in touch with Director Helms."

"Mr. Christian, I…"

"Wheatley, I have to hang up now."

George Christian put the receiver down in its cradle. He adjusted his glasses as he looked sideways at the maps hanging on the wall. He walked closer to the map of Vietnam. He drew a mental line from Hanoi south to Khe Sanh.

"My God," he said out loud to no one in particular, "NVA bombers over Khe Sanh…Uncle Ho's, not ours. Damn, this may be a new war. The President's gonna have a friggin' cow when he hears this."

Christian surmised that several people may have heard the news since the Joint Chiefs knew. The President needed to be made aware of this development now, before he joined the meeting. He picked up the same phone receiver he had just put down.

"Juanita, put me through to the President immediately. It's urgent."

CHAPTER THIRTY-FOUR

THREE MARINES

Estenzo DePasos was teased relentlessly by the veteran Marines as the newbie, or pogue, and more derisively on one occasion as a Mexican maggot. Seldom engaging in conversation, a loner anyway, DePasos withstood the verbal abuse and harassment. This was part of the initiation. When directly challenged, however, DePasos never backed down.

Estenzo DePasos knew how to fight long before joining the Marines. Although never prosecuted, he had run-ins with the local authorities for petty stuff—shoplifting mostly; and for carrying a switchblade. He was always ready for a scrap and stood his ground.

Estenzo's father, an itinerant crop laborer from the Mexican town of Vicente Guerrero sought employment and came to work on ranches in the flat desert around Gilbert, Arizona. He later worked in the onion fields of southern California. Estenzo followed him.

DePasos had grown up with rejection by other kids who, like he, lived on the dusty, rundown fringes of Riverside, California. He dropped out of high school when he turned sixteen.

Estenzo didn't lack ambition, but he had no idea about a direction. He didn't know what having a future meant. DePasos never received encouragement from others. Strangely, at a very early age—he never knew how this happened—DePasos discovered an innate ability. He could draw anything at any time with exacting precision, down to the smallest detail. The perspective and scale of his drawings were perfect. His background scenes were flawless, the figures emotive.

Estenzo's precocious art conveyed genuine authenticity. So natural were his abilities, he didn't think much about them. Often embarrassed when people complimented his work, he rarely displayed his talents to others.

Estenzo sketched all the time, but not on real drawing paper. He would draw on discarded butcher shop paper he found along the back alleys of Riverside.

After the latest incoming barrage from NVA artillery and mortars, DePasos sat alone. He peered out from the small encirclement to observe his surroundings.

The Khe Sanh Combat Base was awash with mud and smoke, shards of timber, damaged shipping containers, boxes and steel drums, shattered shanty buildings, and earth so torn up that walking was difficult. Aircraft and ground vehicle wreckages were prolific. The area, *uno depósito de chatarra* (a junkyard) portended an apocalypse from which no man would escape.

Strangely appealing, the perverse scene resembled Estenzo's old neighborhood which at once made him feel at ease yet long for something more. While the thoughts saddened DePasos, his mind captured the dramatic chaos, the lonely emptiness.

Estenzo DePasos watched as three Marines, walking side by side, still some distance away, approached him. His dark, attentive eyes followed their every move. They came from somewhere on the combat base and were headed to who-knows-where. They didn't talk much. They seemed as much at home at Khe Sanh as they surely would back in the States.

The three Marines came steadily closer. Estenzo DePasos made careful note of the details pertaining to the men.

Their clothes, stained red by the dirt, were salty with sweat and grime. They had faces of ageless, hardened confidence. A certain fearlessness; defiance.

While the boots of the Marine on either side were fully laced, the boots of the Marine in the middle were laced halfway up. The Marine on the right wore two dog tags that dangled on a chain from around his neck.

The Marine on the left as the trio approached him, carried an M-60 machine gun over his right shoulder. He balanced the gun with his right hand placed over the barrel and the retracted bi-pod. Bandoliers of 7.62mm bullets were draped over both his shoulders and around his waist. He wore a floppy field hat with a ring on the right side. His sleeves were rolled up above his elbows.

The Marine in the middle carried a forty-five caliber pistol in a holster embossed with U.S. on his right side. It was hanging from his webbing. His sandy hair was dirty and matted. A small case containing two ammo clips was attached to the webbing on his left. He wore an open, sleeveless flak jacket. The zipper and four buttons were unclasped. He wore no shirt. He had threaded a single dog tag in the laces of his right boot.

DePasos noticed the muscular definition and veins in the arms of each man. These were strong, tough-as-steel, bad-ass Marines.

One Marine carried an M-16 in his left hand. A cartridge magazine was inserted in the magazine well. The selector lever was in the horizontal position, its pointer indicated automatic fire. The Marine carried a canteen attached to the webbing on his left side. A towel hung around his neck.

The Marines walked past DePasos without paying him any attention. The Marine on the right, now on DePasos' left, who carried the M-16, held his helmet with his right hand. A strap around the helmet secured a plastic bottle of mosquito repellant. The Marine had secured his webbing over his shirt, the sleeves of which were rolled up.

The Marine with the M-60 machine gun carried two canteens on his right hip. He had not tucked his shirt in his webbing. It bunched up over the canteens.

The three Marines halted some distance away and stared at the far ridgelines. The stop was abrupt. The man carrying the heavy machine gun placed his left hand on the back of the Marine in the middle to steady himself. DePasos noticed that a large pouch was attached to his webbing on his left side.

The men stood motionless for a few seconds. They were looking to their right at the heights of Hill 950. They murmured among themselves before disappearing behind a red earth embankment and some sandbags.

Estenzo caught site of them again moments later as they walked to the perimeter of the west end of the combat base. Their silhouettes, obscured by smoke, blending with the drab colors around them, faded into the background. A huge surge of red dust from a landing helicopter completely concealed the trio. When the dust abated, the three Marines were gone.

The poignant image of what he had observed moments before was indelibly etched into Estenzo's memory and would linger there forever. The three Marines and their comradeship would make an evocative drawing, a dramatic painting, maybe even a superb sculpture.

CHAPTER THIRTY-FIVE

THE KHE SANH TERRAIN MODEL

And so it was, for a unique group of artisans in Building 213, late on a Friday afternoon on the ninth of February, in mid-winter 1968, that weekend plans had been compromised. With the arduous goal still very much before them, disappointments were put aside.

The team began constructing the Khe Sanh Terrain Model. Four pairs of hands moved continuously over the embryonic model—as if it were a patient undergoing surgery—drawing lines, laying out destinations and coordinates, and outlining features on the base plate with a marking pen. Section by section, the Khe Sanh Terrain Model slowly took shape.

Lora confirmed terrain features through the use of a stereoscope until her eyes hurt. She noted steep slopes, ravines, mountain peaks, and various other relief. More importantly, she identified the lowest elevation in the area. This would be used as the benchmark up from which the model would be built and from which all heights would be reconciled.

Steve, Derek and Matt took Lora's data and correlated scaled lengths of precut matchsticks to the required elevations. They placed them vertically with one end of each matchstick glued to the base plate. The skeletal matchsticks replicated the elevations and contours of the land around Khe Sanh.

Hills 861, 881, 950 and 1015, with elevations given by the height in meters at the crest of the hill, and the Co Roc Massif were all clearly visible from the French maps.

Clay and plaster of Paris were smoothed into the matchstick array to form the hills and valleys. Matt and Lora checked locations, elevations, coordinates and terrain features constantly, making adjustments to the clay base or smoothing out ridges that were not congruent with the data.

Humor was abundant within the close-knit group. Professionals though they were, each member tolerated wry, sometimes ribald abuse which never went without an equally cutting retort. Irrespective of the irreverence and rude commentary, each person pitched in and worked as hard as the next. Off-color jokes were continuous. Nothing was sacred.

Derek pointed at Lora.

"That woman needs money for the lifestyle she wants, right Lora?"

"I deserve it after working with you jerks for all these months," Lora responded.

"Lora belongs in a beauty pageant. Miss Ah-Mer-Ri-Ca. She'll win the bathing suit contest hands down."

"I'll bet that's the only competition you watch, too, you drip."

"Got a cigarette?"

"Man, I'm hungry."

"Who won the game last night? Those jokers haven't played good ball in weeks. Should have had the rebound ten times in the first quarter. I watched the first half. Lousy game."

Matt spoke.

"I was going to change the oil in my car this weekend and give it a tune up. Needs new points, plugs and condenser."

Lora looked sideways.

"You might want to wash it and get rid of those beer cans in the back."

Steve laughed.

"I got a ton of things to do at my cabin in Chincoteague."

"Think Bobby Kennedy'll run for office?"

"No way."

Lora's blond hair fell in front of her face while she worked diligently over the model.

"Castro was on TV last night."

She laughed. "Does he ever change his clothes? He wears the same thing all the time. And that ugly beard. Yuk."

"Don't bullshit me, Lora, you like those kinds of guys…sort of unkempt, the kind you think you can change."

"What are you talking about?"

"Come on. Women marry men hoping to change them. Men marry women hoping they'll never change."

"You heard that from someone. You're not that clever."

What would be offensive to many, the group's endless humor, mockery and jabs at one another—their way of relieving stress—made life bearable during intense assignments.

Friday slipped into the rest of the weekend. The early morning sun of each day shone through the square, industrial windows and cast shadows throughout the workshop. The shadows shortened and lengthened across the floor as the sun rose, shifted to the other side of the building and shone through the opposite windows. Day and night interchanged, but no one noticed. The hands of the clock continued their never-ceasing spin, the deadline drawing inexorably closer.

Someone would go out to buy sandwiches, but the work didn't stop. They all escaped to St. James Café for a quick beer during happy hour on Friday and Saturday evening, but the collection of unruly, iconoclastic individuals went straight back to work. Cigarettes, No-doz tablets and coffee were in constant supply.

The modelers, their backs sore from bending at their waists, were now caught up in painstaking details.

The terrain replication was completed by 10:00 p.m. on Monday evening. Tuesday morning's sun was eight hours before cresting the eastern horizon. Everyone fell silent and breathed a sigh of relief. The worst was behind them.

But Steve, not wanting to lose the edge, was cognizant of relaxing too much.

"Keep at it, guys. Lora, bring the paint and brushes. Let's get started on the foliage. The plaster of Paris is dry enough."

"Hey, don't let Lora near any paint. Remember last summer when she was helping her granddad paint his barn back in Whittier…I dunno, in the middle of the country somewhere?"

Derek laughed as he pointed his finger disparagingly at Lora.

"Yeah, she dumped a can of red paint on her head."

Lora charged back, her bright smile and sparkling eyes radiating her good, easy-going nature.

"I didn't dump the can of paint, dammit. It fell on my head when gramps kicked the ladder by accident. I can paint as well as any of you guys. And it's not Whittier. It's DeWitt, you twit."

For the next several hours, long into Monday night, the team painstakingly painted the terrain, mimicked precisely by plaster of Paris placed over hardened clay. They used various shades of greens and yellows to give definition to the ravines, hills, ridge lines and streams.

Derek began applying a soft grayish, gun-metal blue paint to the sides of the box and the lid.

The hands of the clock pointed straight up to midnight. Monday had lapsed. Crunch day was here.

Hours later, with the sun coming up, application of various colored paints was complete. Lora looked at the model. She pushed her blond hair back off her face to reveal a smudge of green paint on her cheek.

"Holy cow, there's a lot going on with this model. It was more complicated than I imagined."

Steve, Matt and Lora tightened a series of parallel and perpendicular white strings on a square open frame that Derek had specially fabricated. The sturdy frame was slipped into place above the model. It rested on nails that protruded inwardly from the sides of the box. The strings were elevated a couple of inches above the replica terrain. Markers along each side read 30, 40, 50, and so on, while identical markers across the bottom read 70, 80, 90. Each marker and corresponding string identified ten thousand meter grid lines in perpendicular directions as derived from the X-ray Delta series of DOD maps.

Steve unfolded the paper the stranger had brusquely thrown on Steve's work table a few days earlier. The paper showed the various NVA units. Steve picked up tiny red flags that Derek made and placed them on the model's surface to show the enemy's location.

Steve couldn't help but notice.

"My God, the Marines are surrounded."

Derek attached leather handles to opposite sides of the box. A removable plaque was prepared that provided some information. The words "Khe Sanh Area" appeared on the legend. Just below, a map of South Vietnam was glued to the surface. The scale, true north and the declination were also shown.

One type-written label read: "Topographic Rendering Based on 1/50,000 Map Series; Laos and Vietnam, 1965."

And, what Steve was most proud about, a second one proclaimed: "Produced by the Production Services Group, National Photographic Interpretation Center."

And, finally, the model designation number, "NPIC-4811," and date in parentheses, "(2/68)," were provided.

Calipers and a square scale were placed in brackets on the underside of the plywood lid.

By eight o'clock on Tuesday morning, the thirteenth of February, the Khe Sanh Terrain Model was finished.

Steve and his team collapsed from exhaustion. The teasing and mindless chit chat ceased, replaced by fatigue. Each person's weekend had been destroyed, but, working together, the group accomplished something remarkable in a short period of time.

Steve studied the square box. The vertical scale of the model may not have been exaggerated sufficiently to give a viewer an idea of the rugged terrain features, but it did show the geographic layout of the region.

The Khe Sanh Terrain Model was, however, just that: a model of static geography, Plagued with inherent deficiencies, the model didn't show trends of weather, denseness of elephant grass, spider holes, overflowing rivers, angles of ascent up any of the famous hills, concealed ambush points, an impassable Highway Nine or destroyed bridges. It didn't show rain-soaked trench lines or the destruction of the area by constant bombardment. It revealed no decaying bodies of enemy soldiers who had fallen on the battlefield. The model smelled of fresh paint, not rotting flesh.

The pins with red flags may have depicted assemblages of NVA troops in the area but the model could not reveal their movements throughout the night. The terrain model would not give the President an idea about early morning fog that may linger all day. It would not reveal torrential monsoon rains or winds. It gave no indication of diurnal temperatures lowering at night only to rise during the day. Because the model would be artificially lit each time it was viewed, night would be irrelevant. The model would not convey that darkness fell each evening before seven o'clock.

Steve picked up the telephone and dialed the number he was told to call.

"Sir, it's ready.... Yes, Sir...I'll make sure the model is delivered to the White House...A note to the attention of Juanita Roberts and Walt Rostow... Yes, Sir. Got it."

Steve replaced the receiver. He walked over to the work table and laid the cover on the flat box, squared it with the edges and secured its latches.

"Matt, you and Lora gotta deliver the model to the southwest gate of the White House. Good job, guys. There's not a better team."

No one had noticed. When it was Steve's turn to go out for sandwiches the night before, he returned with a small cooler. He opened the lid and slipped his hand into the slush of melting ice. Steve Cooper pulled up a brown bottle. He popped the cap and turned to his group.

"Cold beer, anyone?"

CHAPTER THIRTY-SIX

WEST COVINA AND MOBILE, ALABAMA

The newlyweds returned from their short honeymoon in Hawaii. Sarah would finish her third year as an economics major and Donovan his last year of medical school at UCLA. Married only weeks before, Sarah Dunlap changed her last name to Reickert.

Sarah went to visit her parents for the weekend in West Covina, east of Los Angeles, while Donovan remained in Westwood for his hospital rotation.

A pile of cards and other correspondence were waiting for her on the kitchen table. She thumbed through the congratulatory notes until she came to a strange envelope postmarked "Mobile, Alabama."

Sarah knew no one in Alabama. She opened the envelope and extracted a handwritten note and another flimsy envelope. She read the note first:

Miss Sarah,

I write this letter with a heavy heart. I have come across an envelope addressed to you. I think my son Howard was planning to bring it home from Vietnam to mail to you, perhaps as a favor for a Marine friend of his.

Howie was seriously wounded at Khe Sanh. I am deeply saddened to say he passed on to heaven before he could be brought home to a hospital. His personal effects were returned to me. I have only now gained the courage to look through my son's things. I found your letter.

Howard sang in the Baptist choir. He had a wonderful voice and the biggest smile. God must have urgent business for him.

Miss Sarah, please do not concern yourself about me. I am consoled by reading Colossians1:24: Now I rejoice in my sufferings for your sake, and in my flesh.

I sincerely hope this letter finds its way to you. This is what Howard would have wanted.

May God bless you and your family as he has me and my departed son.

Sincerely,

Amalie Cornelius

Stunned, Sarah read the letter twice. She laid it on the table and picked up the second envelope, a flimsy aerogram marked with red and blue hash marks on the edges and words that read "Par Avion." It had been folded in half. She knew who the writer was. With a sense of dread, Sarah sliced the seams with a paring knife. She opened the aerogram and unfolded the paper that had formed the envelope itself. Tiny words were written in blue ink. She read the opening remarks.

My Dearest Sarah,

You cannot believe how my heart misses you.

Sarah raised one hand to her mouth as she caught her breath.

"Mom, it's from Ben!"

Sarah skimmed the letter, dismissing some paragraphs while absorbed by others.

Do you recall I mentioned a guy named Howard Cornelius from Alabama who I became friends with here at Khe Sanh? He's the one who sings hymns all the time. We call him Corney. He was severely wounded. He's being medevaced out within the next hour. I'm desperate to send you a letter and will give it to him to mail for me. I don't know anyone else I can ask.

"Mom, excuse me for a minute."

Sarah rose from the chair and began walking toward the stairs.

"Sarah…"

Sarah didn't turn. She hurried up to her old bedroom and closed the door. She sat on the bed above which hung on the wall UCLA pennants in a full circle. Sarah read through other parts of the letter cursorily, not paying much attention to the descriptions of the landscape, except for one quick passage.

The terrain is rugged. The deep valleys and hillsides are steep. The vegetation is so dense we can't see ahead even two feet.

Sarah's mother came into her bedroom.

"Are you OK, Sarah?"

Sarah, distraught, held up the aerogram from her former boyfriend.

"Mom, Ben's wounded." Sarah began to sob. "Oh, Mom..."

Her mother ran her hand over Sarah's hair trying to comfort her. She leaned down to kiss her daughter's head softly.

"I'll leave you alone, sweetheart. Come out when you're ready. I'm sure Ben will be OK."

Sarah continued to read.

Sarah, I'm not sure why I dropped out of Fullerton State. None of it made any sense. I felt lost. Now, after two years in the Corps and more than a year in Nam, I know why I should have stayed in college.

And then…

I make this promise. When I return in six months, I will enroll at UCLA to be near you, and finish my degree.'

"Oh, my God. He still thinks we're…"

Her eyes flooded with tears, Sarah continued to read Ben's letter covered with red smudges. The ink had partially run, but Sarah could make out Ben's last sentences through the reddish-blue blotches. She took a deep breath as she read the carefully composed words.

Sarah, from the deepest part of my soul, you are the sun in my life, the life in my heart. Without you, there is nothing. Please wait for me.

Ben

Sarah folded the letter from Khe Sanh and placed it, along with the note from Amalie Cornelius back in the envelope. As she did, she realized—really for the first time—the significance of the rings on her finger.

CHAPTER THIRTY-SEVEN

ARRIVAL AT THE NORTH PORTICO

Startled, Juanita Roberts suddenly looked up from her work. Two Secret Service agents were standing before her desk in the west wing of the White House.

"Miss Roberts, this box was just delivered to the southwest gate and brought to the North Portico."

Juanita, surprised by the cumbersome, flat object painted industrial blue-gray, exclaimed, "My goodness. What a monstrosity. What is that thing?"

"Not sure, Miss Roberts, but it was checked at security. It's safe."

"Who's it from, gentlemen? Heavens, why didn't they deliver it to the West Wing entrance?"

Juanita frowned. "We never receive packages, certainly nothing this unsightly, through the North Portico. It's not a delivery entrance."

"Sorry for the intrusion, Miss Roberts, we were told to bring it to you right away."

"Oh, all right, then. No harm done. Let me read the note."

Juanita Roberts opened a small envelope and read the writing on the enclosed paper:

A three dimensional model of western Quang Tri Province constructed for the President of the United States by the National Photographic Interpretation Center (NPIC), Building 213, Navy Yard.

The two men, dressed in dark suits, held the flat box level between them. One spoke.

"Where would you like for us to put it, Miss Roberts?"

"Certainly not in my office. The study is the best place. Thank you, gentlemen, for carrying it. Goodness, this is the White House, not a museum."

Juanita played a little dumb. "I've overheard Mr. Rostow mentioning a map or something to the President; that it should be here any day now. Maybe this is what he was talking about. Whatever it is, I'm sure Mr. Rostow...and the President, will be very pleased to see it."

Juanita Roberts accompanied the two smartly-dressed men as they carried the wood box several feet away into the study. The men tilted the box and, carrying it on its edge, passed through the narrow doorway. They didn't bother to use the leather handles attached to the sides.

Juanita followed them. She walked to a table and moved some books.

"Place it here."

"Miss Roberts, here's the copy of the gate receipt dated today, the thirteenth of February."

"Goodness, gentlemen, the middle of February already. Next thing you know it'll be Memorial Day...1968 will be by us before we realize it."

"Is there anything else, Miss Roberts?"

"No. Thank you very much, gentlemen."

Amused, Juanita looked at the strange object. She picked up the phone.

"Mr. Rostow, sorry to disturb you, Sir, but I believe it's here."

"Really, Juanita? This should be interesting."

"Well, Sir, I don't know how interesting it is, but it's unattractive. It looks like a cheap card table without legs, something my father would keep in his workshop. I'd never have it in my garage, much less in my house...Yes, Sir. I had them bring it into the study...I didn't know where you'd want it. What?

Oh, no, Mr. Rostow, it's not very big, but it's not small either. Yes, it's completely covered...No, Sir, I didn't see inside. I just don't understand why..."

"Juanita, I'll be right there."

Five minutes later, Walt Rostow entered the study.

"Let's see what we have here, now."

Juanita Roberts pointed to the table.

"There, Mr. Rostow. A big, blue flat box. Like I said, ugly."

"Hmmm. Juanita, I was imagining it would be bigger."

Walt Rostow unhooked the latches and lifted the cover off the box. Two measuring devices were fitted into brackets. The main feature inside the box, the terrain, was expertly painted in various shades of green and earth tones. String lines cut across the top in each direction.

"My God, Juanita, it's beautiful. It could be in the Smithsonian."

"Better there than in the White House, Mr. Rostow."

"Whoever made this did one hell of a job."

Walt Rostow studied the contents closely. "Look at the terrain features and the rivers."

"Mr. Rostow, I have no idea what I'm looking at, really."

"It's a model, Juanita, of Khe Sanh, the place where the Marines are based."

Walt Rostow gestured. "Juanita, here's the airstrip."

"Oh, OK, I see now. Green paint, flags, numbers, place names, valleys, hills. What'll we do with it in the White House?"

Walt Rostow moved his hand over the box to gesture the whole area again.

"Here's the model's scale."

Rostow smiled as he remembered the lecture he and Arthur Lundahl had received from the CIA director two months earlier about perceptions of distances and how Americans can become confused in Europe. He chuckled because he had never been confused in Europe. "This should please Helms."

"Well, Mr. Rostow, I've never seen anything quite like this before. Shall I inform the President?"

"No, Juanita, thank you. I'll call the President in a few minutes and tell him the model is ready for his use. No. Better not call. He's busy. I have to write him a quick message about a communiqué from General Taylor. I'll let the President know about the model in the memo."

"As you wish, Sir." Don't forget the four o'clock meeting, Mr. Rostow. I have copies of the transcript ready for distribution, Sir."

"Thank you so much for your help, Juanita. I want to look at this for a few more minutes. It's like I'm gazing down from thirty thousand feet. The President will be thrilled."

Juanita didn't smile.

"I'll return to my office, unless you need something further from me."

"Juanita, please have the model taken to the Situation Room after I leave."

"I'm not sure why you find it so entertaining, Mr. Rostow. Anyway, the President can do with it what he wants."

Juanita gestured toward the model. "But, don't store that dreadful thing in my office. Give it to the maintenance people to keep in the basement. Next thing you know, we'll have dinosaur models in the White House."

CHAPTER THIRTY-EIGHT

MEXICAN STANDOFF

Art Krim placed his fork on the dessert plate. The Texas-size slice of hot apple pie topped off the main course of barbecue. Dinner with the President and First Lady and with Marvin Watson had been a pleasure. At twenty minutes past ten, it was time, however, to say good night.

Krim usually stayed at the White House, but this trip, he was staying at the Hay-Adams Hotel across Lafayette Park from the executive mansion, not even a ten minute walk. He turned to Watson.

"Marvin, congratulations on your appointment to Postmaster General. You'll assume that post sometime in April, right?"

"Yes, Sir. Probably late April. I'm looking forward to it. But, I must say, I've enjoyed the White House."

Krim sipped his coffee.

"You've been a key asset to the President's administration. You'll do fine, Marvin."

Krim looked across the table.

"The food was delicious, Lyndon, I swear."

Lady Bird smiled.

"Art, you're always welcome. There's nothing better than relaxing with good friends…like being back at our ranch in the spring. We have great get-togethers and wonderful barbecues behind the house."

The President laughed.

"Lady Bird always says behind the house, like it's the back side. She's referring to the front of the house which actually faces the river."

"Lyndon, you're always correcting me. Art and Marvin know what I mean."

Krim pushed his chair backward.

"Very good dinner, Mr. President and Lady Bird. No need to have gone through all that trouble."

"Ah, that ain't nothing, Krim. Just a snack."

Art Krim looked again at the table. This is a snack? As many times as he had dined with the First Family, why did the President always entertain him like this, with so much food? How can he be so casual about it?

"I had it prepared in Texas and flown here this morning on the Jetstar just for tonight. Hell, we just had it warmed up on the grill…and there ya go. Best damned barbecue and brisket north of the Rio Grande. Nothing like it anywhere. No, Sir. Yuki is dying for the leftovers."

"And the apple pie? Who made that, Mr. President? It was yummy."

"Come on, Krim, I can have a few secrets in this place. Lady Bird's pecan pie is even better. She may have a degree in history, but she's one hell of a good cook. That's one thing Lynda and Luci have learned from their mother. They know how to make pecan pie, now."

The President smiled with a father's pride as he looked at Krim and Watson.

Lady Bird, never without her Texas congeniality, laughed.

"Lyndon, don't be silly. Both girls are very talented."

The President reached across and held his wife's hand.

"Those are great girls, Bird, because you're a great mother. It's your Texas savvy, hon."

Lady Bird responded with a warm smile.

"Oh, Lyndon."

"Lady Bird's right. We've had grand parties with chuck wagons and giant barbeque grills in the grove of live oaks next to the Perd'naliss."

The President winked at Lady Bird. "In front of the house."

Krim chuckled.

"I'm well aware."

"Why, hell, kids can swim in the pool, run barefoot and pet the calves. I can bring in Shetland ponies. The evening sun through the trees, the shadows across the grass, the cattle grazing…Watson here knows what I'm talking about. Damn, you can't beat Texas."

President Johnson folded his dinner napkin and laid it next to his plate. He sipped some coffee and placed a toothpick between his teeth.

"Krim, come with me for a minute. I can get you in the Situation Room. I want to show you something you'll find interesting."

The President rose from the table covered with dishes, silverware and wine glasses, each with a red stain at the bottom. He kissed his wife.

"Lady Bird, Marvin, you'll excuse us for a minute."

"No problem, Mr. President," Watson said. "I enjoy visiting with the First Lady. I'll have some coffee and maybe more of that pie."

Krim looked at his watch, but agreeing to the President's last request, laid his own starched White House napkin on the table.

The two men, one from the state of Texas, the other from Manhattan, an island that could fit inside the boundaries of Texas almost twelve thousand times, left the residential quarters. They made their way in the direction of the West Wing.

"Mr. President, I can't even think of another bite of food at the moment. I'm stuffed."

"Most welcome, Art."

The President and his guest descended a few steps leading to the Situation Room.

"We have an issue on our hands in Vietnam, Art, and…"

"Mr. President, I'm not sure I can help."

"Art, I have plenty of military advisors. Some are damned good and some aren't so damned good. I thought I'd get your opinion."

Johnson and Krim entered the Situation Room. The lights were on. Maps covered the walls. Files in neat stacks lay on the conference table and on other smaller tables.

"Art, take a look at that model that was built for me."

The President smiled. "The staff poke fun at me, particularly the younger ones. They say I'm an obsessed old man, but I look at this thing all the time. It's a model of the geography around Khe Sanh…in Vietnam."

"I see that. Nicely done."

Krim noticed that the President fixed his gaze on the model. His facial muscles didn't move.

Krim became uneasy. Here's a model of some part of Vietnam. So what? Maybe he made a mistake to come here. He was a fund raiser, not a soldier.

"Mr. President, I'm at a loss when it comes to things military. I know all about producing movies. I know how to raise a few million dollars, but..."

"Art, look at all the area there."

Lyndon Johnson made a sweeping gesture with his hand over the model. "Mile after mile, thousands and thousands of sections... know what a section is? It's a parcel of six hundred and forty acres. Look at how empty the land is: no villages, no real towns, no trains, no roads to speak of, only paths. Nothing, really."

"Looks vacant to me, Mr. President."

"Krim, I grew up in the Hill Country. It's a desolate part of the U.S., but it's beautiful. Lady Bird and I want to return there one day, back to the LBJ ranch."

"I can understand, Lyndon."

"But, right here, Art..."

The President jabbed his index finger at the model to emphasize his point. "Right in this spot are men of the United States Twenty-sixth Marines and the First Battalions of the Ninth and Thirteenth Marines. Hell, we've got six thousand Marines there and some ARVN Rangers. Even the Navy has people there. Everybody's there. This is the densest settlement of humanity in the entire area, all American. As far as I'm concerned, this is American property. Know what? It's just as hostile as the hills around Johnson City, but it's crawlin' with a different vermin."

"Lyndon, I'm not really the right person to be having this kind of discussion and..."

"Listen to me carefully, Art."

The President thought for a moment. "Each of those brave American boys wants to come back to his home as much as I want to return to mine. They want to be with their families like I do. But they're in a desperate fight for their lives. See all the red flags around here?"

The President pointed to the model again. "Our Marines rule the land, but right now they have to share it with those North Viet-nese bastards."

Krim looked at the President. Why was he telling him this?

Johnson didn't stop.

"You can see the picture taking place at Khe Sanh right now as we tell funny stories and eat barbecue. American boys are surrounded. The enemy intends to annihilate them."

"I had no idea about the terrain, Lyndon."

President Johnson, his hands resting on the edge of the model, leaned over the table. He turned his head to look at Art Krim. The President enunciated his words in a whisper.

"Art, some feel we should not hold outposts that are exposed, unless their value is equal to the cost. We shouldn't seek battles near the border area. I'd say that's clear reference to Khe Sanh…but here we are. We're not talking about the cost of eggs here, we're talking about lives.

"Can you imagine the humiliation that would befall this Presidency if this spot in the model was overrun, if Khe Sanh fell to the North Viet-nese? People will scorn me, saying I didn't learn the lesson from Din Bin Phu, that I was arrogantly careless. I'll have hell to pay if our Marines are massacred and we lose this worthless piece of American-occupied real estate. I can't find the words to describe such a debacle. The families would never forgive me. America would never forgive me."

"But, Mr. President, I'm sure the military has all this figured out."

"Art, I speak to you as a good friend who I can trust."

The evening had taken a strange twist. Krim was feeling awkward. He should've gone back to the Hay-Adams.

"Go on, Lyndon. How can I help you?"

The President's tone, still amiable, became anxious.

"Art, sometimes, solutions become apparent if the problem is talked through with someone who's not in the loop."

Unsure of himself, Krim felt relieved. The President merely needed someone—a confidant—to whom he could vent. He wanted somebody, anybody, to just listen to him.

The President pointed at the Khe Sanh Terrain Model.

"If the North Viet-nese move against the defenses of Khe Sanh, I'm not sure they can be stopped."

The President massaged his face and ran his hand behind his neck.

"Krim, there's a lot of fighting going on all over the place. Khe Sanh may be our only hope at this moment in South Vietnam.

"We were hard-pressed during the Tet Offensive. We didn't know how to fight those kinds of battles, but we didn't lose. In a short time, the North Vietnese may attack Khe Sanh. God, if we were to lose there, it'll be significant because it's exactly that kind of face-to-face battle we can fight. See my point? And this time there will be no mistaking the truth either way, win or lose."

President Johnson pointed at the center of the terrain model. "The balance of what we do in Vietnam hinges right here, in these hills around Khe Sanh.

"I'm told the enemy has embarked on a reasonably predictable program. Weather, Tet, Presidential elections...these are factors Hanoi is taking into account. We can expect them to act aggressively...unless we prevent them from doing so. They want a victory. More importantly, they want a coalition government. But, by God, they're not going to get either one. Not if I can help it.

"Krim, if we lose at Khe Sanh, we've lost the entire war in Vietnam. It'll be a disaster for our South Vietnam policy—our Southeast Asia policy. Hell, maybe even our entire foreign policy. It'll be catastrophic for the presidency. All I have accomplished for this country through the power of the executive office are in ruin. My term in office will fall into disgrace. I may as well go home to those mesquite-covered hills of Texas with my tail between my legs."

Art Krim, silent, clasped and unclasped his hands. He looked down at the Khe Sanh Terrain Model, then back at the President.

President Johnson moved his face to within inches of Krim's and spoke in a low voice.

"Art, the antagonists are lined up. William Childs Westmoreland and Vo Nguyen Giap ten thousand miles away at Khe Sanh. It's a Mexican stand-off. Who blinks first?"

A short silence ensued.

"Krim, we are not going to give the enemy any kind of victory. The Tet Offensive was designed by Hanoi. It was their battle. Khe Sanh is Westmoreland's. A lot is at risk, but I'm just gonna let Westy have his damn battle."

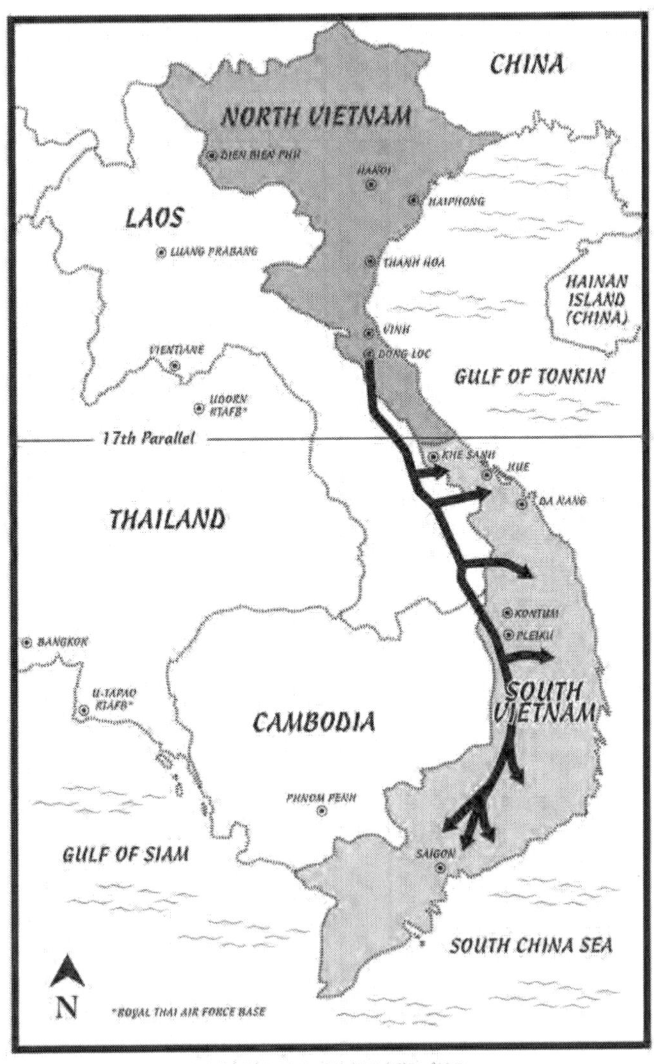

HO CHI MINH TRAIL
(TRUONG SON TRAIL)

CHAPTER THIRTY-NINE

PRESS BRIEFING

The stifling briefing room, located in the Rex Hotel, just down Le Loi Street from the Saigon Opera House, smelling of damp, tropical fungus, was packed to capacity with perspiring reporters. Colonel Ashcroft, a member of Westmoreland's joint staff in Saigon for the last ten months, now dressed in his perfectly pressed uniform, stood at the podium.

Jack Ashcroft, born in Ocala, Florida, earned his college degree in chemistry at Auburn University where he played football. A powerful running back, few people messed with him. He joined the U.S. Army after graduation in 1943 and ended up on the beaches of Normandy. After V-E Day, by a strange quirk of luck, he served on MacArthur's staff in Tokyo for twelve months. His military career was almost shattered when a sailor, tanked up on saki, taunted him as a stupid G.I. and called him Jack Asshole. Those were the last words the drunk could speak for six months. Ashcroft's giant right hand plowed into the man's face like a buffalo, putting him in the hospital for weeks and making him learn to enjoy his meals through a straw. Ashcroft had hell to pay for that incident, but his career was not ruined.

Ashcroft was, however, more than a fighter. He was astute in the office as well as on the battlefield.

Ashcroft leaned forward and spoke into the microphone.

"Ladies and gentlemen, one last piece of information before I open the forum to interrogatives. As you know, the Chairman of the Joint Chiefs of

Staff will arrive in Saigon soon, on the twenty-third of February. He will be visiting us for about a week. I believe that…"

"What's his itinerary, Colonel?"

Ashcroft looked toward the intrusive sound. He recognized Gil Norton, one of the more obnoxious reporters.

"How long is he here?"

Colonel Ashcroft raised his hand to silence the reporter.

"General Wheeler will be in a series of meetings with General Westmoreland. That's all I know."

"What's the subject of the meetings, Colonel?"

"The results of those meetings, to the extent they can be shared, will be made known to all of you. Now, I will take other questions."

The crowd erupted with insistent and competitive shouts. The reporters' concurrent questions were rapid-fire, antagonistic and sometimes irrelevant.

"Colonel Ashcroft, Sir, is Khe Sanh significant to the NVA's overall offensive?"

"Westmoreland has advised not to be fooled," Ashcroft said. "He has stated that Khe Sanh is the next target. Our analysis supports his opinion."

"It's rumored that Giap is now fully in charge of his field forces. Do you care to comment on that, Sir?"

"Any comment would be speculative at best."

"Sir, General Westmoreland assured us the war was going his way. He said we've reached the cross-over point, that enemy troop strength cannot sustain their operations. It doesn't look like that now."

"I'm not sure of your question, Sir."

"What about increases in troop strength? Isn't Wheeler here to discuss additional troops? Doesn't Westmoreland want to be more aggressive? How many men will be slated for Vietnam, Sir? How many will General Wheeler authorize? If we've reached the cross-over point why does he…"

"Gentlemen, please. The discussions between General Wheeler and General Westmoreland have not yet begun."

"Colonel! Colonel!"

"What is it, Norton?"

"Colonel, Isn't it true the CIA and MACV do not agree on enemy strength? Can you confirm that MACV is still discounting the Viet Cong and their cadres from the enemy order of battle?"

"Mr. Norton, that's an old topic. I have nothing to add."

"But, Colonel, surely you have heard about..."

"That's all, Mr. Norton."

Questions from others did not stop.

"Is General Westmoreland thinking about overhauling his strategy in Eye Corps?"

"I have no information on that point."

"Can you give us details about the ambush near Ca Lu on Highway Nine a few days ago, on the fourteenth of February? Kilo Company, I think Sir, Second Battalion Ninth Marines."

"I must defer to answer that at a later date. Details are still emerging."

"Colonel, can you comment about the risk of CINCPAC's permission for B-52 Arclight raids close-in to our positions, perhaps even close to the combat base?"

"All I can say is we're here to win?"

"How are you provisioning Khe Sanh now that the runway is closed?"

"The runway is damaged, true enough, and the Air Force has suspended flights of C-130s, but the airstrip is not altogether closed. We started provisioning through LAPES yesterday along with para-drops. We are developing a new multi-coordinated tactic involving A-4s from Chu Lai and CH-46 supply helicopters from Phu Bai."

"How involved is China in the conflict? Do you have a new timetable? Do you think there are Russian advisors, maybe even some Russian pilots?"

The questions, some of which were asked out of ignorance—an easy trap to fall into—were insinuatingly probing, especially those that naively concerned China and Russia. Ashcroft had been around the block a few times. He wasn't going to fall prey to the insouciance.

"Colonel, looking back, you've described the Tet Offensive as unsuccessful. Do you..."

"Correct. We experienced some tense days. Independence Palace, Tan

Son Nhut, the embassy, the radio station and Cholon, not to mention the provincial capitals, were serious targets. We took hits, but we countered swiftly and repulsed the enemy…not only here but all across the country. I'll say the same thing today that General Westmoreland said in his TV interview and at his press briefing. The enemy is trying to cause us grief, but it's a diversion from the NVA's true intentions in Quang Tri Province. Giap is using the Viet Cong to divert us away from his main, heavily armed NVA divisions. The Viet Cong are on their last leg.

"Hanoi promised its forces they would be resupplied with ammunition. There was no resupply. They confirmed reinforcements. None came. They were counting on an insurrection across the country. Didn't happen, not even in Hue, where there is discontent with the South Vietnamese government.

"The south side of the Perfume River was secured on the ninth of February. We expect all of Hue to be secure within another week. Hanoi completely miscalculated everything which is an indication of their desperation.

"The enemy cannot sustain military or terrorist operations, neither here in Saigon nor anywhere else. Their sideshow is done. Giap's poorly-planned, so-called Tet Offensive, with amateurs acting as soldiers, is a go-for-broke, deceitful tactic and will fail. It has failed, in fact."

"Colonel Ashcroft, Sir. The communist attacks were audacious in their coordination. It seems after three years of fighting, the commandos have demonstrated they can strike at will anywhere in the country."

"Excuse me, Sir. The attackers were cowards, not commandos. They have shown callous disregard for human life. The Viet Cong have executed hundreds of innocent people in Hue, maybe as many as a thousand. The VC took refuge in the Citadel. We've done our best to preserve the historic vestige, but the enemy was so entrenched, we had to resort to other means to rout them."

"And Khe Sanh, Sir?"

"The main battle is yet to come. General Westmoreland's confident it will be with the North Vietnamese regulars. Khe Sanh will be Giap's capstone of his planned three-phase attack. The first phase was the border battles in Two Corps—Dak To and Loc Ninh. The ill-planned Tet Offensive is the second one—it has failed—and the third phase will be Khe Sanh. Giap intends for Khe Sanh to be his second Dien Bien Phu. Giap will sacrifice his men wantonly with the hopes of meeting his objectives. He will fail."

"But Colonel, MACV has moved so many Marines to Khe Sanh, the towns are more vulnerable. Can you address that?"

"The battles of Dak To and Loc Ninh, which I just mentioned, were an attempt by Giap to dislodge our troops away from the coastal plains. The fighting was fierce but his plan was foiled. In the case of the Tet Offensive, the NVA and the VC had surprise, overnight-strength and, in a spineless way, attacked when South Vietnam celebrates its annual Tet holiday, a sacred holiday equally observed by the North Vietnamese. Again, without success."

"But Sir…"

"The enemy is gutless. They have attacked the cities in a pathetic manner to nullify our use of airpower. They are using the civilian population as shields while they inflict unimaginable cruelties and horrors, which is their true nature.

"As far as Khe Sanh is concerned, General Giap must either attack or withdraw. If he has pinned us down, he has also pinned himself down. I'm sure he's calculating his losses and gains, but he's committed. He can attack or he can sit in the hills like a coward and take pot shots at us."

"Colonel, would you care to comment on Nguyen Ngoc Loan's singular execution of a Viet Cong prisoner? Shot in the side of his head…on film, Sir. Can you make a statement about that, Colonel?"

Not expecting this question, Colonel Ashcroft was caught off guard.

"I understand the incident is still under investigation."

"Sir, Senator Eugene McCarthy has speculated about the use of nuclear weapons. Is MACV still considering such measures?"

"We have no plans to use nuclear weapons."

Gil Norton challenged Ashcroft.

"No plans now, Sir…but perhaps later? We know that General Westmoreland drew up plans to use…"

Ashcroft pointed directly at Norton.

"I would be very careful with such irresponsible supposition on your part, Mr. Norton. I repeat, we have no such plans."

"Colonel, given the ambush last week at Ca Lu, Highway Nine is in the hands of the NVA. You mentioned provisioning Khe Sanh with parachute drops and through other measures..."

"Your question, Sir."

"Can you support Khe Sanh by air for very long?"

"I thought I explained that. Yes, we can."

"Colonel, will General Westmoreland pull out? Will he retreat from Khe Sanh?"

The question instantly annoyed Ashcroft.

"Ladies and gentlemen, I want to be perfectly clear."

Colonel Ashcroft walked forward to the edge of the podium. With an eagle on one collar and a joint general staff insignia on the other, his combat boots at their shiniest, Ashcroft stood straight and tall. His physical stature was impressive. He raised his right hand as he spoke.

Every reporter looked at Ashcroft. Cameras, held above the crowd, were aimed at the high-ranking officer. Flashbulbs popped.

"We are at Khe Sanh on an important, morally correct mission, one of historical proportion. We will finish that mission successfully. The enemy will be defeated. His losses will be such that he will be forced to rethink his actions and his position in South Vietnam."

"Colonel, these are similar to statements made before."

The questions became more insistent.

"Is it true that reinforcements from the U.S. may total as many as fifteen battalions?"

"Does the Pentagon want an extension of tours?"

"Westmoreland says he wants to be more aggressive, yet he is not attacking at Khe Sanh. MACV has the Marines in a defensive posture. We've heard…"

The colonel abruptly raised both his hands again.

"Now, understand this."

A hush swept across the conference room. More flashbulbs popped.

The colonel had made presentations at the five o'clock follies many times before, but the questions he was now receiving were irksome. He controlled his composure even though his eyes were shooting darts. He was on completely unscripted territory now. Ashcroft's voice was tinged with anger.

"I will say this one time only. We have the power, the resources, the commitment and the flexibility to win every battle in every corner of this country. General Westmoreland has made it clear. We will not walk away from Khe Sanh. I emphasize we will not forsake our mission in South Vietnam. And we will not retreat from honor. That is all."

The colonel, surrounded by his aides, stepped from the small stage.

"Is Westmoreland going to invade Cambodia and Laos?"

"Colonel Ashcroft, you have to admit, Sir, that defensive measures are..."

Questions were drowned out by the extraneous loud noise of the boisterous crowd.

Ashcroft passed through the front door of the hotel into the clamor of Nguyen Hue Street and the steamy Saigon evening. His vehicle was waiting.

CHAPTER FORTY

SEVEN LAKES COUNTRY CLUB

The general's drive off the tee for the eighth hole was wide. Still in a post-swing stance, he watched as the white golf ball sailed high above the fairway and over a lake, one of seven that dotted the executive golf course. The miniature ball, lost for a moment against the sweeping panorama of an imposing mountain range, landed to the right of a sand trap near the tee of the opposite-facing fourth-hole fairway. Holding his number three wood, the general stood with a puzzled expression on his face. He had sliced the shot.

"My God, and this is an easy fairway, Mr. President. Must've been my grip…or maybe my age."

"Don't worry," President Johnson chuckled. "Your shot'll play."

Lyndon Johnson was taking a break from his west coast tour to visit the world's most famous military personage and the thirty-fourth President of the United States. He'd come to Palm Springs, California to meet Dwight David Eisenhower.

The trip aboard Air Force One from Washington, D.C. began a day earlier. The President's first stop at Fort Bragg to greet soldiers bound for Vietnam was sobering. He stood in awe of the troops who responded with cheers when he exclaimed, "All of you are Airborne."

His trip continued on the same day to El Toro Marine Corps Air Station, California. There, he met a young Marine who had already been to Vietnam. His wife just gave birth to their first baby, but he was going back. Johnson saw no bitterness in the eyes of the young man. Later, the President, standing on the tarmac, watched the plane carrying the Marine and his buddies take off. It faded away at the point of a trail of black exhaust.

The President's tour continued with a short hop in a helicopter to an aircraft carrier steaming fifty miles off the coast of southern California. Minutes before the helicopter landed, the One-MC blared across the flight deck—"United States is arriving."

Eight bells rang out. The President's actual arrival on board the ship was acknowledged by one bell, a stinger.

Piped aboard, the President passed through the traditional receiving lineup of side boys. Again, the One-MC sounded throughout the ship.

"The commanding officer and crew of CV64 are honored to receive the President of the United States of America, the Commander-in-Chief."

President Johnson relished the protocol. He was greeted by Captain W. R. Flanagan, Commanding Officer of the USS *Constellation.*

"Mr. President, welcome on board the *Connie.* We are pleased you are here, Sir."

"Thank you, Captain Flanagan. It's my pleasure to visit this great ship."

The President talked with the officers and received a briefing about U.S. Navy air operations in the Gulf of Tonkin.

"You men are sure pounding the North Viet-nese. Your efforts against the communists are important."

Later, the President gave a press conference before retiring for the evening on board ship. At 3:00 a.m., he asked the Marine who stood guard outside the captain's quarters if he could find another blanket. The Marine would not leave his post.

Johnson called his security advisor just after 6:00 a.m.

"Dammit Rostow, I didn't get a bit of sleep. The captain's stateroom was cold as an icebox."

After attending a sermon on the hanger deck, the President ate breakfast with about twenty-five sailors who expressed their opinion that the war could be won if he let them fight it their way.

President Johnson returned to El Toro by helicopter and continued his trip aboard Air Force One to Palm Springs Airport. He arrived at 11:30 a.m. on Sunday, the eighteenth of February.

The President, ferried by helicopter to the Eldorado Country Club, met General Eisenhower at his home on the eleventh fairway.

After discussion over lunch, President Johnson changed into his golfing attire. He wore a navy-blue turtleneck shirt, dark gray slacks and black and white spiked shoes. General Eisenhower wore his usual golfing clothes and his signature straw hat.

The two Presidents traveled by motorcade and arrived at the exclusive Seven Lakes Country Club, not far away. Developed for those who wanted to live on a golf course among prestigious homes, Ted Robinson's residential design opened in 1965.

President Johnson, upon seeing General Eisenhower's shot go wide, teed up.

"After my encounter with those two trees and that same pond on the fourth, I think I can expect anything," said Johnson.

Eisenhower smiled.

"You know how I feel about this game, Mr. President."

"Damn, Mr. Ex-sitting President, I thought we agreed to dispense with the formalities. Protocol is off. I'm Lyndon and you're Dwight."

"Or Ike, if you prefer, Lyndon."

"Now you're talking. Ike, just like before."

Lyndon Johnson was ebullient. A day on the links with America's best known five-star general in a dramatic setting, with crystal-clear weather, was a welcome respite; just what the President needed.

A long line of Secret Service agents, riding golf carts, causing the occasional traffic jam, followed the two men everywhere.

On the short ninth hole, Johnson just missed clearing a water hazard. He used his executive prerogative and teed up once more. The second shot was better.

Eisenhower sliced his shot again. With their last putts, the front nine was complete. The men stopped in the club house for refreshment.

"Not a bad round, Lyndon."

"Thanks, Ike. I wish I could play more."

The President thought for a second. "Listen, Ike, I really appreciate your advice on Vietnam. Your military leadership provides a perspective that I don't have."

"Lyndon, throughout the history of warfare, victory has been on the side that wears the other side down, either through direct attrition, indirect compromise or through erosion of an opponent's will. In any case, the result is the same: destruction."

A quizzical look crossed the President's face.

"Lyndon, World War Two was complicated, but General Marshall and Winston Churchill were steadfast in their conviction. Those two men could not have been better ordained as leaders at such a horrible time in our civilization.

"On a purely philosophical level, there is nothing keeping us from withdrawing from Vietnam. The same could not be said of the Second World War. All of Europe was at risk. Pulling out was not an option. Germany's cruel transgressions compelled us to stay the course. Our reluctance to become involved earlier was probably our only mistake. We bombed their war-making capabilities until they were so weakened, production was no longer possible."

"Well, we're wearing those communist pissants down, Ike, but I fear we'll have to topple the Hanoi government to bring them to the negotiating table."

"Lyndon, during World War Two, we lost a lot of very brave men—nothing like the Russians, mind you—but I always knew the Allies would turn the tide and win in Germany. The Allies won by applying endless pressure on the Nazi regime. Not to downplay what the Russians did—my God, they could fight—the battle of Stalingrad was the beginning, but the Normandy invasion marked Hitler's demise, and he knew it, too.

"The American people never wavered from the commitment to freedom. America was unified, maybe more than it will ever be again.

"Ike, Vietnam is a different kind of war."

"Lyndon, I have always thought Vietnam would be a problem for us. I knew who the enemy was in Europe, where the front lines were. We put American soldiers on French soil and headed them east. Times have changed. Combat has changed. The structure of geo-politics has changed, too. Even here in America, there's been a change in temperament, a new attitude.

"I can tell you what it will take for us to win the war in Vietnam, but world opinion will not be tolerant of the manner in which we would do it. I'm not even sure America has the stomach for it now...or the pocketbook."

"You know, Ike, I sent McNamara to Saigon last July. Westy told him the war was not stalemated, that we were winning slowly...but, of course he wanted more troops.

"I'm wondering whether Westmoreland's in trouble over there. I've approved General Wheeler's visit to Vietnam. He leaves in about five days. He says we're at a crossroads. The decisions that have to be made are unavoidable. He's expecting my support as well as the support of congress."

"Lyndon, Bus Wheeler's a West Point grad and saw action in Europe during World War Two. I would suggest you listen to what he has to say."

"Ike, there is no doubt about General Wheeler's capabilities and insight. There is growing debate as to whether a new direction is required in Vietnam. The debate ranges from attrition to annihilation. Westmoreland and Wheeler want me to lift the limitations on the conduct of the war. In simple terms, they want to cut the enemy's supply line. That would involve incursions into Laos and Cambodia and maybe an invasion of North Vietnam itself. They want to intensify the bombing of North Vietnam and they want more troops.

"Westmoreland reminds me that he has been fighting with limitations; that for us not to change our way of making war will lead to a conflict that is completely open-ended."

After downing big glasses of orange juice, the two men stepped into their golf cart. Dwight Eisenhower drove while President Johnson sat in the passenger side. The golf clubs rattled behind them.

"Isn't the thirteenth hole up here somewhere? That's your hole-in-one, Ike...just a few days ago, right?"

"Yeah, I used a nine iron. It's treacherous, Lyndon."

"Oh, come on. A par three is treacherous? Can't be. And that mountain, my God. What's its name?"

"Mount San Jacinto,"

"I can understand why you like to vacation here, Ike. This weather's terrific."

"Lyndon, when Kennedy became president of the United States, I briefed him on the benefit of using aerial maps and photo interpretation for military purposes. I used lots of models, too. General Zhukov used models of Berlin when the Russians attacked the city. Mine were crudely prepared with accurate and, then again, not-so-accurate data. Nonetheless, I came to rely on them for Operation Overlord."

The two presidents, continued their attack on the links by teeing off on the fourteenth and fifteenth holes. The sixteenth hole proved hazardous due to a lake in the middle of the par-three fairway. The seventeenth tee was congested. A long line of carts bearing Secret Service Agents crowded a narrow space between the opposing houses.

Johnson won the seventeenth hole. The two presidents moved to the eighteenth tee that faced a lake and a sand bunker slightly left of the green. The clubhouse sat just beyond.

"Ike, I'm sure we'll have to hold a small press conference as soon as we play this last hole."

"I would suppose. I could do with some more orange juice."

President Johnson became more talkative with his host just before his last tee-off.

"And then, there's Khe Sanh. Westmoreland's taking a calculated chance. He seems awfully sure of his tactics. He's trying to lure the North Vietnamese from their hiding places into an all-out offensive and kill them with a combination of air strikes and artillery. He's convinced we need to maintain a forward operating base to block the route of enemy advance in Quang Tri Province.

"Ike, you mentioned models. I have a model of the Khe Sanh area in the Situation Room."

"I'd like to see it someday, Lyndon."

"It was built over a weekend...delivered to the White House less than a week ago."

The President laughed. "Juanita says it's the ugliest thing she's ever seen, but it helps me to understand the geography. It's a good model but I wish I had a better feel for the area."

The President selected a nine iron. As he addressed the tee, Eisenhower pointed with his approach wedge to the eighteenth green, one hundred yards away.

"Wait a minute, my friend. There's a lake in the middle of the fairway, but the real hazard is another lake you can't see just behind the green."

The President's swing was smooth, his shot straight. The golf ball hit the green pin high and rolled toward the back edge.

Eisenhower laughed.

"I thought you were in the drink for sure."

Both golfers parred the hole and cleared the green. They ambled to the clubhouse. Johnson continued talking.

"General Maxwell Taylor is advising me, Ike. I would be negligent not to seek his advice. He questions whether the defense of Khe Sanh will translate into a victory for us. He says if it's feasible to withdraw from Khe Sanh, we should. It may be a liability now."

Sunshine glistened on the snow-capped peaks of Mount San Jacinto, high above the valley floor.

Lyndon Johnson turned to Dwight Eisenhower.

"Ike, I don't like this crap any more than you would, but we're at the apex of perhaps the deciding battle of the war. The future of South Vietnam and our involvement there hangs in the balance."

CHAPTER FORTY-ONE

STAIRWAY OF THE DRAGONS

After days of soaking rain and chilly temperatures, the skies over Hanoi on Monday morning, the nineteenth of February, were clearing up. The thinning clouds revealed patchworks of blue.

At seven o'clock, after a bowl of *pho*, which he had taken outside his two-story home at No. 30 Hoang Dieu Street, General Vo Nguyen Giap, North Vietnam's Minister of Defense, kissed his wife Ha goodbye and walked to work. He rounded the big French-built house with its closed shutters, and past a stone bench placed next to a tree in front of his spacious residence.

Giap dared the winter dreariness to go away. He wore his military uniform and hat, but no overcoat. He carried no umbrella.

Giap turned left from the circular driveway onto the sidewalk shaded by tall trees. He crossed the divided tree-lined boulevard and walked through a narrow stone-arch gate. Old cannons stood guard on either side of the entrance. Reaching his headquarters, General Giap threw his hat on his desk and turned a black knob on the wall. The ceiling fan would rid the room of its musty smell.

Vo Nguyen Giap had arranged for a special noon meeting. At about eleven-thirty, Giap returned to the main square of the ministry compound and waited beneath two magnificent muom trees. He would greet his guests at the foot of the ancient Cau Thang Cua Con Rong (Stairway of the Dragons).

The railings had been carved from marble into undulating serpents that guarded the entrance to the centuries-old Kính Thien Royal Palace, the most important venue in Thang Long, the third name given to the city in 1010, long before it was called Hanoi.

A few minutes before twelve, two Chinese limousines arrived in the courtyard. The *co do sao vang* flew from the front fenders of each vehicle.

Dressed smartly in their green uniforms, Generals Chu Huy Man, Tran Quy Hai and Van Tien Dung, stepped out of the lead vehicle.

Le Duc Tho, a senior ranking politburo member climbed out of the second limousine and stood with the three generals.

"Mr. Minister," Van Tien Dung said, as he saluted his boss. "This is the first time you've greeted us in person outside your office upon our arrival."

Giap laughed at the irony. Since he and General Dung worked in their separate offices not more than twenty meters apart, they would greet each other every day.

"Couldn't resist the bright sunshine. The first day in over two weeks with no rain. What's happened to the American war planes? No air raid sirens."

Giap gave each general hearty handshakes. "General Man and General Hai, I'm sorry to cause you to waste a beautiful day in Hanoi with this meeting, but I must."

He turned to face Le Duc Tho.

"Comrade Tho, thank you for your time."

Giap paused for a second. "Gentlemen, we have an urgent matter to discuss that concerns our efforts with the general offensive-general uprising in the south. Please follow me."

The group made their way to General Giap's headquarters. Each visitor took a seat around the large conference table in the main room.

Giap reached for a teapot and poured tea into the empty cups.

"General Hai, we are all relieved you survived the heavy American air strikes at Sar Lit."

"Thank you, Mr. Minister. I haven't experienced anything more terrifying. We were forced to hide in caves for days. The bombing was incessant."

"Please tell me," Giap continued, "I would like to know our condition in B5T8."

"Sir, as you know, since our success at Khe Sanh village and at Lang Vei, we have complete control of Highway Nine from Laos to the Ta Con area.

"Recent deployments have resulted in the Sixty-sixth Regiment replacing the 325C Division which moved out of the immediate theater on the tenth of February. We cannot discount use of superior weapons by the Americans. We must safeguard our assets.

"We have mobilized the 74th and 75th Anti-aircraft Battalions from Region Four. They're in place in B5T8."

Giap raised his hand.

"General Hai, you should know that the husband of Miss Ngan, my junior assistant, is in a Hanoi anti-aircraft unit sent to Quang Tri Province."

"I see...Anyway, we have maintained strong forces on the ground in the area. Communications are good, sometimes disrupted, but quickly repaired. We are receiving munitions and arms each day. Stockpiles are well concealed. The 675th Artillery Regiment, deployed at Co Roc, has engaged the enemy. We have 61, 82 and 120 millimeter mortars and 122mm rockets. We can adjust to changing situations quickly. The men's fighting spirit is at its highest."

Giap sipped his tea and eyed his field commander.

"Excellent, General Hai."

"Mr. Minister, I've brought something interesting from B5T8. These have become prolific since the middle of January."

A lieutenant carried a long pole in from a side door. Crooked tubes protruded perpendicularly from the shaft.

Giap smiled in surprise.

"What's that thing?"

"Comrade Minister, an electronic sensor. It sends out signals when it detects movement. It's made to look like a plant or small tree, Sir, to blend in with the foliage. The Americans drop these devices from the air. The steel tip buries itself in the earth with the stem and imitation branches above ground. We can hear them clearly when they crash through the jungle. We send out patrols to destroy them. The Americans also drop special bomblets to thwart our retrieval efforts."

Giap picked up the strange, elongated pole that resembled a leafless plant with bare, twisted limbs. It wasn't heavy, but it certainly wasn't light.

"Those Americans are very clever with their technology. How do they think of these things?"

Giap laughed. "You recall the flat bomb the Americans dropped in the Song Ma in 1966, upstream of Thanh Hoa. The bomb was supposed to float down river. When a sensor detected the metal of the Ham Rong Bridge, the bomb would blow the bridge up, but it never worked."

Giap addressed Chu Huy Man, an accomplished and well-respected military professional.

"Do you have anything to add, General Man, anything from your perspective, from B-4 Front?"

"Mr. Minister, I'm sure Comrade General Hai has stated the relevant facts attendant to the Khe Sanh-Highway Nine Front accurately."

Vo Nguyen Giap interrupted.

"Northern Quang Tri Province is vital to our winter-spring offensive."

"I understand, Mr. Minister. Sixty thousand men currently under arms in B5T8 should be sufficient. However, contingency planning is mandatory. We are prepared to support General Hai as may be required."

General Giap adjusted his reading glasses. He turned toward Van Tien Dung.

"General Dung, as Chief of Staff, do you have any comment?"

"General Giap, Mr. Minister, aside from the victories at Huong Hoa and Lang Vei, fighting continues in Hue with some difficulty. Additionally, attacks in the lesser provincial capitals have been disruptive. The people's revolt is expected and we…"

"Gentlemen!"

Giap pointed impatiently to the gadget that General Hai had just shown. "These electronic devices will not be a factor.

"The Americans have mobility but only with their helicopters. However, they cannot respond quickly. We will move against the enemy with lightning speed. We will overwhelm the base before they stop us."

A surprised look crossed the face of each of Giap's guests. Le Duc Tho raised his eyebrows.

Move against the enemy? Lightning speed? Overwhelm the base? What is General Giap talking about? Was this to be a demonstration against the Americans at Ta Con? In the context of the departure of the 325C Division, something didn't add up.

General Van Tien Dung spoke.

"General Giap, are we making plans to attack Khe Sanh?"

Vo Nguyen Giap, remembering his conversations with Ho Chi Minh in Beijing, and more recently, with Pham Van Dong, turned to Van Tien Dung.

"General Dung, you say the general uprising is expected. I maintain there will be no uprising in the south unless the population sees visible signs of a significant, focused military action favorable to us."

The group of highly ranked officers—the very core of the North Vietnamese Army—fell completely quiet. They sipped tea, smoked their cigarettes and ate some orange slices.

General Giap put his teacup down.

"Time is no longer on our side. We must enhance pressure on the Americans in Quang Tri Province."

Giap's guests looked at each other with reservation. Enhance pressure?

"But General, the politburo…"

"Comrade Tho, you are a senior member of the politburo, hence an important participant in this meeting."

Giap walked to a cloth that was draped over what appeared to be a wall hanging.

"I understand President Johnson has a model of Quang Tri Province. Well...," Giap laughed, "I only have this."

Giap removed the cloth to reveal a large map with broad and narrow lines and arrows in various colors with coded numbers and marks. He picked up a wood pointer. "I'm not going to dwell on the tactical details. I want you to know the overall strategy. We will cut off the high points around Khe Sanh, here and here."

Giap pointed to hills located northwest of the Marine base. "This reduces the Marines' fighting strength by about a thousand men."

General Van Tien Dung looked on blankly. Has Giap gone mad?

Giap moved his pointer down the map.

"As for Ta Con, we have nothing of significance on the north side of the base. We will not attack from the northern ravine. The Americans will not know that. They will continue to protect the ravine while denying those resources from defending our other attack points. We will attack from the village and the highway and interdict the base at about here."

Giap tapped the map. "Since Khe Sanh town is in our hands, the thrust will be directed from there. We can move swiftly to the base, invest and neutralize it. We will come from the east and attack straight at the first line of defense, the thirty-seventh ARVN puppets."

Tran Quy Hai, surprised by Giap's revelations, said, "Comrade Minister, a stream at the bottom of the ravine that you mentioned is the primary water source for the Americans. We should destroy their dam or poison the stream. The Americans will not have sufficient water. They'll have no option but to depart the area. Then we would control it."

"Yes, the Americans may leave Khe Sanh," Giap responded, "but they won't leave the Fatherland. Since they won't leave Vietnam, we will annihilate them where they are. The water source will remain unbothered."

Giap set the pointer aside. He removed his glasses and held them in his right hand. "Oh, I forgot. There are two small highpoints that we must also isolate. Highpoint 558—Second Battalion Twenty-sixth Marines—and another redoubt manned by First Battalion Ninth Marines."

General Chu Huy Man, his mouth full of rice cake, spoke.

"Mr. Minister, the battle of Dien Bien Phu affected less than ten percent of the entire French Union force in Vietnam."

"This is true, General Man, but the French were not able to mount a counterattack. They surrendered."

The meeting adjourned. The limousines lined up in the courtyard.

Giap shook each general's hand and, from the top of the stone steps framed by the marble dragons, watched as the three generals were driven off toward the narrow arch gateway.

A second limousine pulled into place. Vo Nguyen Giap and Le Duc Tho descended the stairs.

Le Duc Tho stood pensively while he lit a cigarette. He offered one to Vo Nguyen Giap who politely refused.

"Giap, the old proverb says, 'Even an old turtle has secrets to share.'"

Le Duc Tho inhaled on his cigarette. "Is Khe Sanh that important to us?"

"The Americans think they understand us, Tho. They think they comprehend the situation in Quang Tri Province, but they don't. Their ignorance will be their downfall."

"Giap, there has been controversy about whether to attack Khe Sanh. The point I believe General Man tried to make about the French at Dien Bien Phu was the Americans can and will counterattack. They'll have nothing to lose."

"Comrade Tho, I have been in contact with Chairman Ho by phone and Prime Minister Pham Van Dong. We will give orders for a massive artillery barrage to take place on the twenty-third of February with subsequent probing attacks. On the twenty-ninth, we will attack the lines at the east end of the runway."

Both men eyed each other with slight reservation.

"Giap, we may cause the Americans some damage, but can we defeat them? You and I both know the consequences if we fail."

General Giap rummaged his hand in his pocket. Agitated, he walked over to one of the carved dragons guarding the staircase and leaned against the dragon's stone head.

Le Duc Tho continued.

"Giap, I question whether this fight is to our advantage. Is it a sound strategy? We may have Khe Sanh in our possession, but we will not have *Nam Viet* [South Vietnam]."

Giap reflected for a moment.

"You are aware of the confrontation I had with Le Duan. He makes sweeping decisions based on ego without understanding the implications, or the psychology of our adversary. General Van Tien Dung, my own Chief of Staff, and others have gone to camp and are blind to the reality facing us. The late Nguyen Chi Thanh, too obnoxious for his own good, instilled expectations that cannot be realized."

"Mr. Minister, you are cognizant of the provisions of Resolution Fourteen. Your plan for Khe Sanh is a unilateral deviation from it."

Giap's voice became more pointed.

"Comrade Tho. I didn't agree with all the components of Resolution

Fourteen. Its provisions fall short. The general offensive is not producing results or the insurrection we need. We must first have success on the battlefield. Quang Tri Province is that battlefield.

"We must carry out a plan to annihilate a significant portion of the enemy's manpower. We have no option but to kill as many imperialists as we can. We must poke a stick in the eye of the Americans and make it obvious they will pay dearly. We live by our motto, *'Quyet Thang'* [Determination to Win].

"We will have to make sacrifices like we have many times before, but we need a victory irrespective of definition. Khe Sanh is that victory."

Le Duc Tho stared at the defense minister with some concern. Giap was bordering on insubordination.

"Mr. Tho," Giap continued, "American public opinion, through their own news media, will turn against President Johnson's military adventure in Vietnam. The pressure for American forces to withdraw will be too great in the face of a military calamity.

"We will bewilder the Americans and demoralize the puppet regime. Only at that point will the southern populace revolt. The protracted war that I still support will gain strength through the population, but we need to show positive results now."

"Mr. Defense Minister, I am aware of the comparisons between Khe Sanh and Dien Bien Phu. I recall your paper 'The Big Victory, The Great Task.'"

Le Duc Tho inhaled the last of his cigarette and tossed it to the pavement. "Giap, Khe Sanh may be your great task, but it may not be your big victory."

CHAPTER FORTY-TWO

FLATLANDER

"Know what the best thing about Texas is, John?"

Everyone stopped talking to hear the President.

"You can ride on horseback all month and never leave the state."

Lady Bird smiled at her husband.

"Lyndon, you don't have to tell us how proud you are to be a Texan."

Texas Senator John Tower and his wife, had just finished an informal Sunday brunch with the President and First Lady in the dining room of the White House residential quarters.

"I like Texas, too, Lyndon. I'd better. I'm a Texas senator just like you were, albeit a Republican."

"Why, John, you pretended to be a Democrat. There's still hope for you."

President Johnson didn't interact with Senator Tower that much, but he got along with him well enough. Inviting the Towers to a brunch at the White House seemed a courteous thing to do. After all, they were from the same state.

Lady Bird looked at her guests.

"Coffee?"

John Tower, the first Texas Republican senator since before time and a onetime competitor of Johnson's, recognized brunch for what it was: a token of a casual friendship. He turned to the First Lady.

"I'll have some coffee, Lady Bird. Thank you."

Lady Bird poured coffee into the senator's cup.

"John," Lady Bird smiled back at the President. "If Lyndon can't see the horizon or a sunrise in the distance, he gets irritable, even claustrophobic. He needs the open spaces of the west."

"Just Texas, honey, that's all I need," the President responded. "I remember once I drove from Stonewall to Uvalde. My God, the sky extended forever. Down on the Rio Grande, the sun beat down on us something fierce. I left home once. Went to California, took odd jobs, even operated an elevator—but I missed the openness of Texas."

The conversation fell idle. Senator Tower tried to find a common topic other than politics, but of course the commonality beyond Texas was the very subject he wanted to avoid, but couldn't.

"Mr. President, I must say, your state of the union address several weeks ago was well prepared. I listened very closely to what you said about Vietnam."

"Thanks, John. We worked hard on that address, making corrections up to the last minute. Lady Bird helped me a lot. I think the message was clear to everyone."

"Indeed, but Lyndon, were you not being too optimistic? I mean, the great society and all that. Where's the money going to come from? And, Capitol Hill is not very comfortable with war being waged without congressional approval, irrespective of the Gulf of Tonkin Resolution.

"The Republicans are pulling out all their guns to defeat you in the next election. Plus, certain sentiments within your own party do not favor you."

John Tower had pushed the limit. The table atmosphere became a little uneasy.

"John, I still think of my students when I first taught in that one story, red brick school building in Cotulla. That school was small, but looking back, it seemed big. God, those students were poor. I want to see that reversed. I want our Great Society programs to succeed right here in the USA. The money, this war...well, we'll just have to figure something out."

"Say, Mr. President—I almost forgot—*Time* magazine "Man of the Year," in early January. Twice now."

John Tower averted the awkwardness. "I've been intending to congratulate you."

Lady Bird, relieved the conversation had shied away from controversial topics, interjected.

"Well, it struck me as a back-handed honor. The drawing of Lyndon on the cover, well...my God, it was hideous. The artist made Lyndon look like a disheveled, decrepit man, a dreadful caricature. They called him a McCaw-beaked, jug-eared character. The collection of cartoons and the title, "LBJ As Lear," well, none of it pleased me. I know *King Lear* is Shakespeare's great tragedy, but the comparison left me cold. If it was supposed to be humorous...well, it wasn't. It was hurtful."

"Ah, Lady Bird, don't worry about those news magazines."

Lyndon forced a smile.

"John, I really don't care what they call me. If some congressman, say, from Colorado, calls me a Flatlander, so be it. I've been called worse names. My friends in college in San Marcos called me Rattling Bones or some such name. Kennedy called me Uncle Corn Pone. People in that square state can go ahead and call me a Flatlander all they want. I don't give a crap. Colorado is a great state with great people, but they ain't got good barbecue."

The President laughed at his out-of-nowhere statement—there being no connection between Colorado and Texas barbecue or *Time's* "Man of The Year."

Senator Tower and his wife nodded their amusement as the senator sipped his coffee and she, the last of her champagne. Tower tried to contribute to the conversation in an sociable way.

"Lyndon, I recall your story about your shot at a wild pig when you went hunting a few years back. Whadja use? A Winchester 94, wasn't it? The gun that won the West—a 30-30? The bullet hit the ground way in front of the pig, skipped up and flew right over its head. *Pssung.* You could hear the ricochet."

Lady Bird smiled.

"I think Lyndon used the magnum that day."

"Yeah, I sure scared the shinola out of that critter."

The President placed his napkin on the table. “The ranch is wonderful. We ride horses to the rise and have a picnic beneath the trees overlooking the Perd’naliss. We can hear the cattle at the cattle tanks. That’s the name the hands give the watering ponds. When the sun sets, the entire horizon is on fire.”

Lady Bird tried to include Mrs. Tower.

“Tell me, Lou, have you seen the latest show at the Portrait Gallery? I hear the exhibit is outstanding and…”

“John...”

The President changed the topic. “They built a model of Khe Sanh for me. I have it in the Situation Room. Wanna see it?”

“I’ve heard about that, Lyndon.”

“They did an expert job on it. Lots of colors and shading. It’s better than two dimensional maps. Quite unbelievable, really.

“But. I just don’t understand. If the Marines are fighting the North Viet-nese on this so-called Hill 881, why can’t the Marines…”

“Viet-na-mese, honey. Not Viet-nese,” Lady Bird corrected the President.

“Whatever, Lady Bird. Why can’t the Marines from the combat base go up there? Damnation, John, it’s only this far on the model.”

The President emphasized his point by holding up his hand to indicate the distance by the gap between his crooked index finger and the tip of his thumb.

“Shit, my ranch is bigger than that.”

Lady Bird looked disapprovingly at her husband.

“Honey, please, not while we have guests.”

Both men chuckled at the President’s indiscretions. Johnson continued.

“It doesn’t show all the complications, but I look at the model all the time.”

“Tell me about it, honey.”

Lady Bird spoke wryly. “You’d think it was a model of Gillespie County.”

The First Lady, raising her coffee cup to her mouth, looked at her guests. “Sometimes he goes down to look at it after midnight.”

“Well, Lady Bird...”

The President turned back to Tower. “And the jargon of the cables, my

God. Coordinates, zones and how to relate them to the maps, acronyms, and engagements…I'm inundated in data. It's confusing. The finer points of photo reconnaissance and interpretation and, you know, how to make sense of what is going on from such a remote vantage point…well, quite frankly, are lost on me. I drove a bulldozer when I was a young man. The state constructed the road on the other side of the Perd'naliss from the ranch—I think they paid me a dollar a day. But, I'm no engineer."

The President was beginning to ramble, even to repeat himself.

"Mr. President and First Lady, we thank you for a delightful brunch. You've been gracious hosts. Lou and I don't want to intrude on the rest of your day. I believe you have a reception later this evening. We should say goodbye for now."

CHAPTER FORTY-THREE

BOB ARROTTA AND THE SKYRAIDER

Not easily accessed, Hill 881 South, rising eight hundred eighty-one meters above sea level, played no historic role at any time in its geologic past. Notable only by the three digits that referenced its height, inhabitants regarded it as just another hill in the remote Khe Sanh area.

While there were many knolls, hillocks and mounts, two hills of equal height, Hill 881 South and, two kilometers away, Hill 881 North, became most important in 1967.

By March of that year, the NVA, 325C Division occupied the hills. To counter, the Second Battalion, Ninth Marines moved into the area.

Echo Company Second Battalion found itself in a furious firefight near Hill 861, another giant mound three kilometers east of 881. At that time, U.S. forces lacked sufficient helicopter support to mount mobile maneuvers. Instead, they relied on armed patrols as a way to dislodge the enemy.

On 24 April 1967, two platoons of Bravo Company First Battalion Ninth Marines became engaged with NVA forces around Hill 861 and triggered an offensive intended to overrun Khe Sanh. What came to be known as the Hill Fights began.

In late April, with infantry and artillery assets in place, the Third Marines were sent forward to force the NVA off the hills.

While Hill 861 became the Marines' number one objective, Hill 881 South and Hill 881 North were the second and third objectives.

On the twenty-eighth of April 1967, the enemy, decimated by artillery and air strikes, had been beaten from Hill 861 by Second Battalion. Hill 881 South would not be so easy. But, on the second of May, after bitter fighting, Third Battalion conquered that summit. A few days later Hill 881 North was secured by Second Battalion. The mountains were firmly in American hands.

The NVA 325C Division, so badly beaten by the Marines, withdrew toward Laos. The Hill Fights came to an end. The immediate threat to the Khe Sanh Combat Base subsided.

By mid-May, operational control of the Khe Sanh area passed to the Twenty-sixth Marines. Alpha Company First Battalion occupied Hill 881 South. Fighting around the area continued. By mid-December 1967, Colonel David Lownds, who replaced Colonel John Padley as commanding officer, sent India Company Third Battalion Twenty-sixth Marines and three 105mm howitzers from Charlie Battery First Battalion Thirteenth Marines to the top of Hill 881 South. India Company and half of Charlie Battery, under the command of Captain William H. Dabney, would not fail in the defense of their position.

To snub their noses at the NVA, "To the Colors" sounded wailfully across the hills each morning. The Marine bugler could not have known that the solitary music he played on his tarnished bugle and the hill from where the sound came, would forever become part of Marines Corps lore. The NVA responded with a rain of mortar shells.

On 10 November 1967, the birthday of the United States Marine Corps, Colonel Lownds paid a visit to India Company on Hill 881 South. He told his Marines in a chilling, matter-of-fact way they would soon be in the history books.

Hill 881 South, a small section of the Truong Son Range, had emerged from millions of years of obscure geo-morphology to military importance.

Now, Corporal Bob Arrotta peered out from his position on Hill 881 South. His keen eyes scanned the broad valleys and far ridgelines. The beauty of the area conjured up memories of the green hills of western Maryland, especially around South Mountain where he and his family from Bethesda would visit.

In Vietnam, in Quang Tri Province, and specifically on Hill 881 South—beautiful, but, in this case hostile—far removed from the peacefulness of the mountains of western Maryland, Bob Arrotta and his Marine brothers fought for their lives.

The elongated summit of Hill 881 South, the only defensible location, offered a tidy target for the NVA. Although India Company did not receive many rounds from the smaller caliber mortars, the preponderance of shelling from heavy NVA artillery made the Marines' lives miserable. The enemy took advantage of a horseshoe area to the southwest where they positioned heavy 120mm mortars.

Gritty faced, his body and ripped military clothes reeking from weeks of continuous dirt, and salty sweat, Arrotta stood vigilant in his trench. His beard and thick hair were covered with dust and mud. The dust caked in the corners of his eyes, encrusted the hollows of his ears and invaded his nostrils. Sweat from his scalp continuously slid down his face beneath his beard turning the dust into small rivulets that oozed down his neck.

Arrotta removed his helmet and ran his filthy hands through his dirty hair. His bloodshot eyes, dry as desert sand, were scratchy.

Arrotta unscrewed the cap on his canteen, tilted his head back and poured a few drops of water onto his closed eyelids. He massaged his eyes lightly with his fingers to re-invigorate them.

The PRC41 radio began squawking.

"Dunbar County India One Four, Dunbar County India One Four."

Arrotta quickly replaced his helmet on his head and grabbed the receiver.

"India One Four."

"India One Four, Cherry Bomb Flight Lead. Three A-1s with jelly, one five klicks east, heading two eight zero at zero niner thousand feet. Inbound your site."

"Roger, Cherry Bomb Lead. Continue inbound. Stand by for mission."

"Cherry Bomb Lead standing by."

Bob Arrotta identified a target.

"Lead, I have movement of November Victor Alpha in a deep valley three hundred meters due west of eight eighty-one. Best if you strike north to south. There will be a small ridgeline to your left as you enter the valley. Two and Three, circle at niner thousand for additional targets."

"Roger that, India One Four. Two and Three circling."

"On the smoke, Cherry Bomb Lead," Arrotta said.

A mortar round marked the target.

"Roger smoke."

Arrotta made one last transmission to the Skyraider pilot.

"Cherry Bomb Lead, cleared hot."

Bob Arrotta watched as the lead plane of the flight of three single-seat Skyraiders—commonly known as Sandys—began its dive.

The A-1, soon hidden below the ridgeline, struck the target with napalm. The narrow valley turned into a broiling conflagration of angry red flames and greasy, pitch-black smoke that destroyed North Vietnamese troops positioned for attack.

The pilot pushed the throttle forward and pulled his plane up into a steep banking climb. The A-1 emerged from the destruction it caused in the jungle crevice.

The pilot of the A-1 worked hand-in-hand with Bob Arrotta, who, by default, found himself a warrior goliath, dubbed the "mightiest corporal"—the famous forward air controller known unmistakably on the radio as India One Four.

Arrotta, speaking clearly into his radio with smooth confidence, controlled the sky above him and to a large extent the ground beneath it. Even though the enemy would never see him, he was their worst nightmare.

"India One Four, I see multiple NVA in the open below strike zone. Returning for second pass."

"Roger, Cherry Bomb Lead. Two and Three, descend to seven thousand. Targets in zero one minute."

The pilot of the lead A-1 banked his giant Skyraider hard right. Its silhouette was easily discerned from the ground. The Korean war-vintage aircraft, having completed its turn, now on an opposite heading, drew closer. The plane's radial engine, tandem banks of nine-cylinders each, beat out its incessant, blunted noise as the four-blade propeller chopped through the air. The thunderous noise increased as the distance lessened. The pilot swooped low. The plane's shadow skipped across the landscape.

The Skyraider, descended into the valley. Now, just above the sloping ground, but concealed by the hills, the A-1 bore down on the open clearing.

Intense gunfire erupted from the surrounding crest lines. The unmistakable sound of dual 14.5 millimeter machine guns reverberated throughout the area.

The A-1 reappeared from behind a smaller hill farther away to make another pass with its liquid-gel, fire-making ordnance suspended in canisters from its large, square wings. The whooshed explosion of napalm behind it sent flames and smoke high above the valley, again causing an inferno that consumed the vegetation of the jungle and its menacing inhabitants. No one could have survived the napalm attacks.

Its ordnance expended, the lead A-1 Skyraider departed the immediate area to circle elsewhere. The other two A-1s in the flight continued covering the scene, waiting for their turn. Arrotta guided them through the rugged terrain to their targets.

The flat maps represented the area only by contour lines and shades of color. They did not reveal just how complicated the land could be. No one in Da Nang, Saigon, or Washington, D.C. could comprehend the ruggedness of the landscape as intimately as could Bob Arrotta. He had developed an uncanny feel for the terrain. His maps didn't reveal what Arrotta's eyes could see or what his senses told him. Arrotta knew the enemy, but more importantly, he knew how to kill him.

India Company meant more to Bob Arrotta than his own life. These guys give their best and deserve the best he can offer. He would use anything and everything to protect India Company.

Bob Arrotta was a Marine, but perhaps more an artist—his palette, the landscape around Hill 881 South that concealed the threat; his brush, the air power he could unleash to destroy it.

CHAPTER FORTY-FOUR

THE FOX

President Johnson sipped his coffee from a gold-rimmed cup in the Oval Office while he dashed off a quick memo. Walt Rostow, sitting on the other side of the President's desk, his notebook leaning against the leg of the chair, thumbed through a folder of documents. Other folders were spread on the carpet around him.

The Khe Sanh Terrain Model sat on a portable table a few feet away. Not pleased when the President asked to have the model brought up from the Situation Room, Juanita Roberts was sure it would end up in her office.

Walt Rostow tapped his pen on a folder.

"Mr. President..."

He held up a three page report stapled in the upper left corner. "The NVA are tightening the noose around the combat base."

"Let me see the report, Walt. I can't believe we can't stop those bastards."

"Here, Mr. President; page two, Sir. I was going to submit it to you under memo with a thorough analysis."

President Johnson leaned across his desk and took the report from Walt Rostow. He looked through it quickly.

"Holy mackerel, sixty thousand NVA sonzabitches against...how many Marines do we have at the base now...six thousand or so?"

"About that, Sir...at the base and on the hills. Westmoreland has more soldiers in reserve."

The President took off his glasses.

"But, what about the NVA? Surely they have reserves."

"Well, I would suppose they..."

"Who's the commanding officer at Khe Sanh, again...a Marine general?"

"Lownds, Sir. David E. Lownds. He's a colonel, Sir, not a general. He assumed command last year, in mid-August."

"Then, what the hell does Colonel Lownds say about Khe Sanh? It's his ass that's hanging out, not Westmoreland's."

"Mr. President, there's been some pressure to remove Lownds, but..."

"Dammit, what does Lownds think?"

"To quote Colonel Lownds, he says Hell no, I'm not worried. I have the Marines on my side."

The President laughed loudly.

"A Marine is a man you have to hold back, not shove."

The President studied the maps and photographs that Rostow had laid in front of him.

"Isn't Lownds the guy with the mustache, who smokes cigars?"

"Correct, Mr. President. They call him the Lion of Khe Sanh."

"Well, by God, I'm gonna buy the Lion of Khe Sanh a box of cigars. He's gonna have one hell of a fight on his hands."

The President adjusted his glasses. "What're the North Viet-nese waitin' fer? Santa Anna didn't wait for shit. He marched his soldiers across the Rio Grande and east from Dell Rio somewhere—I dunno where—through Knippa, I suppose, straight to San Antonio. He took the Alamo within ten days. The actual attack lasted less than three hours. Slaughtered every one of the defenders—Bowie, Dickinson, Travis, Crocket. The whole lot."

"Sir, Westmoreland says it's only a matter of days before the NVA attack. He feels the trap is set."

President Johnson stood from his desk. He walked to the trio of doors that led to the Rose Garden. A cardinal had landed on the ground. Spring was surely near. Johnson scratched the back of his head.

"Rostow..."

"Sir."

"Ever try to catch a fox?"

"Sir?"

The President turned to face Rostow.

"Just 'bout the time you think you got 'em by the..." the President clinched his right hand into a fist, "they're gone." The President smiled. "Clever little bastards. Wily as hell."

"No. Mr. President, never tried, Sir."

"Walt, when I was a boy in the Hill Country..."

Walt Rostow had a sense of what was coming.

"Oh, I guess I was about ten or so at that time. We had moved about six years before from Gillespie County where I was born, you know, west of Hye…just a small cross-roads town."

"Mr. President, your birthplace is through the grove of oak trees, past the pecan orchard from the Texas White House on the Pe-der-nal-es River."

Rostow made sure he pronounced the name of the river like it was spelled.

"Perd'naliss, Walt. We say Perd'naliss down there."

Walt Rostow nodded his understanding.

"I've even drawn water from that old iron pump on the back porch, Sir."

"That's right. You know the place. It could get damn cold in that little house in winter."

Walt Rostow didn't comment.

"Anyway, like I was saying, we moved east into Blanco County, to Johnson City. Walt, this ain't Houston I'm talkin' about. I was without shoes most of the time."

The President's eyes shifted outside again to the Rose Garden. The cardinal had flown off. The President walked back to his desk.

"I used to see a fox almost every day. I first saw him right in the city limits loping along the edge of Town Creek, not far from our home on Elm Street. He ran behind the cotton gin; a building of corrugated metal—not a big building, but big for Johnson City. He'd cut across the highway right in front of Withers and Spaulding's General Store."

The President became more animated by a story that he embellished with each telling. "He'd run up Pecan Avenue right past the Johnson-family cemetery plot …you know, with a small fence around it. He'd stop next to a big tree and the headstone of James Polk Johnson's grave. He'd look around, then run right into the center of town, past the bank, the hotel and some shops as if he owned the place, and cut across Nugent Street. He'd dash right smack-damn across the lawn of the Blanco County Courthouse. That fox wasn't scared of nothing. He could sure run, too, I'm tellin' ya. I followed him all the way to the Perd'naliss many times. I watched him cross the river and head up toward Marble Falls, but he didn't go that far. He stayed around.

"One day, I was with my papa and some folks who came from Blanco town, not far away. We were cuttin' wood in the hills just south. You know, not really big hills."

The President held his hand out flat. "Now, I'll grant you, there're some good-size trees up there, but no real timber. You could see the entire Perd'naliss valley and smoke coming out of chimneys in town. You could even hear the mill running and the blacksmith's hammer clanging away.

"We were stacking wood on the bed of a wagon. I happened to look up and there he was. That damned fox was just staring at me. I swear, he followed me all the way up those hills. We eyed each other for, oh, I dunno, ten minutes, or so. I saw him yawn, scratch his face with his paw…then he just ran off."

The President clasped his hands together in front of him and quickly slid one in front of the other to indicate a quick motion. "Somebody pulled out a rifle but never got a shot off. They'd never have hit him. He was too fast. I followed the fox down a draw but lost him. He sure knew his way around. That fox made Blanco County his home. I saw him more and more. He was paying attention to my movements as much as I was paying attention to his. Damndest thing."

"Mr. President, Sir…"

"Hang on Walt, the story gets better. That fox taunted me every day. We have foxes, coyotes and bobcats in the Hill Country. But that fox was the smartest of them all. He had the prettiest reddish-brown coat and the bushiest red tail.

"I was lying in bed one night, the windows were open—man, it was hot as hell. I decided I was gonna nab that fox. I started settin' traps. I set one near Town Creek, I set one near my family's little cemetery in town—the one I just mentioned, you know, with James Polk—and I set one near the much larger Masonic cemetery north of town. Never caught him. But, I never gave up trying, either. One day, I set a trap with a lot of chicken meat and some broken eggs nearer to the Perd'naliss—you know, that was a bit of a walk from my home—I thought maybe the fox would feel more comfortable outside of town. He hung around there a lot. Next morning before dawn, I got up and woke my brother Sam and Lucia, one of my sisters."

The President laughed at the irony. "She was only about four. Dad always told us that if we didn't get out of bed early in the morning, we'd never catch up with the other folk. 'Come on, Lucia,' I'd say. 'Let's go see if we caught that fox.' We jumped out of bed, got dressed, climbed out the window and ran through town to the river. We arrived at the site of the trap completely out of breath.

"Well, let me tell you, the trap was sprung, but guess what? No fox to be seen. Not even the hair of the fox. And all the bait was gone. Intelligent damned critter. Later, I saw him runnin' through town. Rostow, I swear, that fox was laughing at me. He thought it was a game."

Lyndon Johnson enjoyed telling this story. It's not that he was living in the past—well he was, of course—but really, he was just talking about a youth's discovery of the world around him.

To the core, Lyndon Johnson, as well as Lady Bird, were genuine, easy-going Texans. This was a far-cry from Rostow's Jewish, New York City upbringing and the cultured life he had experienced.

"Mr. President…"

"Damn, Rostow," the President's tone changed, "with sixty thousand NVA pissants, they could destroy Khe Sanh like a twister in Amarillo, carve that base up faster than a hot knife through butter."

"Sir, we're pounding them daily with air strikes. The aerial photos show nothing but scorched, pockmarked earth around the base. Look at this aerial photo, Sir. See the lines of bomb craters? Straight as an arrow, crater after crater, Sir."

Walt Rostow stood up to point to the lines of bomb craters on the photo. He ran his index finger across the photo tracing one of the lines.

"My God," the President exclaimed, "the bomb lines crisscross and cross again."

Stunned by the extent of devastation, the President correlated what he saw on the photo to the same area on the model that depicted lush-green landscape.

"Walt, they should have inserted some bomb craters on the model...made it more realistic."

Walt Rostow didn't respond.

"So, tell me, Walt, how can anything survive? How can they still have so many troops? I know there's a lot of territory out there around the Marine base, but the NVA have to be holed up somewhere."

"Mr. President, nuclear artillery shells would solve the problem."

Momentarily tripped up, President Johnson pondered what he had just heard.

"Now, you listen to me, Rostow. I don't wanna hear that crap. We ain't gonna do it. I want all such talk stopped toot-sweet."

Rostow could just visualize the President's pronunciation of the French expression *tout de suite*, meaning immediately, and smiled to himself.

"I understand, Mr. President. I was just making the comment, that's all, Sir."

The President realized Rostow's comment was off the cuff and eased off on his cutting tone.

"These photos...the terrain, even on the model, looks flat to me. Is the terrain as rugged as they say, Walt?"

"Sir, you can see from the model, the immediate area around the base is relatively flat. There's a steep drop-off to the north to a ravine and to the east toward Highway Nine and the Quang Tri River Valley. But to the west and a little bit south, the area is pretty flat. Farther away, the hills are very steep. The enemy is completely dug in throughout the area. I don't think our patrols venture far from base now."

"And the road to Khe Sanh?"

"Completely cut off, Sir, bridges destroyed."

"Our artillery can't return fire?"

"Sir, not exactly. We have 105mm and 155mm artillery stationed on the combat base to return incoming enemy fire. But they cannot return fire effectively against the NVA guns positioned at Co Roc or at another place called 305. The NVA artillery are too far away, Sir. The base artillery supports the hill encampments. And then, we have some 105s on Hill 881 South. In addition, Khe Sanh is supported by long range artillery at Camp Carroll...and at a place called Rockpile...here...and here."

Walt Rostow pointed at the locations on the map and continued. "The longest-range artillery piece we have, the Army's M-107, a 175mm gun, falls short of Co Roc from where the bulk of the NVA artillery fire is coming. It can fire a one hundred fifty pound projectile about thirty-two kilometers but it still falls short of Co Roc."

"So, move a few 175s to Khe Sanh. Shoot back at the little pissants."

"Mr. President, last July, we tried to move a few 175s to Khe Sanh from Camp Carroll. The 175s are not towed, Sir. They're too big. They move on their own tracks, under their own power, but they can't move fast. The big guns never made it. They came under attack."

"How far along the road did they get?"

"I believe to Ca Lu, Sir…or just beyond."

Rostow gestured toward the terrain model. "We'll never move those guns to the combat base without a major fight."

President Johnson looked at the model.

"The Twenty-sixth Marines are facing bad odds, Walt. Tell me honestly what you think."

For the first time during that morning session, the Oval Office fell completely quiet. President Johnson seized the advantage as if he was anticipating it. He leaned forward over the desk. The Johnson treatment was about to rear its ugly head.

Lyndon Johnson moved his face close to Walt Rostow's, breathing into his mouth. The President stared unblinking straight into the eyes of his security advisor, burning holes through his glasses into the back of his skull.

"Answer me, Rostow. What do you think?"

"Well, Sir, I think Khe Sanh…"

The President jabbed his security advisor's chest with his index finger.

"Rostow! Dammit. Westmoreland keeps saying he's going to use the Marines at Khe Sanh to draw the enemy out, you know…like bait. You said it. He's settin' a trap."

"Mr. President, we think Giap will attack…"

Walt, what if the NVA don't fall for the bait?"

"Sir, it seems…"

The President raised his eyebrows. He looked straight at Walt Rostow.

"Walt, what if they're as smart as that damned fox?"

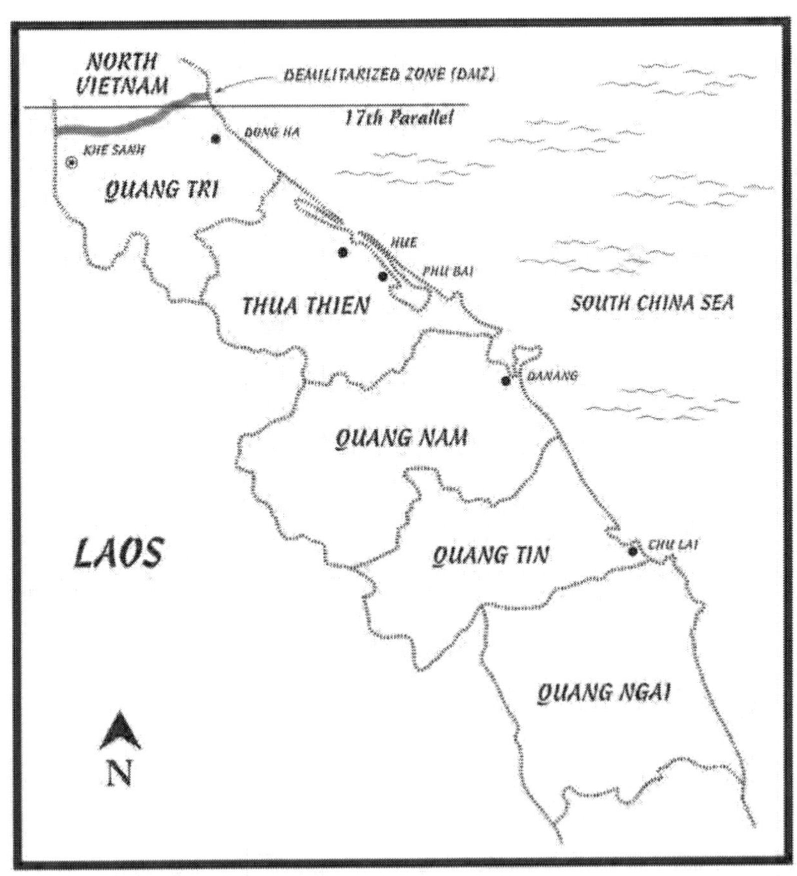

I CORPS TACTICAL ZONE (EYE CORPS)
FIVE NORTHERN PROVINCES IN SOUTH VIETNAM

CHAPTER FORTY-FIVE

PLAYMATE

"Look at that dynamite body. I've never seen such curves. Sweet Jesus, that's one gorgeous chick."

Entertainment for men, or certainly what the cover promised, surreptitiously arrived at the Khe Sanh Combat Base in February in the form of the January 1968 edition of *Playboy*.

Undeterred by the current, yet indifferent shelling from the North Vietnamese, the salacious, for-men-only monthly publication made its way around the combat base, into the hands of young men overburdened with high-octane testosterone. Deprived of living, breathing female company, sweet fragrances, soft hair, or anything even remotely sensuous, the inhabitants of Khe Sanh were suffering from an understandable loneliness. Their plight would be at once appeased and exacerbated by such enticing fantasy images offered up by Hugh Hefner.

The occupant of the Playboy Mansion made a fortune satisfying, if not preying on, the vicarious needs of young men. No one cared. They were gonna look. An unspoken public demand, albeit male, was being commercially fulfilled at a sales price of not much more than a dollar per copy.

By the time the magazine fell into the possession of an unshaven Corporal Mark Russell and his comrades in their below-ground hootch, the binding was in tatters, the pages dog-eared and torn. The purple cover sported the smug, iconic *Playboy* bunny surrounded by photographs of four very fetching young women.

No red-blooded American male really cared about the cover. The real attraction lay within. Straight to the centerfold of the Playmate of the Month which surprisingly, had not been removed.

Mark Russell, having grabbed the magazine out of his fellow Marines' hands, turned it on its side. He saw the pages cascade down as they unfolded to reveal the forbidden feminine delicacies every man desires. There, for his eyes to feast, sat a partially covered, perfectly shaped, very young female body; stunning beyond belief.

"My God! Look at this woman."

NVA shelling continued. Debris flew in all directions from the explosions.

Russell and his buddies, oblivious to the hazard above, gained a glimpse of the young, blond-haired, soft-eyed woman who stared straight into the camera, immediately into her admirers' eyes. The youthful perfection of her form was partially concealed by a black, see-through negligee draped enticingly across one shoulder. The January Playmate was proof of God's desire, or at least that as contrived by Hugh Hefner, for all men to be happy. She was the manifestation of this destiny and the modern-day fulfillment of any man's erotic fantasy.

Deep in their dugout, the inhabitants talked hurriedly at once. For a moment, the hellish world of Khe Sanh was suspended in place and time.

"Hey, look. I think she's from somewhere around Detroit, Michigan. She rented an apartment in a suburb. It says she swims at Blind Lake near Ann Arbor. That's where I wanna go. God, she'd be scrumptious in a bikini."

"What's wrong with the way she's dressed now?"

"Man, they don't make women like that in Michigan. Only in heaven."

"And in Malibu, where the golden sun shines on her creamy skin."

"I don't even know where Detroit, Michigan is."

"Isn't Michigan two states?"

"Where in hell is Blind Lake?"

"I don't give a damn where she's from, I just wanna look. My God, she's perfect."

"We gotta pin her up. We can't let those guys in Recon make away with her. God sent her to us. She's our playmate."

"You mean, *my* playmate. I saw her first and I think the FPO had something to do with her being here, not God. But OK, FPO or God, either way, she was sent to me."

"Bullshit, Russell! Like hell you saw her first. She's not your playmate."

The eternal human phenomenon of desire emerged. The emotion common to all mankind; that of jealousy, was surfacing over something visual, not tangible.

The title of the playmate spread, "Moving up in the World," provided a puerile, empty theme.

"She may be moving up, but we sure as hell aren't."

"What are her measurements, man?"

"Doesn't say."

"What, *Playboy* didn't give us her measurements? What kind of deal is that? It's important to know. Look at those two guys in the photos. What's with the white socks? Those jerks, they don't care about her."

"Man, she's so delicate. She's only five foot five."

"Look at the red jump suit she's wearing."

"There're only three nude pictures of her. I wanna see more."

A waif, a sylph—there could be no doubt about it—this playmate was, in no uncertain terms, exquisitely ravishing.

"And, she's twenty."

"You're too inexperienced for her, you idiot. You're only eighteen. She needs someone to take care of her, to protect her, and lavish gifts on her… and massage her body every single day, maybe three times a day with hot oil. I'd start right at her waist. It wouldn't matter in which direction my hands would go on her sleek skin."

"Massage? You got hands like a damn gorilla."

"Man, she's as sweet as they come. She's too perfect to give anyone a difficult time. I wonder if she's got sisters."

Russell checked to be sure his M-16's selector lever was in the safe position, then slung his weapon over his shoulder. He grabbed his Viceroy cigarettes. The shelling continued, but he had learned to live with it. He pointed to the image of the sensuous semi-nude girl, lit a cigarette and inhaled.

"When I get home, I'm gonna marry you, honey. I'm taking you everywhere."

Mark Russell, reminded of a song by the Spencer Davis Group, sang a portion of the lyrics: "I had a girl, she was my queen."

"Russell. What's a beautiful girl like her going to do with a stupid, unwashed jarhead like you? She's being wined and dined by the rich and famous and ridin' in big-ole limousines to uptown Beverly Hills, with the palm trees and the ocean and the beach and the money, the glam and the friggin' glitter. You're not included in this parade, man."

"Can you just imagine her on a deserted island?"

"Forget the island. I can imagine her wearing her negligee in this hootch right now holding a glass of champagne in her hand and all of you gone. I just close my eyes and I can see it all."

"You wouldn't know what to do next."

"Man, she doesn't know about Khe Sanh, much less what a hootch is. She's never even heard of Khe Sanh."

"Just look at those eyes. She's lookin' only at me. She can wear that red jump suit all the time as far as I'm concerned...and it'll always be open. God, I can just smell her perfume all over her body."

"Oh, bullshit. The only time you're gonna see her is in this photograph. She don't care about any of us over here in these rat holes. She's got all the rich celebrities drooling just to catch a glimpse of her."

"Yeah, I'm catching a glimpse of her right now."

"Turn the page. Hey look, she's wearing a number seventy-six jersey. That was my football number."

Everyone stared at the photographs. Suddenly, all was silent. The thick dust in the hootch began to settle.

"The shelling's stopped."

One of the Marines removed the centerfold and stuck it to a low wood cross beam.

Russell slapped his buddy on the back of his head through his helmet as he pushed him through the opening.

Corporal Mark Russell, his M-16 hanging at an angle across his back, stared at the centerfold suspended at eye level.

Do they *really* make women this beautiful?

The young woman who, as if sent by special messenger, made her presence known by her sheer beauty. While she existed only in a photo, in two dimensions, the playmate was fully manifested in his mind.

The blond playmate graced Mark Russell's life at a time when there was despair; when the future was uncertain. Through her virtual presence, this seraph cast a bright light of cheerfulness over the gloom. She gave sustenance to him in spite of the pervasive carnage.

Although Russell was well aware that she knew nothing of his existence, his past or from where he came, she filled an infinite void. This enigmatic but alluring young woman transcended all heavenly creations.

Russell would make her, not his playmate, but rather his hope. She had become his beautiful guardian angel.

Russell walked closer to the hanging centerfold. Her light blond hair, parted in the middle, gracefully framed her soft face. He ran his fingers along the outline of the blonde's form on the foldout. He traced her young face, the fall of her hair and the slightness of her shoulders.

Her supple, peach-skin cheeks accentuated her cherubic mouth perfectly formed with the softest of lips. He scrutinized the details of her femininity, but returned to her warm eyes. Russell stared into their mystifying depths. He saw a hint of distant sadness, an eternity of forlornness in their expression. He wondered why. They guarded an unknown storm, a deep mystery that would never be revealed. He could dive into those blue pools of sensual tenderness and dwell forever.

Like Mona Lisa's stare, *Playboy's* temptress charmed her unwitting victim relentlessly with her beguiling gaze. Her entrancing eyes defined the abandoned enchantment of her exquisite face. Inquiring and searching, seeking and unmoving, they stared at Russell. They looked into his fragile, yet precarious life, into the very depth of his being.

Comfortable with her nudity, at ease in front of the camera, from the foldout page, the January playmate, who appeared from nowhere, ignited Mark Russell's passion in a part of the world where the devils of hell prevail and earthly mortals live, but only on borrowed time. Russell raised his hand and blew an enduring kiss to the blond goddess who would gaze from a photograph forever.

A deep longing swept over Mark Russell. He would never actually meet her. Russell couldn't bring himself to utter it, but the thought was real. She had come to Khe Sanh to save his life. Thanking her, Mark Russell said her name softly out loud.

"Connie Kreski."

CHAPTER FORTY-SIX

RUNNIN' THE INJUNS OFF

"Daddy, I got you a delight I'm sure you'll like."

Lynda Bird Robb-Johnson, carrying a plate with a slice of pecan pie and a big bowl of vanilla ice cream, walked through the door of the Oval Office

The more reserved of President Johnson's two daughters, Lynda found living in the White House to be difficult at times. A student at George Washington University, a few blocks away, Lynda was subjected to lots of attention and ridicule.

The press became too intrusive. She received criticism for her selection of attire when she attended the wedding of Princess Anne Marie of Greece.

Lynda Bird married Charles Robb, a captain in the Marine Corps, in December 1967, about six weeks before the start of the siege of Khe Sanh. The wedding took place in the East Room of the White House.

Lynda's name-change, as well as Luci's before her, was the only regret the President had about either marriage. It disrupted the initials, LBJ, common to each member of his family.

"Thank you, sweetheart. Damn, that looks good."

"Why are you working so late, Daddy?"

"How'd you know I was down here?"

"Dad, come on, the White House isn't that big. You're either upstairs or in the Oval Office."

"Yeah, you're right. I'm wide awake and didn't want to disturb your mother. Even when she's in her bedroom, she can sense when I'm not sleeping. I hate to bother her, so I come down here.

"During the day, the damn phone rings off the hook. If I ever do this job again, I'm not gonna give out the number of my direct line. Every congressman tries to call me about some budget thing or…I dunno…some tax issue. They call me sometimes at three in the damn morning."

"Daddy, I think you've called several congressmen and more than a few senators at three a.m., so I'm not certain that…"

"They all say the same thing: 'I hope I'm not disturbing you, Mr. President.' Sometimes, I don't get a bit of work done."

President Johnson slipped a piece of pie into his mouth. "Damn, this pecan pie is yummy."

Lynda smiled.

"I made it for you, Daddy, just yesterday."

"Lynda, you are such a dear. I can't wait to harvest the new crop of pecans at the ranch next fall. We always have fun. The weather's crisp. We build a big fire and cook hot dogs and roast marshmallows."

Lynda smiled.

"And mom makes the best potato salad ever."

"Yeah, fall at the ranch is special."

"Daddy, it's lonely late at night down here, even a bit eerie."

Lyndon Johnson laid the plate on his desk, stood and took Lynda's hand. They sat down on one of the couches. Lynda snuggled up against her father and laid her head on his shoulder, her soft hair cascading down.

"Daddy, you're on pins and needles. I'm concerned about you."

"Don't worry about this big ole, ugly Texan, kitten. It's this whole damn mess…this siege thing at Khe Sanh. I'm not sure the cavalry will arrive in time to run the injuns off."

The President stood and walked back to his desk. He picked up some cables from the USS *Ranger* and USS *Ticonderoga*, two U.S. aircraft carriers on station in the Gulf of Tonkin. He walked to the table with the Khe Sanh Terrain Model which still sat in the Oval Office. Lynda stood beside him and stared down at the flat, square box.

"Lynda, I've looked at this thing so many times,"

Lynda pointed to a tiny type-written note on the surface of the model.

"Dad, what's *Xom Cham* mean?"

"That's the Khe Sanh Combat Base where the Marines are. See the runway? It's not as long as the one at the ranch.

"The press calls Khe Sanh a dusty cow town waiting for the shootout. I doubt any of those journalists have ever seen a real cow town, let alone a dusty one. Here's Highway Nine and here's Laos and the Ho Chi Minh Trail way over here.

"These are the mountains the Marines are occupying around the base. See? Here's Hill 861—Kilo Company. They've been fighting the NVA for weeks now. The NVA trench lines are only a few feet away from ours. Every day, the NVA creep closer and closer."

The President moved his finger a little to the west to hover over Hill 881 South.

"They call this Dabney's Hill."

"Who's Dabney, Dad?"

"He's the company commander, a captain just like Chuck. They say India Company raises an American flag every morning on that hill...pisses the NVA off. Over here are Hills 950 and 1015. And, here's the DMZ, not too far up north."

"What's with the strings across the top?"

"It's a grid, honey. Latitude and longitude. Each interval is about six miles or so."

The President pointed. "Those little red flags represent the enemy. The Marines are just about boxed in."

The President moved the conversation along. "Those reporters never say anything good about what we're doing over there. The American public's understanding is tainted by what the media prefers to show on the news.

They think we're losing in Vietnam. Some of those newsmen...well, I just shake my head."

"Dad, I understand, but I don't understand. The history is so complicated. I have to wonder... "

"Lynda, if you read *Why Vietnam* that I authorized to be published months ago, you will understand. Your new husband will deploy to Vietnam within about six weeks."

"Don't worry about Chuck. He'll be OK. I'll see him in California before he goes."

Lynda completed her earlier thought. "What will keep North Vietnam from invading South Vietnam when we're gone? Maybe the reporters and the networks are not supportive, but I get the sense the South Vietnamese government can't manage its own affairs."

"Lynda, South Vietnam has the right to democratic self-rule. We gotta defend that."

"Daddy, you need some sleep. Let's go back up to the residence."

"You go on up, sweetie. I want to stay here a little longer. Please look in on your mother."

Lynda Bird Robb-Johnson kissed her father. She stood up to leave the Oval Office.

The President, sadness showing in his eyes, looked at Lynda's soft face.

"Sometimes, I may not have been the best father to you and your sister, but I only want good things for both of you."

"I know that, Dad. You're the greatest father anyone could have...gruff like an old bear, but still the best. Come on, Daddy, give me a Texas smile."

A grin swept across the President's face. Nothing pleased him more than the attention of his daughters.

"Go to bed now, honey. Maybe we can make some plans for the weekend. Maybe Camp David."

"Dad, you need to exercise more often. It would be good for your spirits."

Lynda kissed her father on his forehead. "I'll see you bright and early, Daddy."

"Thanks, Lynda. If I'm not looking at the cables..."

The President laughed. "Juanita told me she's having the model taken back to the Situation Room. She says it's too ugly for the Oval Office. Anyway, I'll be here with my own newswires."

"No matter, Daddy, I'll bring you a mug of hot coffee first thing, maybe even another slice of pecan pie."

"See you in the morning, sweetheart."

As the President spoke affectionately to his daughter, half a world away, across the vast Pacific Ocean, the deadly struggle between the U.S. Marines and their foe was still being played out at Khe Sanh.

The North Vietnamese were about to send a grim message to the Marines.

CHAPTER FORTY-SEVEN

WHISPERS IN THE WIND

In a quiet moment of early morning in Quang Tri Province, on the twenty-third of February, when the sun had not encroached on the horizon sufficiently to give color to the sky or cast shadows on earth, weary combatants half-stirred to life. Hollowed eyes of the exhausted Marines at the beleaguered Khe Sanh Combat Base and on the nearby hills, and those of the equally-spent enemy who surrounded them, gradually opened to slits.

The North Vietnamese general offensive-general uprising, with an attack on the U.S. embassy in Saigon as its hallmark, fizzled. Fighting in Hue continued, but the enemy's momentum stalled.

The downpours, typical for this time of year at Khe Sanh, were subsiding. Heavy dew, covering everything, formed rivulets that slid from shanty roofs and canvas coverings, off sandbags and equipment and down poles and stems.

The American occupants of this hellish corner of Southeast Asia had endured weeks of NVA bombardments, but today would be unlike any other.

Earlier in February, NVA trenching began to appear around the combat base, sending an unwelcome sign to its inhabitants. North Vietnamese commanders gathered in a small village to the west. They planned something new, this time directly against the Americans. On the twenty-first of

February, the NVA launched more than three hundred rockets against the eastern end of the base. Several probes followed, but all were repulsed.

NVA units conducted a number of maneuvers. Either to mask these movements or to tighten the containment—no one knew precisely—Vo Nguyen Giap sent orders to bombard the Marines at Khe Sanh.

The intensity of the barrage on the twenty-third of February took everyone by surprise. The incoming shelling was incessant.

The American encampment became a giant outdoor shooting gallery, an amphitheater of deadly explosions.

The Americans protected themselves in trenches, bunkers, behind embankments and under piles of sandbags. To fight is to live. To live is to survive, to take cover. The Marines may take a beating, but they would not be intimidated.

The sun, on its ceaseless arc, rose higher.

Dampness had enveloped the tropical foliage in the valleys below. Mother earth sucked up the warmth of the nurturing sun, further distilling the tiny water droplets into microscopic particles that formed a dense, murky mass of gray. Floating fog, *le crachin*, rose from the valleys and crept high up the sides of the mountains, erasing them from view. The Khe Sanh plateau succumbed to the blanketing shroud that smothered the base, turning it into a sinister fairytale land with no beginning, no end. NVA forward artillery observers could not precisely locate targets, hence no pinpoint shelling. The barrage was random.

The early morning fog dampened the brightness of the instantaneous explosions that moved in arbitrary waves the entire length of the east-west axis of the base. Like giant footsteps of impending destruction, the sounds of each report reverberated across the scarred plateau. The world rumbled as shock waves penetrated the depths of earth. During momentary pauses, dirt and rocks, blown into the air, made crunching sounds as the random material came crashing back down.

The base, rendered an indescribable wasteland, was strewn with an overwhelming abundance of debris. Everything above ground was being destroyed. None of the structures built within the U-shaped roadway that looped around the COC was usable. The roofs, made from plywood or pierced steel planking or any other haphazard material, covered with dirt, were blown away. Portions of the trench lines around the COC had collapsed.

Fog began to lift in the Khe Sanh area. NVA forward observers relayed target information back in fast order to the North Vietnamese gunners at Co Roc.

Range, gun-azimuth and firing angles were calculated and plotted. The din of resulting artillery fire, in and around the caves of Co Roc, was clamorous. After so many rounds, the barrels, too hot to touch, almost glowed from the intense heat. Still, the sweating NVA gunners, shirtless and breathless, loaded the big guns and pulled on the lanyards pouring withering indirect fire into the American encampment.

There would be no reprieve for the Americans, no tomorrow.

The Khe Sanh Combat Base was suffused by deeply pulsing detonations. The dreadful inventions of war wrought by mankind; inventions that could hurl destruction from remote locations, that altered the manner in which warfare was manifested, was a fact of life at Khe Sanh.

The NVA guns, manufactured at Artillery Plant No. Nine in Sverdlovsk, on the eastern edge of the Ural Mountains in Russia, and the projectiles fired from them, designed by ordnance engineers, shot through barrels made from steel forged by metallurgists—their bores rifled by machinists—propelled by high-explosive charges developed by chemists, wreaked havoc on the Americans. The Russian-made guns accomplished the only thing artillery was created to do: propagate destruction.

The Marines responded with American artillery pieces fabricated in like fashion as their Russian counterparts, but on a piece of isolated land called Rock Island in the middle of the Mississippi River. The constant whistling of deadly, outgoing projectiles fired from the Marine base and the clank of the empty, hot brass casings ejected from the back of the 105s signaled the devastation that American artillery was imposing on NVA troops.

The U.S. howitzers, with flat tires on either side of their carriages, each shredded by shrapnel, and jagged gouges in their steel armament were in continuous action against the North Vietnamese. The cacophony of their signature sounds rang out across the plateau.

Incoming enemy rounds didn't stop.

The antagonists, coming from very different cultures, with their own motivation for being in the same place at the same time, some farther from their homes than others, may meet face-to-face on the battlefield and burn malevolence and death into each other's eyes. Far from families, far from young wives, younger children, far from the laughter of friends and for reasons they may never understand, comrades would stand with comrades of like uniform and militate against enemy comrades in other uniforms who found themselves in the same situation.

For now, through the remoteness of an impersonal artillery exchange, soldiers on both sides were free from the intimate deadliness of individual combat only to experience the more invidious trauma of not knowing when or where the next shell may land and whether they would live long enough to see another sunrise.

The NVA guns, then those of the Americans, fell silent. Smoke, like whispers in the wind, wafted from the muzzles of the barrels.

By noon, the fog evaporated. Magically, the last remnants of *le crachin*, nature's fleeting spirit, disappeared mysteriously. Fantasyland, if ever and to whatever extent, was no more. The lush greenness of the deceptively smooth, but altogether hilly countryside was disclosed. The Khe Sanh Combat Base sat exposed.

The North Vietnamese didn't waste time pinpointing their artillery and mortars. Heavy shelling began again sometime after noon. The targets were selected with precision.

Radio calls from Captain William Dabney on Hill 881 South again crackled with urgent warnings.

"Arty, Arty, Co Roc!"

Artillery rounds were coming from the Co Roc Massif. They flew in an arc south of his position. "Arty, Arty, Three Oh Five!" They were coming from a more northerly location and passed over Hill 881 South.

The shells slammed into the combat base. The deafening explosions reached a crescendo toward mid-afternoon. By evening, about a dozen Marines had lost their lives while others who lived waited for the anticipated ground attack. Khe Sanh was at the precipice of eternity.

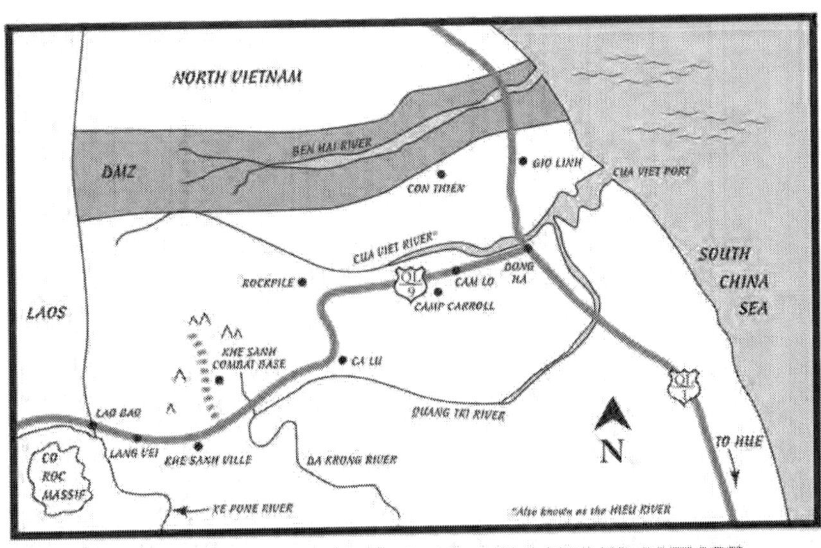

HIGHWAY NINE AREA IN QUANG TRI PROVINCE

CHAPTER FORTY-EIGHT

"HEY, HEY, LBJ..."

Juanita Roberts entered her office to retrieve a gift she wanted to give a friend with whom she was having a late lunch. She was meeting her near the church in which Abraham Lincoln worshipped on New York Avenue, a fifteen minute walk. She heard the President end a phone call in the Oval Office. She'd better look in on him.

"Mr. President, are you all right?"

President Johnson, his hands clasped beneath his chin, looked up without removing them.

"Oh, hi, Juanita. Yes, I'm fine. No meetings this afternoon, thank God. Thanks for arranging some free time for me."

"Mr. President, your calendar is completely full. I take calls constantly from people asking for an appointment. There aren't enough time slots."

Born in Port Arthur, Texas, Mary Juanita Duggan graduated from Texas State College for Women. Upon graduation, she enlisted in the United States Army Women's Corp. She began to work for Johnson in the mid-fifties, but quickly found she could hardly keep up with his energy. She undertook mundane tasks such as sealing envelopes and sending out free seed samples.

Forever loyal to her state, Juanita married Texas Senator Ray Roberts during World War Two who, as a Navy officer, survived the sinking of the USS *Hornet* in the Pacific in 1942. She never forgot the ship's number: CV8. Years later the couple divorced.

Lyndon Johnson lost his first senate race but, undeterred, ran again in 1948 and won. Juanita Roberts proved a valuable asset during his campaigns. Juanita assumed the role of Johnson's personal secretary in 1962 and followed him to Washington.

"Would you care for some hot chocolate, Mr. President? It's chilly in here."

"Thank you, Juanita…Oh, I dunno, I guess…nah, forget it."

The President pointed to the furniture ensemble. "Juanita, sit down. You and I haven't visited for a long time, just the two of us. We used to have long conversations in east Texas during my senate campaigns. I miss those days."

"Mr. President, I'm sorry, I'm not trying to be impolite. I heard you on the phone and…"

"Nonsense, Juanita, have a seat. Let's talk."

"Mr. President, it's past 1:00 p.m. and… Oh, I almost forgot, you do have a quick coffee appointment early tomorrow at seven thirty with the senator from Georgia, and a mister…oh, I can't recall his name just now."

"Me neither."

Juanita and the President chuckled. They shared a private joke about the President's sometimes real, sometimes deliberate absent-mindedness.

"Juanita, sometimes I wish the damn North Viet-nese would just attack Khe Sanh and get it over with. Dammit, I don't understand Hanoi's strategy. And that terrain model…it helps a lot, but all I do is stare at it."

"Mr. President, I'm sure everything will work out. You shouldn't fret too much."

"Juanita, you're a military officer, let me ask you. What do you think about Khe Sanh?"

"Mr. President, I've got my own problems right here. I've enjoyed a good career in the military, but geo-political matters…well, the thought of war is never appealing."

"Juanita, I'm being called a baby killer. It's even appeared in the press. Have you been hearing the chants outside the north fence, in Lafayette Park? 'Hey, hey, LBJ. How many babies did you kill today?' I can hear almost any insult and not take offense. About the only way a person can insult a Texan is to insult Texas."

"Texans are a special breed in many ways. I don't pay a lot of attention, Sir."

"And you sure as hell can't be a weeny in this town, Juanita. Why hell, I've hurled insults myself, sometimes right on the House or Senate floors, sometimes right in the face of my good friends."

The President laughed. "But, mostly at the Republicans."

"I know that, too," Juanita said, rolling her eyes.

"But that chant hurts. I have two daughters, one has a baby boy, you know, Luci's son, Patrick Lyn. Lynda will have children, too, one day. Hopefully, I'll have a granddaughter."

"Mr. President, you'd spoil that child too much."

"Juanita, my mother Rebekah—I always thought she was very pretty—she had it tough. It was not an easy life for her. She was so ashamed of her hands. There was no way she could have elegant hands with all the work she did. It hurt like hell to see her work so hard. But momma was keen to take care of us, to keep up her children's personal appearance. My father, ole Sam Ealy, was pragmatic, but not too intellectual. I think this may have been a disappointment for momma.

"I'd hear her crying at night. She was afraid and, well, I didn't know what to think. I'd touch her arm and say, 'Don't worry, Momma.' She'd smile at me to reassure me, but I was scared for her. Shit, I was only about five.

"She had few wants, but she would like to have been able to dress up of an evening and attend a tea in Johnson City—even then, it was pretty uncivilized—or maybe go to a restaurant or do some shopping in Austin, stay at some fancy hotel. But where we lived, none of that was possible. Nights on the farm were dark and lonely. She had no amenities, no friends. It was an austere life. We were poor as dirt.

"When Daddy died in 1937, I moved momma to Austin and found her a small place to live. I tried to make her remaining years as comfortable as I could. She deserved the best. Momma was a strong woman, Juanita. God, she was strong."

The President gazed off. "And a strong Texan, too."

Juanita nodded her head while the President continued.

"The best place a boy can grow up is in the country. I spent endless hours catching frogs and tadpoles in the Perd'naliss River right in front of our house. I remember I fell off a rock downstream of the house and cut my knee. No bother.

"Man, how the clouds could build up in summer. They'd billow up right over our heads, I swear, in the bluest sky…and the lightning storms, my God."

President Johnson leaned back in his chair. "My mother took care of all of us. The neighbors, too. She even took care of their children. That's what we did in Texas. Still do. I don't want to kill babies anywhere in the world, not in Texas and not in Vietnam."

Juanita Roberts had a long history of working for the President. His life was politics. She felt comfortable with him under any circumstance. She knew his moods. He could be sentimental, sometimes overly so, but he could be mean as a bull and tough as leather, even downright rude. His tolerance was short as a fuse. When he ran out of patience, it was best not to be in the way. She had felt the brunt of more than a few of his verbal tantrums. However, Juanita Roberts, steadfast in her loyalty, had her own core of strength. She knew when to stand her ground and when to talk back, but she also knew when to remain quiet.

"Juanita, I've tried to understand why the mood of Americans is so different from what we saw during World War Two. We fought to free Europe from Hitler, to defeat the Nazis; and also to stop Japan. Aren't we doing the same for South Vietnam? Aren't we trying to help a new nation? Ah, Juanita, you don't have to answer that. I'm just thinking out loud."

Juanita looked at her watch. "Oh, my, it's almost two in the afternoon. I promised to have lunch with a friend. Goodness, I hope she's still waiting for me."

"Juanita, enjoy your lunch. Is your mother still in town?"

"No, she left yesterday. She told me to thank you for the flowers."

"Go on now, Juanita, take the afternoon off. I won't forget the seven-thirty meeting tomorrow with the senator. I'll check in on the First Lady. She's got a cold."

"Oh, Mr. President, The senator's office was asking me the other day about the bombardment of Khe Sanh. He's received many calls. He'd like to see the Khe Sanh Terrain Model."

Juanita smiled coyly. "Couldn't wait to have it removed from the Oval Office."

"Yeah, no problem. Please arrange a viewing for him."

"I'll leave you now, Mr. President."

CHAPTER FORTY-NINE

STAR

Mail to Khe Sanh had been sparse through the latter part of January and into February. The incoming shells and the threat of an NVA attack—imminent battle—presented too much of a risk when bringing in non-combat, non-essential material.

There was not much room in cargo holds for mail for six thousand people. Mail from the U.S. stacked up in Da Nang. Marines needed guns and ammunition. Letters from home, however much a morale booster, would have to wait.

Once in a while, a chopper pilot would have a soft spot for the Khe Sanh Marines. Even if his helicopter's load was maxed-out, he would take on a bag of mail in Da Nang, spirit it through the air across Eye Corps, along the Quang Tri River valley and throw it on the ground at Khe Sanh.

However difficult it was to supply the main combat base, the hill redoubts were worse. The Marines on the hills received supplies through a new coordinated technique involving fighter jets, helicopter gunships and CH-46 cargo helicopters carrying external sling loads of badly needed medicine, food, water and light military hardware. Termed super gaggles, the first resupply through this method occurred on February twenty-fourth, the day after the intense, day-long shelling of the base. A crazy concept perhaps, but damn if it didn't work.

Ronald Sacklund, of India Company Third Battalion Twenty-sixth Marines had been in ferocious firefights more than once, but he escaped unscathed. Not long after the first super gaggle mission, he looked up in time to see a flat box being tossed at him.

"Holy Jesus, look at what I got."

Known to his fellow Marines as Red Sack, Sacklund had just received mail from Laramie, Wyoming.

"Man, this came quick. How did that happen?"

"You got lucky, Sacklund. I ain't had no damn mail for months. Go on, open it, you selfish bastard. Share the moola."

Sacklund held the box with reverence. His father had wrapped it. Tape had been cut and placed expertly on the precise folds and edges.

Ronald Sacklund ripped the brown paper open and cut into the lid of the box with his knife.

"This better be good, Sack. I'm not sure I can waste much more time on this package thing. I got too much else to do here at the Khe Sanh resort."

Sacklund paid no attention to the remark.

"Two letters from my Aunt Hazel. Mailed to Laramie."

"Jesus, Sacklund, why can't she just mail them to you direct?"

"She can never remember the FPO address."

"For Christ's sake, Ron. All she needs to do is write 'Sack-o-Shit, Hill 881 South.' It'll make it, right here to this very hill. Tell her I want an angel food cake, too."

The other Marines, now curious, laughed.

Sacklund continued. "Letter from my sis at the University of Wyoming."

"Man, I didn't even know you had a sister."

"One, two, three letters from Mom and Dad. A letter from a guy I worked with two summers ago. Hey! This is great! A card and a letter from my cousin Judy in Modesto, California, a letter from my older brother with a photo of my little niece Ginny sitting on Star, and some newspaper clippings.

"Jesus, get a load of this headline. 'January 26th, 1968, President Johnson Signs Executive Order. Reserves Called Up. Ten thousand, five hundred more troops going to Vietnam.' That was weeks ago. Friggin' terrific. We got company."

"This war's gettin' outta control, man."

Sacklund continued reading headlines. "'Vets of Dien Bien Phu appraise situation at Khe Sanh.' Where did this come from? Those Frenchies were never gonna win."

"Oh, man, this is some bad shit. 'G.I. Deaths hit four hundred per week.' Wonder how many are from Khe Sanh?"

"Too many, my friend. All taken outta here by chopper."

"Get a load of this. 'Nixon says use of A-weapons neither necessary nor desirable.' And, 'U.S. worries that NVA attack at Khe Sanh may not happen.'"

"Jesus, they're worried now that we won't be attacked?"

"Who wrote that crap?"

"Guys, look at the cover of *Time* magazine. Holy shit, this is the second time Giap's been on the cover. I saw the first one in 1966."

The cover, edged in red, featured a garish, almost satanic drawing of Vo Nguyen Giap's face in devilish yellow and red hues. The title, "Days of Death in Vietnam," cut diagonally across the top.

"Hey, it's dated the ninth of February. Man, this is really current. Right on the cover, 'Hanoi's General Giap.' I'll bet Westmoreland's pissed as hell."

Sacklund laid the magazine down as he scoured through the other clippings. They focused mostly on ranching, animal shows at the fairgrounds, Presbyterian Church outings and, of course, rodeo news.

Corporal Ronald Sacklund would read the magazine and each clipping after he read the various letters he received. He picked up the picture of his niece on the back of Star.

How Sacklund longed to ride in the hills and hunt pheasant with his new Browning twelve-gauge shotgun. He missed the sight of big blue skies, the jagged mountains and the high plains. He remembered how his six year old niece would get all duded up with cowboy boots and a Stetson hat too large for her. She would sit bareback on a big, gentle Percheron workhorse which, because of the white mark on his forehead, she named Star, and feed a colt that would nudge up against her leg.

Sacklund's niece and Star were best of friends. She would lie on Star's back in the sun while he slowly grazed in the wind-swept grasslands. Star never moved abruptly.

Sacklund, with his niece in front of him, would ride Star to a high vista to see the redness of the setting sun on Devil's Tower beneath gold clouds. He recalled how she laid her head down on Star's neck and talked to him while they rode through the openness of Wyoming.

Of all the clippings received from home, some of which Ronald Sacklund had yet to read, there was one headline that went thus far unnoticed: "General Pershing's Grandson Killed in Vietnam."

CHAPTER FIFTY

THEY'RE ALL PROBABLY VC

Glenn Townley served in Vietnam in 1964 as an Army helicopter mechanic. He was honorably discharged and earned a college degree in surveying in May 1967.

Glenn wanted to return to Vietnam to serve in the U.S. Army Corps of Engineers. A back injury precluded him from serving again. USAID had some opportunities, but instead, he accepted a position with an American contractor. He was assigned to projects located at the U.S. military base at Bien Hoa, northeast of Saigon, on the other side of the Saigon River.

Glenn had been in and out of Saigon, all around Cam Ranh Bay and Da Nang, and as far north as Dong Ha. The rigors of his job were never ending. While the days were very long, the weeks flew by. Glenn managed about twenty surveyors, most of which were Vietnamese, and of those, quite a few were female. Of all the surveyors, the ones he found to be the most diligent and exacting with instrument procedures and record keeping were the women.

Glenn, still worried about the recent Tet Offensive and the attacks on the Bien Hoa base, was excited to have a three-day leave from the project. He hitched a ride by helicopter to Saigon.

Months before, Glenn met Beverly Davros sitting at the bar enjoying a vodka tonic at the Honolulu airport. Glenn dropped his shoulder bag and a box he was carrying and sat next to her. He ordered a Rusty Nail.

"What's in the box?" she asked.

"New mitt. I bought it on the way to the airport, but no room in my suitcase."

That sparked the conversation. The two strangers hit it off immediately. More importantly, they were on the same flight to Vietnam.

Over the intervening months, Glenn and Beverly frequently wrote letters to one another and talked on the phone—a secure military line—when they could. Now, more than friends, the two single expats arranged to meet in Saigon on Glenn's approved leave.

Beverly Davros, an operating nurse, lived in a flat on a small street near Lotus Garden Park. She had returned to Saigon from attending a medical conference in Japan one week before the Tet Offensive.

Settled at a table on the famous open-air terrace of the Continental Hotel, Beverly waited to surprise Glenn. She saw him emerge from a taxi. Glenn checked in at the reception desk while Beverly, holding his favorite drink, sneaked up behind him.

"Hey, you hunk. Thirsty?"

Beverly gave Glenn a big kiss and handed him the cocktail which he downed in one gulp while he squeezed her body with his other arm. Thrilled to see each other, both were laughing.

Glenn wore jeans and a short-sleeve sport shirt. A Rolex watch was wrapped around his left wrist.

Quite the simple, but fashionable dresser, Beverly, a ray of sunshine, wore a white dress and an elegant silver necklace. Thin and shapely, with flowing light brown hair, Beverly was easy on the eyes.

Porters took Glenn's luggage to his room on the second floor overlooking the broad intersection of Tudo and Le Loi Streets.

Glenn returned with Beverly to her table on the open terrace facing the side of the Opera House.

The conversation lively, Glenn stole more than a few kisses from his girlfriend.

A torrential downpour passed through the city, but the sun soon came out from behind the dark clouds. Steam was rising from Saigon's asphalt-paved streets.

Honda motorcycles roamed throughout the city. Their two-stroke engines polluted the air with their piercing, high pitched sound and bluish smoke. Parked in front of the Continental, motorbikes were prolific. Their drivers; the cowboys, so named due to their floppy hats with draw strings under their chins, and their tendency to rip off unsuspecting people, were on the prowl. A few sported pistols, some blatantly. Wallets and purses were not safe.

"Are you sure about Westmoreland, Bev? Why do you think the President's bringing him home?"

"I dunno, Glenn. Promotion."

"A promotion?"

"Yeah. That's what they say. Chief of Staff."

"Holy cow, the top dog, I'll say it's a promotion. One in a million officers ever get that far. At any other time, Westmoreland would eat it up, but I'm sure he's fuming. He doesn't want to sit behind a desk in Washington, D.C. He wants to be here where the fighting is. The promotion will sideline him from the action in Vietnam. This is where it's all happening. It's the only war we got."

"Westmoreland asked for two hundred thousand troops, says we can win the war if we invade Cambodia and Laos and stuff like that."

Glenn reached for Beverly's hand.

"Holy crap, Bev. Two hundred thousand troops! And, he's thinking of invading Laos. *And* Cambodia? Where'd you hear that?"

"You've been at Bien Hoa too long, Glenn. It's all over town. Even the New York Times reported it."

"Beverly, I never have time for the news. My days are completely full."

"Yeah, I was talking with a patient at the hospital, a colonel who had an appendectomy. He told me."

"Ah, man, after Tet, this is serious news. Ho, boy."

"That's what I heard, Glenn. But, I'm a nurse, not part of any inner circle."

"It'll take a million men to invade Cambodia and Laos."

"Glenn, All I know is what the colonel said. President Johnson feels it's time for a change in command...may have made the decision back in January. All the optimism Westmoreland showed last year about turning the corner and winning has evaporated."

"For Christ's sake, Bev, aside from Tet, the military's got this one year tour of duty thing so there's no consistency. In my job, I've got good people. Never any turnover. But, for the army, people are coming and going constantly. Westmoreland's got to deal with new people all the time. There's no continuity. Westmoreland's been here four years. That's four generations of new personnel.

"And Khe Sanh. I was up there last November doing some survey work on the base, but left after about three weeks. Never went back. I can tell you, that's one crazy place. Remote as hell...impossible to get around. The jungle is so thick and the mountains, my God. Westmoreland has his hands full, that's for sure."

"Glenn, I don't know much about Khe Sanh."

Beverly pointed over her shoulder in some direction. "Other than it's up there somewhere. I'll tell you what I've heard at the hospital. We don't get the combat wounded, only the people with non-combat issues, like the colonel when his appendix ruptured. Some think General Westmoreland's taking a big chance at Khe Sanh."

"I don't know, myself. Could be, Bev, but what's he supposed to do?"

The two friends sipped their Saigon drinks. Glenn changed the topic.

"Where would you like to have dinner, sweetheart?"

Beverly smiled.

"I haven't even thought about it. It feels good to just sit here and have a few cocktails with you. These are the best drinks."

Outside the terrace, the high pitched squeal of Honda motorbikes continued to fill the air and drown out all conversations. Beverly turned her head to look down Tudo and Le Loi Streets, then back to Glenn.

"These motorcycles make a god-awful noise. I can't stand it. Those guys shouldn't ride those damned things on the sidewalk...punk cowboys. They're all probably VC."

"Hey, how about the floating restaurant? Or, the food's real good at the Majestic. Let's go there, Beverly. Great bar."

"The Majestic? Oh, Glenn, it's going to rain again."

"Come on, Bev, we can take one of those small French taxis. What do they call them? *Du sha-vo*, or something like that?"

Beverly pulled Glenn's face to meet hers.

"I have a better idea. Let's go to your room and order up a bottle of champagne."

"The motorbikes will make a racket."

Beverly bit Glenn's earlobe gently.

"Silly man, we won't notice."

CHAPTER FIFTY-ONE

LION OF KHE SANH

Colonel David Edward Lownds, standing in the dank Combat Operations Center, the COC of the Khe Sanh Combat Base, stuffed a Dutch Masters cigar into his vest pocket. He filled his dirty mug with old coffee and took a sip of the acid-tasting liquid.

Nothing elegant, the COC was definitely a bunker, a rectangular concrete structure built underground several years before. Originally used for ammunition storage, it consisted of six rooms, two on one side of a corridor and four on the other. The single corridor, sixty feet long and four feet wide, exited at either end of the bunker. Recessed mortar pits crowned the top of the concrete steps. Because of a low concrete lintel, entering the COC required above-eye-level awareness, lest the visitor hit his head.

The COC was dominated by the operations room, the largest room in the complex. A myriad of communication gear, rifles, packs and tables covered with maps filled the area. The Fire Support Coordination Center, the FSCC, a source of constant radio chatter, sat adjacent the operations room. A small room for the S2, the regimental intelligence officer, opened off to the opposite corner and down a few steps. Lownds and his executive officers used a room across the corridor from the operations center as a place to sleep.

Although they could bed down at night in other facilities not far from the COC, they seldom left the command post.

Now armed with a loaded M-16 across his back and, more importantly, with stale coffee and a cigar, Lownds ambled toward the steps. Underground for twenty-four hours, he needed some early morning fresh air to clear his head. He passed a chessboard sitting on a table in the open alcove opposite the bunk area. Chess pieces sat haphazardly in the squares.

Lownds looked at his watch: 3:45 a.m. He climbed the concrete stairs to the surface.

Although he was not a reclusive person, Lownds enjoyed his solitary time. The moments just before dawn were the best.

The colonel stopped and sipped his coffee. He felt a pang of guilt when he took his cigar from his pocket. Both he and his wife had been warned to quit smoking. His wife would never quit; but Lownds had to admit, he enjoyed his cigars as much as she her cigarettes. Lownds bit off the tip of the Dutch Masters and spit it on the ground. He crouched behind some sandbags and struck a wood match.

The cigar tasted good, very good; even in the pre-dawn morning. But, oh, how much better one would be with a Beefeaters gin martini.

The debris-strewn trails, the results of the last NVA bombardment, could hardly be discerned. The obscure outline of destroyed and damaged equipment took on a ghastly appearance in the fog. Lownds walked past Charlie Med and continued toward the west end of the base.

"Good morning, Colonel."

A Marine was sitting on a sand bag smoking a cigarette. "Captain James Bryant here, Sir,"

"How's the battery, Bryant?"

"Guns are good, Sir. The base is awfully quiet."

"Yeah, unlike the twenty-third of February, just two days ago, with so many incoming rounds. That was the most intense barrage we've had to date. Over thirteen hundred shells fell on the base."

"We heard the gooks digging trenches until two thirty this morning. The sound stopped. Must be in bivouac."

Colonel Lownds thought it an odd word to use in this case, bivouac.

"I would say they are, Captain."

David Lownds lived by military protocol. It was the correct way for a Marine officer to conduct himself. But, Lownds was also a person who enjoyed conversations. At roughly four in the morning, he dispensed with reference to rank, especially with someone who had gone through Quantico like he had and who was at Khe Sanh with him.

Lownds inhaled on his cigar while he shielded the tip's glow with his other hand.

"Where're you from, James?"

"Maine, Sir."

"Oh, yeah? What part of Maine?"

"Small town of Jay, on the Androscoggin River, Sir. Just north of Livermore Falls, way downstream from Mexico."

"Captain, I'll just bet you and I are the only two people on the entire Khe Sanh Combat Base who know there's a Mexico in Maine."

"Sir, and there aren't even two people in Maine who know where Khe Sanh is."

Lownds blew out smoke as he nodded.

"You're a very long way from home, Marine."

"Like you, Sir. You're from the Northeast, too."

"Yeah, the birthplace of volleyball is the only claim to fame my hometown has...that and the canals, I suppose. How did you know it was me approaching just now, Captain?"

"Your cigar, Sir. I could tell it wasn't a cigarette. You were coming from the direction of the COC and you always smoke cigars. I surmised it must be you."

"Good observation. I should have shielded the tip from view."

"Sir, I doubt the NVA can see it through the fog. I only saw it when you were about ten feet away."

Lownds flicked the ashes off his cigar. He sat down next to the captain in the damp fog.

"Sorry, son, I don't have another cup to share my coffee with you."

"That's all right, Colonel. I'll just enjoy my cigarette."

Bryant could never be so nonchalant with an O-6, but the mood was relaxed.

"Colonel, what do you think of our being at Khe Sanh?"

Lownds drew on his cigar.

"MACV and IIIMAF must have their reasons for a static defense, but… well, it doesn't matter what I think."

Both men, understanding the nuance, chuckled quietly.

"The press is always hounding me for drama. Every day there's a new reporter with some crazy theory. I'm not sharing anything. They wouldn't understand. They come, they go. They never stay long enough to be conversant about the situation. The press always like to use the C-130 that crashed on the tenth of this month as a dramatic backdrop. I hold sessions by the sandbags just outside the COC.

"But, I'll tell you one thing, Captain. We have our orders. The NVA aren't gonna push the Twenty-sixth Marines around."

"Or the Thirteenth Marines, Sir," Bryant responded with what could have been considered impertinence but, in fact, it was a statement of pride.

"Yes, of course. Sorry, Captain."

Lownds' rejoinder showed he was not without quick wit. "Well, at least the First battalion of the Thirteenth Marines."

Both men shook hands; a show of camaraderie.

"What about General Giap, Colonel?"

"Funny you mention that. I was reading about his campaign at Dien Bien Phu just yesterday."

"Really? I heard you told some news reporter you had never heard of Dien Bien Phu."

Lownds removed his helmet. He ran his hand through his graying hair, then his fingers stroked his moustache.

"Yeah, the NVA may eventually read what he reports. It would make a big splash with the press. You know..."

Lownds raised his hands above his head and moved them apart as if spreading out a banner. "Khe Sanh Commander Knows Zip About Dien Bien Phu. Now that would get the commies' attention. The truth is, I'm far from uninformed."

"I wouldn't think anything less, Sir."

"The French were never prepared. Christian de Castries was the wrong person to be CO. He underestimated Giap's smarts."

Lownds blew cigar smoke out his mouth. "What do you like to do, son… back home?"

"Fish and hunt north of Presque-Isle. Just me, my pack, fishing rod and my rifle. I enjoy making fresh coffee on an open fire early in the morning."

Lownds laughed.

"I can smell it brewing now. What sort of rifle, Captain?"

A Savage .243 bolt-action, Sir. I restored it. There's nothing like being in the woods with a rifle."

"I can understand. I've got a keen interest in dendrology…the study of trees. Woodworking is great. I'm going to order a grandfather clock kit and assemble it from scratch. It'll end up with my son someday."

"Colonel, we've been here for a whole lotta weeks now and…"

Lownds interrupted.

"One reporter asked me if I thought the NVA were really trying to take Khe Sanh."

Lownds sipped his cool coffee. "Was he joking? Giap has moved some units away, but the NVA are still poised at us…. Married, Captain?"

"Yeah, married, no kids—not yet, anyway. My wife's an accountant."

Lownds inhaled on his cigar, then spoke.

"I'll probably go back into business, perhaps be a bank manager. I need to stay in one place. I've moved my family around too much."

Lownds exhaled smoke and took the cigar from between his chapped lips. "So, no children yet, Captain?"

"No, Sir. I'm thinking about law school, then maybe children."

"Well, I don't know much about law school, but get ready for a big change in your life when the first child arrives. I have six girls and a boy.

"My son liked to go crabbing at Camp Lejeune His bucket was always full. My daughters collected their fair share of cockles, too. We'd go to the beach early and watch the sun come up over the Atlantic. It would be a fiery yellow-orange. And then late afternoons, the ocean could turn so blue beneath huge clouds on the eastern horizon. Absolutely terrific. I wouldn't have changed a thing."

"Colonel, I know you were at Iwo Jima. How does Khe Sanh compare?"

"Well, there, we attacked the Japs. Here, the NVA are attacking us. Not quite the same."

Lownds placed his helmet on his head and adjusted his M-16 on his back. His cigar had burned down to a stub. He looked at his watch, lit by the glow of his cigar, which he held near the crystal.

"It's a little after four-thirty, Captain. It'll be light soon. Thank you for the conversation."

Bryant looked at Colonel Lownds, the Lion of Khe Sanh.

"Thank you, Sir."

"You know...the anniversary of the attack on Beatrice at Dien Bien Phu is March thirteenth, a little more than two weeks from now."

Lownds dropped the butt of his cigar and squashed it underfoot. "Giap's spoiling for a fight. He knows where we're weak. He'll attack, but he'll get punched up."

Captain Bryant flipped his cigarette away. It hit the ground in a shower of sparks.

"Colonel. I don't think there's a single Marine here who would prefer to serve under another CO, Sir."

"Captain, there're a lot of excellent COs out there...better than me."

"Sir, I think..."

"Keep your eyes out, Bryant."

CHAPTER FIFTY-TWO

SUNSETS. . .BEFORE THEY END

Alan Pierson liked to record trivial facts in a small spiral binder. Quick to jot down thoughts and observations, he kept a pencil in the metal spine. His friends made fun of the way he kept track of everything.

After the artillery barrage on the twenty-third of February, Alan maintained a running tally of the incoming enemy rounds that hit the base.

Away from his position when the current shelling began, he dove for cover among a haphazard placement of sandbags and debris at the north edge of the runway.

Ever mindful of his diligent record keeping, Alan, now prone and hard up against something that might protect him, withdrew his notebook. He wrote down the date, 26 Feb 68, and began recording the incoming rounds.

Alan Pierson counted out loud—no one could possibly hear him—while making a series of hash marks—four strokes down and a fifth line cutting diagonally across the short vertical lines. He filled two pages of his notebook with five blocks of five lines on each page. Near the back of his notebook, Alan had written *A Poem for Sally,* lengthwise at the top of another sheet, for his girlfriend back home in Knoxville, Tennessee. Just beneath her name, he wrote the poem's title, "The Mists of Khe Sanh."

The NVA artillery rounds kept crashing into the base.

"Holy Christ, they're all over us."

Alan began his fourth block on the third page.

"Sixteen…Seventeen..."

He kept counting. "Eighteen…Nineteen..."

Alan was only a diagonal hash mark away from twenty marks on that page when an enemy shell exploded near him. The explosion ripped through the sand bags.

Knocked unconscious, Alan came to a few seconds later to discover he was seriously injured. Shrapnel had torn into his torso, arms and legs. He instinctively felt his body. He still had all his limbs, but his right leg was torn above the knee. He was bleeding profusely from a deep gash on the back of his thigh. His ears were ringing from the concussion, but he could hear nothing else.

Alan grimaced at the excruciating pain and yelled out.

"Corpsman! Corpsman!"

Sweat poured from his every pore. Alan's eyes were stinging. Blood flowed down his face. He felt for his helmet but it had been blown away. Fear swept over him. He would never see Sally again.

Shells continued to slam into the base. Explosions occurred everywhere—all around him. The sharp ringing in his ears turned to loud roars.

"Corpsman!"

His own words were inaudible to him, but he felt the vibration in his jaw when he yelled out. "Corpsman! Oh, God."

The artillery shelling stopped. But, enemy mortar rounds and the scream of rockets filled the void as they careened toward the base.

Alan saw his notebook with the poem he had written lying in the dirt only a few feet from him. He pulled himself across the ground, grabbed the notebook and put it in his pocket. Then he began to claw his way to get help. He had a long way to go from the revetments on the north side of the airstrip to the hospital on the south side. He could cover the distance quickly on foot, but at a crawl and with so many wounds, the journey would take an hour. Blood flowed non-stop from the bad gash in his leg.

The dust and smoke in his eyes obscured his vision. Out of breath and light-headed from loss of blood, Alan did what any person in desperation would do. He yelled out louder.

"Help me. Somebody help me. Oh, God. I'm hit bad."

Exhausted and weak, soaked in sweat and covered in dust and muddy blood, Alan Pierson lay his face in the red dirt. He felt for his notebook to be sure he had it—no way was he going to lose Sally's poem—then passed out, face down.

Pierson was revived when corpsmen turned his body over. His hearing somewhat restored, Alan Pierson heard the corpsmen talking faintly, but the voices seemed distant, floating, as if in a hollow room without walls. The jumbled talk of his rescuers sounded like children. He thought he heard birds.

"Over here! Bring the stretcher over here. He's still alive. Let's get him away from the strip."

"My God," a second Marine cried out. "Look at the gash on his leg. Jesus, it's clean through the bone."

"Quick, put a tourniquet on his leg. He's lost a lot of blood."

Alan heard surreal words: "This one's bad." Were they referring to him? He stared up at the sky. What were they talking about? What bone? Why are my hands painted red?

Alan's eyes opened wide. Where was Sally's poem?

The NVA shells came back with the same fierceness as before.

Marines rolled Alan's body onto the stretcher and, braving the explosions and flying shrapnel, stood at each end. They lifted Alan's body off the ground, then ran in a low crouch. They arrived at the medical receiving point and ducked behind some sandbags before entering the shanty structure known to everyone as Charlie Med.

Alan Pierson was mumbling incoherently.

"I'll get more fish from the stream. Where's Sally? Don't lose Sally's poem."

A stretcher bearer yelled out.

"Doc, quick...almost bled to death."

The doctor, the bottom half of his face covered by a bloody, sweat-soaked surgeon's mask, immediately placed his stethoscope on Alan Pierson's chest.

"He's alive, but barely. I need plasma, quick."

A needle was stuck in Pierson's left forearm. Plasma began to flow into his body from a plastic bag elevated on a wood pole.

Alan Pierson's eyes grew wider.

"Tennessee fish are the best. Brown trout in the Clinch River...Kentucky Lake...Best bass...walleye up on the Cumberland."

Pierson coughed up dirt. "Where's my darling Sally? She needs to read my poem."

Alan Pierson's bloodshot eyes narrowed to a distant focus. He saw Sally's hair pulled back. She smiled and winked at him. The image faded.

"The sunsets. Sally will go away with the sunsets...before they end. Sally, come back to me...Sally, your poem!"

The doctor listened to Alan's heart again. "Very faint. This Marine's hamburger meat. Lacerations on his right shoulder and right arm. His right leg is barely attached. It's hanging by a thread. Femur completely cut."

"We put the tourniquet on him out there, Doc."

"His leg has to come off. I can't repair it. By the time we get him to Da Nang, it'll be septic."

CHAPTER FIFTY-THREE

TANGLEFOOT

"When you gonna stop lookin' at that dead gook? He's been a goner for days, man."

"I should know. I nailed his ass good when he got snarled up in the tanglefoot. He managed to pull the trigger on his rocket launcher. The rocket shot straight up in the sky. It exploded in the valley. Now, he just hangs out there. Even his own pinko bastard buddies don't want him."

"Man, that attack last night…it was worse than last week."

"Scared the hell outta me, man…they attacked the perimeter screaming and shooting, AKs blasting, RPGs, grenades…the entire NVA army was coming in here. The last mortar round had just slammed into the hill. All of a sudden, they were everywhere, like friggin' cockroaches.

"That one gook doin' circles, screamin' and shootin', sprayin' bullets. He was nuts. The fifty-cal blew him away. His putrid body's over there behind the sandbags."

"This place really reeks with all these corpses lying around…whew."

"How many did we kill?"

"I dunno. Ten, maybe fifteen."

"Somebody has to bury 'em otherwise this place'll be a cesspool in no time."

"I ain't volunteering. Lotta hard work diggin' a hole with these play shovels. Throw the dead bastards over the wire. Let them assholes bury 'em.

"Know what's amazing about that gook out there?"

"He's dead, I dunno. What?"

"He gets skinnier and skinnier each day. The skin on his face has shrunk, pulled tight. You can see his teeth, the shape of his skull. His nostrils are like two big holes in his face. Every day the skin falls off. I can see his jawbone. He just stares back at us from those empty eye-sockets."

"Too freaky! He's almost a skeleton."

"Are you kidding? They all look like skeletons even when they're alive."

"The birds are ripping meat from his body. They tear off a piece of bloody flesh and fly away."

"How many did you shoot?"

"Three or four. Got 'em before they made it to the trench line, just before we pulled back. I was able to toss two grenades, then I got hit in the arm. I tried to fire Meredith's grenade launcher, but couldn't find no shells. I had to move away from my position. Doc says I'll be OK."

"Man, the choppers ain't never coming to get us outta here. There's only one place for them to land and the gooks've got that zeroed in with their mortars. They control the countryside and we control this hilltop. Eventually we just wake up one day and...there ain't no way off this hill except fightin' off it."

"Ah, man. Stop worrying. We'll get outta here...some of us may not be breathing, that's all...but the choppers'll come and get us."

"Think the gooks'll attack again?"

"Damned if I know. You know as much about this joint as I do. Maybe tonight. The com-radio says the other hills were attacked, too."

"Smitty got hit in the head."

"Bad news. Good guy, Smitty."

"And Turner got it from shrapnel—cut to pieces—and Belton is dead."

"No shit! Belton was supposed to go home to Oregon, or... I dunno where, next month. His thirteen months are about up and he gets shipped up here, gets KIA and now he's going home one month early. Zapped."

"There're sixty thousand NVA out there waitin' to overrun the base."

"Sixty thousand? Where'd you hear that?"

"There may be even more. I wouldn't be surprised if it was a hunnert thousand NVA."

"Man, you're scaring me to death."

"The NVA and VC and their so-called Tet Offensive…they ran out of steam, or bullets, or something. They're pissed as hell. We're open season now, buddy."

"They tried to shoot up a few choppers on Hill 950. They were low on water up there a few days ago and Lownds flew some up to them."

"Ah, what the hell?"

"I'm just about bingo on ammo."

"They oughta nuke the sonzabitches and get this thing over with. Drop one big bomb way out there and, boom, blow the bastards to smithereens. The war is over, we can go home."

"That ain't gonna happen."

"God, this place stinks! We gotta get those damned bodies outta here."

"Wonder how long he'll hang in the wire before one of his commie buddies pulls him down?"

"Been too long already. I look at that stupid corpse and it just stares back. Every day, it shrinks to bare bones. He's a scarecrow trying to tell us something."

"Yeah, we're next."

"There'll be so many NVA skeletons out there. It gives me the heebie jeebies just thinking about it. It'll be an NVA ghost valley."

"This place'll never be the same."

"I don't give a crap."

"Here, take the binoculars and keep your ass here. Gotta take a leak. I'll find some ammunition and a few grenades."

"Don't bring back none of them baseball grenades. They ain't worth shit. Lotta Marines been killed by those damn things."

"I'll be back in a few. Oh, man. I've got a baaad-aaass feeling."

CHAPTER FIFTY-FOUR

THANH PHO MY: A POEM FOR SALLY

The dark green of the hills around Da Nang gave way to a soft blue pastel. The distant profiles of the moisture-laden peaks and ridgelines rolled across the horizon. Monkey Mountain, the more prominent of the hills, formed the picturesque Son Tra peninsula. Like a fist intruding into the Gulf of Tonkin, it shielded the serene waters in Vinh Da Nang (Da Nang Bay) from the larger tidal influences and tempestuous storms of the South China Sea.

Da Nang city, home to a sprawling airbase surrounded by other American military installations, had become corrupted by the cultural lifestyle of the United States. The clash was evident everywhere.

Hamburgers, French fries, plenty of cold beer and unending nightlife, promulgated by gaudy, flashing neon lights, pervaded the city. Nightclubs, cocktail bars and massage parlors proliferated. Young Vietnamese women, always available and seductively dressed, would satisfy the needs of any soldier if he was willing to accept the risks. The sordid invitations were endless. 'Hey, G.I., America number one. Me number one, make big boom boom with G.I.. Do G.I. like me? We have fun tonight, boom boom."

Overwhelmed with ostentatious materialism—anything could be bought in the city—Da Nang was a lively bastion of U.S. personnel; so much so the Vietnamese called it "Thanh Pho My"—the American City.

Sergeant Geoff Brenner never dreamed he would be stationed in such an exotic place. Surely, this was not the Vietnam he had seen on TV.

Brenner had been in the Army for twenty-three months. He'd learned to accept the military way, even to thrive within its organizational bureaucracy. Little did he know he possessed a professional talent that would be in great demand.

Sergeant Brenner grew up in an affluent family near Conway, Arkansas. Brenner's education and training in civilian life had little to do with attacking enemy positions. His upbringing didn't have any connection with the usual professions.

Quick with a smile, but more as a cover-up, Brenner had one passion. He rebuilt big-block V8 engines.

Brenner was being groomed for his father's prosperous mortuary. Not long after high school, still learning at the knee of his father who was the principal owner and a professional practitioner, Brenner became a licensed mortician. He honed his skills of taking care of the deceased.

Brenner went on to college to earn a business degree, but his grades didn't reflect much promise. In 1966, his second year of regular college, Brenner knew he would be drafted. He joined the United States Army.

After basic training, with his professional talents apparent, Geoff Brenner was assigned to Graves Registration. He received quick promotions. Not long after postings in Virginia and Hawaii, he received orders to Da Nang, Vietnam and arrived there in August 1967.

Geoff Brenner learned to look at the remains of the deceased in the same way he regarded car engines. He had seen many dead bodies, some mutilated in highway accidents. He was accustomed to the bloating and decaying odor of a corpse, the escaping of foul gas, the discoloration of the skin—no two bodies were the same—the smell of formaldehyde and the overall process of preparing a body for burial. He was well acquainted with the stages of decay, had become accustomed to microbial proliferation—autolysis and putrefaction—and rigor-mortis, algor-mortis and the ultimate Cadaver Decomposition Island, or CDI. Brenner even took an interest in a bizarre phenomenon called spontaneous human combustion. In short, he was no stranger to the terminality of life.

But, Geoff Brenner was not quite prepared to tackle the morbid assignment given to him in Vietnam.

Brenner sat on a low wall smoking a cigarette outside the U.S. Army Morgue. Pieces of rind from an orange he had eaten lay scattered on the ground beneath his dangling feet. The day started at four a.m. and finished at two p.m. He and his team had prepared twenty bodies. They were loaded onto a C-141 for the flight back to Travis.

Brenner overheard a radio on a vehicle parked a few feet away. The radio was tuned to the air traffic control frequency at the airbase.

"Da Nang Tower, Hardball Seven Two. Five miles south, for landing."

"Hardball Seven Two, runway three five left, altimeter, two niner niner two, wind, three six zero at eight, cleared to land."

"Roger, Da Nang Tower, three five left."

The call sign identified the aircraft as a helicopter.

"Hardball Seven Two, state cargo, internal, external."

"Internal. Two pax, three walking WIAs, one WIA litter."

Then, Brenner discovered his day was not yet over.

The pilot continued. "And six KIAs."

"Roger Hardball Seven Two. Cleared to land."

Ground vehicles were standing by to transfer the wounded to the naval hospital. Two large trucks, deuce-and-a-halfs, their tailgates lowered, backed up to where the CH-46 would land.

Not far away, an empty cargo plane operated by a private air shipping contractor, was scheduled to leave at midnight for Honolulu. If Graves Registration could process the bodies, all of them could be on their way to the states late that night. There would be no residual work the following morning. The embalming tables would be empty...and ready to receive more deceased the next day.

The chopper touched down at Da Nang, settling on its three landing gears. The pilot shut down the helicopter's engines. The back ramp opened as the overhead rotor blades slowly spun to a stop. The crew chief walked down the short metal plank beneath the rear of the fuselage. He shouted.

"We need lots of muscle, boys. This cargo's heavy shit. Get ready for the smell."

The concentrated stench of human bodies quickly permeated the outside air from inside the chopper.

The passengers and walking WIAs disembarked and were taken to their destinations. The KIAs were removed while a corpsman entered the helicopter and tended to the WIA on a litter at the front of the fuselage. The litter had been loaded into the CH-46 at Khe Sanh first with the KIAs stacked longitudinally behind him.

Now with some KIAs off-loaded, the ground crew could carry the stretcher off the helicopter ramp to a waiting ambulance. A tag with a big "I" written on it signifying immediate attention had been attached to the Marine's blood soaked shirt.

Inside the ambulance, a corpsman placed a stethoscope to the Marine's chest and listened.

"Man, we gotta get him to the hospital fast."

The ambulance sped away.

Meanwhile, the macabre collection of deceased that had been placed in the deuce-and-a-halfs arrived at the morgue for final processing by Graves Registration.

Geoff Brenner and his team began preparing the bodies on the embalming tables for their last trip home. The ventilation could not keep pace with the intense foulness. Time was short. A lot had to be accomplished before midnight.

An hour later, the litter with the Marine who'd been taken to the naval hospital was brought into the morgue. The Marine's lifeless arms fell below the body from beneath the sheet.

"Lay him down there. We'll take care of him."

Sometime afterwards, the body was lifted up onto a vacant white porcelain embalming table. The Marine's face was ash white with a slight yellow coloring that extended down from his mouth to his neck. His expression was composed and tranquil, as if asleep.

Geoff Brenner spoke to a new staff member who had been in the morgue for less than three days.

"Brunstom, let's remove his boots and utilities."

"What happened to this guy?" Brunstom asked. "He doesn't look too shot up. Lots of gashes, but he should have lived. Did you see that guy over there with half a face? The only thing left was his right cheek, an eye, his tongue and half his lower jaw."

"Yeah, I saw it. Now help me."

Brunstom didn't pick up on the hint, he didn't stop.

"Or the guy yesterday without a face at all..."

Brunstom made a slicing gesture with his hand. "My God, that was a hideous mess."

"Brunstom, cut the crap."

Brenner had the same reaction, but his prior training helped him maintain his composure. Brenner had learned to detach. "You'll get used to it, Private, and if you don't, you can always quit. Lots of people have. I can't even begin to describe the horrors I've seen over here. This ain't bad today.

"If there's lots of fighting, there's going to be lots of corpses. During the Tet Offensive, we got so many bodies from Hue, we couldn't process them fast enough. Each day more arrived. They just kept coming, stacking up. The odor was overwhelming."

"I'm not sure I can do this."

"Listen, Brunstom, this ain't easy duty. It's gruesome, OK, but that's the way it is. We gotta prepare these soldiers before we send them home. That's our job.

"Now, you and others are here with me. We have no way of knowing what will happen tomorrow. Let's get the deceased ready to ship out on the DC-8 tonight."

"Ah, Sarge, I can't stand to think of the families when they open these boxes."

"Brunstom, it doesn't work like that."

"But, Sarge…"

"Brunstom! Get a grip, man. The military will make arrangements. Each body will be escorted home. The remains will be transferred to a proper casket for shipment to a professional mortuary."

"How do you know all that, Sarge?"

"My father owns a funeral home in Arkansas."

"This is bullshit, man."

"It's a shock to me every day, Brunstom. I never know what I'll find when I unzip a body bag. War, for all its glory, is about death. We're at the drop-off point of the conveyor belt. Now, help me get this Marine prepared for repatriation. We got to go through his pockets and record everything and give it all to the Private Property Depot."

"Lots of cuts. Doesn't look like anything that serious to me."

"Brunstom, his leg...almost gone, bone sticking out...probably bled to death."

"I have everything off his person, I'll catalogue it all: Identification card, dog tags—I'll keep them here with the paperwork—watch, cigarettes, lighter, class ring, twenty dollars, can opener, empty AK casings in his pocket, a small notebook with numbers and words."

"Brunstom, there may be valuable information in his notes. Give the notebook to me. I'll take care of it."

"Hand-written notes are valuable?"

"Brunstom, I don't make the friggin' rules. Notebooks and documents are submitted for analysis."

Brunstom handed Brenner the notebook. He put it in his side pocket.

"We need postmortem records for the ante-mortem comparison. Let's measure the body, get fingerprints, do the dental examination and chart the wounds. Let's get him and the others embalmed and on that plane tonight."

Brunstom tried to act as if he was an old hand at this. But he was not as hardened as he wanted to show.

"God, this makes me sick."

"Brunstom, this war is ...well...look, just forget it. Tomorrow and the day after, and next week and the week after will be the same."

Later, with the embalming complete, the Marine's body was wrapped in a clear plastic sheet and secured with tape. The remains were lifted off the table and placed with accompanying paperwork in an elongated aluminum coffin-like container with rounded corners that was resting on a cart. After the lid was closed and sealed, the container was rolled out of the morgue and placed on a pallet. Others containers were stacked on top, loaded on a truck and driven to the airbase apron. All six KIAs plus the Marine who died at the hospital, were embarking on their final trip home.

Brunstom lit a cigarette.

"I worked in a warehouse two summers ago and we stacked boxes containing air conditioners. Here, we stack boxes with bodies that only a day or two before were walking around, talking and breathing. Man, I can't stand seeing this every day. I don't know how you do it, Sergeant."

"Quit talking, Brunstom. First of all, they're not boxes, they're transfer cases. And you're just making things worse."

Brenner would not allow himself to look at Brunstom's face as he spoke. "To be here, you have to fortify yourself. You have to dig deep, man. Some guys can eat a sandwich in here. I can't…and I'm a professional mortician. The man you replaced a few days ago literally broke down. Nobody in Nam gets shot like in TV westerns, you know, like in Bonanza."

Brenner and Brunstom drove to the waiting plane to help with the loading.

A large forklift arrived at the back of the truck. The operator slid its tongs beneath the large platform-size pallet and lifted the stack of aluminum transfer cases. The forklift backed away from the truck. The operator drove to the cargo plane and stopped at its side. One by one, the metallic cases were carried inside the waiting Flying Tigers aircraft. The cases screeched as they were slid along the aluminum floor. Six transfer cases were lined up inside the plane and secured into position.

"One transfer case to go. Let's get it off the forks and moved into position. The pilots want to take off as soon as they can. It's almost midnight."

Working in the dark under the ramp lights, the men moved the last transfer case of human remains off the forks.

Geoff Brenner caught sight of the tag illuminated by the flood lights. It identified the same Marine he had processed hours before. He read the destination first—Knoxville, Tennessee—then the name—Pierson, Alan.

Brenner reached into his pocket and pulled out the spiral notebook that had been taken from Pierson's body. He flipped through the pages as he murmured.

"Some kind of diary or haphazard notes with numbers and hash marks. Wonder what this Marine was keeping track of?"

Brenner turned one page sideways and read, "A Poem for Sally." A period appeared after each line of the poem. He was reminded of his tenth grade English teacher who scolded students who hadn't placed periods after each line of their poetry assignments. Geoff Brenner read Sally's poem softly out loud.

Through the clouds, horrors shriek, their wickedness on high.
Destruction near, arriving here, from deep the prism sky.
Hugging the dirty red clay of my desolate abode.
Errant not, targets sought, enemy shells explode.
Bursting of the banshee's scream, a universe of fear.
Harking sadness, projectiles endless, far and falling near.
Spirits aloft, free to fly, comrades brave, proud and tall
Of those who gave their best, smiled, then turned and gave their all.
Sacrificed unknown, to an endless, timeless death.
Rockets beckon, they call to me, seeking my own last breath.
My full soul, not long for earth, saddened, but not whole.
In the crevice of wondrous eternity, forlorn, a longing, desolate heart.
My desire, your warmth next to me, rapture shall never part.
Beneath the shadows of the moon, daylight comes, from night till noon.
Surrounding heights, depths of space—silent—a mystery dawn.
Wandering, seeking, ephemeral ghosts—lonely—the mists of Khe Sanh.

Brenner slipped the notebook back into his pocket. He would submit it for analysis the next day. It would eventually reach Alan Pierson's family.

His tortuous work day finally over, Brenner looked to the northeast, to the stars in the sky and saw beneath them the glow of the lights of *Thanh Pho My.*

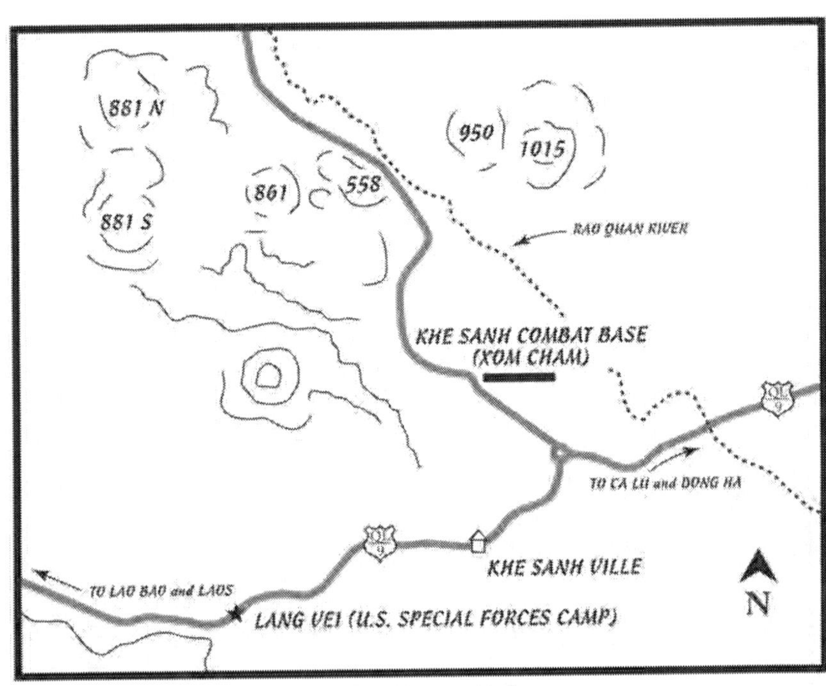

KHE SANH AREA
(WESTERN QUANG TRI PROVINCE)

CHAPTER FIFTY-FIVE

THROWN OFF COURSE

"Marvin, I don't like this kind of crap."

The President tapped his desk with his pen. "The press keeps calling Vietnam McNamara's war. It's not his war. The press trumped that up two years ago, or so, I dunno. Mac's personality gets in his way, I swear. If it's anybody's war, for better or worse, it's my war. Ole Bob McNamara, assuming responsibility for the conduct of the war...well, to be honest, Marvin, it's chewing him up. He's damn near a nervous wreck."

Marvin Watson, a Texas native from Oakhurst, a graduate from Baylor University and a proud ex-Marine, stood in front of the President's desk in the Oval Office listening to his boss.

Watson served Lyndon Johnson faithfully for years. He worked for LBJ in the 1948 race for the U.S. Senate. He served as the head of the Democratic Party in Texas and he organized the 1964 Democratic Convention. In 1965, Watson became the White House Chief of Staff in all but title. He was soon to leave the White House for his new post. Watson scratched his chin in a feint of contemplation.

"Mr. President, there's a logjam of people wanting to meet with you. Oh, about that file you asked me to review. I'll get on it first thing in the morning, but if you don't mind, Sir, I'll excuse myself just now."

"Marvin, that logjam can wait. Don't worry about that damn file. I'm calling Mac now. I'm gonna clear the air. I don't give a hoot if he is leaving the Pentagon. Pour yourself a scotch."

The President dialed McNamara's direct number. A perfunctory voice answered.

"McNamara."

"Bob. The press keeps painting the wrong picture 'bout Veet-nam being your war. This war is on my shoulders and no one else's."

"Mr. President…"

"I want to bring this thing to conclusion, Mac. I want to get the hell out of that stinking, two-bit country, but I want to end the conflict as victor, not as loser. I'm not going to be the first president to lose a war. I got FDR, Andrew Jackson and George Washington staring down at me from their paintings right here in the Oval Office."

The President was just getting started. "It would be a disgrace to lose this war. You can imagine how history would portray me, what historians would do to me. You understand what I'm saying, Mac?"

"Sir…"

"Bob, they won't be talking about you; they'll be talking about me. I'm the one who lost the war, not you."

"Mr. President…"

"Westmoreland keeps asking for more. More, more and more. Vietnam is an empty hole. During World War Two, we bombed Germany's cities and Japan's, too, but in Vietnam we bomb the hell out of the countryside."

"We bomb the targets you approve, Sir, and…"

"Mac, dammit, that's in North Vietnam. I'm talking about the jungles around Khe Sanh."

"Because it's a conduit for the NVA, Sir. Mr. President, the statistics…"

"This Tet Offensive thing has thrown us off course. I thought we had the enemy all sewn up in the northern part of South Vietnam. Isn't that what your numbers showed?"

"Sir…"

"Reporters say fifteen thousand NVA and VC were killed in the Tet fiasco. Fifteen thousand! How many more were there? They destroy one hundred of our planes and attack the provincial capitals. How did that happen?"

"Mr. President, they infiltrated the towns from outside at night and..."

"McNamara, the VC bastards were right in the middle of the damn towns. They live there, for Christ's sake."

Just because the conversation was on the phone, the Johnson treatment could be equally intimidating.

The President rose up in his seat while he talked. "Do you mean to tell me that with five hundred thousand American troops in Vietnam, we can't detect what's goin' on over there, we can't put a stop to it?

"Mac, six American missionaries were killed in some town, Ban Me Tuit, or something like that—damn these names—and fourteen American civilians working in some pacification program were killed near Hue. Slaughtered like cattle.

"Ain't never heard of the city of Hue. Now look at it. It's all over the front page of every newspaper in the world. Bodies are floating in the Perfume River. The city and its bridges and that citadel site are destroyed. The world press is making it out that we're to blame, that we destroyed everything."

"Mr. President, we used machine gun fire and small rockets to minimize damage to the citadel, but we had to resort to heavier ordnance to rout the VC. We caused some damage, Sir. Couldn't be helped. Hue was secured by the twenty-fourth, Sir...last Saturday. Tet is over.

"The Marines report that just over one thousand VC were killed in Hue. Sir, we're winning and..."

"Winning? You guys over there on that side of the river...Jesus criminy. Three thousand VC invaded Saigon. Walked right in. Rode through town, took taxis...hid their weapons in vegetable carts and coffins. Brought them in by bicycle, clever little bastards. They even struck the U.S. embassy at three o'clock in the morning and killed a bunch of people. A brand new embassy that Bunker inaugurated. Impregnable...shit almighty...or so we thought."

"Mr. President, the attack was more than three weeks ago, Sir."

"I don't give a damn if it was three months ago. The sappers marched right in, right into the embassy of the United States of America, just down the street from the Catholic Cathedral, right in downtown, flower-filled Saigon, and killed Americans. Went right in past our gates."

The President's voice rose in pitch. He became more strident "Right through the front damn door of our embassy, Bob!"

"Well. Not quite, Mr. President. The VC attacked the embassy sometime after midnight. They riddled the guard post with their AKs. An RPG round blew a hole in the compound wall near the gate and the VC slipped in through the hole. Time Magazine showed the picture of the hole. That's how the VC gained access to the grounds. They came through the hole, Sir. Not through the gate, and they..."

"Gate, hole, door...I don't give a rat's behind, they got in."

"The Marine guards killed two or three of them, but yes, Sir, they kept coming through the hole and over a wall. Brought in explosives to blow the place up. A Marine guard, a Ronald Harper, I believe, was able to close the heavy doors to the main building. We lost four Army MPs and one Marine, a James Marshall, a southern boy.

"The Saigon police didn't come to help our people. Said they needed U.S. protection at night. One by one, all the attackers got picked off. By mid-morning, it was all over. We killed nineteen VC. The attack was insignificant."

"Crap. You may call this embassy thing insignificant, but I can damn sure tell you, it ain't. The VC sonzabitches got inside the grounds of the United States embassy in Saigon. The United States embassy! That's a pretty big embarrassment, if you ask me. Turn on your television. They're still showing the film clip all over the world. Westmoreland's over there talking about consternation. The public must be wondering...consternation or constipation."

"Mr. President, I'm confident we're winning. First, it was Loc Ninh last October and then Dak To in November, both on the western border. We lost a lot of men, but Giap lost many times more. He gained no clear objective. He was defeated.

"Giap's men are growing tired of defeat. Their morale is flagging. The Tet

Offensive was their new hope, but it's over. The same thing happened. Defeat. The attacks across the country were a cute tactic, but none of it worked. We've regained the initiative throughout South Vietnam."

"Bob, what the hell happened to the so-called big attack at Khe Sanh? Wasn't Khe Sanh supposed to be the real target? It's almost March first. Shouldn't they have attacked by now? What kind of intelligence do we have, anyway?"

"Mr. President, Giap is trying to divert our attention away from Khe Sanh, Sir, just like Westmoreland said on TV. I spoke to Westmoreland this morning. He's confident Khe Sanh is still the target. The shelling has not stopped.

"Sir, Giap may have surprised us everywhere on the last day of January, but he didn't win. He needs a victory. He'll go for Khe Sanh, now. The barrage on the twenty-third is proof."

The President leaned forward on one elbow.

Marvin Watson shifted his weight from one foot to the other. The fact that Robert McNamara was leaving the Pentagon in a few days made the conversation no less awkward. Plus, no one wanted to be on the other end of the stick when the President was in top gear.

"Mac, Khe Sanh better hold. That's all I can say. You make damn sure those Marines have all the support you can give 'em."

"We will win, Sir," McNamara said. "The body count is on our side. There's more than a ten to one kill ratio and..."

"Body count? Jesus, Joseph, Mary. We can't win a war based on body count. Have you completely lost your mind?"

The Lyndon Johnson steamroller was unstoppable. "What do you think the American public will do to me if I continue to show a scorecard that provides kill ratios? This isn't a basketball game with rebound statistics or a football game with—I dunno—average yards per pass. This isn't the leader board at Augusta."

"Sir..."

"McNamara!"

The President's face was beet red. He was breathing hard. "You listen to me. No American, not one single American family…Bob, are you listening? No parent, no father, no mother will be pleased to see their son Johnny's flag-draped casket knowing that ten or twenty or more North Viet-nese were killed for their son. What do you think they'll care? Do you think the parents of that young boy will say, 'Thank God, at least there are a bunch of Viet Cong dead'…huh, Bob? They wouldn't care if a thousand Viet-nese were killed for their brave son. They just want their son back alive."

The President breathed in. "How in the hell can anyone explain that business-sounding data to the dead soldier's family? Use your brain, man. We're talking about Vietnam, not IBM. We're talking about American boys—coffins being off-loaded from planes—not cars coming off some assembly line."

"Mr. President, the body count shows that our tactics are effective and the NVA have…"

"Have what? Dammit, Mac!" the President roared.

The silence that followed was more disconcerting than the exclamation.

"You are not understanding me. To date—see if my math isn't correct—we've lost about twenty thousand American boys. That's the population of a small town. That's the size of San Marcos where I went to college. Using the kill ratio of ten to one doesn't make me feel better. A ten to one ratio means the Viet-nese have lost two hundred thousand soldiers to our twenty thousand, right? Now, if I understand the number of men per one NVA division, that means they have about twenty divisions. Dammit to hell, Mac, you and I both know they don't have twenty divisions. Statistics be damned."

"Sir, they're receiving supplies from Russia and China…you know that, Sir."

"Mac, I just don't understand what with all the bombings on that Ho Chi Minh Trail thing, why the NVA can't be eradicated. I hear CINCPAC has approved B-52 bombing raids at Khe Sanh…Arc Light raids, I suppose they're called, as close in to our boys as a half mile."

"That's right, Mr. President, as close as a kilometer, to be exact. Admiral Sharp approved that on February eighteenth, Sir."

"Damn, you'd think they would have run for home, the little shits."

"Mr. President, the terrain there is difficult. Just look at the Khe Sanh model, you can see how crazy the ground is...ridges, steep hills, deep valleys. It's a maze of geographic complications. The NVA are well dug in. But, when they attack Khe Sanh, they'll be out in the open and we'll..."

"Bob, I look at that model of Khe Sanh every single day."

"Mr. President..."

"Now, I don't know the first thing about geology, but I just can't imagine that Khe Sanh is any worse than any other battlefield. Hell, we beat the Japs throughout the Pacific. What about the Chosin Reservoir? What about Italy?

"And what's this I hear about C-130s being prohibited from landing at the base?"

"Mr. President, over the last month, or so, until the tenth, we delivered over thirty-five hundred tons of supplies by C-130. That's over seven million pounds, Sir. Tonnage increased from sixty tons of supplies in January to almost two hundred tons so far in February. But, it's very dangerous. Incoming flights have been suspended, but re-supply has not stopped at the base. Beginning about the sixteenth, we began provisioning the base with a system called LAPES."

"Which means?"

"Low Altitude Parachute Extraction System, Sir. A C-130 flies just above the deck and supplies are extracted out the back ramp by a parachute. We will soon begin using GPES, Sir. Ground Proximity Extraction System. It's a controversial technique. Plus, the super gaggles have been successful."

"Lapes, geepas, super gaggles...Whatever it takes to keep our Marines provisioned."

"Mr. President, our paradrops just west of the base have been effective, too. There may be no shaving cream, but there is no shortage of combat provisions. Like I say, when they attack us and are in the open, we'll destroy them, Sir."

"Mac, you're leaving Defense at the end of February—not even a week from now—for the World Bank. We got North Vietnam, we got North Korea, a crisis on our hands in Berlin and we got problems in the Middle East. King Hussein wants a bunch of F-4 Phantoms and a shit load of tanks. God knows what the Chinese or that idiot Castro are planning. With this Pueblo thing now and American sailors in the hands of the North Koreans, I hope you're right. No…let me re-phrase that. The Pentagon damn well better be right."

"Mr. President, in fact…"

"I want our young men home, but I want a sovereign, secure South Vietnam."

"I understand, Mr. President."

"Talk to you later, Mac."

The President looked up at Marvin Watson as he brusquely placed the phone receiver back in its cradle.

"Marvin, I'm going to the Situation Room and then to lunch with Lady Bird."

The President stood abruptly from behind his desk. He walked in front of the three television sets and out the door. He paused and turned around.

"Marvin, I didn't mention this to McNamara just now, but when I met General Max Taylor, he recommended again that we evacuate Khe Sanh. I read some report that's been circulating. An NVA deserter said the NVA were going to use FROGs…some acronym."

"Free Rocket Over Ground, Sir. I heard about it, too, from Rostow, days ago."

"Free rocket? Over ground? Almighty Jesus. I'll be back before two to prepare for the press release about the Middle East. Tell Secretary Rusk I want to see him at four p.m. Oh, and tell him I want him to stay for an early dinner with the First Lady and me. Put in a call to Bunker in Saigon. I'll be talking to him—me and the Secretary, together—about eight tonight, our time. I need the latest info from Bunker. I'll be talking to General Wheeler, too. He's been in Vietnam a few days now. I'll also talk to Westy after I read his daily report."

The President thought for a moment. "But, Marvin, I'm thinking I would like to have an untainted account about Khe Sanh."

"Mr. President, I'll get a hold of Rostow and tell him to put that Terrence Kerley guy on the next plane to Saigon."

"Marvin, Let's see what Wheeler brings back this week."

"I'll at least have Mr. Kerley on alert, Sir."

"Well, tell him to wait for instructions. He's to go, get the information and come back. That's it. Stay out of the bars. No bull-shittin' around."

"I understand, Sir."

The President turned and strolled from the Oval Office door, mumbling.

"First, it's beagles, then gaggles. Now it's frogs."

CHAPTER FIFTY-SIX

PAPA 27 0308 ZULU FEB 68

"Lieutenant Sterling, find Colonel Lownds quick. I think he went to visit Bravo Battery. He should read this cable from MACV. Here, take it with you."

Lieutenant Sterling headed to the east end of the base and arrived at Bravo Battery.

"Seen the CO? I've got a message for him."

"He was just here, but he's gone to visit with the one-five-five guys."

Sterling quickly walked to the west end. He passed Alpha Battery where the men were positioning 105 shells and replacing one of the rifled gun tubes. Only twenty minutes earlier, all the batteries had been in heavy counter-battery exchange with NVA artillery. The barrels, so hot, radiated heat for several feet.

Sterling was soon at the 155mm battery. Lownds was visiting with the gun crews.

"Colonel, apologies, Sir. I was told to give this TTY straight to you, Sir."

Colonel Lownds unfolded the sheet of paper and read the message. When he finished, Lownds handed the message back to Sterling.

"Lieutenant, MACV's giving us lots of praise. Here, read it yourself."

> FM; COMUSMACV TO CO 26TH MARINES
> INFO ZEN/DEP COMUSMACV FWD
> PAPA 27 0308 ZULU FEB 68
>
> YOU, YOUR MARINES, AND THE ASSOCIATED U.S. ARMY AND VIETNAMESE TROOPS ARE AT THE CENTER OF THE INTERNATIONAL STAGE STOP YOU ARE FACED WITH A MILITARY CHALLENGE UNPRECEDENTED IN THIS WAR STOP I WANT YOU AND YOUR TROOPS TO KNOW THAT I HAVE THE UTMOST CONFIDENCE IN YOUR FIGHTING SPIRIT, PROFESSIONALISM, AND ALERTNESS STOP THESE ESSENTIAL QUALITIES, PLUS THE INDOMITABLE COURAGE OF THE U.S. MARINES ARE DESTINED TO PREVAIL OVER THE ENEMY STOP. THE ENEMY WILL TRY EVERYTHING IN THE BOOK, BUT YOU WILL DEFEAT HIM AT EVERY TURN STOP BE ASSURED THAT THE CHAIN OF COMMAND IS WATCHING YOUR SITUATION HOUR BY HOUR AND PROVIDING YOU FIRE POWER NEVER BEFORE EQUALLED ON ANY BATTLEFIELD STOP
> MY PERSONAL COMPLIMENTS AND BEST WISHES TO YOU STOP.

"Sir. At least we've not been forgotten."

Colonel Lownds laughed slightly.

"We should send this on to General Tran Quy Hai, maybe even to General Giap, just to keep them informed, of course...as a favor. I'm sure they'd be amused."

"Sir?"

"Lieutenant, it's not what the message says. It's what MACV doesn't say. We're about to be attacked."

Colonel Lownds looked across the denuded area to the airstrip and the wreckage of planes that had been pushed to the side. He saw the carcass of a giant CH-53 helicopter in the distance. The helicopter sustained a hit in the tail section while it was lifting off. The pilot fought to keep it from crashing, but the vibrations were so violent, it smashed hard on the ground. The main rotor blades dipped down. The giant planks sliced through the cockpit killing the crew before tearing loose and flipping through the air. The engines whined as the behemoth pulsated on the ground like a wounded animal in its death throes. Now, the destroyed helicopter sat lifeless, abandoned. The event was so horrific, Lownds couldn't forget the pilots' names—James Riley and Cary Smith of HMH-463.

"Tell me, Lieutenant, you've been here as long as I have. If the NVA attack us, just where do you think they'll attack?"

"You're asking me, Sir?"

"Sure, why not? You see the situation every day."

"Sir, the S2 would know better. I'm sure Major Hudson would be better informed, Sir."

"Thank you, Lieutenant. Jerry Hudson's an excellent S2, but I like to hear other opinions. That's why I get around the base. I need to know everything. Tell me what you think."

"Colonel, if I was Giap, I would saturate the base for several days with non-stop artillery, mortar and rocket fire and blow everything to pieces."

"Preparing the battlefield, Lieutenant."

"Exactly, Sir, then attack before dawn."

"Did you forget about our airpower?"

"No, Sir, but I understand Giap takes risks at the expense of his men."

"Where do you think they'll come from, Lieutenant?"

"Not sure, Sir. They could come from anywhere, from everywhere. They control the town and the highway so that may be the springboard. Could be, they'll attack the Ninth Marines first, sometime after midnight, Sir, and then they'd have easier access to the base."

"Interesting, Lieutenant."

"Sir?"

"Everyone compares Khe Sanh to Dien Bien Phu. In your scenario, you would attack way before dawn. Giap, on the other hand, attacked the main French stronghold at Dien Bien Phu with the full assault at midday. The battle was over by dinner."

The lieutenant looked down. Had he said the wrong thing?

"Lieutenant, did you ever hear about the battle of Na San?"

"No, Sir."

"We all know about the French debacle at Dien Bien Phu, but few recall the French victory at Na San. Giap is not invincible. He's made plenty of mistakes. In 1950, The French suffered losses at the battle of Cao Bac Long, but the French devised a new tactic. The main base at Na San was surrounded by strong points with interconnecting trenches and defensive lines. They called it hedgehog. We don't have that here. The hill positions are not connected except by radio, helicopter and artillery.

"The objective of this new French technique was to thwart the Viet Minh. The French successfully beat them back. Giap suffered five thousand casualties with two thousand killed…not sure how many, really. The French officer, Colonel Jean Gilles, I think his name was, beat Giap at his own game.

"As for parallels with us, the French were surrounded like we are and prevailed. Na San was higher up on a plateau, like us. Na San was resupplied by air, same as us. The air links at Na San were never completely severed, just like us here.

"Giap screwed up at Na San. He committed his forces into futile attacks without properly preparing the battlefield.

"Giap had learned how to fight the French in their hedgehog position and applied those lessons two years later at Dien Bien Phu, which is situated in a relatively broad valley surrounded by hills. The French base was easy to observe. Simply put, the Viet Minh had the high ground.

"The French had about fifty artillery pieces. The Viet Minh had over two hundred. Giap spent several months building roads, stockpiling ammunition and placing heavy artillery in the mountains in preparation for the attack. Some of the guns were made at Rock Island Arsenal.

"Dien Bien Phu became famous because it was the last hoorah for the French. It was their last stand. People fancy this is our last stand, too, our Little Big Horn. That's what they want…more for the sadistic drama.

"Ever notice how the press makes Giap out as more intelligent than any of us? They've been shelling us for weeks. Enemy activity is all around. The sensors keep picking up heavy movements of NVA. People talk about Giap's brilliance at Dien Bien Phu, but fail to remember he lost in a very big way at Na San. He will lose here, too…in the same manner. Giap has miscalculated. Khe Sanh will be Na San all over again.

"My bet, Lieutenant? The NVA'll come from the east. The east end of the base was inadequately defended, so I put the ARVN there. The NVA want to punish them. They're always probing the Rangers, but with Captains Walter Gunn and Hoang Pho in command, they won't get far."

CHAPTER FIFTY-SEVEN

MINOT, NORTH DAKOTA

North Dakota's bleak winters are interminable. Night falls quickly, the wind is ceaseless and the temperature never rises above zero. Snow drifts across plains like a wandering soul, settling against fences and in the ditches that line the country roads. And against the door of the Eggenhofer home, thirty miles from town, that had withstood many such winters.

Manfred, who shortened his name to Fred, and Eva were first generation German-Americans. Their parents immigrated to the United States from Witzhave, just east of Hamburg, Germany in 1913. They carried on the family farming tradition and spoke to each other in the language of their ancestral country. They taught their children the German language, too.

Manfred Eggenhofer saved three thousand dollars, enough to purchase a small farm in 1946. Over the years, running the risk of over-extending their debt, the Eggenhofers were able to purchase several more parcels of land. Through years of dedicated work and a lot of sweat, the Eggenhofer farm grew from less than twenty acres to well over three thousand; from a small white, two-room house and a simple barn to a comfortable home and a large farm complex.

Every time Eggenhofer looked at the barn painted a rust-orange, he smiled. His young daughter, wearing handed-down, torn jeans, had asked why barns were always painted red. She was allowed to choose a color for a new barn. She chose bright Halloween orange. Her sister objected. A compromise was reached. Rust-orange was selected. Not the most agreeable color, it would at least resemble autumn leaves.

Fred Eggenhofer overestimated the amount of paint needed. A smaller building and the chicken coop were also painted in the same color, much to his daughter's delight.

Fred Eggenhofer enjoyed seeing his farm grow and be productive year after year. He took comfort knowing all his equipment was parked in the machine shed after work each day. He derived personal enjoyment from working the rich soil of the land he would never give up. His farm was a business, but it was also his family's legacy.

Fred Eggenhofer seldom ate at the table in the evenings. After a day on his property that stretched beyond the flat horizon, he preferred to kick off his worn boots and relax in his armchair while he ate straight from the plate.

Now, on this winter's night, Manfred sat in his comfortable chair to feast on a big ham steak with dressing, and a side of green beans with real bacon bits.

Eva's meals were always delicious. She filled a bowl with large Polish pickles as an added treat. Her husband never tired of pickles. Sometimes, not often, he'd have an occasional cold beer, seldom any wine and never hard liquor.

The black and white TV, with its rabbit-ear antennae on top, cast its white glare across the cozy room. A small reading lamp on a small table next to the couch where Eva always sat provided softer light.

A familiar face stared stoically from the TV screen. Like an arrow straight into the mind of every American, to the heart of the country, to Minot, North Dakota—to Fred and Eva Eggenhofer—the commentator, at the conclusion of the CBS evening news on the twenty-seventh of February, began to deliver a somber speech about Vietnam.

Tonight, back in more familiar surroundings in New York, we'd like to sum up our findings in Vietnam, an analysis that must be speculative, personal, subjective. Who won and who lost in the great Tet Offensive against the cities? I'm not sure. The Vietcong did not win by a knockout, but neither did we. The referees of history may make it a draw. Another standoff may be coming in the big battles expected south of the Demilitarized Zone. Khe Sanh could well fall, with a terrible loss in American lives, prestige and morale, and this is a tragedy of our stubbornness there, but the bastion no longer is a key to the rest of the northern regions, and it is doubtful that the American forces can be defeated across the breadth of the DMZ with any substantial loss of ground. Another standoff.

Both Fred and Eva stopped eating and listened intently, their eyes glued to the image of the bespectacled man who was talking on the screen.

On the political front, past performance gives no confidence that the Vietnamese government can cope with its problems, now compounded by the attack on the cities. It may not fall, it may hold on, but it probably won't show the dynamic qualities demanded of this young nation. Another standoff.

We have been too often disappointed by the optimism of the American leaders, both in Vietnam and Washington, to have faith any longer in the silver linings they find in the darkest clouds. They may be right, that Hanoi's winter-spring offensive has been forced by the Communist realization that they could not win the longer war of attrition, and that the Communists hope that any success in the offensive will improve their position for eventual negotiations. It would improve their position, and it would also require our realization, that we should have had all along, that any negotiations must be that—negotiations, not the dictation of peace terms. For it seems now more certain than ever that the bloody experience of Vietnam is to end in a stalemate. This summer's almost certain standoff will either end in real give-and-take negotiations or terrible escalation; and for every means we have to escalate, the enemy can match us, and that applies to the invasion of the North, the use of nuclear weapons, or the mere commitment of one hundred, or two hundred or three hundred thousand more American troops to the battle. And with each escalation, the world comes closer to the brink of cosmic disaster.

To say that we are closer to victory today is to believe, in the face of the evidence, the optimists who have been wrong in the past. To suggest we are on the edge of defeat is to yield to unreasonable pessimism. To say we are mired in stalemate seems the only realistic, yet unsatisfactory, conclusion. On the off chance that military and political analysts are right, in the next few months we must test the enemy's intentions, in case this is indeed his last gasp before negotiations. But it is increasingly clear to this reporter that the only rational way out then will be to negotiate, not as victors, but as an honorable people who lived up to their pledge to defend democracy, and did the best they could.

This is Walter Cronkite. Good night.

Manfred Eggenhofer sat bewildered at what he had just heard. He recalled he joined the Marines two months after Pearl Harbor and one month after he married Eva. He fought at Guadalcanal where he was wounded in the stomach in late August 1942. He recovered through a prolonged convalescence and returned to the Pacific to fight for America again. Later, he continued with the Marines, battle after battle, on so many inhospitable islands, until his days as a fighting Marine came to an end in November 1943 at Tarawa.

Manfred Eggenhofer was severely wounded in his upper torso on the first day. Bandaged up, he later fearlessly attacked a stronghold of Japanese soldiers armed with rifles. He killed three. When he took aim on his fourth victim, he was riddled several times by bullets from a hidden machine gun. He survived the battle and the massive killing on Betio Island, but was shipped back to the U.S. wrapped in bandages.

Eva looked at her husband as he sat absorbed in front of the TV. She remained quiet. An expression of apprehension crossed her face while despondency showed on his.

Walter Cronkite's news presentation was as grave as the North Dakota weather. Fred put his fork down on his plate.

"Eva, that guy makes it like we're losing. Who is he to lecture us about negotiating and stalemates? He sounds like he's apologizing for our government, like he's speaking for America. He's in Vietnam for a few days… and what, he's an expert now?"

Fred Eggenhofer motioned to the TV with his right hand. "Our boys got caught off guard, maybe got beat up, but they aren't losing. Those Marines at Khe Sanh will never stop fighting. Marines don't give up.

"Those damn Japs were so well dug in at Tarawa, we had one hell of a fight. Eva, our farm is bigger than the Tarawa atoll. We were attacking strongly fortified positions, but we knew we would win in the end. A lot of Marines got killed there. My God, the sight of so many dead bodies..."

Because of the heroism of Fred Eggenhofer and other Americans just like him, and technological advances, the Japanese would eventually lose the war. The American onslaught was too overwhelming, but American victory came with a heavy price.

"The Vietnamese can be resupplied, but we may not be so fortunate. We're going to have one hell of a time flying in ammo, food and water for our Marines. Eva, there must be tens of thousands of those Vietnamese out there. The cost in blood won't be cheap, but the Marines will hold. Dammit, I wish I was at Khe Sanh to help those young men. Poor bastards, to be stuck fighting in a place like that."

"Now, Manfred, please honey. You know you can't be there. It's time to pass the torch to those much younger than you. You can't keep fighting our wars. You did your part and you came back home to me—twice—all shot up, but in one piece, thank God. Many others weren't so lucky, Fred."

Eggenhofer fell silent. He cast his eyes across the room, focusing on nothing in particular.

"Eva, America is a great country with hard-working people—people like our parents and you and me and our children—who made the United States what it is. Our parents back then and our family today would never have had the opportunities in Germany this country has given us. America, this land and this farm have been good to us. We've been blessed with good health, prosperity and a future for our kids. Both girls have gone to university. We labored hard for what we earned. We worked this land. No one else did. We asked for nothing that we could not provide for ourselves and our neighbors. This is why we fought for America."

The moroseness that captured Eva's facial expression deepened. Fred Eggenhofer continued. "Eva, during World War Two, we knew why we went to war and what we fought for."

"Fred…"

"We had to beat Japan and Germany. I knew we had to stamp out the Nazis. I didn't want to go to war against the German people, but I had to do my part. I went to the Pacific to fight the Japanese. That's why I joined the Marines. No one asked any of us to go. We went because we felt obligated to defend America against that scourge, Hitler, who ruined our grandparents' old land and that silly Hirohito who was foolish enough to bomb Pearl Harbor. We expected no handouts in return. America sacrificed a lot of its men in the Pacific and in Europe, yet we won. Our only desire was that America would remain free and our country and our families would be safe and prosperous."

"Honey..."

Eva could see the sad empathy in her husband of twenty-six years when he watched the evening news report.

Vietnam bothered Fred Eggenhofer, but something more disconcerting troubled him. He could not understand the demonstrations that were occurring across the country by Americans against America. He had a hard time comprehending America's emerging loathing of his fellow servicemen and why they would be so hated for wearing his country's military uniforms. What's the new generation doing to the America he fought for?

"Eva, no one can choose the war they're in if they're in the service. Drafted or enlisted, it makes no difference."

"Fred, I know how you feel, dear, but you mustn't fret."

"Eva, we say we're trying to help another country build, we're blocking the spread of communism. But when those young Marines come home—some all shot up—what will they think when they're treated with such hostility? Will America be as grateful to them as the country was to my generation?"

"I'm sure it will be, Fred."

"Eva—damn—I don't want to go to bed angry. Look, what if some young Marine ends up a paraplegic? That Marine's made a mighty big sacrifice for his country. He'll come home not to the thankful cheers of those honoring a hero, but to the terrible taunts, insults and jeers against him. Hell, Eva, all he did was serve his country. He can't quit, he can't come home. He's a Marine. He has to fight. He has to do what he's told. That's what Marines are trained to do. They're faithful. That's called serving your country. It's called honor."

"Fred, please..."

"Some Marine comes home, say from Khe Sanh, and now what? What's he to think when people won't sit next to him on a plane or when they spit on him at the airport and curse him and call him a murderer? What's he to do?"

"Manfred, I've seen you do this too many times. You're working yourself up. Finish your ham, take a hot shower and go to bed. You have to go into Minot early tomorrow for the equipment auction. The road will be bad."

But Fred Eggenhofer wouldn't stop.

"Eva, I swear to God, if I could, I'd be there with those Marines. I'd kill every Vietnamese soldier that crossed the barb wire into that base. And when I ran out of ammunition, I'd throw rocks, kill them with my bare hands, if need be. I'd stand and fight with those young Marines right there."

Eva's melancholy slipped further. She couldn't hold her tears back.

"Oh, Manfred, when you joined the Marines, I was so afraid I would never see you again. The many letters you wrote gave me so much anxiety, so much fear, sleep was impossible. I was alone in North Dakota, while my handsome husband was fighting on some unknown island so far away. The loneliness was unbearable. Would I ever run my hands through your blond hair again and feel your strong arms around me? What would I do without you, Manfred?

"The painful memories I have of you in the Pacific and then coming home two times on a stretcher. I don't want to be reminded of those lonely days. I don't want any more war in this house. Can you understand how I feel?

When you talk like that, the fear comes back. I get scared something will happen to you. I couldn't bear to lose you, not then and not now."

Eva wiped her eyes.

Fred stood and walked to Eva.

"Eva, I didn't mean to make you cry. Nothing is going to happen to me. But my thoughts and prayers are with those Marines. God help them. After World War Two, I wanted to do my part again in Korea, but couldn't."

"That's what I mean, sweetheart. The medal you framed and hung above the fireplace is something I know you're proud of, and you have a right to be. I'm proud of it for you and I am equally proud of you. It's bestowed on only a few brave men, many of whom are not with us now. But, when I think back to what you did to deserve it, I shudder."

Beside herself with memories of the fear of losing her husband, Eva kissed Fred Eggenhofer on his cheek and ran her hand through his hair. She retired to her sewing room to regain her composure.

Eva picked up a specially made cedar box that sat on a shelf. It held her husband's wartime letters. It was the one possession she cherished more than any other. Eva sat with the box on her lap and cried.

On each side of the door that now separated a caring, dedicated wife from her devoted husband, emotions that could not be easily quelled surfaced in each.

Fred Eggenhofer's depressed contemplation would be visible to anyone as he pondered what had just transpired. Hurt Eva, the woman he cherished? No. Hurt the woman he had known since he was fourteen, the woman who stood by him, who waited for him and who gave him two beautiful daughters? Not in a million years.

Fred held his head in his hands and whispered, "I never knew that medal scared you, my darling Eva. Why didn't you tell me?"

To frame and hang it with the photos of his children and his farm had been a mistake.

With his own memories of the Pacific islands on which he fought implanted in his mind and the long boat ride home with his body shredded by Japanese bullets—the fear he also had of never seeing his beautiful wife again—Eggenhofer felt tears well up in his eyes.

He looked at the contents of the wall hanging—a medal, characterized by an inverted, dark-gold, five-pointed star suspended beneath an anchor with thirteen white stars on a field of blue above both. Unknowingly, this very medal that had been bestowed upon him as he stood at attention in his Marine Corps uniform had caused immeasurable heartache for his wife. He reached up and removed it.

For now, until a better place could be found, Manfred Eggenhofer put in a drawer the same award that had been placed around his neck more than two decades earlier: the Congressional Medal of Honor.

CHAPTER FIFTY-EIGHT

M-1 THUMB

A little west, but mostly north of the Khe Sanh Combat Base, ringed with a tangle of wire, sandbags, bunkers, lookout posts, claymore mines and trench lines that snaked through the dirt, the top of the hill was unlike any place on earth. It bristled with guns.

The Marines owned the fortified redoubt, at least its summit. They fought those who tried to assault it. Many times, the Marines had thrown the NVA back. Still, they came on.

The North Vietnamese soldiers dug their own communication and circumvallation trenches up to and near to those of the Marines. They placed mortars in deep pits and ringed the hill with heavy machine guns.

Fighting had taken a break. The air was filled with the stench of rotting NVA corpses and exposed entrails from the fighting that had occurred during the days and weeks before. The hideous odor, corrupting the atmosphere, hovered over the area.

Inside the perimeter, Marines, tired, sweaty and hungry, bloodied and bandaged, were portraits of somnambulant ghosts. Dark lines, accentuated by red dirt that would never wash away, creased their faces. Their hollow eyes, recessed in their sunburned faces from lack of sleep, reflected the persistent strain and ubiquitous horrors.

While the American occupants of the hill took badly needed breathers, they resolved that the hill would never be conquered by the North Vietnamese.

Without benefit of construction material or equipment, the Marines continued to improve the ramparts. They dug deeper and placed more dirt on top of their fortifications. They strengthened their trench lines, strung new concertina wire and repositioned claymore mines. They cleaned their weapons and reloaded them. Ammunition was distributed. Lookouts kept a constant vigil.

A sudden shot from a Marine's rifle rang out.

Brent Chafner was proud of his shooting abilities. He started shooting with his father at age six. At eleven in 1959, Brent's father gave him a single-shot Anschutz .22 caliber rifle. It was the best twenty-two money could buy. "Son," his father said. "This may be just a twenty-two, but it's not a toy."

A few years later, Brent, at fourteen, shot a M-1 Garand rifle at a range with other teenagers. The recoil was so violent, it knocked him down. His right shoulder was black and blue for days.

The thing he remembered about the M-1 wasn't its weightiness or its kick, but something that had nothing to do with marksmanship. The instructor, an ex-Marine and a Korea Vet, explained to him and the other teenagers how to load the en-bloc clip of eight 30-06 rounds so as to keep their fingers out of the receiver and their thumbs away from the bolt when the operating rod was released. He hadn't paid close enough attention. He held the operating rod open with the side of his hand and pushed the loaded en-bloc clip into the magazine with his thumb. But, he didn't lift his thumb from the top of the clip before his hand allowed the operating rod to release. The instantaneous action triggered the bolt. The result was exactly as the Marine instructor had warned. The bolt slammed immediately shut, severely injuring his thumb. His hand was bandaged for two weeks. Since then, every time Brent fired at a target, he was always reminded of that incident and his self-imposed injury that he learned was given the name M-1 Thumb.

Brent didn't give up. He never stopped practicing his marksmanship. He became expert with the M-1. He never got his thumb caught by the bolt again.

The bullet from the muzzle of Brent Chafner's Remington 700 snapped through the air faster than the speed of sound, hitting its human target three hundred meters away.

The North Vietnamese infantryman who just finished his breakfast of dried fish, not thinking he had been spotted, turned his head to the side at the same time Brent Chafner squeezed the trigger. The bullet smashed into his neck just below his ear. A pink-red spray of blood spattered his terrified comrades crouching nearby. The bullet passed through the base of the man's skull in one ten-thousandth of a second. Undeterred, it continued its straight flight and, in what seemed to be the same instant, ripped into the side of a shattered tree, splintering a large piece of wood from its trunk.

The soldier's nervous system did not register the sudden trauma, but his body immediately reacted to the energy the bullet imparted upon impact. The once walking North Vietnamese soldier never knew what happened. Locked in the crosshairs of the Marine's .308, he died before the sound of the shot reached him. Rendered inert by a potent rifle bullet, the soldier crumpled lifeless to the ground.

The violent impact was seen only by the prone Marine through a Redfield rifle scope and by his spotter next to him through his powerful naval binoculars.

"Kill confirmed, Brent. Good shot."

Brent, still aiming the Remington rifle, worked the rifle's bolt and slowly ejected the empty, brass shell. The hollow casing, still smoking and smelling of expended powder, flew out of the chamber to the right, bounced off the sandbag embankment and fell to his feet. That was the last round in the magazine.

"See that bastard go down?"

The spotter gestured thumbs up.

"That son of a bitch just woke up dead."

Brent reached down and picked up the empty casing. He looked at the base of the cartridge and noticed the initials "LC." The cartridge was manufactured in Lake City, Missouri. He placed it in his vest pocket as a souvenir of his most recent enemy kill. His fingers felt three other casings which he also kept in his pocket for the same reason.

The Marine and his spotter slid farther down behind the sandbags into the shallow perimeter trench and quickly moved some fifty feet away to a new shooting position.

Brent extracted the bolt and placed it in his pocket. He reached for the ramrod. It's best to swab the barrel after several shots. He poured just a drop of light cleaning oil on a small patch of cloth and slid it into the breech of the weapon. He pushed the ramrod slowly forward the length of the barrel, then withdrew the aluminum rod out the muzzle. Brent made a second pass with a clean patch. He removed the bolt from his pocket and wiped it, paying close attention to the firing pin face. He slipped the bolt back into position, then ran a cloth the length of the rifle. He cleaned the front and aft lenses of his scope.

Brent opened the bolt again, this time without removing it from the rifle. He loaded the magazine with live rounds and then, keeping the rounds depressed, slipped one into the breech. Brent slid the bolt home slowly, forcing the new brass shell, tipped with a sharp, copper-covered bullet, into the firing chamber. He relished the intricate mechanically-precise sound of the action as the bolt would slide home. Brent lowered and locked the bolt's handle with his M-1 thumb and reached for his canteen.

If Brent Chafner could extend the lethal limits of the hill's weapons with long range, pinpoint rifle fire, kill enough of the enemy to strike fear in their minds, he may weaken any enemy assault.

Brent would again take careful aim through his rifle scope from a new concealed position.

Two rules hadn't changed since he began shooting at age six: patience and accuracy.

CHAPTER FIFTY-NINE

TURNING POINT

In a peculiar twist of the universe, days and dates don't repeat with perfect regularity. Through man's observations of the celestial heavens did he figure how to compensate for the drift of time. In the Gregorian calendar, even-number years evenly divided by four are adjusted by one additional day. The recipient month for the extra day of every fourth year is February. That anomaly is the trademark of Leap Year. Only then does February have twenty-nine days.

The intercalary year was unique in 1968 for the Marines at Khe Sanh, indeed for all U.S. military personnel on a one year tour of duty in Vietnam. They would endure, more so than in a normal year, an additional day in theater.

On the twenty-ninth of February of that leap year, the day General Wheeler returned from his Vietnam fact-finding trip and Robert McNamara resigned his post as Secretary of Defense, the Situation Room, instead of providing a place for analysis and discussion of global security issues, had assumed the look of a war room for only one international crisis: Vietnam.

Walt Rostow, central to the events, entered to attend an evening meeting and took his seat at the table.

"Mr. President, Sorry to be late. Just received some news. It seems the NVA have tried to attack Khe Sanh, Sir."

"What? The little buggers are actually…"

"For the last ten days, Sir, we've been aware of enemy movements toward the base."

Walt Rostow motioned for the terrain model to be moved closer to the President. "Trench lines have been excavated up to the east end of the base, and the south side, too. The Marines are doing everything they can to thwart them, but it's been shown that taking out trenches is not easy. The NVA are evidently digging tunnels under Khe Sanh. The Marines are using stethoscopes and divining rods to find them. The Vietnamese think they can blow Khe Sanh up like they did at some hill at Dien Bien Phu or what the Yankees tried at Petersburg. The Australians tried something similar somewhere in Belgium during World War One. So far, though, none have been found. I did see a report about a tunnel on Hill 861, Sir, but nothing has come of it. Regardless, the NVA are advancing their belligerence."

"Rostow, you just said they attacked."

"A major thrust was imminent, based on revelations back in early January by that deserter...his name was Lieutenant Tonc. The Marines were convinced the attack would come from the east. The enemy massed its forces, Sir, about here. Then, a company-size probe attack was made against the Thirty-Seventh Rangers...ARVN, Sir."

Rostow pointed to the model. "Here, Sir. But, the assault was unsuccessful. The Marines claimed about twenty-five enemy dead."

President Johnson looked down at the model.

"Jesus, will this Khe Sanh shit ever end?"

"Then, on the twenty-third of February, Sir, Khe Sanh sustained the highest concentration of incoming artillery fire to date. However, the enemy didn't follow up with ground forces.

"Two days later, a patrol led by Bravo Company First Battalion Twenty-sixth Marines ended in disaster. The patrol was ambushed with terrible consequences. We have not retrieved the bodies of the dead Marines.

"The NVA continue to be threatening in the area immediately south and east of the base."

The President's hand moved over the terrain model.

"What about our airstrikes, Walt?"

"Right, Sir. The weather is improving. The Vietnamese know this and have to act quickly, if they are to act at all. The NVA moved heavy ordnance into Khe Sanh Ville. On the twenty-seventh of February, two days ago, Arclight raids were conducted against the village and wiped it out.

"Today, at about 9:30 at night in Vietnam, a battalion of the Sixty-sixth Regiment of the 304th Division launched another attack at the east end of the base. I know it's small on the model."

Rostow pointed. "Here, at the end of the runway. However, combined strikes by our fighter-bombers and intense artillery fire from the base and from the 175s at Camp Carroll and Rockpile compromised the enemy's plans. The high fragmentation COFRAM rounds did a number on the enemy as they emerged from the bombing. It was withering, Sir. The NVA had nowhere to go but into the teeth of the base artillery and the ARVN. The enemy advance was stopped. They tried with probes two more times, but never closed the gap. The last attack occurred after midnight, but it failed."

"So, what are you telling me, Walt? Have we reached a turning point?"

"Sir, reports confirmed that several trench lines were filled with enemy bodies annihilated by the COFRAM rounds. They were evidently poised for attack and were killed on the spot. In other areas to the east of the base, our bombing and shelling were so intense, the entire Sixty-sixth Regiment may have been wiped out."

The President smiled.

"So the Tiger of Dien Bien Phu didn't roar after all."

"Or, he's about to roar in a big way, Sir."

CHAPTER SIXTY

SERMON IN THE CLOUDS

A solitary, close-shaven man of about thirty, one of the chaplains on the Khe Sanh Combat Base, climbed the concrete stairs and left the COC at the double-quick. His helmet bounced on his head. A dirty flak jacket on which he had drawn a cross covered the man's torso.

The Chaplain made a brief stop at Charlie Med. A Marine covered in grease emerged with fresh bandages on his arm.

"Worship Service on Sunday, right, Chaplain? I'll be there, if I'm alive."

Black humor, serving as a psychological defensive measure, pervaded the base. No one, not even the Chaplain, was immune to the rampant, dark absurdities. Marines were always talking about death and yakking derisively about God and destiny. They made fun of the sermons, but the Chaplain went about his business calmly.

"I'll believe it when I see it, Corporal."

In a crouched position, the Chaplain ran hastily across the width of Khe Sanh's east-west metal-plank runway that was pockmarked with incoming NVA mortar and artillery rounds. Jagged metal planking lay in crumpled piles near the craters and at the edges of the runway.

Two photographers, an American and a Frenchman, followed the Chaplain who stopped next to a bunker and some sandbags stacked knee high.

The Chaplain reached for a Greek New Testament Bible in his pocket. An American missionary couple, on assignment in the Khe Sanh area since the early sixties, had recently loaned the Bible to him. Unfortunately, it would not be returned in the same condition it had been lent. The protective plastic covering melted when the Chaplain sat too close to a fire one evening to ward off the bitter wet-cold. He never warmed up, but the heat turned the plastic cover into a crinkled mess.

The Chaplain took out a candle holder, a white cloth and a silver chalice from a knapsack-type bag that served as his altar kit. He also pulled out a shiny brass cross. He took special care to place the cross perfectly upright on the sandbags.

A long ridgeline above which towered Hills 950 and1015 stood several kilometers to the north. Characterized by its upside down, teacup-shaped profile, Hill 1015 was prominent. The Marines controlled Hill 950, but not Hill1015; and not the slopes below it. The serene beauty concealed the North Vietnamese artillery observers who were positioned on the forward-facing slope. They spotted targets on the American base and called in artillery rounds from Co Roc. Congregations of people on the base were prime targets.

Mindful of the instructions the Chaplain had received not to congregate more than six Marines at any one time, he visited as many sites on the combat base as he could each day to lead the men in prayer.

The Chaplain opened a small circular container from which he extracted a few wafers. He looked up, cupped his hands to his mouth and shouted in a stentorian voice.

"We're gonna have a short worship service. All denominations are welcome."

Just as the Chaplain was about to begin his service, artillery rounds and rockets were already piercing the air toward the combat base. The incoming shells screamed and howled as they arrived. The loud impact was a shocking end to the menacing death-sound they made.

NVA rockets screeched shrilly like so many tormented demons. The sound suddenly shrieked from all directions. Nothing else could be heard. They crashed in violent explosions.

Marines learned to discern the sound of incoming artillery shells and rockets. Those who immediately took cover, usually escaped the enemy shelling unharmed, but there was no guarantee.

The ground erupted not far from the makeshift altar. Red earth showered the area along with flying jagged metal. Smoke and red dust were thick. An acrid smell of expended high explosive stung everyone's lungs.

The Chaplain rose from a nearby trench. Through the haze, he saw his battlefield-altar was unscathed. A single shaft of sunshine beamed through an opening in the clouds. It illuminated the brass cross which, in contrast to the gray backdrop, glowed in totemic silence.

The irony was not lost on the Chaplain. The highlighted cross sent a clear message. The microcosm of the struggle of man against evil was enduring, but salvation was at hand. The sunbeam of light was a signal of eternal blessings. *Keep me safe, oh, God, for in you I take refuge.*

The Chaplain, dusting himself off, grabbed the helmet which had fallen off his head and made his way to perform the brief service.

"Men, be not afraid. Nothing can harm us."

He motioned with his arms. "Let us congregate and give thanks to our Father. Strength is found by coming together in his divine presence."

Five Marines assembled at the Chaplain's makeshift, open-air church. No one asked them to be in harm's way, yet here they were.

"We gotta be quick. He'll understand."

Then, with a confident grin, "The NVA may not want us here, but God does. This hostile land is also God's creation."

The Chaplain bowed his head and placed his hands together in front of his body. He began his service. "Our Father, we have been sent here to do thy will. You guide us through dangerous times. We pray to you, our Lord. We ask you to accept us into thy Holy Kingdom as your servants."

The silent men, some with rifles at their side or across their back, lowered their heads. They took off their helmets to communicate with God in their own way.

Oblivious to cynical onlookers and their vapid prattle, the Chaplain thought of a little-known passage he felt was apropos to the precariousness in which he and many others now found themselves. The bleak hills that surrounded the cradle of land that came to be known as the Khe Sanh Combat Base and the tens of thousands of people who had gathered there for hostile reasons conjured the passage perfectly. The Chaplain recited the fourteenth verse of the third chapter of Joel, one of the twelve minor prophets whose writings were apocalyptic.

"Multitudes, multitudes, in the valley of decision. For the day of the Lord is near in the valley of decision."

The Chaplain spoke extemporaneously as he opened the tattered Greek Bible.

"God provides comfort in times of loneliness and sorrow, in times of suffering, fear and temptation. We only have to heed His divine wisdom through His only begotten son, Jesus Christ."

The Chaplain, having lost track of time, continued with his eyes closed. "The Scriptures teach us to be strong in the face of adversity. They remind us to have faith in our Savior."

The Chaplain recited a verse from John.

"Here on earth you will have many trials and sorrows. But, take heart..."

The words of Psalm 91 which always struck the Chaplain as so appropriate now took on a more poignant meaning. Taken by the cogent symbolism revealed in the passage, he paraphrased key words.

"Arrows that fly by day"—the rockets. "Terror by night"—the artillery shells that flew unseen or the enemy's attacks on the outposts under the cover of darkness. "Thousands falling at your side"—friendly casualties. "Ten thousand by your right hand"—the strength of the Marines.

The Chaplain recited other salient passages which he had underlined in his borrowed Bible, every page of which was dog-eared, torn and stained with red dust. But, the Chaplain, haunted by a new epiphany, returned to Psalm 91. With full understanding of God's message, the Chaplain bowed his head in supreme reverence and recited the first line out loud.

"Surely He will save you from the fowler's snare..."

The Chaplain raised his head and repeated a simple word.

"Amen."

The Chaplain looked toward the ground. His boots were worn. His lower pant legs were half eaten away by the red dirt and humidity. He touched his sweating forehead as he pushed his glasses back into position.

He had over-extended his sermon, but the Chaplain persisted: Psalm 139:

"You hem me in behind me and before me and you lay your hand upon me."

The Chaplain was very much pressed for time. He quickly flipped to the eleventh verse of Jeremiah, the second longest book in the Bible.

"Let me see your vengeance on them, for to you I have committed my cause."

Oh, how the Chaplain wanted to read from Acts, Romans, even from Philippians, but these readings would have to wait.

"We'll have a quick communion."

The ceremony, already too long, never reached that far.

NVA artillery rounds smashed again into the combat base on the opposite side of the runway. The North Vietnamese gunners marched the shells across the airstrip toward the assembly. The Marines dove for cover in all directions.

The Chaplain hurriedly placed the articles of his sermon in his altar kit. He grabbed the cross and ducked for cover.

The shelling stopped abruptly. Two Marines lay dead not far from him. The Chaplain was shocked at the horrible sight.

Semi-conscious, the French photographer was lying on his side with his cameras on the ground. His American colleague was kneeling next to him.

The Chaplain, gathering strength, steadied himself and knelt down. He touched the photographer's face.

"God bless you, my son."

The Chaplain uttered additional words, from the Twenty-third Psalm, meant for those who had just been wounded, but perhaps more for himself. "Yea, though I walk through the valley of the shadow of death, I will fear no evil: for Thou art with me."

CHAPTER SIXTY-ONE

BACK AND FORTH

President Johnson called his vice president at his winter retreat in Waverly, Minnesota to discuss the $186 billion budget that he had submitted to Congress weeks before.

Hubert Humphrey hailed originally from South Dakota, a state far to the north of Texas. He attended the University of Minnesota where he received a degree in pharmacy. His interests eventually turning to politics, Humphrey became a professor of political science and, later, the mayor of Minneapolis, serving that city between 1945 and 1948. He helped stomp out the influence of the communist party in Minnesota and was elected to the United States Senate in 1948.

Hubert Humphrey and his wife enjoyed their vacations in cooler summers and colder winters on their tranquil lakeside acreage.

"Good morning, Mr. President."

"Hubert, thank you for all your help on this year's budget. I knew you would lead the effort for me."

"Mr. President, I'm sure as the winter snow that we've got the support."

"You've always been a steadfast supporter, Hubert, even if we've disagreed on some topics."

The topics to which the President referred, of course, revolved around the war in Vietnam. Hubert Humphrey had higher political aspirations. He would seek the presidency in the future. While showing loyalty to Johnson's administration, Humphrey would have to distance himself from the President's unpopular war in Asia. Humphrey would have to present a counter position, perhaps an antagonistic, or at least a more palatable policy to the American public. This little scenario could become politically sticky if the war dragged on.

The conversation quickly shifted to Vietnam. It couldn't be helped.

"Mr. President, these newspaper articles about the war are disturbing."

"I know, Hubert. The NVA attacked Khe Sanh on the twenty-ninth of February. Didn't succeed. But, even more disconcerting, on about the eleventh of February …early last month, it was a Reamer Argo in Saigon… a colonel on Westmoreland's staff, who did some analysis of sieges. He came to the conclusion that sieges have some things in common, namely, the force under siege becomes rigid and loses the initiative. He goes on to say that supply problems develop.

"Rostow tells me that Vauban, some ancient French guy who built forts, said the defenders become demoralized, that those besieged can't last more than a month. Argo says that Khe Sanh is following the same pattern of other historical sieges. He concludes that if we maintain a defensive action, the North Vietnamese may succeed with their siege efforts. The fortress can't hold out."

"Interesting."

"Westmoreland was not impressed. Felt it was defeatist."

"What did Argo recommend, Lyndon?"

"Argo says we must use an outside force to gain the initiative. I've heard from so many sources that Khe Sanh can hold and then again, it can't hold; the Marines can survive, then they can't survive. Back and forth."

Hubert Humphrey, holding the phone to his ear, looked out the large window of his one-level ranch-style home across the frozen lake. He spoke candidly in a straightforward voice.

"Lyndon…Mr. President…you have to bring this war to conclusion. I support any decision you make and your stance on Khe Sanh, but it must be balanced with the understanding that we need to get out of Vietnam soon."

"Hubert, they say we need Khe Sanh and can defend it successfully, and that's the story. Wheeler signed the memorandum in January, remember? Said we should hold Khe Sanh."

"I understand Wheeler's point, but I have concerns about an outcome that's uncertain."

"Yeah. Thank you for your candidness, Hubert. We occupy huge, sprawling bases, but the North Vietnamese and Viet Cong hold the entire countryside. Hue is secure and Da Nang is safe, I dunno, like Des Moines."

The President chided, "The mayor of Da Nang could learn a few things from the mayor of Des Moines. You were a mayor once, Hubert, in that up-north country of yours…in some town called, what was it? Minneapolis, right?"

The President liked to poke fun at northerners.

"What's the latest news from Vietnam, Mr. President?"

"Ho Chi Minh says the Tet Offensive set a foundation for future victories."

"What are you hearing exactly about Khe Sanh itself?"

"The hill positions are being hit daily. I can't keep the dates and the damned hill designations straight. Things move so fast over there, it gets confusing. I need to look at that model every day to locate the places.

"A Sir Robert Thompson, some English pacification guy, says the purpose of the Tet offensive was to dislocate U.S. Forces. He thinks Khe Sanh is a major diversion contrived by Vo Nguyen Giap. The *New York Times* has made a similar analysis.

"The French veterans of Din Bin Phu are chiming in now with all their bullshit. General Navarre says the North Vietnamese cannot win. That's exactly what the French said in 1954."

"Mr. President, the French are playing both sides of the game. We all know the French are supportive of Ho Chi Minh, if for no other reason than revolution is in French blood, more so than wine. France has always been a hotbed of discontent with socialist leanings. Ho Chi Minh is a revolutionary. The French are sympathetic toward him."

"French people. All they do is eat pâté and snails with sissy forks. They like that stinky cheese and drink that licorice-tasting pastis God-awful stuff.

We saw how effective they were at Din Bin Phu. Navarre, de Castries... just gave up."

"The French got beat up pretty bad, Mr. President. They lost a colony and their prestige. They harbor bad feelings toward Americans."

"Hubert, General Wheeler was at the White House this morning for a breakfast meeting. He got back from Vietnam before March. He is convinced that Hanoi will try to consolidate power by seizing enough territory to force our hand at negotiations with some kind of trumped-up government.

"The Joint Chiefs of Staff say if I want to realize my objectives, I need to send even more troops to Vietnam. Wheeler's re-iterating the need for two hundred thousand men. I'm perplexed. Is the troop mobilization intended to meet an emergency or are we anticipating unforeseen difficulties? I've directed Clark Clifford, who took over at Defense on the first of March, to review the request. Bunker wants all two hundred thousand troops. I'm not sure yet where Clifford stands on this issue."

"Mr. President, this is tough. But I must stress we need to end the war as soon as we possibly can."

"Westmoreland and his generals and the Joint Chiefs say we need a strong military presence in Eye Corps to stop the infiltration of the North Vietnamese into South Vietnam."

"It's problematic, Mr. President."

"General Max Taylor keeps urging an evacuation of Khe Sanh. He made his feelings well known some time ago. And, the Marines are not keen about reporting to Westmoreland. There's a big rift between MACV in Saigon and Marine headquarters in Da Nang."

The President was now openly venting. "Hubert, I told you a moment ago, I have to believe my generals. I listen to Wheeler and Westmoreland and I listen to President Eisenhower, and Max Taylor, too. I want to believe their expertise. I become more worried every day about what's happening over there. Colonel Argo's analysis doesn't help a damn bit...gives me the jitters.

"That Route Nine highway is probably the most dangerous road in the world right now. Can't get nothin' through."

"Mr. President, it would seem that..."

"And of course, early on, the Marines themselves came under criticism for not being prepared for such a campaign as they are experiencing at Khe Sanh."

"Mr. President, I'm sure we'll win at Khe Sanh."

Hubert Humphrey was sounding like a dove and a hawk at the same time, to the point he was on the cusp of contradicting himself. There was silence between the two men and then Humphrey spoke.

"Lyndon, we're losing a lot of Americans in a war that most people don't understand and for a country that most Americans don't care about. Based on what I've seen thus far, we need to win and get out, or if we can't win, negotiate. If Hanoi isn't forthcoming, we have to find the solution."

CHAPTER SIXTY-TWO

TRAN QUY HAI

"Gentlemen, General Tran Quy Hai will be with us shortly."

NVA officers had traveled for many hours and, in some cases, for several days through mountains and jungle to be present for this meeting. They were now seated on crude wood benches or standing idly in the underground B5T8 headquarters. Each man, showing respect, wore his rank on his battlefield uniform, a custom not typical with the North Vietnamese soldiers in the field.

The original B5T8 command center, deep in the Laotian jungles near Sar Lit village, destroyed by American bombs less than two months before, in January, had been reconstructed. The newly-excavated headquarters functioned as well now as the old one did before the bombing; maybe even better. But, it was already showing signs of intense use.

Chicken bones, picked clean, lay scattered in the dirt. The humid, musty air in the bunker ten meters below the surface of the ground, crowded now with so many sweating bodies, was stifling.

General Hai entered the bunker, his arrival heralded by the noisiness of his entourage. The general wore solid red collar boards and, more specifically, his rank insignia on yellow shoulder epaulettes. He removed his green *mu sat* (pith helmet) with a star on the front and laid it on the table in front of him.

The table was draped with a red cloth. Above and behind it, a sign written in yellow letters on a field of red, proclaimed: *Vinh quang nhan dan Viet nam, Vi nhan dan.Tien len* (Glorious Vietnam. For the People. Forward).

Tran Quy Hai exuded a composed confidence. He turned to a large map of Quang Tri and Quang Binh Provinces and eastern Laos that hung on the wall to the left of the banner. A picture of Ho Chi Minh hung beside it.

"At the time I was given command of B5T8 or, if you wish, the Khe Sanh-Highway Nine Front, the Central Military Party Committee and the Ministry of Defense developed a strategic plan that called for attacks throughout South Vietnam. The primary targets were the provincial capitals. Saigon and Hue were paramount objectives. Perhaps not obvious to you, Highway Nine and northern Quang Tri Province have been important to those efforts.

"The general staff divided Quang Tri Province into two military areas, east and west. The dividing line was established at kilometer forty-one on Highway Nine. Battlefield A extended from that point to Laos. Battlefield B ran east to the Cua Viet Port and included Vinh Linh and Southern Quang Binh Province. The 320th Division and three regiments of the disbanded 324th Division were responsible for the eastern sector while the 304th and 325C Divisions commanded the western sector. Of course, there have been some displacements of the divisions since then. Hanoi decided to make Battlefield A the primary focus. Because of the mountain terrain in the west, we can exploit our traditional fighting strengths.

"I briefed Minister Giap in person a week ago, after the attack on the twenty-ninth of February. I re-affirmed we are prepared for a new thrust.

"As you know, wide-spread military action is underway in the south. There has been a lot of fighting in Hue by your comrades. Due to the attack on the American embassy by the NLF, Saigon remains in complete turmoil. The city is gripped with fear."

Tran Quy Hai did not mention that fighting in Hue, though vicious, ultimately was not in North Vietnam's favor, that by the twenty-fourth of February, the Americans declared Hue to be secure. He did not say the attacks on the provincial centers had been quickly repulsed. Nor did he reveal that the attack on the American embassy was short-lived, that daily life in Saigon, though tenuous, was restored. He did not inform the men that the North Vietnamese Army and Viet Cong had lost a lot of fighters throughout South Vietnam, that the losses were staggering. He did not tell the men the truth. The Tet Offensive was a complete fiasco.

"The next several weeks and months will determine the fate of the war against the imperialist Americans. The role of our efforts in Quang Tri Province, specifically Battlefield A, has been to draw American forces in and pin them down far away from the cities. The Americans have obliged us. Their goal was to create a barrier in the Khe Sanh-Highway Nine area so as to block the flow of support from North Vietnam to the southern battlefields. As a result, they've invested a large number of troops and military assets in Quang Tri Province."

Tran Quy Hai could be vague, even taciturn, but in the grip of this suspense, his dramatic preamble was ominous.

General Hai fingered a cigarette out of a crumpled pack. He flipped open the brass lid of an American Zippo lighter given to him by a junior lieutenant in the 304th Division. A map of the northern part of South Vietnam and the letters I CORPS and USMC had been engraved on one side of the lighter. Intrigued with this American invention, Hai had his name engraved and VUNG I, to mock the American military region, on the other side.

The roller struck the flint. The wick inside the perforated wind cell burst into flame. General Hai tilted his head to one side as he placed the Zippo near his face and lit the cigarette. The smell of kerosene filled the air. The brass lid clanged shut with the solid metallic sound for which Zippos were famous and, for some mysterious reason, the sound North Vietnamese soldiers cherished.

"At the highest of priorities, our enduring strategy is to reunify all of Vietnam."

General Hai waved his hand with the cigarette at the men while he balled his other hand into a tight fist in front of his face to make his point.

"It's for the *quan doi* to reduce the American invaders to complete rubble. We must nullify the slovenly rat-soldiers who support the puppet Saigon regime."

Tran Quy Hai threw his smoking cigarette to the dirt floor and rubbed it into the soil with his boot. He became more assertive. "There is much more, however."

Tran Quy Hai spoke in a measured tone. "Our original objective was not a sole victory at Khe Sanh, but rather a nation-wide general offensive-general insurrection against the illegal Thieu regime.

"We have been instructed to bombard the Americans at Ta Con continuously as harassment. We are to catch them off-guard through two or three major artillery barrages. One occurred on the twenty-third of February."

Again, General Hai did not elaborate on the failure of the attacks against the ARVN line on the twenty-ninth of February, or the resulting losses. He made no mention of the deadly effectiveness of the ordnance the Americans used.

"Even though there have been differences of opinion about how to conduct battle in Quang Tri Province, a large number of American troops can still be eliminated.

"I bring you to the point. February has passed. We have sent propaganda teams into the area to spread the word. The final attack on the American Imperialists will occur soon. I cannot disclose the date, but within a short time, we will attack the Americans at Khe Sanh again.

"The new plan of attack has been submitted to the central committee. It has been received favorably. In anticipation of Hanoi's non-objection, we are making preparations now and are moving combat elements closer to the Americans.

"We will not use large frontal infantry assaults or risk entire divisions. However, we will not shrink away either. Our tactics are a departure from those we used at Dien Bien Phu, but will be no less effective.

"The combat formula we must utilize is flexibility, close coordination and the launch of a powerful, but focused attack at a precise moment. The artillery barrage preceding the attack will compromise the American defenses."

Tran Quy Hai lit another cigarette. The Zippo lighter clanged shut again. "B5T8 will explode like a volcano. We will severely damage the American Imperialist army. Our success will be the pillar of our magnificent 1968 triumph."

The audience of young officers applauded.

Tran Quy Hai relished the moment. Using all his guile, he had accomplished something very important. He had stirred the very passion in each man who sat or stood before him. This collection of young men, some of whom he would never see again, would honor the Quan Doi Nhan Dan and carry forth Ho Chi Minh's mandate of a united Vietnam.

But, Tran Quy Hai did not quantify success, nor did he reveal exactly what he meant by damage or triumph.

CHAPTER SIXTY-THREE

MACV

Better known as MACV, the two story building housing the American command in Vietnam, located near Tan Son Nhut Airport in Saigon, was built by an American contractor. Although it sustained damage during the Viet Cong attacks during Tet, the building still functioned.

The chow line in the cafeteria of the American command was not yet open for lunch, but if requested, the cooks could prepare an early order.

If the Vietnamese couldn't do anything, they could sure cook good burgers at MACV; at least that is what Terrence Kerley was told before he left the States. It may turn out to be the only good thing since Kerley was flying straight back to Washington late that night.

Terrence Kerley's position in life was strange. He worked for the Department of the Interior, but felt he would be successful as an independent lobbyist and quit. Kerley tried to pass himself off as a street-savvy intellect. Really more of a gopher, he made his mark by sometimes undertaking ad hoc assignments for the White House. Although he was never contacted by the President directly, he presumed an air of importance that was not commensurate with his station in life.

Garnished with lettuce, tomatoes, pickle relish and a thick slice of Vidalia onion, the delicious-looking burger, accompanied by a side order of French fries, was served in front of Kerley on a big plate. He was starving.

Kerley spread mustard on the bun and promptly bit into his juicy cheeseburger.

"Mr. Kerley, the colonel will see you now."

Kerley looked up to see a young, smartly dressed Army lieutenant standing next to his table.

"You're kidding me. I just took the first bite out of my cheeseburger."

"Sorry, Sir."

"Come back in a few minutes."

"Can't do that, Sir."

"All right, Lieutenant."

Kerley wiped his mouth cursorily with his napkin. He had put too much mustard on the bun. Still chewing, Kerley stood up.

"Christ, they could have waited twenty minutes."

Kerley followed the tall, young Army officer whose uniform was creased like a razor blade, whose shoes were shinier than black obsidian. In contrast to Kerley who had no hair—out of ironic teasing, people spelled his name Curly—the lieutenant had a full head of thick hair that was closely cropped.

Kerley was shown into a small briefing room. An Army colonel, a full bird, whose name on a black plastic nametag over his right shirt pocket read "Ashcroft," stood facing the door. An Army major and a Marine lieutenant colonel, members of the joint staff, stood on either side of Ashcroft.

The escorting lieutenant left the assembly of men and walked into the hallway. He closed the door behind him, sealing off the conference room.

The walls were lined with maps showing the manner in which South Vietnam had been parceled into corps by the U.S. military.

Kerley immediately recognized First Corps, which he knew was referred to as Eye Corps, at the top of the map of South Vietnam, and the five provinces that comprised it—Quang Tri Province being the most northern, the most important and certainly the most active.

Colonel Ashcroft held a lit cigarette between his middle fingers. He threw down the pack of Winstons on the table as he breathed smoke out through his nostrils.

Ashcroft did all the talking.

"Mr. Kerley, I trust your accommodations at the Caravelle Hotel are satisfactory."

"Only just so, Colonel."

"You have chosen a precarious time to visit Saigon. The city is almost back to normal after the attacks, but I would not recommend that you roam the streets. The VC are still in town."

"Thank you, Colonel. Now if we can..."

"Exactly what is your mission here, Mr. Kerley?"

Momentarily tripped up by the interruption, Kerley paused for a moment.

"Gentlemen, I'm on special assignment. I need all the details about Khe Sanh firsthand."

The three officers did not speak. They stared incredulously at the pudgy, bald man. Their face muscles didn't twitch.

Colonel Ashcroft took a drag on his cigarette and blew out smoke without a hint of emotion.

"Mr. Kerley, let me get this right. You have come all the way from Washington, D.C. to find out about Khe Sanh in one day...all the details, to use your words. Not about the Tet attacks, only Khe Sanh. You need all the information now, is this correct?"

"That is correct, Colonel Ashcroft."

"And who sent you? I believe we have the right to know that."

"A very highly-placed individual."

"And you expect to learn all there is to know about Khe Sanh in one briefing and report back to this highly-placed individual, whoever that may be."

"That's right. I'm expecting your cooperation, Colonel. I'll be straight and tell you..."

"No. Mr. Kerley, I'll be straight. I will tell you. Maybe you are not aware, but General Westmoreland sends briefing cables directly to Washington every day. Plus, for your information, General Wheeler was here for a week. What can you provide from this trip that would be different or better?"

"I have my instructions, Colonel Ashcroft. And, yes, I'm well aware of Westmoreland's cables and Wheeler's visit. Like I say..."

"Mr. Kerley, I don't have time to brief you and neither does anyone higher in rank than me...or lower."

Ashcroft looked down at Kerley and squared with him. "I was made aware of your visit an hour ago. I can afford only ten minutes."

"Colonel..."

"What do you want to know, Mr. Kerley?"

Kerley was brought up short by the clipped tone of the colonel's voice.

"OK, if that's the way it is..."

"Ten minutes, Mr. Kerley. I have more important things to do."

"I'll have to report your recalcitrance, Colonel. My boss will be displeased."

"Mr. Kerley, I believe you may be misinformed. I work directly for, in capital letters, the COMUSMACV. That would mean, in case you do not know, The Commander of the United States Military Assistance Command, right here in Vietnam. Let me be clear. There is no other top commander in this theater. His office is down this hallway. The person who occupies that office is the one who sent me to talk with you. Now, can we get on with it, please?"

Kerley's face was turning red.

"Colonel, I have just one question then."

"Shoot."

"Can we successfully defend Khe Sanh?"

Ashcroft's patience was about exhausted.

"Mr. Kerley, I don't know who the hell you are, but if that is all you have come to Saigon for, under some pretense to learn the details, the answer is yes, short and sweet. We will continue to successfully defend Khe Sanh."

The cool air in the room, clammy from the constantly loud, window-mounted air conditioning unit, and now somewhat smoky from the colonel's cigarettes, matched the cold tension between the two men.

Kerley's anger was boiling. He looked directly at Ashcroft and responded dead-pan, but in a petulant tone.

"Enlightening."

The colonel's face hardened.

"Don't be insolent, Mr. Kerley. Not with me."

"Colonel, some people believe the terrain around Khe Sanh renders the base indefensible."

Colonel Ashcroft lit another cigarette.

"And you have come all this way to express the uneducated opinion of others about terrain in a part of the country several hundred miles from here, in a part of the world I doubt any of them have ever seen. A trifle presumptive, wouldn't you agree, Mr. Kerley? Perhaps boastful is a better adjective."

"Certain people in Washington want an answer, Colonel and..."

"I've had enough, Mr. Kerley. Now, you listen to me."

Ashcroft pointed first to the Marine officer in front of him, then turning obliquely, to some distant, imaginary point in the opposite direction. "Those Marines in Eye Corps will do their job. They'll defend Khe Sanh and they will win. Giap and his field generals have miscalculated. They'll be defeated just like the Tet attacks in Saigon and elsewhere. That's the message with which you may return to Washington, D.C."

"Now, Colonel..."

"Let me try again, Mr. Kerley. You will pardon my directness."

The colonel leaned forward. "Vo Nguyen Giap will slink back to Hanoi with that ragtag army of his. Am I clear?"

Colonel Ashcroft spoke one last time. "Now that you have no further questions for me to entertain, this meeting is immediately terminated. Your ten minutes are up, Mr. Kerley."

Colonel Ashcroft opened the conference room door. The young lieutenant immediately stood up from a wood bench. Ashcroft's voice echoed the length of the hallway.

"Lieutenant, Mr. Kerley is to be returned safely to the Caravelle."

CHAPTER SIXTY-FOUR

CREATION OF STRIKE GROUP CT43

Major Hieu Phat turned through some pages of a folder while other officers took seats around the wood table. Unlike the B5T8 headquarters, his command post, located only a few kilometers away in eastern Laos, served a singular purpose. It was the final transshipment point for soldiers slated for Quang Tri Province.

"Gentlemen, I'll come straight to the issue. General Tran Quy Hai reports there will be another attempt against the American base at Khe Sanh.

"We have been ordered to consolidate soldiers into two strike groups, codenamed Chien Thang, a total of two thousand men in a big surge. Chien Thang 42, comprised of nine hundred soldiers can be configured easily since it will be made up mostly of experienced men. We will move that Chien Thang group to Huong Tan Cong So 3 [Attack Sector N3] within the next six days."

Captain Phan Cong Nho, standing at the back of the room, spoke.

"Major Phat, Sir, our capabilities..."

"Let me finish, Captain. You haven't heard the bad news yet. Even before the jumping off of Chien Thang 42, we must organize and equip Chien Thang 43.

"Raw troops are arriving by the hour. Deserters are being given one last chance to fulfill their obligation. Stragglers are being rounded up.

"CT43 will consist of eleven hundred men. A company of experienced soldiers from Highpoint 845 has been withdrawn from that sector for this operation and will join with CT43 to augment and inspire the new troops."

There was a brief pause. "Gentlemen, that will be all for now."

The North Vietnamese officers, stunned by the abruptness but more by what they heard, stumbled up the steps from the underground tunnel and emerged into daylight. A few men cursed while others scratched their heads in bewilderment as to how they would arrange for the successful launch of two large strike groups. Working with new troops was always difficult.

Captain Nho, who never talked out of turn, felt compelled to express his thoughts.

"Major Phat, may I have a word with you, Sir?"

"Yes, Captain. Go ahead. Get it off your chest."

"You'll excuse me, Sir. This has never been accomplished before. We can hardly move three hundred men as a group on schedule now. It's not possible to equip two thousand disorganized men into consolidated groups and jump each one off consecutively. A force of this magnitude will require thirty days, Sir. We are already stretched too thin to be able to manage a huge concentration."

"Stretched too thin, Captain? I will attribute what you say as an observation, but let me caution you that further talk of this nature will reflect badly. Colonel Hoang Dan will move the strike groups suddenly to drive the attack to victory."

"Major, we need to scale back the effort."

Major Phat's patience with his junior officer's reluctance was at an end.

"Captain Nho, I said drive the attack to victory. We are not scaling anything back. We are under orders to send two CT strike groups to Attack Sector N3. That is exactly what we are going to do. The CT strike groups need to be in position to move quickly and in force. Colonel Dan will not turn them back."

"But Major…"

"Captain, enough! You have explained the risks as you see them. But, I have told you what we are going to do. Am I clear, Captain?"

"Yes, Sir."

"I have a feeling the new attack will happen before late March. Time is critical. The attack at the end of February failed. We won't fail now."

"Right, Sir, understood."

"See to it, Captain."

CHAPTER SIXTY-FIVE

MEDEVAC

In a shocking incident, more than forty Marines were killed when their C-123 crashed five miles east of Khe Sanh on the sixth of March. This came on the heels of a previous downing of another C-123 about one week before. The siege was taking its toll on the American defenders of Khe Sanh. The Marines had suffered more than a thousand casualties thus far.

Still, the NVA's harassing artillery bombardment of Khe Sanh from Co Roc did not subside. It began anew.

Lieutenant Guarino yelled at a Marine standing nearby. He had worked with him for days evacuating the wounded.

"Jordan, the choppers are landing in zero five minutes. Two 46s. Whadawe got?"

"Two KIAs and two critical WIAs, one Marine all shot up and one civilian with a head wound. I believe he'll live, Sir, but he's hurt pretty bad."

"Let's get the civvy the hell outta here. What else?"

"We got fourteen Marines trying to get on board—all wounded but walking."

"OK, find eight walking wounded. They can carry the KIAs. You and I need another six men to help us carry the critical WIAs."

"We're covered, Lieutenant. The Marine with severe body wounds—we have to be careful of the transfusion tubes, Sir."

"Got it, Jordan."

"Sir! The shells are coming up the runway toward Charlie Med!"

"Corporal, get yourself in the trench."

"Sir, I'm staying with these guys. They can't move at all and I can't move them."

The lieutenant yelled out.

"Everyone stay low! The NVA will spot a new target."

"Sir, we are the new target! They know the choppers are coming in here. They've shifted their shelling. Their guns are zeroing in."

"Juliet Hotel Seven, this is Kilo Sierra Charlie Med. Delay landing. Lima Zulu hot. Delay landing for one zero. Acknowledge."

"Roger, Charlie Med, Juliet Hotel Seven and Eight delay landing one zero. Advise when clear."

"Corporal, they're delaying. Keep low."

"Lieutenant, the men are stable. Both are breathing, but the Marine's bandages are seeping lots of blood. Not sure he'll…"

NVA artillery shells slammed into the earth near Charlie Med. The overwhelming explosions were deafening. Dust rose in dense columns. Suspended in the air, it lingered, choking everyone.

Jordan choked, He gulped in dry air. He tasted the bite of the red dust and suffocating smoke as he coughed.

"Not sure he'll make it, Sir, but the civvy is OK."

"Son, we'll get him on board."

Jordan talked to the Marine.

"Listen to me, buddy. This is Jordy. I'm with you. Choppers are here in a few. You'll be sittin' in first class with good company. The Purple Foxes will get you to Da Nang in no time."

Lieutenant Guarino yelled again amidst the explosions.

"Corporal, you all right?"

Jordan, still prone in the dirt and holding his helmet on, yelled back.

"OK, Sir. OK."

The NVA cannonade stopped as suddenly as it had begun.

Lieutenant Guarino spoke back into the radio.

"Juliet Hotel Seven, proceed inbound. We have two KIA, two WIA critical, one's a civilian; and fourteen WIA walking."

"Roger, Charlie Med, good copy. Juliet Hotel Seven and Eight inbound with water and ammo. Off-load and on-load in zero one minute. Fuel low. Must land in Quang Tri on return."

"Jordan, they're coming in. Too many men running for one chopper. Gotta divide them into the two choppers. Place the critical WIAs in the second chopper. You take control of the Marine and I'll manage the civilian with the head wound. You'll run first and I'll follow. After we get them on board, we move away from the choppers and drop to the ground. Got it?"

"Roger that, Sir."

The choppers crept up the Quang Tri Valley, slid behind Hills 950 and 1015, banked sharply to the south and approached from the west. Skimming just above the ground, they made their presence known through their rotors' loud shuddering, chopping noise. The mammoth helicopters slowed their forward speed, their noses pitching up for the controlled descent onto the red dirt of the Khe Sanh Combat Base. The turbines whined, the exhaust blew hot. The blades, now directly overhead, stirred the dust into a dense red cloud. The pilots pressed the collectives down in their respective cockpits.

Cargo was being kicked out the back loading ramps beneath the choppers' whirling blades. What looked to be cartons of Coke taped together were thrown out the side door.

At the same time, Jordan, with the aid of three others, lifted the stretcher of the severely wounded Marine, while another Marine kept the plasma flowing from the clear bag that he held above his head.

The choppers were still being off-loaded as Jordan and three others ran with the litter to the helicopter's back ramp. Jordan's legs got crossed up as he moved with his load. He fell, losing his grip on the handles. The litter with its injured Marine hit the ground hard. The wind was knocked momentarily out of Jordan's lungs. His helmet fell off and rolled several feet away.

"Jesus Christ!" Jordan admonished himself out loud. "Get up you bumbling dumb shit! Got to get this Marine on board."

Jordan finally reached the ramp and immediately began lifting the litter into the back of the helicopter. Wounded Marines who had already boarded the chopper pulled the stretcher into the fuselage. Although others were struggling to climb on board, they tried to help the casualties.

Lieutenant Guarino, trying to breathe as the thick red dust choked him, was also having trouble carrying his litter, but he didn't fall. He wasn't running as fast as Jordan who yelled back to the lieutenant.

"Sir, Marine in. Civilian next on board. We can do it, Sir."

Jordan ran back to help Lieutenant Guarino.

The helicopter pilots circled their fingers to let everyone know they were about to lift off. Each pilot began raising the collective and moving the cyclic to control the ascent.

"Lieutenant, gotta move him now."

The two Marines, an officer and an enlisted man, fought through the dust and placed the litter carrying the civilian on the loading ramp. The timing was none too soon. The thick sound of the rotor blades, as they tilted and chewed into the air, deepened. The rear of the helicopter lightened. Marines, already on board, dragged the litter inside the fuselage. Jordan got the attention of a Marine. He threw him a bag with cameras and pointed to the civilian's litter.

Lieutenant Guarino and Lance Corporal Jordan sank into a shallow trench as the choppers were lifting off. Dust and debris blew over them as they covered their faces with their forearms.

The pitch of the blades on each helicopter dug into the air to tug the machines skyward. The red dust blew again in thick clouds. The thunder of the rotors and the shrillness of the turbines were as earsplitting as they had been during landing.

The two CH-46 helicopters sped the length of the runway and gained altitude. They turned slightly southeast, then south and headed for Quang Tri to refuel before continuing on to Da Nang.

Once the dust had cleared from the landing zone, Jordan noticed a blue object lying in the dirt. He picked it up and discovered it was a French passport. He opened it quickly and read the name: René l'Escalier.

CHAPTER SIXTY-SIX

FRIENDS AND FAMILY GATHER HERE

Men wearing heavy topcoats invaded the restaurant. Their bearing, as well as their sheer numbers, underscored their portentous presence. They posted themselves at the entrance, in the kitchen, behind the bar, at the stairs leading to the second floor, near the upstairs restrooms and at every window.

Outside, stern-faced men stood on the sidewalk just near the corner entrance to the establishment, on each corner of the intersection and along each street for many yards. The interior and exterior of the building and surrounding neighborhood were under heavy guard.

Established in the 1930s, the unassuming restaurant in Georgetown, a quaint enclave of Washington, D.C., was always a welcoming venue for locals. The sign inside, displaying a spoon and fork, said it all: *Friends and Family Gather Here.* Sunday mornings were special. Brunch began at eight o'clock sharp. The restaurant would come alive with the smile and the wry humor of the Maître d' from Brooklyn, who always wore a tie. Glasses low on his nose, he always sat at the corner of the bar reading the newspaper before the restaurant's doors opened. Equally scathing toward democrats and republicans, he was never without a sarcastic opinion about the political scene.

The restaurant enjoyed the patronage of many well-known people, not least of whom had been John Kennedy and his future bride Jacqueline Bouvier. He, then a promising Massachusetts senator, and she, a ravishing, sophisticated beauty from New York, became engaged in the early summer of 1953. John Kennedy proposed to Jacqueline in the restaurant while sitting at a window booth overlooking the street.

Now, another person, coming from many blocks away, was about to visit the famous neighborhood restaurant. But, he was not a common person with an ordinary job. He was the thirty-sixth President of the United States. His name was Lyndon Baines Johnson.

The President's motorcade, preceded by motorcycles, had made its way around the semi-circular driveway of the White House to Pennsylvania Avenue. A scarlet oak tree near the gate stood strong.

The motorcade exited the northeast gate, turned left on Pennsylvania Avenue and motored past Lafayette Square—thank God the protestors had taken a break—around Washington Circle to Georgetown's M Street. The President's Continental limousine with the presidential flag on each front fender turned right on 33rd Street. It passed colorful row houses on the right starting with the address 1211 clearly visible on the stone and brick façade of the first home.

The presidential vehicle turned right and finally came to a stop at the junction with Wisconsin Avenue, beneath a sign that read "Martin's Tavern."

"Mr. President, once you leave the limousine, walk immediately through the doorway."

An agent opened the rear door of the limousine. A fire alarm call-box was the only obstruction on the sidewalk. The President exited the vehicle to his right and walked not more than eight feet to the entrance of the restaurant.

"Good morning, Mr. President. Your table is ready, Sir."

"Thanks, pardner. Can't wait for a big breakfast."

"Yes, Sir. Absolutely, Sir. We'd thought you'd never arrive. Damned near drank all the coffee."

A young, wide-eyed, short-haired blond waitress dressed in a white apron and a man's white shirt with a black vest and tie, welcomed the special guest. She spoke in an east European accent.

"This way, Mr. President. Your guest is waiting at your table, Sir."

"Just dandy."

The President relinquished his overcoat. He made his way through the maze of tables, then past the amply-stocked bar to his left.

The surprised guests all watched in awe as the large man strolled through the restaurant with the Secret Service standing guard. Lyndon Johnson passed two patrons having breakfast at the corner of the bar. Above them on a shelf sat a wood carving of what looked to be a jockey dressed in a red and white pin-striped uniform. Tall glasses, each with red liquid inside and adorned with celery stalks, sat in front of the two customers.

"A bit early for stiff drinks, isn't it, gents? Hair of the dog?"

"Good morning, Mr. President."

The President smiled at the two men and shook their hands.

"Enjoy your Bloody Marys, gentlemen."

The President pointed to their plates. "Bacon and eggs and hash browns. Mix that with some onions and Texas chili peppers…can't beat it."

Johnson entered a small wood-panel chamber at the back of the restaurant that contained three narrow booths on the left and two small tables to the right.

"Well, I'll be damned. Jim, how the hell are ya?"

"Mr. President, good to see you. You look good."

"Really?"

Lyndon Johnson slid across the bench of the last booth in the room.

"I don't recall these booths being so damn small. This is the same table ole Sam Rayburn and I used to play dominoes on. Jesus, I can hardly get in now. I know I ain't put on that much belly fat since I was here back then."

Both men laughed.

"Thanks for inviting me, Lyndon. I haven't been here before."

"No problem, Jim. I should come here more often, but the Secret Service frowns on it. We'll have a good brunch, but I don't wanna beat around the bush. I thought we could come here and talk instead of at the White House. Sometimes, it's good to get out of that place."

"Mr. President, what can I do for you, Sir?"

The President asked a crisp question.

"Jim, can we win at Khe Sanh?"

"Holy Jesus, Lyndon…I wasn't expecting that."

"Jim, I need honest talk. I got the Pentagon…you know Clark Clifford replaced McNamara on the first of March?"

"Yes, Sir."

"I got Wheeler, Rusk and Westmoreland. I got the CIA, the DIA and the NSC. I've got battleships, aircraft carriers, helicopters, bombers, fighter jets and a half million men."

The President pointed back over his left shoulder with his right hand. "I have the whole damn State Department over there in that ugly building in Foggy Bottom. I got Ellsworth Bunker in Saigon, I got Rostow—he drives everyone nuts—I got Helms and Max Taylor…and I got the so-called wise men."

The President laughed as he continued. "I got maps, photos, drawings… you name it. They even built a model of Khe Sanh for me. I have it right in the White House."

The President cleared his throat. "But, I don't feel I'm gettin' the straight poop. I had Rostow send a guy to Saigon. Wasted trip.

"I've tried to correspond with Ho Chi Minh, but it went nowhere. You're a military analyst. You know the Vietnamese and their abilities. You visited North Vietnam before the war. You've even met General Gee-ap and Ho Chi Minh."

"Yeah, we spoke in French. Giap's a dapper guy who likes art. He's a devotee of classical music. Studied and law and likes an occasional sip of Cognac.

"Ho Chi Minh's a sour-puss. He was a cook on some ship prior to his revolutionary days. Smokes like a chimney, wears pajamas all day and speaks a bunch of languages…must have a good ear. He's a loner, a prolific writer who comes across as a sweet, smiling uncle. But he's a multi-invented, ruthless communist who never spent a dime that he earned. He's rather indolent."

"Damn Communist leaders. All they want is money for themselves. Anyway, I'll ask it again. Can we win at Khe Sanh?"

"Mr. President, look at it this way. If the NVA disengage, it's because they have dictated it on their terms. On the other hand, to embarrass the greatest power on earth, they risk annihilation by staying and fighting. Giap is probably willing to throw human lives at the fight, but, *only* if he sees a clear victory. He knows the odds. My feelings are the NVA do not care that much about Khe Sanh...not like they cared about Dien Bien Phu."

Jim scratched his forehead. Does the President really want to hear this? "Lyndon, what would Giap do with a victory at Khe Sanh except rub our noses in it? He couldn't keep it. What the North Vietnamese fear the most is what the French were incapable of doing."

The President raised his eyebrows and looked at his guest across the narrow table in the most recessed part of the restaurant.

"And that would be?"

"A major reprisal, an immediate retaliation."

The waitress delivered two cups of coffee, the cups and saucers rattling slightly as she set them down.

"Interesting, Jim. Hey, we don't have to order brunch quite so fast. Continue."

"Our winning or losing at Khe Sanh is an issue that's easily decided but there's a much broader issue that's not so easily determined."

"Go on."

"There are a lot of similarities between the war in Vietnam and the Civil War, if none other than the north was fighting to re-unit the country. From a purely military perspective, logistics and resources are key in any conflict. It was Nathan Bedford Forrest who summed up all military strategy in exactly six words: 'Get there firstest with the mostest.'"

Johnson smiled.

"I thought Patton said that."

Both men laughed.

"During the Civil War, the South was blessed with a superior commander. Ole Bobby Lee. He was something else, alright. He had better field commanders. The Confederates were better led and better motivated.

"In the beginning of the Civil War—most of the battles were set-pieces—

the major engagements were separated by time and distance. The North wasn't inclined to pursue the Confederates after a battle. In fact, after each confrontation, the North retreated to the safe haven of Washington, much to Lincoln's dismay. The South, staying in the field, was able to re-equip in between battles.

"Even after Antietam and Gettysburg, the only two times Lee invaded the North, neither McClellan nor Meade pursued the Confederate army. Well, maybe Meade did, but he didn't cause much damage. Lee's retreat from Gettysburg may have been his finest hour. He moved the entire Army of Northern Virginia back across the Potomac.

"But, the Confederates had grown old. Stonewall Jackson, killed a year earlier, was gone. Supplies dwindled. As for the Army of the Potomac, General Grant took overall command. General Meade was subordinated to him. The North changed its approach.

"The Army of the Potomac crossed into Virginia to press the Confederates. Lee moved his army south of the Rapidan River. He camped near Orange.

"Grant had well over a hundred thousand men. Lincoln sent out a call to raise seven hundred thousand recruits to reinforce his army. The response was overwhelming. Lee, on the other hand, had only about sixty thousand men.

"One morning in early May of 1864, General Lee, observing from atop Clark Mountain, saw Grant's army stir on the other side of the Rapidan. Grant was moving his force toward Germanna and Ely Fords to cross the river. Grant's overland campaign to destroy the Army of Northern Virginia and capture Richmond had begun. The two armies were about to clash.

"Lee, knowing he must keep his army between Grant and Richmond, moved his force to an inhospitable place called the Wilderness. He would meet Grant there amidst entangled brush and thick forest. The fighting was dreadful.

"A day or so later, Lee's army, though completely exhausted, checked the Union lines. Grant's army didn't succeed. After two days, the battle of the Wilderness was over.

"Grant moved his army to the southeast. Lee, protecting Richmond, moved his army, too. He correctly predicted the next engagement would occur at Spotsylvania Courthouse. The Civil War had entered a new phase. The battles were now bunched much closer together. Lee was pressed harder.

"Some say that Grant was basically a drunk. I don't know. Maybe he was. But, Grant got one thing right that no other union commander understood. Not Meade, not Hooker, not McDowell and not McClellan."

The President leaned forward to listen carefully.

"Grant didn't disengage or retreat after a battle. He constantly militated against General Lee's Army. Interestingly, while Grant lost close to twenty thousand men, Lee suffered a lot less. Lee wrongly surmised Grant would sue for peace. He thought Grant could not continue to tolerate such losses. But, Lee also knew he couldn't either.

"Even with high casualties, Grant was still capable of delivering staggering blows.

"Grant didn't quit the battle at the Wilderness. He just moved it farther down the road. Lee had no choice but to counter. The battle at Spotsylvania was a repeat of the Wilderness. The Federals sustained another twenty thousand casualties while the confederates lost twelve thousand men. Grant was losing two thousand men each day, but he didn't stop. He moved again, this time to the North Anna River. Lee reacted accordingly, always keeping his army between Grant and Richmond. The two armies clashed twenty times during May.

"Of all the fighting to date, none would be as intense as Cold Harbor. In early June, Grant charged the Confederates in their trenches before sunrise. Within one hour, Grant had lost seven thousand men. Confederates losses were much less. Although Cold Harbor was an outright victory for the Confederates, Grant was winning the war.

"Robert E. Lee could not overcome the momentum Grant had gained. Lee's army was shattered with no respite and no hope of replenishment, Grant, on the other hand, could command any amount of resources on any timetable...*the mostest.* While the overabundance stacked up at City Point, Lee's men were reduced to eating grass.

"Petersburg was the beginning of the end for the Confederacy; and, with the loss of the Southside Railroad at Richmond, Lee had only one option. He ran for the hills. A few weeks later, General Lee trotted his horse Traveler up a road from his last headquarters to some house in Appomattox. With the stroke of a pen, he surrendered. It was all over.

"Ulysses Grant, the so-called drunk, had just won the American Civil War. He became a hero…and eventually President of the United States."

Lyndon Johnson pulled on both of his ears and sipped his coffee as he listened. His guest continued on, more than he needed to, but Lyndon Johnson was entranced by the recounting.

"Neither Lee nor Grant stayed around for the formal surrender ceremony the next day…Lyndon, the point I'm trying to make is this. Both sides can muster the resources. Russia and China are supplying a lot of weapons to North Vietnam. But, Americans and both houses of Congress are becoming increasingly antagonistic toward the war. It's costing a lot of money. Logistically speaking, our supply line is too long and it can be cut off instantly by congress. Neither Russia nor China will curtail shipping armaments to Ho Chi Minh. Can the U.S. win at Khe Sanh? Most assuredly. Win the overall war? That's the larger question."

For all his histrionics and bombastic rhetoric, Lyndon Johnson wasn't a fool. The person sitting across the table from him spoke with candid simplicity. This was no bullshit.

"Jim, my speech at Johns Hopkins University in April 1965 presented the foundation of our involvement in Vietnam. It's far away, I know, but it's also very close. Every president since 1954 has supported South Vietnam… *three* presidents. I said as much later, in my speech last September. We have a promise to keep and I intend to keep this promise. I remember my words exactly. Our objective is the independence of South Vietnam and its freedom from attack. We want nothing for ourselves, only that the people of South Vietnam be allowed to guide their own country in their own way. We have no territory there, nor do we seek any."

"Lyndon, it seems to me we sometimes confuse the situation with other objectives such as the containment of Red China."

The President removed his glasses.

"That argument will continue for a very long time."

The President raised his coffee cup to his mouth, then lowered it. "Jim, you mentioned the word motivation, that the men under Lee were more motivated. It does seem to me that Ho Chi Minh has motivated all Vietnamese people, even more so than President Thieu. I'm just wondering..."

The President stopped for a half second. "Let's get some steak and eggs. Maybe they have Canadian bacon, too. Damn, I'm hungry as a coyote in a west Texas winter."

CHAPTER SIXTY-SEVEN

RUY LOPEZ OPENING

Colonel David E. Lownds laid his helmet on a box in the underground command bunker. He wiped the sweat from his unshaven face with his forearm.

The combat base had just withstood another shelling from NVA artillery and rockets. The barrages, sporadic at times, were a daily occurrence.

Unfazed, Lownds moved an aluminum lawn chair, its nylon netting frayed and torn, closer to his makeshift plywood desk. He sat down. Lownds rested his foot and worn-out boot on the desk while he looked at his wristwatch. An open cardboard box sat inches away. Words on its side read "Oven Fresh." He sipped his day-old, cold coffee from an unwashed mug and placed it next to a black plastic ashtray.

A large floor fan with a burned-out motor stood useless behind Lownds. A crude box, serving as a bookshelf, hung on the wall to his right. It was crammed with notebooks and files. An overhead light provided the only illumination in the command nerve center. A pervasive gritty film lay on the surface of everything, especially his coffee.

At forty-eight, a father of seven, Lownds was living like a rat in some forsaken part of the world, going for weeks without a shower, breathing dust and gunpowder and still being shot at. He wasn't the only one.

Born in 1920, Lownds attended the University of Rhode Island. He enlisted in the Marines in 1942. Wounded by shrapnel at Saipan and by a Japanese bullet clean through his left hip at Iwo Jima, Lownds knew what it meant to face a formidable enemy. He left the Marines after attaining the rank of full colonel to pursue a business career. But, David Lownds was still an officer in the United States Marine Corps. He would honor the call of duty that his country might someday ask him again to fulfill. That someday came. Lownds was called back into service. He accepted this inconvenience with dignity and pride.

Again in uniform, David Lownds went first to Okinawa. He was worried that he might be the only Marine colonel not to serve in the Southeast Asian conflict. He was pleased when he received orders to Vietnam.

The real fight that would determine America's success or failure in Vietnam would probably occur in Eye Corps. Khe Sanh represented an annoying intrusion to the North Vietnamese. They wouldn't stand for such an impudent infringement for very long.

Lownds looked up to the low concrete ceiling in disbelief that the command bunker was still intact after the last shelling. Regardless of orders that all bunkers must withstand 82mm mortar rounds, nothing could stop the NVA's heavy artillery.

Lownds twirled his mustache with the fingers of his left hand. He held the stub of a cigar in his right hand. He bit into his lower lip. His face and sharp eyes showed the strain of the previous days of shelling and lack of sleep. Lownds was operating on his training. His nerves were running on adrenaline, his mind on his wits and his body on caffeine.

Colonel Lownds stood up and spoke to Major Hudson, his S2 intelligence officer.

"Jerry, let's look at our options again."

Lownds leaned over the scarred plywood plank. He swept his right hand over sweat-smeared maps, gesturing toward Laos. "The NVA came here via Highway Nine from Lao Bao and via trails that circumvent Hills 861 and 881. We can't maneuver to the north for the same reason the NVA won't attack us from that direction. Repositioning our forces south would be ruinous. We'd be chopped up. We can't move east. The road is in the NVA's possession, and maneuvering west would be extremely risky. We're gonna fight."

Jerry Hudson spoke.

"Colonel, if I may."

Lownds, motioned with his mug to Hudson.

"Go on, Major."

"Colonel, shouldn't we bring some Marines off the hills back to the base and strengthen our position here?"

Lownds thought through the question.

"I understand where you're coming from, Major, but we can't weaken the hills right now."

Lieutenant Colonel Edward Castagna, the operations officer, picked up on the S2's comment.

"Colonel, bringing the Marines here by helicopter will be risky. The air operation would require a lot of coordination."

"If the NVA were to occupy the hills, they'll pour artillery and mortar fire right down our throats just like Fairview Hill at Chancellorsville. The hills control the corridors."

"Colonel, if the NVA were to put guns on 861 or 881, they will be susceptible to our airstrikes, counter-battery fire from the base and the big guns at Carroll. I'm not suggesting the hills be abandoned. I'm pointing out that we may need the help of some of those Marines. If we're overrun here on the base, the Marines up there will have little chance of survival."

Castagna responded.

"The hills would be on their own."

"Gentlemen, both of you make good points, but I can't risk losing the hills right now. I need 861 and 881. Captain Dabney can see everything from 881. I'm sure if we were to do as Hudson suggests, we'd have to get approval from as high up as Westmoreland. MACV would not approve such a plan. Anyway, we aren't gonna do it."

The colonel sat back down in his lawn chair and thought for a moment. With absolutely no emotion—a sobering statement of fact—Lownds said to anyone who cared to listen, "The enemy's infantry is under their big guns. They're inching toward us under the umbrella of long-range artillery fire."

Lownds thought back to an almost humorous statement made by a young captain at a recent briefing when describing the enemy's deployment. With nonchalance the captain simply said, "The NVA's everywhere."

Lownds ran his hand over the maps to flatten them out. Through upturned, alert eyes, partially hidden by his eyebrows, he looked at the men around him. "The Army's 175s can't reach the NVA emplacements at Co Roc from Camp Carroll or Rockpile."

Lownds touched the map at the locations he mentioned to make his point. "Our own 155s on the base are limited in range, too. The NVA have to assemble near us if they are to be effective with a major assault. If we concentrate all our firepower from Camp Carroll, the Rockpile and from here at the base, in pre-designated geographic cells within a three to six mile radius of the base, this will cause the enemy to disperse. He won't be able to concentrate his units and supplies near us.

"Giap's probes tell me his attack will be focused, not like the circumferential assault at Dien Bien Phu.

"The TPQ strikes have been effective but close air support will not always be available. We need to make more use of our artillery. We can survive the enemy's barrages. It's their ground attacks we need to stop, so we concentrate our artillery fire in pre-planned cells to cut off their infantry. We create a box developed by rounds hitting on four sides, close in the sides and collapse the box with saturation barrages. We hit each cell at the same time for five or ten minutes or stagger the shelling to frustrate the NVA."

"Colonel, there's a lot of area out there. Can we afford to deplete our ammunition on supposition as to where the NVA are, Sir?"

"It won't be based on supposition, but rather on information provided by the sensors and other reconnaissance devices.

"Hudson, I want you to gather as much intel as you can about enemy strength, concentrations and movements…and anything else. Prepare a systematic schedule of fire missions by cell based on what you learn."

Colonel Lownds turned to his Target Information Officer standing next to him.

"Captain Baig, your intel expertise and capabilities will be indispensable."

"Absolutely. Thank you, Colonel. I'm working on some important intelligence now, Sir."

"Castagna, visit the batteries in person and get a visual report. Find out about their ammo, quantity and type.

"We'll meet here tomorrow at oh four hundred. I'm going up to take a look around. The NVA's guns are tearing us to pieces."

Lownds picked up his M-16 and made his way to the stairwell. He noticed that the chessmen had been arranged in proper order on the red and black chessboard. In the classical Ruy Lopez opening, he slid white's king's pawn two squares to the middle of the board. Moving the queen, a bishop and a knight would subsequently complete the opening strategy and allow the queen to assume both an early defensive and offensive position. It was black's turn to counter.

Colonel Lownds climbed the steps, being careful not to hit his head on the lintel, and emerged from the underground command post. He surveyed the wasteland with incredulity. Tires on damaged equipment were flat or cut to ribbons. Water tanks were punctured, wood poles and frames were splintered and sandbag embankments were in tatters. The ground, cratered from the explosions, was littered with debris. The air, redolent of sulfur and cordite, also smelled of urine and excrement. The burned-out carcasses of aircraft sat as testimony to the peril of the NVA shelling.

The Khe Sanh Combat Base couldn't have looked worse if junk had been pushed out of a cargo plane and allowed to crash to earth in random heaps.

Wounded Marines were being carried to Charlie Med. Navy Corpsmen were treating those who had received severe injuries. Others with lesser wounds were being tended to by their comrades.

The colonel, with cigar in hand, spoke in soliloquy.

"OK, Lownds, here you are. This is the famous Khe Sanh. They're hammering you hard with their artillery and rockets. Dig a foot a day and get ready to fight back. There's no other way to survive this."

Lownds looked at the distant hills. "We need those Marines here but we need the hilltops too."

He thought back to the chessboard in the COC and his very opening move. The Khe Sanh Combat Base was the king who was now deprived of the protection of the pawn in front. Without the support of Hills 861 and 881South, likened with the protecting bishop and the subsequent movement of the knight that would complete Lownds' Ruy Lopez opening, the king would be vulnerable.

CHAPTER SIXTY-EIGHT

RAIN

Gus Delaney leaned back against the damp wall of his earth hootch on the south side of the Khe Sanh Combat Base. He placed his M-16 against some crates and removed his helmet. His arms were covered in scratches from the patrol he and his platoon had just completed. It wasn't a long patrol, only two hundred meters outside the wire. There was some gunfire but no serious engagement. After about four hours, the twelve man patrol returned to base.

"Damn these mosquitoes. They never stop buzzing my ears."

Gus reached for a green, military-issue aerosol can of insecticide spray. Instead of spraying the area around him, he used it as a repellent and sprayed the atomized toxic liquid directly on his ears, neck and face. The harsh mist stung his eyes.

"Little bastards."

Gus struggled out of his flak jacket. He inhaled the smoke from the cigarette drooping from his sunbaked lips and blew it out through his nostrils.

Duane Carter sat across from him on a wood box.

"Gimme a cigarette, Gus."

Gus threw the pack and lighter to his buddy.

"Yeah, here, take one."

"The gooks were watching us all the way, Gus. Never saw them but I could hear them. They could've hit us at any time."

"Scary shit out there, man. Didn't see much. A few broken shovels. We did find those abandoned boxes of ammunition."

"They weren't abandoned. They were placed there. The other patrols found new RPGs and crates of grenades. They've moved most of their men back, but they're bringing munitions forward. The dinks are planning something bad. It's been too quiet these past several days. They're waitin' and watchin' our every move. They're gonna nail our asses good."

Gus looked down at the flicker of the candle.

"Patrols are goin' out early tomorrow."

He lit another cigarette. "How long you been in the Corps, Duane?"

"Nine months. Before I enlisted, I went to California to see some friends. I wanted to learn to surf so I borrowed a board. Drove to a place called Trestles near San Clemente. My friends said that was the best place to surf. Shit-for-brains me, I didn't know the beach was part of the Marine base out there—you know, Camp Pendleton. My buddies never told me it was a restricted area. Shit, I had no idea. I'm in the water fifteen minutes, next thing I know, my ass is arrested by Marine security. They gave my surfboard back to me on the base and told me to get the hell outta their sight."

Gus laughed.

"Now look at you. You're a jarhead yourself."

"Yeah, I stayed in California for a few months. I was broke. No job. No gig. My buddy says, 'Hey, man. I'm joining the Marines. Come with me. We can join together.' And here I am at Khe Sanh. Instead of a guitar, I'm carrying an M-16 that plays only one loud note."

"What happened to your buddy?"

"Wounded badly near Hill 55. Got shipped home."

"And you're still here having all the fun."

"Yeah, I miss the guys in the band, the music. We played surfer sounds. Beach Boys and Jan and Dean songs...you know, stuff like that. That's why I wanted to learn to surf."

"Oh, you had the suntanned girls all over you then, man. You're even dumber than I thought to give that up. This is your punishment for joining the Marines."

"Don't remind me. I was just visiting. Drove my car out west and I dunno, ended up joining the Marines. I'm from Chesterfield, Missouri, originally."

Gus looked at his pack of cigarettes.

"You mean like these?"

"Same name; Chesterfield...outside of St. Louis."

"Never heard of it. What was the name of your band?"

"The Galaxies. I played lead guitar. We're gonna change our music when I get home."

"To what, that hippy crap?"

"Ever hear of Jimi Hendrix?"

"Who?"

"The guy can play guitar. Comes out of nowhere—Seattle someplace—and blows everyone away. I heard he was in the Army...Airborne, I think...but got out. Probably a dope head by now. He's got an album called *Electric Ladyland*, got all those weird psychedelic colors and wild, friggin' hair. My folks can't stand it.

"I played his album while on home leave. I tried to imitate what he was doing on my guitar, but couldn't keep up. God, he's fast.

"Once in St. Louis, I stopped in some sort of tavern pub. The place had a low ceiling and a bar that wrapped around the room. In front of the stage, there were three stand-up tables made from barrels. A wood statue of a woman, the type you see on the bow of an old ship, stood in an alcove.

"An English couple was performing on stage under bright lights. I didn't think much of it, until I listened closely to the guitarist. My God, he hit all the chords perfectly. He played a red Fender...the chords, the timing, the sounds...incredible.

"The singer's voice was crystal clear. She could sing anything. Someone in the audience kept yelling, 'Let the beautiful girl sing.' She was from somewhere near Liverpool. The guy with the guitar was from the other coast, near Lincoln. Man, they were friggin' unbelievable."

"What was the band's name?"

"Not sure. Can't recall. Man, after each song, the crowd kept screaming,

'Play it again, play it again!' They went crazy, man. During the last set, people surged forward to the edge of the stage. They were waving their arms. Everyone was singing with that duo. It was wild."

Duane wiped sweat from his brow. "You know, Gustof, my man, the old U.S. of A is changing. This war is unpopular as hell. People are pissed at us for being here…as if we had something to do with being in Vietnam."

"We do, man. We joined the Marines and they sent us here. Got to make the most of it. But, yeah, being back in the world isn't what it used to be. It ain't what we think."

"I don't care, Gus. I still wanna go home. I don't give a damn 'bout being a hero or gettin' some kind of medal, I just wanna strum my guitar. Shit, the gooks are out there preparing for another attack, maybe the big one. I can feel it. They don't give a crap 'bout playin' guitars."

"Duane, they come, they come. They don't, they don't. Nothin we can do, man."

"Rain!"

Duane Carter's eyes lit up. "That was the name of the English group."

CHAPTER SIXTY-NINE

BURIAL GROUND

Not many people in Hanoi could afford to buy a newspaper. To compensate, the government plastered *Nhan Dan*, the communist people's daily paper, on walls throughout the city for anyone to read. The buildings that lined famous Trang Tien Street and the Bu'u Dien (Post Office) a block away, afforded wall space to allow printed news to be posted early each morning.

Reports on the fighting in Quang Tri Province dominated the news.

By two in the afternoon, loudspeakers, mounted high on street light poles throughout Hanoi, would supplement the printed news with commentary. Political slogans, propaganda and party announcements were never in short supply.

Doan Ngoc Tinh lived across the Red River from Hanoi all his life. He grew rice and melons in plots of land and harvested fish from a nearby pond. He sometimes rode his bicycle from Xuan Thu to Mai Lam and then to the main highway across the Red River on the giant bridge into Hanoi. Designed by the Paris engineering firm of Daydé and Pillé, the bridge, coated with faded silver paint, was majestic. Originally named Le Pont Paul Doumer (the Paul Doumer Bridge) the Viet Minh renamed it Cau Long Bien.

Beginning in October 1967, American warplanes attacked Cau Long Bien mercilessly. It was destroyed twice, but the Vietnamese repaired it sufficiently for traffic. The third strike was the most vicious. The Americans used fifty planes to drop the structural icon. The repair would take many months.

Tinh didn't like ferries, but he boarded a small boat that took him across the Song Hong to Hanoi. He was to meet his cousin who would arrive later by train.

Tinh had another reason to spend time in Hanoi. He wanted to read the latest news of the war in the south; perhaps there was something pertaining to his grandson Que.

Tinh pedaled to Trang Tien Street and turned up Dinh Le Street. He stopped at the intersection with Pho Nguyen Xi and leaned his bicycle against a tree. He began to read *Nhan Dan* glued to the façade of the building. Tinh focused on the main article.

> *Leaders of the Central Committee declare that criminals Johnson, McNamara and Westmoreland, and the U.S. military cannot win against the glorious Vietnam patriots, men and women, who have picked up guns to fight. The American imperialists will be vanquished from the Fatherland. Quang Tri Province is the deadly lesson the imperialists will learn. Ta Con will be an American burial ground.*

He read further with the hopes that a related topic would shed light on Que's whereabouts. Tinh remembered the handwritten note from his grandson, dated many weeks earlier.

> *Ong Noi [Grandfather],*
>
> *I leave Vinh tomorrow for Dong Loc and then to the south. I heard it will take us several weeks to reach our destination. I do not know where I am going but I believe it is Ta Con. I can only send this one note so I send it to you. Please tell Me oi va Bo [Mom and Dad] that I miss them very much. I miss you, too, grandfather. And please tell Hang to study hard. I think of her every day.*

Tinh had some time before the train carrying his cousin would arrive. He would take a circuitous route to the station.

He pedaled his bicycle around the corner to tree-lined Ngo Quyen Street, past what used to be called the Metropole Hotel. Tinh stopped briefly to look at the mysterious fountain covered in algae that sat in a park across the side street from the hotel. Stone toads sprayed water toward the center of the strange structure. A girl was washing fruit in the water.

Named after Léon Jean Laurent Chavassieux, the French constructed the park in 1901. The Vietnamese called the square Dien Hong Park and also by a more commonly used name, Vuon Hoa Con Coc (Toad Park).

Tinh then rode to the intersection with Ly Thai To Street. Thirty minutes later, he made his way past the imposing walls, topped with glass shards, of Maison Centrale, the old French prison, renamed Hoa Lo.

As Tinh pedaled steadily toward the train station, his mind was troubled by the news he had just read and the note from his grandson. Tinh knew that Ta Con had another name: Khe Sanh.

CHAPTER SEVENTY

NO WAY TO START A MEMORABLE DAY

Lyndon Johnson yelled after George Christian at the same time his breakfast was being rolled into his bedroom suite.

"Thanks for the files, George. See you in a bit. I'll be right down."

The President, throwing a tie around his neck—the collar of his white shirt turned up—spoke to his wife.

"Lady Bird, gotta eat and run. Meetings in forty-five minutes. Damn these tight collars."

Lyndon Johnson sat down and tucked a starched napkin beneath his chin.

"Chipped beef. That's what breakfast is all about. It's the best."

"Lyndon, aren't you supposed to award the Medal of Honor today, to a couple of Marines?"

"Can't wait. Lady Bird. The citation for each award is very descriptive."

"I'm sure, Lyndon."

"Staff Sergeant John J. McGinty III charged through heavy fire to rescue men of his platoon. They were shot up pretty badly. He reloaded their weapons. He beat back the North Vietnamese attack by directing fire and calling in artillery very near his position. He shot five with his pistol. He was wounded, but never failed to organize and encourage his men. He directed fire to repel the enemy attacks."

"At Khe Sanh, dear?"

"No, no. The incident occurred in 1966. I think he became an officer."

"And the second Medal of Honor recipient?" Lady Bird sipped her coffee. "What happened to him, Lyndon?"

"Another Marine...I can hardly pronounce his name...Captain Robert J. Modrzejewski. I think I said it right—*Mod-dra-jew-ski*—from Milwaukee. He's now a major. His men were surrounded and he called in artillery. He was also wounded."

The President buttered a slice of toast and bit into it. He dug his fork into his breakfast and shoveled the tasty food into his mouth while he continued to talk.

"Great Marines."

Lady Bird dipped her spoon into a grapefruit half.

"Lyndon, I read the report this morning in the *Post* about Nixon and the New Hampshire Republican Primary. He may win by a wide margin."

"The Republicans don't have crapola."

"Lyndon, I know how you feel but that doesn't help."

"And Robert Kennedy's impending announcement of his candidacy...It seems the little runt's going to run after all, even if he's not in the primary."

"McCarthy may give you a problem, dear. He's had quite a run around the country. He was going to skip New Hampshire and go after Massachusetts, but decided to join the fray after all. I figure it may be close, but you'll win, honey. As goes New Hampshire, so goes the nation."

"Oh, I don't know, Lady Bird, it may or may not be close...hard to say. As goes New Hampshire? Honey, it's just the primaries, not the general election. McCarthy's riding to prominence on my bad fortune with the Tet Offensive. And now we'll have to deal with gnarly Nixon."

The President dabbed his mouth with his napkin. "Bobby Kennedy was just waitin' for this opportunity...arrogant, know-it-all, smart-ass. That damn accent—I swear."

"Oh, Lyndon, don't let Kennedy vex you so much. It's counter-productive."

"Nixon ain't got a chance of winning. His bullshit talk is bordering on treason. He has no plan about Vietnam, that phony SOB. I don't care what he says. He don't know shit."

"Lyndon, honestly. Such crudeness so early in the morning. This is no way to start a memorable day in honor of two worthy Marines."

"You're right, Lady Bird. It'll be a pleasure to meet these two brave men."

The President consumed his breakfast.

"Lyndon, slow down. You're always in such a mad rush."

"Lady Bird, I ain't no gourmet. I know what I like to eat...and I eat it."

Johnson pointed to his plate. "They really know how to prepare this stuff. Next time we're back at the ranch, I'll have this for breakfast every day."

"Lyndon, maybe we'll have chili con queso and tapioca pudding tonight. How would that be?"

"Sounds perfect to me, Bird."

Lyndon Johnson shuffled through the files given to him by George Christian. He picked up a cablegram dated that day, the twelfth of March 1968.

"What the hell? The CIA is indicating movement of Giap's forces. They turn yellow all of a sudden?"

The telephone rang. "Yeah."

"Mr. President, I'm sorry to bother you, Sir."

"Whatcha got?"

"Sir, first thing this morning, would you mind coming down to the Situation Room for a quick briefing? We have received some surprising news about Khe Sanh. We can show you the latest developments on the terrain model, Sir."

"Is it about the NVA shifting?"

"Yes, Sir, to the southwest of Khe Sanh. But, Sir, there have been some other threatening developments. We are receiving reports of another enemy build-up."

"For Christ's sake, they're shifting troops and there's another buildup? What's this about?"

"It's best to show you on the model, Sir."

"I'll be there in ten minutes, but I can't stay long. I have a meeting with Treasury that can't be postponed."

"Understood, Sir. Thank you, Mr. President."

The President removed the napkin from beneath his chin. He put on his suit jacket and started for the door.

"Damn good breakfast, Lady Bird."

The President kissed his wife on her cheek and stepped back.

The First Lady's eyes followed him

"Lyndon..."

The President turned around.

Lady Bird was smiling. She reached out and took her husband's hand.

"Lyndon, this will be a great day for you."

CHAPTER SEVENTY-ONE

CROSSING THE TRAIL

The North Vietnamese ambush of a Marine reconnaissance patrol near the Khe Sanh Combat Base was quick. The perpetrators couldn't be seen but the noise was overwhelming.

Pinned down in a broad swale that offered minimal protection, the Marine platoon found itself in a lethal crossfire of enemy machine guns, assault rifles and rifle-propelled grenades. Hand grenades came from everywhere. The platoon, which had left the perimeter of the Khe Sanh Combat Base only three hours before, was reduced to less than a fourth of its strength. Many Marines, their bodies chopped up by a hail of lead, lay in pools of deep crimson and black blood that covered each man, soaking his utilities before seeping into the red dirt. Rifles, helmets, packs and other equipment were scattered around the bodies, littering the tall grass of the killing field. Of the Marines not yet fallen, everyone had received some sort of bloody wound; some were in serious need of treatment, but the two medical corpsmen who had accompanied the patrol were dead.

Lieutenant Rick Sweeney's face was bleeding heavily from an angry cut above his right eye. His left arm was limp from a bullet that smashed into the bone of his forearm. Another bullet ripped into his right hand, almost severing it. He bled profusely, but quick attention by another Marine who subsequently died from his own wounds checked the flow of blood. Sweeney experienced shock but regained his senses.

A potent force when it left the combat base, the Marines were now badly mauled. Going forward on this recon patrol with a depleted unit made no sense. The platoon would be slaughtered altogether if it didn't regain the safety of the base. When the firing became sporadic, Lieutenant Sweeney gave the command to the surviving men in his patrol to disengage. Losses were too high.

To First Sergeant Greg McCurry, the short firefight seemed to last an eternity. He wasn't spared any injuries. McCurry was hit by grenade shrapnel in his left side. A bullet passed through his right shoulder spinning him around. His shirt and right arm were covered in blood. He pulled back with the others but stopped short. Maybe as many as twelve Marines had fallen around him. They couldn't all have been killed. Maybe there was at least one Marine who was so badly wounded he couldn't move.

Greg McCurry grew up near Geneseo, Illinois on a small farm north of town and the Hennepin Canal. His home, painted white, surrounded by cedar trees, was located at the top of a crest of Highway 82. He would watch violent thunder storms and dazzling sunrises from his upstairs bedroom window. He would often walk to the nearby river or just a little farther to the canal with his uncle to fish.

One winter day, when he was nine, he and his father drove into town on Highway 82. As they reached a concrete underpass beneath the train tracks in Geneseo, a car coming in the opposite direction began to slide out of control on the slushy snow just at the opposite opening of the underpass. Greg's father veered to the right, scraping the concrete wall. His quick reaction avoided a collision.

Three days later, his mother and five year old twin sisters were not so fortunate. They were returning from the town of Joy when the driver of an on-coming truck lost control on the ice. The truck hit the ditch and rebounded into the opposite lane and hit McCurry's mother's car. It rolled several times and came to rest upside down seventy feet off the side of the road. His mother and his twin sisters died instantly. Greg never recovered emotionally from the tragic loss to the family. He and his father remained in their humble house sitting on the low hill on Highway 82.

As Greg gained age, he worked his father's farm and eventually as a lathe operator at the Springfield Armory on West Main Street. In 1965, when faced with college, or remaining on the farm with his father, McCurry enlisted in the Marines. He would make a career as a military man. Maybe after this tour in Vietnam, his second, he would finish his college degree and apply for Officer Candidate School.

McCurry became familiar and even comfortable with South Vietnam's jungles, having been on many patrols. The combat experience would make him an acceptable OCS candidate. He was confident he would become a capable field commander.

McCurry, ignoring his wounds, started back.

Lieutenant Sweeney called out in a loud whisper.

"Sergeant, where the hell are you going?"

"Sir, they can't all be dead. I'm going back to see."

"McCurry, you are not going back. You don't have a chance and there's nothing you can do alone."

"Sir, I don't give a damn, I'm going back. There may be a Marine back there who needs help."

"Sergeant! Negative! The radioman was killed, the radio destroyed. We can't call for shit. We're on our own. You're staying with us. We're returning to base."

"I'm going back, Sir."

"McCurry, you're a brave Marine, but don't be a stupid Marine. I say again. We've lost our radio man and our radio. We've lost a lot of men. We don't have the firepower. We cannot continue. The recon mission is over. Do you understand?"

"I'm going back. There may be some survivors."

"You stubborn ass! You can't bring in a wounded Marine by yourself in that terrain. How in hell's name do you think you're gonna do that? We have to return to the combat base. The patrol has to stay together."

Lieutenant Sweeney's reasoning was futile. Sweeney didn't have the energy for a major personnel confrontation. He stared at McCurry's contorted, blood-stained face.

"I can't stop you, McCurry, but your bullshit will not go unreported. Understood?"

McCurry didn't respond. With the wounds the lieutenant suffered, chances are there would be no report. He would be flown out immediately.

The lieutenant, breathing heavily and losing his strength from lack of blood, looked at McCurry angrily.

"You asshole. Here, take my M-16. Yours is too shot up and I can't use mine with my arm and hand the way they are."

McCurry looked at his own weapon. The plastic butt had been shattered and the forward hand-stock was partially blown off. He threw it to the ground, grabbed the Lieutenant's assault rifle and started to make his way back.

"McCurry, for the sake of God, don't do this, man. You'll not make it back to the base."

In a second, Greg McCurry had disappeared into the tall grass.

Wounded in the shoulder—the entrance and exit wounds felt like a thousand hot needles sticking in him—McCurry moved as quietly as he could. He carried two canteens, the lieutenant's rifle and some magazines of ammunition. He crept along, then stopped to listen. He moved again, but stopped after a short distance. No sounds. The NVA must have pulled back after the ambush.

Farther on, McCurry came across a Marine lying face down, his legs crossed, a damaged M-16 and a helmet next to the body. He crawled up and turned the body onto its back. The Marine, his front soaked in blood and mud, a large gaping hole in his shoulder so deep it exposed his still heart, was clearly dead.

He found another Marine, this time on his side. He rolled the body onto its back. The Marine's head, nearly severed, moved as if on a tether. Where his neck should have been, there was a deep gash of a hole.

McCurry stayed still and listened. He heard nothing. He remained motionless for several minutes, then slowly crept forward.

McCurry saw boots and legs of a torso almost concealed from view by the thick brush. McCurry crawled up to the body and moved the grass to one side. The Marine's utilities were covered in blood. McCurry could not tell exactly where the Marine had been hit, but he could see he was still breathing.

"My God, he's alive," McCurry whispered out loud.

McCurry placed his ear to the man's chest and detected a faint heartbeat. He poured some water from his canteen into the Marine's mouth. The Marine's eyes opened in a disoriented state of shock.

McCurry covered the man's mouth with his hand and placed a finger to his own lips to signal to his comrade to remain quiet. He removed his hand from the Marine's face and gave him a little more water. He whispered.

"You're new to the company. What's your name?"

The man tried to speak, but his voice was weak.

"What?"

McCurry lowered his ear to the young Marine's mouth. The Marine tried again, but his reply was swallowed by the gurgling in his throat and the blood he coughed up.

"Staffor..."

McCurry whispered the answer back, "Stafford?"

The weakened man nodded.

"Listen to me, Stafford. I don't know how I'm gonna to do this, but I'm gettin' you back to base. Understand?"

The Marine nodded his head again.

McCurry was five foot seven. This Marine was well over six feet and big. McCurry continued.

"We've gotta go back out of this ravine, move through an open area and stop short of a trail just outside the wire. It's just you and me, Marine. We're on our own, brother. I can't lift you. I have to turn you around and drag you by your arms."

McCurry slung the M-16 to his back and slid his arms beneath the bloody Marine's shoulders. McCurry's upper body wounds were piercingly painful, but how else could he help his comrade?

Greg McCurry pulled and tugged the Marine through the tall elephant grass for the rest of the day, sometimes only a few meters at a time. Continuously out of breath, McCurry often became faint from the sweltering heat and loss of blood.

Each time McCurry checked on Stafford, he was grateful to find he was not dragging a corpse through the jungle.

Evening came. McCurry, moving, stopping, moving again, always dragging Stafford, felt exhaustion throughout his body. He had to stop. McCurry covered Stafford with large banana palm leaves and grass, then laid down.

At about eight,well after dark, McCurry began the arduous trek again with his wounded charge. He whispered.

"You with me, Stafford? We still have a ways to go, buddy. Here, drink some water."

The NVA shelling began again, a relief to McCurry. Enemy troops would be less inclined to be roaming about. The explosions provided some cover while the flashes of light guided the way.

Thick swarms of mosquitoes blitzed McCurry and Stafford, biting them incessantly. There was no respite from the hungry insects.

McCurry was covered in sweat. His shirt was a bloody mess. He stood, picked up Stafford's shoulders and began to walk backward again. McCurry tried to give some encouragement to Stafford.

"Just a few hundred meters and we're drinking beer and eatin' hotdogs. The women'll be all over you, man. You're a hero."

Stafford reached out to grab McCurry's arm. For the first time, he spoke faintly.

"You get Silver Star for..."

"All I'm gettin' is you outta here…plus, I'm gettin' mighty thirsty. I'm ready for that beer. How 'bout you?"

McCurry attempted to improve his grip on Stafford's shoulders to drag him closer to safety. He also tried to show some humor.

"God, you're a heavy SOB, Marine. Ever figure out why the Marines call our battle uniforms utilities? Why does the Corps say cover when it's a hat? I never figured that shit out."

Stafford smiled weakly.

"Hey, Stafford, seen all the propaganda the gooks have been sending our way? Their artillery shells litter the base with paper with all their communist crap. I read one that said, 'All Marines soon be killed at Khe Sanh. You not see America again. Time now near you to die.' Such hogwash. They're even using loudspeakers now. Giap don't know shit."

Even McCurry was grinning at his own embellished pantomimes. "Three weeks ago I went to Da Nang to get a tooth fixed. Everyone made fun of me because my boots were red. Nobody else wore red boots. That's what you get for being at Khe Sanh, man…red clay and dust."

McCurry continued to drag Stafford toward the combat base. Exhaustion quickly set in again. McCurry felt his head go faint. He lowered his head to improve the blood flow. Perspiration ran down his face and back and chest. The air was stifling, even hours after darkness had fallen.

"One good thing about losing blood, Stafford, the damned leeches don't bother you. I've lost so much blood they've gone elsewhere."

McCurry's shoulder was hurting intensely. His heart was pumping near its breaking point. His lungs burned. His arms and his thighs ached with fatigue. Still, he continued to drag Stafford toward safety. He was not going to abandon his Marine brother.

McCurry stopped many times throughout the night to regain his strength. At one point, he thought he heard something behind him in the jungle.

Finally, after so many hours of darkness, the eastern sky turned a shade lighter than black. As dawn approached, McCurry, his body scratched and cut, covered in perspiration and old blood, his wounds aching and continuing to bleed, accomplished the impossible. He had dragged Stafford all the way near to a low berm on top of which sat the trail he and Stafford needed to cross to safety. They waited for daybreak. The two wounded Marines, one much worse than the other, had somehow survived the night's trek through the dense foliage.

McCurry left Stafford alone and crawled to the top of the embankment of the trail directly in front of the base's line of defense. The early morning light suffused the area in a dull grayness.

McCurry knew better than to approach the base. He knew all about the NVA bastards that were shot many weeks before just outside the perimeter when challenged by the Marines. The Marines would not hesitate to open fire. McCurry was taking a chance. The NVA tried so many ruses to fool the Marines and lure them out. They yelled out, they tried to talk like Americans, tried to read off names from dog tags, even whistled.

The Marines answered with gunfire.

McCurry could barely see the Marines as they moved in their firing positions in the semi-darkness. How was he going to do this?

"Ah, man, they'll lob grenades at me."

But what was McCurry to do?

He called out in a subdued, but clear voice, "Marine outside the wire!"

M-60 machine gun fire from the perimeter raked the area where McCurry lay. The slugs passed overhead and thudded into trees and into the ground around him.

"Oh, man," he whispered to himself. "They're gonna send in mortar rounds next."

McCurry thought of something.

"One Marine with one whiskey mike," he repeated.

McCurry didn't know if anyone would understand whiskey mike for wounded Marine. He made it up. No NVA could have thought of that. This would convince the Marines that he was for real, or so he hoped.

A voice from the perimeter challenged. "Who are you? What's your name? What unit?"

"First Sergeant Greg McCurry, Recon."

"What state you from?"

"Illinois. Geneseo, Illinois. I was on a patrol that got ambushed yesterday."

"OK, Mr. Illa-noise. You can see us but we can't see you. Move a bush."

McCurry, lying prone, smiled to himself. That guy ain't from the Midwest. There's no *noise* in Illinois. He moved some tall grass which could barely be seen in the dullness of the early morning hours.

"OK. We got ya. When the fifty opens fire above your head, run for the trail. When you cross it, we'll have Marines waiting with a corpsman and a litter."

"Roger that, compadre," McCurry whispered, to himself. "But I'm not sure how the hell I'm gonna run with Stafford."

McCurry shook the bushes again in acknowledgment. He went back to Stafford, knelt down and whispered into his ear.

"Stafford, listen, we have to wait until they open fire over our heads for cover, then we cross the trail. Once on the other side, we'll still be outside the base, but they'll be waiting for us. Understand?"

The supine Marine nodded feebly. He was lapsing in and out of consciousness.

Stafford nodded.

"I unnerstand..."

"Good. Here's some water."

McCurry tilted the canteen to his comrade's mouth.

"Let's get closer to the trail so we don't have so far to go when the signal is given. Help me."

Stafford mustered some energy and spoke just above his breath.

"Tell Denise that I..." His voice faded.

"Stafford, when we get back to the base, you can call Denise and tell her yourself. You can talk to your girlfriend all day."

Stafford tried to sit up, but slumped back to the ground. He tried to kick the ground with his feet in a feeble effort to push his body along while McCurry tugged on his arms.

"Come on, Stafford, only about thirty meters. Don't give up. Come on, Marine. Help me."

McCurry and Stafford made it to a low point just at the edge of the trail.

NVA gunfire and mortars had erupted several hundred meters away but posed no threat to the two Marines. McCurry heard the explosions as the mortar rounds fell on the Khe Sanh Combat Base. Mortar rounds from the base were being fired in return. McCurry looked over the berm and saw the perimeter of the base. Completely worn out, he lay on his back. He breathed heavily and waited for the signal.

The sun came up and shone eerily through the low, thinning fog across the plateau. The unmistakable outlines of Hills 950 and 1015 were visible. Up above, white clouds were turned into sheets of fire, as the rays of the morning sun colored their undersides.

McCurry tried to give Stafford more water.

"Drink it. You need it more than me. I don't have much more."

The water spilled from Stafford's slightly open mouth.

"Stafford!"

Stafford remained quiet.

"No! Don't die on me. We are close to making it, so close to safety, just have to cross the trail, man. Stafford! Don't do this to me. Come on

Stafford. All this way...ah, man, hotdogs, beer, it's just waitin' for you, buddy."

McCurry placed his hands on the Marine's jaw and turned his head. Stafford's mouth fell open. His vacant, dilated eyes didn't focus or register any movement. They only reflected the bright copper sheen of the clouds above Khe Sanh.

"Dammit, Stafford! We have to cross the trail! That's all we have to do and we're home free. Come on, man. The beer is cold."

McCurry shook the limp Marine's shoulders.

"Stafford!"

Fifty-caliber machine gun fire erupted from the Marine perimeter, the signal for McCurry to move quickly to the safety of the Khe Sanh Combat Base. Thick lead bullets whizzed and snapped overhead, ripping at the thick foliage, cutting branches, splintering trees and ricocheting. McCurry hugged the ground until the covering fire from his comrades stopped.

Stafford was no longer of this world.

McCurry could do no more. He had to save himself.

McCurry's eyes caught something move into the open to his right. He saw the muzzle of a short-barreled assault weapon and the angry, obsidian eyes of the brown-skinned person who held it. McCurry could not react fast enough. The distinctive, deep throated sound of the Russian-made AK-47 opened up. Slugs punched through McCurry's body, wrecking every organ. McCurry, his stomach and lower chest nearly disemboweled, spewing gushes of blood, dropped his weapon. He clutched his sides in excruciating pain as he fell to the ground face down on the edge of the trail less than fifty yards from safety.

The North Vietnamese soldier walked over to where McCurry lay and looked down on his prey. McCurry's fingers dug into the red earth. The American was still alive.

The NVA soldier who had been following him all night lowered his weapon and pointed it at McCurry's back. He squeezed the trigger twice. The weapon erupted loudly. Two empty shell casings were immediately expelled to the side as the couplet of slugs exited the muzzle in a flash and burrowed into McCurry's back.

Quickly, the North Vietnamese soldier picked up McCurry's M-16 and disappeared into the bush.

Sergeant Greg McCurry's blood-covered body lay near the trail, no more than ten feet from that of Stafford's, the fellow Marine he tried to save outside the wire at Khe Sanh.

CHAPTER SEVENTY-TWO

BINH TRAM HAI MUOI

“Stop!”

A man with steely eyes stood sharply from the brush and raised his hand. “Show me your paper.”

Bui Van Que reached into his pack for the document that had been given to him weeks before in Dong Loc.

“Here, Sir.”

The man unfolded the damp, rumpled paper and read: DL/B5T8/BT20 ((7)).

He put the document in his shirt pocket.

“You’ve arrived at *binh tram hai muoi* [Waypoint Twenty]. I will show you the rest of the way. I’m the giam doc for this waypoint.”

Dressed in a light-green shirt with its sleeves rolled up and dirty shorts with large pockets on each side, the giam doc wiped the sweat from his brown face. He slipped one foot covered in bleeding sores out of his rubber sandal and rubbed it over the infected scabs on the calf of his other leg. Betel juice oozed from the corners of his mouth. He motioned to the men to follow him, but he stopped quickly. The giam doc pulled out the note. He pointed to the encoded line.

“The last number on the paper is seven. There were seven soldiers in your group. I see only three. Where are the others?”

There was no answer.

"I asked you, where are the other four men?"

"They…they didn't make it. They…"

"Doesn't matter, they'll be found and sent down here. I'll see them soon enough."

After thirty-two days of walking through jungle, over mountains and across rivers, Bui Van Que and two other comrades—the residual of the original seven—had reached the last waypoint of their trek along the Ho Chi Minh Trail. The supply line extended for hundreds of kilometers farther south, but their journey down the Truong Son Trail was finished. They had arrived in eastern Laos, south of the DMZ, but with less than a third of the equipment they had been given in Dong Loc.

Of the four soldiers who did not arrive, two became so ill neither could continue. Another person fell and broke his leg. All three were left behind. The fourth person deserted during the sixth night.

Bui Van Que wanted to turn back, too, but realized he couldn't. Duty or patriotism or the fear of execution didn't drive him on. He could not bear the humiliation that would befall his mother and father. Dishonoring his family, especially his grandfather, was something he could not bring himself to do.

The other two members of his group who had survived the ordeal were in no better shape. One of them, so exhausted, couldn't rise once he had fallen to the ground. Each man begged for water and was given only a sip.

"Follow me, you three. We have five more kilometers to the waypoint. I will make sure you are fed and given hot tea. You've been told we have plenty of medicine and a number of infirmaries…a load of monkey shit. You'll be able to rest for about three hours."

Bui Van Que had heard the muffled booming of heavy artillery during his last two days on the trail. Now, the explosions, no longer muted by distance, were more menacing, more foretelling of the horrors he would soon see.

"Five more kilometers?"

Que could barely walk five meters more.

The giam doc looked sternly at Que.

"Is this all they gave you to carry? An assault rifle and one magazine of ammunition? That's all?"

"The equipment...I couldn't carry it all. I didn't want to lag behind the others so I started leaving things behind, but I lost some of it...like my canteen."

The giam doc repeated derisively.

"You say you lost some of it? You left some things behind?"

And, with an angered look on his face, "Did you think someone would pick up your gear and carry it for you? I wasn't born yesterday, you stupid idiot. How many times do you think I've heard the same excuse? You didn't lose anything, soldier. You just threw it away, that's what you did. All you spoiled babies from Hanoi do the same thing. We are dependent on everything that comes down the Ho Chi Minh Trail. And then, you have the guts to tell me you left it behind. To hell with your canteen."

Que didn't know whether he was going to be shot, but shaking from deep fatigue, he didn't care.

The giam doc continued the diatribe.

"We need material any way we can get it. It comes by truck, motorbike, *xe dap* [bicycle] mule, horse, *xe cong nong*, even by old women carrying *quang ganh*...and with you boys. Right now, we're in the middle of the biggest fight of this war to crush the American criminal invaders...bigger than anything with the French. We could probably win the war with the crap you bastards threw away along the trail."

Bui Van Que and his two companions finally reached binh tram hai muoi. It was nothing more than a clearing beneath the denseness of the overhead jungle foliage. Next to a large tree, a hole was covered by a frame of tied bamboo and tree branches. The giam doc lifted the frame to one side.

"Go in here."

Steps, carved out of the dirt, led straight down. A faint light glowed at the bottom.

Que and his two comrades descended the steep dirt steps to an underground room. The odor was that of old, wet clothes, dank red soil and fetid water. Que sat down on a low bench and leaned against the earth wall. His head fell to his chest. His cohorts collapsed on the dirt floor.

A lone voice sounded from the dark recesses of the tunnel system.

"You must be exhausted."

Bui Van Que answered.

"My stomach hurts too much. I can't continue."

Que buried his face in his hands as the man responded.

"You have no choice but to continue. You'll sleep here, along with others when they arrive later. The ventilation is not good, but the bombs cannot reach us. These tunnels are stronger than the ones at Vinh Moc."

"Who are you?" Que asked.

"You don't need to know. You won't see me after tonight."

"Are there others?"

"A lot. They're located in other tunnels not far from here. You'll be on your way by four a.m."

Que looked at his watch. It was almost midnight.

"I can't believe I have to move again in a few hours. I haven't had two hours steady sleep in weeks."

"You can forget about sleep. Here, drink some tea. Eat this banana."

Que heard footsteps descending the dirt steps. A man appeared in the room.

"My name is Captain Nho. I'm from the assembly area, not far away."

He checked his notes with the aid of a candle.

"Strike Group CT42 is on its way to Attack Sector N3. CT42C formed up—an auxillary communications sub-group…about fifty men. They've been sent, too.

Strike Group CT43 is being consolidated and will form up tomorrow to move to Attack Sector N3. You are assigned to that group."

Bui Van Que, so hungry, devoured the slightly-spoiled banana. Evidently, that was the food he had been promised. Exhausted, he lay down on the dirt floor of the underground chamber. Within seconds, he was fast asleep.

Above ground, distant North Vietnamese artillery roiled constantly. Single and combined flashes momentarily colored the western skies. The artillery retaliation of the Americans lit up the east with similar sharp flashes that, hovering near the horizon, punctuated the darkness. American jets made horrible noises.

More soldiers straggled into the waypoint in the same exhausted state as

Que. Each man had a serious ailment. All were malnourished. Thirty men were crammed into the subterranean cave where Que slept.

Three hours after he fell asleep, Que barely heard Captain Nho's voice, but he felt the violent kick to his legs.

"Get up! The war is on!"

Chaos filled the room as men scurried and fumbled about in the darkness.

Que rubbed his face and tried to stretch, but he was too weak. He fell back. He rose up on his arms and stood. Wobbly, he searched furtively for his things.

"Where's my rifle, my ammunition?"

"Everything's been collected."

Que climbed the dirt steps, pushed up the horizontal bamboo door and stepped into the early morning darkness. Other soldiers staggered toward the assembly point two kilometers away.

Strike Group CT43 was about to take shape but its formation baffled Que. Where are the others?

Instructed not to congregate until the last minute, one by one, the *bo doi* emerged from the jungle. Marshals began to huddle Que and other men closer into individual groups. The assembly grew as more men were assimilated into formations. Dust rose from the ground.

Captain Nho pointed to an area to the left of Que's group.

"That pile of combat equipment will travel with you. Sort it out. Each man must carry the maximum. Make damned sure all of it arrives with you."

Never before had Que been near so many people packed together as tightly.

Each man was encumbered with hand grenades and ammunition. Some men carried two AK-47 assault weapons, one for him and the other to be held in reserve. Designed by comrade Mikhail Kalashnikov, the AK-47 wasn't light, but it was rugged and reliable.

Several soldiers were burdened with mortar tubes or base plates or mortar shells. Others carried loaded B-40 rocket launchers with oddly-pointed rockets in packs on their backs.

Each soldier would forage for food, but there would be little time to hunt or fish.

"You men of CT43, you will leave the assembly area with these guides in one hour to your destination at Attack Sector N3."

Captain Nho pointed to several barefooted men, one of whom twirled a stick between his blackened teeth.

"You will move as units, but with separation. You will proceed along the route until you are met on the other side of the Xe Pone River.

"From now on, you will be vulnerable. You must move forward quickly. I repeat again. Quickly. There is no time to waste. CT43 will be joined at Attack Sector N3 by a company of two hundred men arriving from Highpoint 881."

Bui Van Que remembered a sign written on a plank of wood that had been posted on the way south: "The trail is like octopus tentacles. Each tentacle is headed in the same direction for the same purpose: Death and Victory!"

"Attack Sector N3 and after that, *Diem Tan Cong Mot* [Attack Point One] against Khe Sanh, are about fifteen kilometers that way."

Captain Nho pointed to the east. "The enemy is there."

CHAPTER SEVENTY-THREE

HOW'S ALL THIS GOING TO END?

President Johnson and Luci, his second daughter, were watching the evening news on one of the three televisions that cluttered the furniture landscape in the White House residence. At least one was always turned on. Often, all three TVs were alive with network broadcasts.

While the rooms inside the White House seemed unusually chilly, even drafty, the blustery night outside was less hospitable.

Luci sat lengthwise on a sofa with her knees bent up. Wrapped in a comforter, she sipped hot lemon tea.

Luci enjoyed attending social events of any kind, in and out of the White House, but being a president's daughter necessitated that she be chaperoned, even though she had a driver's license. In 1964, she gave a tour of the White House for her high school classmates. Luci was fond of dancing and learning new dance steps. The Frug and the Watusi became her favorites.

Luci married Patrick John Nugent at the Basilica on Michigan Avenue in Northeast Washington sixteen months before her older sister took her own nuptials. The reception was held in the Blue Room of the White House.

Coverage of the war in Vietnam continued to dominate the television news. The reporting from Vietnam was alarming. Recaps of the Tet Offensive, the destruction of Hue and the fallout of the attack on the U.S.

embassy in Saigon—now several weeks past—remained key stories. But, it was the ongoing drama of Khe Sanh that captured the viewers' attention.

President Johnson turned the black and white television off immediately after the news report. The screen became a lifeless, brown-gray slate.

"Luci, I don't know about this. The coverage of the war over there is... well, I dunno what to say."

President Johnson took off his glasses and, reacting to what he had just seen and heard, massaged his fatigued face with his fingers.

"How's all this going to end, Luci?"

"Dad, everything will be OK. You wait and see."

The President sighed.

"Just a few days ago, I received a memo from the Pentagon in reaction to a newspaper article that talked about President Eisenhower leaving the door open for the use of nuclear weapons. I'm sure they misquoted Ike. He would have conferred with me first. But this sort of talk by anyone, quite frankly, makes me uneasy."

A moment of silence passed between the young woman and her troubled father.

"Luci, they starve me in this White House."

The President's voice rose out of frustration. "What I'd give for some real food, a big ranch-style meal, a bowl of Texas chili...that's what I want. I'm sick and tired of this dieting crap."

"Daddy, I'll call down to the kitchen and have someone prepare you a steak or a pork chop with some potatoes and maybe some chili."

"Ah, those darn cooks. They cook all this state dinner stuff like we was dining at the Waldorf in New York City. I don't need all that high-falootin' food. I just want a good, hot country meal that I can sink my teeth into...a juicy slice of roast beef, some mashed potatoes and black gravy—Texas style."

"Dad, maybe..."

"Know what, Luci? A really big ear of fresh corn would be great. Iowa corn on the cob is the best."

The President smiled and pointed his index finger to Luci. "But don't you go lettin' on to Senator Miller. I don't want those people up there in that state thinking they have something better than we do in Texas. Come this summer, those Iowans'll send me a truckload of corn and dump it right under the North Portico. I can just see Juanita throwing a fit over the mess those Hawkeyes would make. She'd have a conniption."

Luci smiled. There were two things about her father. He knew what he liked and he was never without a sense of humor.

"Don't worry, Daddy."

Luci's smile turned to a feisty laugh as she poked her father in his side. "I'll get you something that'll stick to your ribs."

Luci poked her father's side again.

President Johnson twitched suddenly as he laughed. He reached out to wrestle with his daughter.

"You do that again Luci Baines and I'll…"

"Yeah? You'll do what, Mr. President?"

Luci egged her father on. "Make me live in the White House? Send me to Texas?"

Luci tickled her father in the ribs.

"Listen here, young lady…"

"Ticklish, Dad?"

Lyndon Johnson smiled.

"Luci, you remember back in Texas how I'd throw each of you over my shoulder like a sack of potatoes."

"Yeah, one Easter Sunday, we were on our way to church on the other side of the river. Lynda and I were all dressed up. You picked me up and almost dumped me in a cow paddy."

The President laughed.

"Oh, man. Was Lady Bird ever angry…hooo wheee."

"Dad, I was wearing that new dress mom bought in Austin. It had bright colors. Mom was so proud of it."

"Luci, if the kitchen asks you if I want any wine, just say 'no.' I don't want no wine. Maybe some lemonade. And don't be tellin' your mom I fell off my diet, young lady. I may be the President of the United States but she'd sure 'nuff give me the what-fer."

Clearly anguished, the President slouched down in his big chair and kicked off his polished shoes. Luci tried to cheer him up.

"Dad, the Texas bluebonnets will be in full bloom at the ranch soon. Remember the drive we made to Harper when Lynda and I were still in grade school? The sun was shining. The sides of the highway were covered with purple color. I never saw so many wildflowers, and all the same color. I will never forget how beautiful those bluebonnets were."

The President looked fondly at Luci. Such sweet memories of earlier times with his two daughters.

"Yeah, you and Lynda liked to play among the wildflowers. Your mother never stopped talking about how bright they were. They were everywhere that year."

"Dad, bluebonnets are always the first to bloom…"

"You and Lynda were in the backseat."

The President laughed. "You knocked my hat off and pulled my ears. You hollered into my left ear and Lynda into my right ear. Stop! Stop! Daddy, stop! Damn near wrecked the car."

"Dad, when we first came to Washington, we hated to leave Texas, and..."

Luci fell silent as she watched her father's gaze drift away.

The President became detached, withdrawn.

"Luci, can you imagine what President Lincoln must have felt a hundred years ago? Lincoln's army was almost annihilated so many times. After one of those big battles in Virginia, or maybe it was in Maryland, Lincoln asked out loud, 'What is my country going to do?' Now, a little more than one hundred years later, I'm beginning to ask the same question over Vietnam. Jesus Christ, Luci."

The President caught himself. Mindful of his daughter's conversion to Catholicism a few years before and remembering his promise to attend mass with her at St. Dominic Church the next Sunday, his spontaneous comment in her presence was an awkward thing to say.

"Sorry, Luci. I didn't mean that."

"That's all right, Dad."

"Dang it. I don't know what to think about what's going on in Vietnam."

Luci picked up the phone and called down to the kitchen.

The President paused for a few seconds, then shouted with great exasperation, "You know, those God..."

Lyndon Johnson stopped himself quickly. He put his shoes on. He started for the bedroom door as he rephrased what he was about to say. "Those scoundrel Viet-nese!"

"Daddy, where're you going? You've got to eat something."

"I'm gonna get some fresh air."

Luci's face lit up. A pretty young woman, she had the most winning smile. "Wait, Daddy, I'm coming with you."

President Johnson enjoyed the balcony that President Truman had constructed in 1947. A controversial addition to the White House, the Truman Balcony added an inviting grace to the south façade as it overlooked the South Lawn. Straight out from the balcony, the dome of the Jefferson Memorial, its elegant rotunda lit by giant floodlights, stood gleaming. The statue of Thomas Jefferson faced the White House. Hidden by buildings and trees to the right, the imposing edifice of the Lincoln Memorial sat bathed in light. To the south and slightly to the east of the White House, in between Constitution and Independence Avenues, the colossus of the Washington Monument pierced the bleak sky, towering over all other structures. The horizontal demarcation of two different colored stones of the monument, a third of the way up the obelisk, couldn't be discerned, but the red aircraft warning lights near the apex of the monument were clearly visible.

"Luci, after all these years in Washington D.C., I know very little about the history of the monuments or who designed them."

Once back in the residence—the mansion—his meal, covered by a brightly polished silver cover, sat on the table. The President didn't pay much attention.

Luci removed the cover. "Daddy, I had this meal specially prepared for you and now you're not hungry. What happened to your appetite?"

"Oh, Luci, I dunno."

"Hey, Daddy, after Sunday Mass, let's go to the Shoreham Hotel, just you and me, and have a relaxing brunch. You know how proud I am to be seen with you."

"Let's do that. Your mom would probably like us to be out of the house. This old haunt would be a lot quieter for her."

Luci admonished her father.

"Eat your dinner, Mr. President."

Lyndon Johnson smiled at Luci as she turned for the door.

"Be sure to see if Lyn's OK and get some sleep."

Alone, the President ate a bite of his meal. Tormented, he put his fork down, moved his plate to one side and went to bed.

CHAPTER SEVENTY-FOUR

THE POLITICAL OFFICER

"Gentlemen, your party and country have called upon you to lead all people of Vietnam to freedom from the American imperialists. It is incumbent upon you to defend our righteous self-rule over our ancestral land."

Not really a combatant. Major General Le Quang Dao, a senior-ranking officer in the Quan Doi Nhan Dan, the party commissar, the political officer attached to B5T8, made sure cadres adhered to party values and guidelines.

Not often was the political officer near areas of combat, but Dao thought it important to talk to the officers at Attack Sector N3. His presence ensured cadres fighting the Americans in Quang Tri Province would adhere to a proper attitude. The men needed arms, food and ammunition, but they also needed nurturing in the ways of the party…not the government, the party.

Born in 1921 in Dinh Bang village, Bac Ninh Province, not far from Hanoi, Le Quang Dao rose through the ranks of the army. After thirty years in service, he was promoted to the rank of major general. He stood now in front of the Sao Vang-centered red flag spread across a wall behind him. Le Quang Dao, with full hair, a high forehead and wearing glasses, continued with his message.

"You officers are here for a special reason. Forget that you are far from your homes. Without your sacrifice, American imperialists will continue to destroy the Fatherland and subjugate our people.

"Vietnam has been downtrodden for centuries by invaders who rape our land, and our women, and exploit our toil for their selfish gain. My home was attacked viciously by the French. Later, we exacted our revenge. We ambushed them in 1946. They paid with their own warm blood. The French continued to cause us humiliation until Vo Nguyen Giap destroyed their will at Dien Bien Phu eight years later.

"Outside powers have chained us to the soil, but in so doing, that pernicious restraint has confirmed that it is our land, our country. It's time now for our people to unchain themselves and flourish for the survival of the Fatherland. We are privileged to fight for Ho Chi Minh's vision of one Vietnam. Our motto, *Doc lap, Tu do, Hanh Phuc* [Independence, Freedom, Happiness], is the guiding principal as we seek to liberate the southern provinces from the imperialists. We will unify our country, now unjustly divided."

Some of the officers were eager to hear Dao's words, but most preferred for the meeting to end. Major General Dao, gauging the men's attentiveness, continued with his inflated speech.

"The fight for liberation of the south and our victory are now concentrated at Khe Sanh. This is where we will beat the criminal President Johnson, his immoral imperialist forces and their South Vietnamese puppets.

"*Nhan Dan* newspaper in Hanoi reported on the radio that Khe Sanh will be the final chapter for the Americans in Vietnam."

Dao didn't bother to tell the men that several hundred soldiers of an infiltration group had deserted. Instead, he quoted Radio Hanoi. The North Vietnamese Army killed over four thousand troops, more than half of which were Americans.

"Gentlemen, we will kill every imperialist who violates our country, who fights against our cause and our devoted forces. The glorious Quan Doi Nhan Dan will crush the Americans and conquer Khe Sanh."

Major General Le Quang Dao was stretching his rhetorical abilities too far. His phraseology would soon bore the men, some of whom were already jaded by so much propaganda. He drew on his cigarette and exhaled the smoke. "The Americans are here because they are required to be here. We are here because we want to be here. They fight so they can go home. We fight to save our home. The Americans do not want to die for a foreign cause. We willingly die for our glorious cause. While their motivation is like the smoke from this cigarette—that blows away—ours is solid, like the ancient soil on which we stand and beneath which our ancestors are honorably buried.

"Our undertaking is of historic significance to Vietnam, to the communist movement and to the world. Reunification of our Fatherland and national salvation are greater than all of us. The Americans are unwelcome guests, but their arrogance precludes them from leaving Vietnam."

Major General Dao stood at semi-attention. "Your comrades, dead and alive are expecting you to join them in this glorious fight. This is the place from which Westmoreland and the Americans will be vanquished into the East Sea."

Le Quang Dao held up a fist. "*Chien Thang*!"

Dao's eyes scanned the room. "Your sacrifice will glorify Nguyen Hue [Emperor Quang Trung] and Ly Thai To. Those of you who will die will do so in honor of the Fatherland. Those of you who survive will fight until you no longer have luck."

Le Quang Dao smiled ruefully. "Your spirit will remain here in Quang Tri Province forever."

CHAPTER SEVENTY-FIVE

BATTLEFIELD INTERLUDE

"Douglas, Jesus Christ, man! Gunny's gonna chew your ass good for dropping that last round down the tube after the cease fire."

The eighty-one millimeter mortar crew enjoyed teasing its oldest member. The ribbing was endless, but Lance Corporal Larry Douglas, age twenty-two, didn't care. His rebuffs were just as colorful.

"I don't want those prissy Air Force assholes to get all the glory."

Everyone laughed, mostly out of anxious release.

The intense exchange of mortar fire with the North Vietnamese had lasted ten minutes, during which time Douglas's mortar team had fired fifteen rounds.

The humid air was stifling in the trench and the dugout mortar emplacement. The up-right mortar tube was burning hot.

Wesley Woodman, wearing a sleeveless flak jacket, lit a cigarette and inhaled deeply. He rubbed the back of his neck. Words on his flak jacket read "Las Vegas."

Stewart Matlock, a big Polack who everyone called "Stewey," removed his helmet and poured water down his throat from his canteen. Sweat poured from his forehead, stinging his bloodshot eyes.

"So, what happened next, Douglas?"

"So, what happened next what?"

"Come off it, old man. You started the story. Finish it. After you sat below the senior tree at your high school...you know...what happened to the girl?"

Larry Douglas smiled half-heartedly. A look of embarrassment, perhaps regret, crossed his face. He wished he'd never brought the topic up.

"OK, so I sat down on the benches beneath the senior tree. That and the patio outside the cafeteria were the only places where students could smoke at my high school. She sat on the bench on the opposite side of the tree with all her books."

This is where Larry had left off before the brief attack. Now he was on uncharted ground.

The incident happened just before he graduated from high school, after the spring prom in Wheeling, West Virginia. Still fresh in his mind, he didn't like to be reminded of past feelings. As long as the memory was suppressed, Larry could deal with the pang of affection that would sometimes surface. Recounting further details of the story to his comrades was difficult, too personal, but what the hell? We're all gonna die anyway.

Woodman spoke mockingly.

"She was dating some basketball player, right? That's what you told us. You're not making this crap up, are you?"

"When I saw her sitting in the shade, my heart skipped a beat...I was so close to her. I looked right at her. She was the most beautiful sight I have ever seen."

"You mean, more beautiful than the chicks in Khe Sanh?"

"Hey man," Stewey chimed in, "what was she wearing?"

"I dunno."

"You asshole, of course you know. Douglas, come on, man. We want the juicy details."

"OK, OK. She was wearing a dark blue skirt, a white blouse and a white sweater casually over her shoulder."

"What about underneath? That's what we wanna know."

"Do you guys wanna hear this story or not?"

"No, no, Larry, go on," Woodman said. "This is just getting good. I want to find out how she rejected your ass and how you had to slither away."

"Listen butt-face, she didn't reject me."

Reggie Murphy, another member of the crew, who had remained silent up to this point, spoke.

"His heart skipped a beat. How touching."

Murphy blew smoke out his nostrils and scratched his face. He put his helmet back on while shaking his head. "Man, she had plans for her boyfriend after school that day—oh yeah...you can count on it and you weren't the lucky guy, asshole. Go on, mortar man, tell it to us straight,"

Larry, framed by the distant hills in the background, lit a cigarette. Why he had started smoking was beyond him but everyone else smoked, so why not?

"I tried to talk to her at school but that didn't work. And now, here we were sitting not more than ten feet apart. I moved closer to her and said hello. Our eyes met for a moment."

"That's the only contact you made? When's this story gonna get good?"

"Stop it, Murph, you short-timer, let Larry finish. I wanna hear how this ends."

Larry Douglas continued.

"I can still see her. She had short jet black hair, shiny as silk, and the softest, most gorgeous dark brown eyes."

"This is really getting good now. Tell us more, Casanova. We have all day. We ain't going nowhere but this stinking mortar pit. So let's hear it."

"We started talking. Her name was Chrisandra."

"I knew it. What we got here is a classic Romeo and Juliette romance. Casanova and Chrisandra."

"I found out she was a dancer auditioning for a part in a musical in Cincinnati the day after we were to graduate."

"Man, I would say Chrisandra was on her way to the bright lights. She had you and Wheeling, West Virginia in the rearview mirror."

Douglas looked across the base.

"I saw her alone in town a week later. I didn't have to report to boot camp for another three weeks. I figured I'll never get another chance. I asked if she'd go out with me."

"Well, Jesus criminy Christ. Finally! Let me guess. She said no to you, right?"

"No, dumbass, she smiled and said yes. We walked down Market Street and stopped in the Wheeling Cafe. A fast Elvis song—can't recall the name of the song—was playing and then they played 'Strangers in the Night'... you know, a Frank Sinatra song."

"You mean a stand real-close, body-rubbing kinda song."

"I looked into her dark eyes. She stared right back at me. Sent shivers down my spine. I've never felt anything like that in my life."

Woodman, laughing at Douglas, described a scene in a mock movie.

"Guys. I get the picture. Here's Douglas in the restaurant with this girl. The music is playing. He's being mister debonair and all, but he didn't tell her he joined the Marines. He makes a play for this girl, but guess what? The asshole's got no money. She suspects this, but she's trying to be nice to mister cool-hand Larry. She's just hoping he'll disappear. I can see it all now"

"Yeah, the old man couldn't pay for squat," Murphy said.

Douglas paid no attention.

"After we ate, we left the table... and I paid, you assholes. I had money. I stood next to her and little behind her. I placed one arm around her waist and then an amazing thing happened. It surprised the hell out of me."

"What? This better be good."

"She slipped her fingers in between mine. I could smell her perfume. I felt her soft hair with my cheek...my God."

Douglas took comfort in what he had just told his buddies if for no other reason, it was a story of home. It was a special moment for him and it gave him courage. Each person had a story. That was his. He saw a different composure on the faces of his mates; a look of empathy, or perhaps envy.

Douglas fell into a contemplative mood that exuded the respect that brothers-in-arms come to have for one another when facing the same fate. Larry Douglas had revealed something trivial, but deeply personal. He accepted their bawdy jokes and silly insults as harmless taunts. He understood their cutting humor was a cover-up of their emotions, a concealment of their own longings. Larry's comrades were as lonely as he was—he knew it and they knew it.

"Is Lance Corporal Larry Douglas in this unit?"

The Marine officer, appearing from nowhere, stood on the edge of the embankment looking into the mortar pit. A Colt forty-five caliber automatic pistol hung from his webbing and an M-16 was slung over his shoulder. It was the sheet of paper the major was holding, however, that made his sudden appearance odd.

"I'm Douglas, Sir."

The major removed his helmet and tucked it under his arm. "I need to talk you, son."

Larry Douglas climbed out of the mortar pit. The two men walked about ten feet away.

"Douglas, do you have a brother?

"Yes, Sir. Four years younger."

"He's in the Army, right?"

"Yes, Sir."

The major looked at the slip of paper.

"His name is Mathew, right? From West Virginia."

"Wheeling, West Virginia, Sir."

"And, to confirm, he's in-country, correct?"

"As far as I know, Sir. Is there something wrong, Major?"

"Douglas, your brother was killed north of Hue three days ago."

CHAPTER SEVENTY-SIX

WE WILL MAKE IT TO N3

Lieutenant Nguyen Cuong, almost lifeless with fatigue, gave the order to halt. The forced march stopped in an unspoiled area beneath the towering trees of Quang Tri Province. The soldiers in Cuong's company unslung their weapons. They fell to the wet ground beneath the overhead foliage that denied the jungle floor of sunlight.

Cuong's uniform was in bloody shreds from the battles of the past many weeks. Dirty bandages covered a large wound in his left side just above his waist and a smaller wound in his right shoulder. The blood that seeped through the gauze was black. It dried to a crust. He wore torn sandals. His feet bled from open sores.

Hungry to the point of severe cramps, Cuong, his AK-47 beside him and several banana-like magazines of ammunition strapped around his body, led the men through the jungle. His company, a consolidation of two hundred men, had been instructed to rendezvous with Strike Group CT43 at Attack Sector N3, southwest of Khe Sanh. A large number of troops were being massed for an attempt against the Americans.

Cuong thought about the horrific fighting he left behind at A-1 Hill. Not the official military designation, of course, A-1 Hill was the name used among Cuong's comrades to identify the taller of two mountains located next to each other, both of which were occupied by the Americans. The Americans called it Hill 881 South. The name A-1 was borrowed in commemorative honor of General Giap's famous attack on the real A-1 Hill at Dien Bien Phu. The French had named the same hill Eliane. It was one of the last strong points to hold out before the collapse of the main French base.

Fighting in B5T8 was just as savage. The Americans fought ferociously. Their airpower was too much. The rain of bombs and the terrifying cluster bomb units, what with the widespread destruction they caused, were invented in hell. Napalm was the worst of it. Cuong watched so many of his comrades writhe in pain, their skin burning in a dark red blaze, their screaming voices emanating through the fire as the flames completely consumed them.

The captain of Cuong's company and the other officers had been killed, their bodies abandoned near the giant mountain. Cuong assumed command of the men remaining in his company until a new captain arrived.

The company retreated. Few soldiers escaped without serious wounds. The men marched north for two days to the DMZ, then west to a safe valley to re-assemble the unit's emaciated pieces, then finally southeast, through the dense rain forest.

Cuong stood and slung his weapon over his back. He adjusted his ammunition belt and the pack that contained a day's ration of rice. He put his helmet on.

"Company, we have to move. We need to be at N3 tonight. Pick up your weapons."

"Lieutenant, we can't make it by nightfall."

The words came from Kua.

Kua's real name was Kanh. The diminutive was corrupted from *Cua* (crab). When much younger, he tried to imitate how crabs walked at the fish market. Kanh spelled the nickname incorrectly with a K because he thought all words beginning with a hard phonetic kah-sound started with a K, just like his name.

"Kua, when we were ten, we defied our parents and caught trucks to Ha Long Bay for the day. We hid in the back of the trucks, remember? We were scared we would be caught by the gendarmes. Yet, we didn't get caught. We were afraid to swim to that small island in the bay. We made it, didn't we? And returning to Hanoi that night, we were scared of what might happen to us on the highway. Nothing happened. We made it back to Hanoi safely. The hard part is not the doing, but rather making up one's mind to do it. We will make it to N3."

Cuong gave an encouraging nudge with his fist to his friend's shoulder. He drank a slug of water from his Russian canteen. The purification tablets gave it a horrible acidic taste.

"Here, drink some water, Kua."

Cuong smiled at his friend. "We are brothers from Dong Da. Always remember that. And always remember the hard part is not the doing."

CHAPTER SEVENTY-SEVEN

AGONY

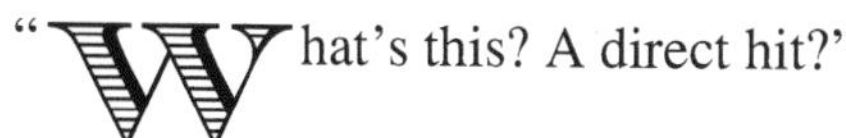

“What’s this? A direct hit?”

President Johnson picked up the copy of *Newsweek* magazine lying on the table in the Situation Room. The cover photo showed a Marine ducking to protect himself from a reddish-orange explosion, the result of North Vietnamese artillery and rocket attacks.

“Mr. President, I brought this in for you to read. I didn’t know if you’d seen it. Great photos of Khe Sanh, Sir.”

The President thumbed through the magazine, then looked around the room as he took his seat.

“All right, everyone, please sit down.”

The President looked at his watch. “My schedule is very tight. Let’s hit the highpoints.”

He moved the magazine to the side.

Walt Rostow leaned forward.

“Sir, first thing. Israel and Jordan are fighting and…”

“Damned Middle East. Everything that happens over there draws the world closer to a major war—everyone’s so trigger happy. Those Arabs and Israelis will fight for the next ten thousand years.”

Lyndon Johnson tried to make a joke. “Just like Longhorns and Sooners in the Cotton Bowl. Ain’t nothin’ we can do about it.”

"Mr. President, State believes Antonin Novotny will resign his office as President of Czechoslovakia. Warsaw Pact countries may meet in Dresden to discuss the crisis"

"Those Warsaw SOBs. Yeah, keep me up to date on that. Right now, though, we gotta stay focused on Vietnam."

The President glanced at his watch again. "Let's move along."

"Mr. President, MACV has requested use of Agent Orange as an additional measure at Khe Sanh and along Highway Nine to remove the cover of the jungle canopy. I think they…"

The President adjusted his glasses.

"That request's on my desk now."

The President looked around the Situation Room. "Now listen here, everyone. Things south of the DMZ remain unsettling. Westy's reports lead me to believe that..."

The President pointed to the copy of *Newsweek* askew on the table. He thumped the table with his fingers then gestured to the Khe Sanh model sitting close by. "I know those Marines are in peril. Damn, I live with it every day. Those few days in early February when we thought the NVA would pour over our lines like an open sluice gate drove me crazy. I felt as if every decision I made about any damn thing had some bearing on Khe Sanh. They…"

"Mr. President, if I may weigh in, Sir."

Lyndon Johnson looked at Walt Rostow. The President tolerated interruptions from those who might make a significant contribution. Rostow could be pushy at times. He always had an opinion—not necessarily a bad one—and he seldom failed to express it. But, the President held up his hand.

"Let me remind everyone here. I am willing to meet with the North Vietnese anytime, anywhere to reach an agreement that recognizes both governments. I want to negotiate with North Vietnam, but we will do so from a position of strength. I have asked the American people for their understanding and patience. I have urged austerity measures telling every American that we have to tighten our belts.

"The Tet Offensive was a disaster for the North Vietnamese. The NVA and the Viet Cong didn't destroy our embassy in Saigon. Bunker tells me our embassy is completely functioning as before. They didn't topple any government and they didn't succeed with their general uprising, or whatever that dumb plan was they thought would work…I dunno, some resolution thing. And they didn't…well…I'm not sure now if they'll attack Khe Sanh at all."

Walt Rostow raised his hand furtively.

"Sir, we can't drop our guard. MACV Forward in Phu Bai…Prov Corps, and III MAF in Da Nang confirm the enemy is still active. As you know, we've observed a new build-up. Recent action south of the base indicates more of the same. Indications are the NVA will attempt a new thrust, Sir."

"For Christ's sake, Rostow, that's exactly what Westy's been waitin' fer. If the North Vietnamese won't negotiate, then it's time to take the little bastards down a notch."

The President, breathing heavily, looked over the top of his glasses. His eyebrows raised, he glowered around the room. "Ho Chi Minh may as well come to the negotiating table now. It'll be a lot easier."

Johnson stopped talking and caught his breath. No one spoke. He pointed to the magazine again.

"The Agony of Khe Sanh. *Newsweek* chose the correct word: Agony."

The President thumbed through the magazine and stopped to read the headline on page twenty-five: *More of the Same Won't Do.* He read the article's opening sentence. "President Johnson's strategy for Vietnam has run into a dead end." And, the next paragraph, "The United States is seized by a crisis of confidence."

It was the very last sentence, however, that completed the subtlety of the headline: "Indeed, to do more of the same might lead to more of the same kind of failure."

Failure? Is this what his presidency has been about? The President breathed deeply. He spoke without looking at anyone in particular.

"Dammit, we gotta stand by South Vietnam."

The President fell quiet. "I'm sorry for this digression. Y'all work tirelessly in support of my administration. I just felt a need to express my frustration, and...well, that's the way we do things in Texas."

What was the President up to? Clearly exasperated, his comments seemed shrouded in vague meaning.

The President composed himself while he straightened some papers. "I just learned this morning that total American losses have exceeded twenty-five thousand deaths."

"That's correct, Sir, by latest reports."

"Kennedy, McCarthy and that phony Nixon are having a heyday with that statistic."

The President looked at the *Newsweek* cover again. "I'll read this later today, maybe at lunch."

"Mr. President, the cover photo was taken on the first day of the siege."

"Man, the NVA scored a bullseye."

"Yes, Sir. Hit the main ammo dump."

Rostow used an expression he had just learned. "Square in the V-ring, Sir. Unfortunately, Mr. President, the photographer was killed in a C-123 crash not far from Khe Sanh with about fifty Marines on March sixth, Sir."

"So, you're saying these photos are published posthumously."

"Sadly, yes, Sir."

The President looked at the magazine, then at those around him.

"Who was the photographer?"

"Robert Ellison, Sir. His name is inside. He was twenty-three."

CHAPTER SEVENTY-EIGHT

BEO NHAY TIEN

Colonel Do Thi Tu, a veteran of the 304th Division of the People's Army of Vietnam, was aware his men knew the ground attack against the Americans at Ta Con just after the middle of February met with disaster. Later, at the very end of February, the NVA attack on the ARVN forces on the east side of the Khe Sanh Combat Base met the same fate. The American airstrikes were too well placed. The pounding artillery and the 37th ARVN were more effective than surmised. Had Tu's men broken through the outer line, the *bo doi* would not have been able to penetrate the second line manned by the Americans. The NVA assault plans, half-baked, were a complete failure.

Talking about the debacle would serve no purpose. Colonel Tu would focus on the new attack instead. It would come from the south and face only one line of defense.

Colonel Tu gathered his men, a semi-commando sapper group informally dubbed the *Beo Nhay Tien* (Leaping Leopard Unit) at Attack Sector N3 at midnight. Located about fifteen hundred meters southwest of the American encampment, Attack Sector N3, consisted of a complex of valleys and draws separated by hills. The Leopards were instructed to bivouac in canyon C of N3. They would find no amenities, but it didn't matter. They wouldn't be there long. Strike Group CT42, arriving a day earlier, was located not even one kilometer away, in an adjoining valley, still part of Attack Sector N3. CT43 would arrive at N3 within a day and would be staged in canyon D.

The colonel smoked nervously while he adjusted his helmet. He spoke to each company of the famed *Beo Nhay Tien*, collectively a total of three hundred specialists.

"Once the CT strike groups are in place, we'll be poised for decisive action."

The colonel, his cigarette dangling from his mouth, clapped his hands together in prideful enthusiasm. *"Chung ta se khong that bai* [We will not fail]!"

He drew a map on the jungle floor while he talked. "The new attack will be preceded by a prolonged artillery bombardment by the 675th at Co Roc and by mortars. The barrage will continue for about twenty hours spanning two days. During this time, we will follow CT42 into position at Diem Tan Cong Mot, only three hundred meters from the American perimeter. We will stay there with Strike Group 42. CT43 will move with and behind us to Diem Tan Cong Mot.

"The end of the barrage on the second day will be the signal to attack. Force A of the Leopards—seventy men—will be the first in. They'll destroy the barb wire aprons with Bangalore torpedoes. That accomplished, CT42 will be the spearhead of the attack. CT42 will storm the American trenches, invest the base, and overwhelm the Americans' primary line of defense.

"Forces B, C and D of the Leopards will immediately follow CT42. Once inside the perimeter, Force B, consisting of ninety men carrying large satchel charges, will go straight for the first target, the underground headquarters, and destroy it.

"Force C and Force D, a total of one hundred forty men, will attack artillery and other targets. The Marines have two batteries of 105s at the east end and a battery each of 105s and 155s toward the west end. Mortar positions located on the south side will also be taken out by Force C and Force D.

"CT42 will continue to cause as much destruction as possible and neutralize smaller fighting units. CT42 will shoot a flare to signal that the gates to liberation have been opened. CT43 will attack decisively in the wake of CT42 to reinforce the momentum. CT43 will be the *Bua ta* [sledge hammer] and press the attack to a successful conclusion.

"I have elected to lead the Leopards personally. Our combined attack on the Americans at Khe Sanh will carry historical importance equal to the attack on the French at Dien Bien Phu. I know something about that campaign. I attacked the hill the French called Beatrice."

A career soldier from Yen Bai Province, the colonel stood perfectly erect. "Gentlemen, we have been observing the Americans for many weeks. The Americans are weak here, in the middle section of the south perimeter of their base. You will encounter the usual barb wire, aprons, mines, etc. Fighting and machine gun fire will be heavy. The command post will be heavily defended. It is located about one hundred meters from the south perimeter. The line of attack is straight toward the headquarters.

"The American commander never leaves the base. His name is—I can't pronounce it—Londs, Lunds…not sure. It would be a prize if we took him captive, like de Castries at Dien Bien Phu, but… well..."

Colonel Tu smiled. "I recall when General Giap placed a call to Hanoi. Madam de Castries, staying at the Metropole Hotel, was informed that the French Union forces were defeated at Dien Bien Phu. General Giap respectfully passed the word to Madam de Castries that her husband was alive, though he was now a prisoner of the glorious Viet Minh. I doubt Giap will call the American commander's wife this time. I believe you understand what I'm trying to say.

"Reports indicate he has not studied the battle of Dien Bien Phu, but, since he fought against the Japanese, we must assume he is a hardened veteran with significant combat experience."

Tu laughed. "Londs likes cigars, not that that matters."

The message was perfectly clear. The Quan Doi Nhan Dan was going to attack the Americans again and destroy them.

But, Colonel Tu, full of pride and courage, harbored reservations. Military headquarters had analyzed every aspect of the impending battle, but they may be reaching too far. Would nine hundred soldiers in CT42, combined with the Leopards' three hundred specialists, be effective as the driving wedge? CT43 was somewhat larger, but together, were the two CT strike groups sufficiently strong? The base may be in shambles after the artillery strike, but the Americans will still have fighting capacity.

Colonel Tu thought back to the fight for Beatrice. The Viet Minh won, but the steep hillside was literally covered with the dead bodies of his comrades.

Now, fourteen years later, to win or lose at Khe Sanh could decide the fate of the military efforts of the Quan Doi Nhan Dan in South Vietnam. The cost incurred at Dien Bien Phu was significant. The price they will pay now against the U.S. Marines may be higher.

Tu lived through the battle of Beatrice Hill. He doubted he would be alive after the attack at Khe Sanh.

The section of the line the Americans call the Gray Sector may be the weakest, but do any weak spots really exist in the American defense? The answer would be revealed soon.

But, one question nagged Colonel Tu. If we win, what then?

CHAPTER SEVENTY-NINE

THE TIO

The strange man, exuding a poised demeanor, entered the underground Khe Sanh Combat Operations Center, the COC. Well-manicured, of slight-to-medium build, and with salt-and-pepper hair, he was a mystifying personage. Few took note of his arrival at Khe Sanh two months before, in mid-January. Personnel, some cloaked in secrecy, came and went all the time. Not more than a handful of Marines knew how the commanders at Khe Sanh came to rely on him.

The individual was dressed in precisely-creased Marine utilities. He was not burdened with any weapon except an inward curving Gurkha knife strapped to his belt that substituted for a side arm. He wore a gold ring inset with a noticeable ruby stone bearing crossed swords—perhaps a family crest. He also wore the twin silver bars of an O-3. The mysterious individual was, in fact, a captain in the U.S. Marine Corps.

Colonel David E. Lownds nodded acknowledgement of the officer's presence.

"Gentlemen, the captain has something to tell us. Please give him your undivided attention."

Colonel Lownds' introductory remarks resonated with diffident respect. "He's been with us at Khe Sanh as the Target Information Officer, the TIO, as you may know. He has worked with Major Hudson to assist us with target intelligence."

Lownds held the coffee pot.

"Care for some coffee, Captain? It's not the best. It's not even very warm."

"Thank you, Colonel Lownds, but no. That's what you American infidels drink."

The captain flashed a friendly smile. "The coffee in the COC is not to my specific liking. English breakfast tea, perhaps, with some fresh biscuits, would be the more appropriate choice...certainly a better one, I should think."

"Infidels?" Lownds smiled back and spoke as if the captain was visiting for the first time. "Sorry 'bout that. Bad coffee and stale C-ration crackers... that's all we got in this restaurant."

The captain played along.

"No bother, Colonel."

Colonel Lownds raised his eyebrows at the effusiveness of the junior officer's response.

The captain turned to the men around the table.

"Thank you, gentlemen, for your time. I will intrude no more than necessary."

The captain cleared his throat. "I have important information you will find to be of interest, even beneficial."

An odd way to talk by someone who had been at Khe Sanh since the start of the siege. No Marine officer was that cultured with his verbal exclamations. The captain spoke with an articulate accent.

He unfolded and arranged two maps on the table beneath an overhead light.

"Sound and vibration sensors that have been air-dropped indicate the 304th has pulled back to the southwest of the combat base. We don't know why. The whole division is no longer an immediate menace. Interestingly, aerial surveillance provides evidence of tracks and new paths and development of storage depots in the area. The influx of refugees is also an indication that something is developing in the absence of the main division."

While the captain's intelligence was derived from technology, some of his sources were more curious.

"Montagnards who I have enlisted, have confirmed strange ground movements."

"*You* have enlisted Montagnards, Captain? You said *I* enlisted, not *we* enlisted. Is there something I should be reading into this?"

"Colonel, my respects, Sir. Please bear with me for a few minutes. The NVA are planning a new ground attack against the Gray Sector."

The captain pointed to the south side of the combat base that was protected by Bravo Company First Battalion Twenty-sixth Marines and farther to the east by the 37th ARVN Rangers.

The captain smiled.

"However, the NVA infidels are ignorant of what we know."

The young officer's ironic humor surfaced again with a word he had used before. To the captain, everyone, NVA and Americans alike, were infidels.

"Captain, our defenses have been strengthened with double aprons of barb wire, tanglefoot, concertina, mines, trenches and additional bunkers. We are using fougasse on the hills. We are monitoring the approaches to the base closely. We've had a lot of enemy activity south of the base and..."

Colonel Lownds hesitated. His fingers made sweeping gestures above the maps. "You could be right, though."

Lownds tapped the maps. "The last time they made a serious attempt was on the last day of February at the east end of the base. Two days ago they tried another probe with about six hundred men. In each case, they were cut down before they could reach the perimeter."

"Colonel, that deserter Lieutenant Tonc gave us credible information. At least, we could rely on it to the extent we were prepared. The timing of the attacks was way off, but they attacked the east side of the base first which correlates with what he told us. Fox and Golf Companies Second Battalion on 558 became an obstacle for an attack from the west and gave pause to the NVA.

"However, Giap has devised specific plans for Khe Sanh. The enemy is maneuvering troops into position now."

"Captain…"

"Colonel. Please allow me to continue, Sir."

Baig bowed slightly at the waist. "If I may, Sir"

The captain's eagerness, combined with smiling enthusiasm, a bit contrived, was contagious. Lownds breathed in.

"Please do, Captain."

The captain pointed to an area again to the southwest of Khe Sanh.

"Now, there's a special sapper unit. I can't pronounce the Vietnamese name but in English, the translation means—somewhat sophomorically—Leaping Leopards. They came from Laos and paralleled the 689 ridgeline to a position about here. The North Vietnamese call this Attack Sector N3 which is located near a small place named Ta Du, at coordinates X-ray Delta eight three eight, four zero five, about one and a half kilometers to the southwest of the base. The sapper unit will join with what we have learned are *Chien Thang* strike groups.

"*Chien Thang* means victory. The CT strike groups are specially formed to insert large groups of soldiers quickly, as inertial bulwark, into the enemy's ranks. Napoleonic tactics, Sir."

Baig bowed slightly. "Napoleon believed that battles are won by intrusion of large masses at strategic places at the most propitious moment. Historically, Grenadiers with fixed bayonets served this purpose. Of course, these tactics were quickly antiquated with the advent of the machine gun. Giap, a student of Napoleon, is applying a variant of that tactic here...but with his own machine guns.

"CT42 will be the vanguard of the attack. Together with the Leaping Leopard Unit, they have dispersed in canyons around Ta Du. A second strike group, CT43, reinforced with a company from Highpoint 845, is also consolidating there."

The captain pointed at the map with an enlarged layout of the base as he looked around at the silent men. "The Leopards and CT42 and CT43 will move to the attack point at coordinates eight four seven, four one three, very close to the base. They will attack right through the garbage dump with CT42 leading the way. The Leaping Leopard Unit, who will provide initial sappers against our perimeter, will follow in the immediate footsteps of CT42. The COC is their target...that and the artillery batteries. They'll be carrying satchel charges."

The captain moved his hand over the map, his gold ring clearly visible.

"The NVA eighth company has been digging trenches just outside the wire, an insidious activity, if I may add, Sir."

"The trenching seems to have tapered off now, Captain. The trenches aren't being maintained."

Captain Baig continued.

"Colonel, the bulk of their ammunition is being stored at coordinates eight one seven, four zero four, southwest of Khe Sanh. Ammunition is being transferred closer to Attack Sector N3 at coordinates eight three four, three nine six, near Tom Bang. Our patrols have discovered caches of ammunition brought forward.

"The attack will be preceded by a sustained barrage of artillery and mortar fire. The signal for the cannonade will be broadcast through a secret signal on Radio Hanoi The barrage will begin about dusk and continue through the night. The most severe artillery bombardment will occur the next day and it'll last most of the day. It will sweep across the base, but will come to concentrate most heavily on the south side."

Colonel Lownds, observing the captain's eccentricities, stared at him as if he was watching a character in a stage play. He seemed unafraid, but was he for real?

"Captain, heavier than on the twenty-third of last month?"

"I should think, Colonel. The NVA have concentrated more artillery in one place than at any point in its army's history. As we all know, they have 130, 152 and new 122 millimeter long range guns and heavy mortar and rocket batteries. It's all pointed right here, Sir."

Lownds, clearly concerned, became intrigued.

"Captain, come with me topside for a moment. Let's talk."

"Pleasure, Colonel."

Colonel Lownds and Captain Baig passed the chessboard. They climbed the concrete stairs and walked to an area not far away. They stood behind a wall of sandbags.

"All right, Captain, now let me just ask you."

The captain bowed slightly as a gesture of high respect.

"As you wish, Sir."

"Captain, how can someone less than field grade officer know all this information so precisely and with such confidence?"

"Colonel, I'm well aware how strange my elaborations may sound. What I am saying is the undisputed truth. What I have gleaned is the result of the sensors and aerial photos, but, more importantly, much of what I know comes through contacts I have in a certain capital city."

"Contacts? In a certain capital city? Captain, what are you saying?"

"Colonel, you can appreciate the incipient threat. Now..."

Baig spoke in supplication. "If I may."

Lownds motioned for him to continue.

"The NVA's new plan to attack Khe Sanh was submitted to the politburo in Hanoi. Consent was granted. Even though Giap has moved his main divisions away, CT groups have been specially formed and equipped. Unorthodox as the plan may be, it is not to be taken lightly."

"Are you certain of the attack?"

"As certain as tomorrow's sunrise, Sir. The Khe Sanh Combat Base will be attacked again."

The statement was ominous.

"If you are so confident of what you know, why did you wait to inform me? You can talk to me at any time. And, if you know where the enemy is and where he will be, why not obliterate him from the air right now? You are, after all, the TIO."

"Colonel, your questions are completely logical. The intelligence congealed late last night as I corroborated the information. I'm sharing this with you here in person because you and I, and all the Marines are in the direct line of fire."

Not given to tones of wryness, Colonel Lownds could barely contain himself this one time. A slightly sarcastic remark escaped the colonel's lips.

"Tell me about it, Captain."

"Colonel, my maps have nothing on them. No notes, just maps. I'm carrying no documents. There is no coded message. I cannot allow a security breech. I have complete faith in what I have revealed."

David Lownds ran his right hand through his hair.

The captain continued.

"Now, Colonel, I come to the point, in answer to your second question. We will catch the enemy in a vice and eliminate his forces before the attack. Air strikes are being developed now. They will prove most effective and demoralizing if the enemy consolidates in one place. The airstrikes will be devastating. But Colonel, some of the strikes will be close to the base perimeter, perhaps closer than a thousand meters."

"Captain, when the air strikes hit the enemy on the twenty-ninth, body parts rained down on our men inside the perimeter. The men could see bodies blown into the sky. With 500 and 750 pound bombs, even two thousand meters is already too close."

"Correct, Colonel, but the NVA know that. For protection, they will hide within that *cordon sanitaire*, if I may, Sir—the safety zone.

"I would advise your men that any movement may tip the NVA off."

"Captain, I'm not moving the men away from their lines. The positions have to be manned continuously."

Colonel Lownds threw the soggy cigar stub to the ground. He reached inside his flak jacket for another. "You're Asian…born there, right?"

"Correct, Sir. India, to be more precise. Some may even say Dravidian… from the Deccan, southern India, but not Hindu, Sir."

Colonel Lownds broke the military façade.

"Cigar, Captain Baig? I have two."

"Very kind of you, Colonel, but no thank you, Sir."

"Harry," Colonel Lownds said, using the captain's nickname because he was never sure if he could pronounce his real name correctly, "you've enjoyed a lot of targeting successes using sensors dropped in the region."

"And sadly, a number of failures, Sir. I must be honest. The lack of secondary explosions disappoint. Also, Sir, I am dependent on the bomb damage assessments. Quite honestly, I am wrong sometimes. I have to be aware of NVA disinformation. The NVA are not stupid…and I'm not infallible."

"You were an artillery officer at one time. You went through Fort Sill. I'm pleased you're here."

"Very kind, Sir. I am honored to be under your command."

Lownds narrowed his eyes.

"You'll recall my anger when Khe Sanh ville was the target of an Arclight raid you directed a few weeks ago."

"Colonel, the NVA were coming. We put an end to that danger."

"Harry, put yourself in my shoes. Help me to understand how you come about this intelligence. I need to know that your information is completely accurate. My question again. How can I trust what you say is true?"

[*Born to an aristocratic family in Panchgani, Maharashtra State, in 1932, Mirza Munir Baig was raised in India; France, the United Kingdom and what came to be called Pakistan. After college, he sometimes lived in the United States. During the 1940's, his father was the commanding officer of the Khyber Pass in what was then northwest India.*

Mirza came to understand he was different. Born into noble ancestry, he took strength from the integrity and attributes he inherited from his family.

Baig's acceptance at Clifton and Trinity Colleges and Cambridge taught the young man culture and sophistication. He eventually studied at McGill University in Canada and received a graduate degree in business.

Mirza Baig became disenchanted with the private sector. He desired a military career. He tried for selection at Sandhurst, but due to a bureaucratic mix-up, was not accepted.

Mirza's father encouraged him to join the United States Marines. The Marines were the only real military organization remaining in the world.

An appeal was made directly to the Marine Corps Commandant. Mirza was accepted into the Corps. He began his Marine career as an enlisted man. Later, he survived OCS at Quantico.

The Marine officer became a U.S. citizen, but Mirza Munir Baig was English all the way.]

"Colonel, Baig is my family name, but it's a title connoting achievement in the privileged presence of an emperor."

Harry Baig bowed again slightly. "At your service, Sir."

Harry paused for a few seconds. "My traditions, rather atavistic, Sir, allow me to understand Asia. I have contacts that many in the U.S. military do not have. I can rely on my contacts one hundred percent."

"Captain Baig, I intend no disrespect to your ancestry or your rank, but I must say..."

"Colonel, I, too, intend no disrespect to either you or your rank, Sir. I may not be a field grade officer. I may not look like you or speak with an accent from Georgia—I may not be a Georgia Peach. I can be crude and swear with the best of the men, but I find cursing less than fructuous. I prefer to embrace the alacrity of the English language.

"I have studied the NVA. I have a plethora of knowledge from my research. I know the enemy's rates of travel, how they provision, what and how much they carry, when and how they move and how many men move at a time. I know how they come down the trail and their order of battle. I am aware of their fighting doctrine.

"I understand the NVA military philosophy as developed by Vo Nguyen Giap. He is ruthless, but cautious. Giap has high regard for his army, but will not hesitate to put his soldiers at risk. He has said, 'Use all one's power and strike at once.' Napoleon, Sir. But he tempers that with his own theory, that of steady attack, steady advance. He will incur sacrifices that no one else would consider, but only if the outcome favors him.

"Vo Nguyen Giap's Dien Bien Phu campaign was built on the premises of high resolve, provision for a continuous fight, close coordination and development of encirclement positions.

"Colonel, what I just told you in the COC is the honest truth."

Colonel Lownds puffed his cigar for a few seconds—*an accent from Georgia. A Georgia Peach.* A *plethora* of knowledge. *What in the world does plethora mean...and atavistic? Fructuous? Alacrity? What a vocabulary*!

The captain had a genuinely soft graciousness. Void of any conceit whatsoever, convincing in a matter-of-fact style, he spoke without ambiguity. There was little not to like about this courteous, engaging individual. He projected an eccentric, cultivated persuasiveness in a courteous, casually ingratiating manner. Erudite, but not obnoxious, the captain, a consummate gentlemen, was clearly no amateur.

Colonel Lownds drew on his cigar.

"Harry, most of us infidels smoke cigarettes, but I prefer cigars."

"I can confirm that now first-hand, Sir."

"My offer of a cigar is still good."

Mirza Baig, raising his hand, declined the offer again and, remembering his joking reference about Americans being infidels, smiled at the gentle jab the colonel was directing toward him.

"I will leave the enjoyment of cigars to others whose tastes are more refined."

"Do you drink, Captain Baig? Not that I have anything to offer you."

"Very seldom. I did enjoy a sip of a peculiar scotch from a small island off Scotland's west coast. Isle of Jura whiskey, aged in used bourbon casks from America, is best consumed around five o'clock."

Lownds broke into laughter.

"Yup, 'bout right. Seventeen hundred. That's when I enjoy a cigar the most and an extra-dry Beefeaters martini. A big, juicy steak for dinner, and a Bordeaux wine are soon to follow."

Colonel Lownds looked at the dark eyes of Mirza Munir Baig as he blew smoke out his nostrils. "India. I have never been to India."

"You should visit sometime, Sir. You'd enjoy meeting my family."

"I'm sure it would be interesting, Captain."

"And, Colonel, we refer to the evening meal as tea."

"Captain, we should return to the COC."

Colonel Lownds began to walk back to the command bunker.

"Colonel..."

David Lownds stopped and turned back to face Harry Baig.

"Sir, have you ever heard of Resolution Fourteen?"

"I don't believe so, no."

"Colonel..." Harry Baig gauged what he was about to say. "Resolution Fourteen calls for a sweeping offensive to incite a country-wide uprising in South Vietnam. The resolution envisioned large, all-inclusive battle areas—basically the entire country under siege. The Tet Offensive, Sir."

"You mean, Captain, the Tet Offensive that did not achieve success. The enemy could not sustain the general assault on such a wide basis. It was doomed from the start."

"Aside from the Tet Offensive, Giap saw that Resolution Fourteen could work, but *only* if he could win a visible victory from a well-defined battle...a Dien Bien Phu-type engagement. Colonel, where else could that happen other than here at Khe Sanh?"

"Captain, Giap has moved forces away from Khe Sanh. Giap's success is questionable."

"Colonel, only through my most current intelligence has something emerged that is surprising, casting doubt on that assumption. In a separate policy that emerged earlier this year, to reinforce Giap's premise, a stated objective is to annihilate a large number of American troops in a single action. Again, this can only point to Khe Sanh. Contrary to military logic following a dislocation of his forces, Vo Nguyen Giap smells blood."

Baig paused, then continued. "Colonel, it's not lost on you that Khe Sanh has not been attacked by a force sufficient to overrun the base. His futile attacks at the end of February, the slaughter of his men that ensued, proved the effectiveness of our measures. We have not been attacked, really. Not yet, anyway...not the ground-swell attack the French experienced."

"Captain, you mentioned..."

"In Giap's mind, the North Vietnamese need a victory from a major battle, but Giap is a calculating individual. He's prepared for the risk of committing his forces, but *not* all. Giap knows an attack on Khe Sanh by his divisions could be catastrophic. Yet, he is convinced that if he can show the world he can kill a lot of Marines, compromise the garrison with an acute thrust directly at the COC and withdraw, he will have achieved success, perhaps equivalent to Dien Bien Phu, regardless of the men he may lose. Hence, the scenario involving the CT strike groups."

"Giap cannot occupy Khe Sanh, Captain."

"Colonel, Giap does not intend to occupy Khe Sanh. He will dissolve back into the jungle while leaving behind a large number of Americans dead in his wake. The impact of his attack on the world will be far more significant than an unquestioned victory.

"Sir, they will follow a master plan. Individual units are not allowed to think for themselves. Field commanders will not deviate from this plan."

Lownds held his smoking cigar at chest level as he pondered the captain who wore the exact same, but freshly pressed utilities.

Something wasn't adding up. Is Giap really going to take this chance? But more absorbing, Lownds thought back to a book he once read: *The Quiet American.* Captain Baig may be the regimental TIO, but did he spring from Graham Greene's novel? Was he Alden Pyle incarnate? Was it possible that Baig was really a CIA operative?

The colonel looked at the south Asian who stared right back.

"And you, Mirza Munir Harry Baig, are a Marine Corps captain."

"Sir, I went through the mud along with other OCS candidates. I'm an officer in the United States Marine Corps, just like you. "I'm proud of my commission. I am also your TIO, Sir, as you have so correctly reminded me."

Lownds exhaled cigar smoke. He recollected—*achievement in the privileged service of an emperor.*

"And you know all this with certainty."

"Indeed, I do, Sir. This time, unequivocally."

CHAPTER EIGHTY

KHU TAN CONG SO BA

Every challenge that Bui Van Que encountered on the long walk south from Hanoi to Vinh and Dong Loc, along the Ho Chi Minh Trail, into and out of Laos and finally into Quang Tri Province was frightening. Danger lurked everywhere. Que was prepared neither for the remoteness of the landscape nor the hostile environment. The hills and valleys were rugged, the trails difficult to negotiate. The difficult terrain and treacherous rivers, including the mystical Xe Pone River, had severely weakened him. The rain had been an overwhelming deluge from which he could not protect himself. He shivered constantly, even when standing in the sun.

Que stayed in underground bunker waypoints at night, slept in trees, on the cold jungle floor or in tunnels hewn from the sides of mountains. Suffering from near starvation, he ate leaves, berries and rodents. He sucked on fresh bark to take his mind off his virtual starvation.

Que developed acute intestinal disorders. Diarrhea, afflicting him for weeks, was on the verge of crippling dysentery. The abdominal pain and severe cramps were unbearable. He had lost twelve kilograms.

Blood-sucking leeches attacked his upper legs and torso. He cut them from his body one by one, leaving bleeding sores and nasty scars. Next day, he was attacked again by the slimy urchins. Que's arms, legs and face were covered with ugly lacerations. He battled mosquitoes, parasites and insects that tormented his skin. He scratched the insect bites so vigorously the welts had become red with deep infections. The sores filled with thick white puss. Que's left foot and the glands in his armpits, reacting to his body infections, became painfully swollen. All of his toenails were ripped from his toes. His black gums were bleeding. His clothes, ripped as they were, hung on his ravished body like the rags of a *bu nhin* (scarecrow).

For all his hunger, lack of sleep and sickness—his constant companions—Bui Van Que could do only one thing. He pushed himself forward.

Even though Que had finally reached as far as he needed to go down the Ho Chi Minh Trail, at binh tram hai moui, he found himself in a Chien Thang strike group. After an additional three day march across streams, along the sides of steep hills and into a deep ravine that opened into a valley, Que and his malnourished comrades arrived at Khu Tan Cong So Ba (Attack Sector N3).

Now, far south of his home, in an extremely remote and intimidating area at the very edge of the battlefield, Que and others were being pushed and jostled into lines. There was no separation between men. The muzzles of AK-47s strapped to the back of the man in front protruded menacingly in the face of the man behind.

"Men, we are not more than fifteen hundred meters from the Americans. Look around you. This is Strike Group CT43, a glorious force of eleven hundred men. All of you have been moving simultaneously in this direction.

"CT42 and the Leaping Leopard Unit are in canyons not far away. We will move with them to the attack point during the artillery barrage. We no longer have the luxury of time. There will be no stragglers. From this point on, deserters will be summarily shot.

"CT42 will lead the Leaping Leopard Unit into the American base. As soon as CT42 attacks, CT43 will move into attack position vacated by CT42. Group CT43, strengthened by a company of two hundred men from Highpoint 845, is the largest strike group and will augment the attack and overwhelm the remaining defenders."

Bui Van Que desperately needed a rest from the many sleepless nights and the constant movement down the trail. After the formation was dismissed, he walked up a side slope from the valley to give himself some space and to rest his legs. He unslung his weapon from his shoulders and removed his rucksack filled with ammunition and grenades. It was not with small trepidation that Que, collapsing next to his equipment, contemplated a future that would be even less comfortable and much less certain.

Que breathed heavily as he bumped a Nhi Thanh cigarette out of a crumpled pack. He lit it and felt the sting of smoke in his mouth when he inhaled, which only exacerbated his hunger. He leaned back against a tree and removed his rubber sandals. Que massaged his bleeding feet and bruised, bloody toes.

Que remembered his grandfather and how he used to ride with him on his bicycle across the Red River on the giant steel bridge into Hanoi. He was still angry with himself for having lost his diary in Dong Loc. Reading the special letter from his girlfriend Hang, and seeing her picture he had tucked inside would have been comforting.

Que's mind slipped back to happier times, just five months earlier, when he and Hang would stroll around Hanoi's famous Hoan Kiem Lake in the temperate, fall evenings.

Que, wearing the uniform of the Quan Doi Nhan Dan, walked arm-in-arm with Hang. Dressed in her favorite *ao dai,* Hang would snuggle into Que's shoulder. Que remembered every word spoken during their leisurely strolls around the lake—the lake of the rising sword that contained ancient, heroic-size turtles—and past the island pagoda.

Que thought of Hang's plaintiff words.

"You will come back to me, my darling? You know how I already miss you."

Que remembered how they embraced near the twin trees whose trunks had grown out horizontally over the lake. He recalled they kissed on the other side of the lake beneath Hoa Phong (Harmony Tower), a small, ancient four-arched pagoda across the street from the Post Office. Built in 1865, it was the only remaining trace of the much larger Bao An Temple. Tradition held that people who vowed affection for one another beneath the small tower would find eternal peace and happiness.

Hang's tender words, "Em Yeu Anh," were captured for all time in the hollow of the stone archway.

Que could not stop imagining Hang's warm eyes. He buried his grubby face in his bleeding hands. Would the images just go away, please?

"Hang, I have to serve my country. You would never want to live with a coward."

"But, Que, you are not a coward."

"Hang, I am not the only one to go. So many of our friends have gone south to fight. One Vietnam will rise just as the eternal sword rises from Hoan Kiem Lake. I will come back to you. I promise."

Those tender memories saddened Que, but they also emboldened him with much needed courage. He fought not for himself but for his country. He fought for Hang.

Que rubbed his face. Sadness overwhelmed him. Without even knowing it, amidst such warm thoughts while sitting against a tree at Attack Sector N3, Que, completely exhausted, closed his eyelids.

CHAPTER EIGHTY-ONE

SOMETHING'S FIXIN' TO HAPPEN AT KHE SANH

Ten thousand miles distant, on the other side of the globe from Vietnam, just after the first day of spring, but still in the grip of winter, the citizens of Washington, D.C. slept. On the North Lawn outside the White House, skeletal elm and linden trees, bracing against the wind, stood stark in the night. Inside the White House, calm and quiet prevailed. All unnecessary lights were turned off. A chill pervaded the rooms and hallways of the historic dwelling while the occasional creaks and ghostly moans revealed its age.

The President and his wife, occupying separate suites, were asleep. Luci, with her baby son Lyn snuggled warmly next to her, slept beneath heavy comforters in her bedroom down the hallway.

Lyndon Johnson stirred. He threw back the covers, sat up on the edge of the firm mattress and turned on a table lamp. He looked at the clock on the nightstand.

"Damn. Two a.m."

The President, half-sitting, leaned over and picked up the scattered cables he had read prior to falling asleep the evening before. Khe Sanh, Khe Sanh. The cablegrams, intruding into his conscience during the night, caused him to sleep fitfully.

One cable indicated the NVA were focusing some of their efforts elsewhere. The CIA confirmed the NVA 320th Division had moved to the coast and the bulk of the 304th Division had moved away from Khe Sanh.

But, Rostow's concern was strengthened by a counter report from the CIA that indicated special strike groups had been formed. Walt Rostow repeatedly warned the President not to abandon the idea of an NVA attack at Khe Sanh. Actions were imminent.

Lady Bird's sleep was disturbed by a bothersome sound in the President's suite. Reminded of the late-night emergency of the *Pueblo* incident, she went to investigate.

"Lyndon, why are you awake?"

The President didn't bother to look up.

"Lyndon, what are you doing?"

"Gettin' up, dammit. Can't sleep. Something's fixin' to happen at Khe Sanh."

The President held up the cables. "And it ain't good."

"Lyndon, it's late. Go back to sleep, honey. "

"How can I sleep when those fishhead-eatin' Viet-nese cause me so damned many problems? Another Din Bin Phu, for sure, I swear. The Viet-nese aren't gonna make me look like a fool."

"Lyndon, you'll wake Luci and Lyn."

The President scratched his head and adjusted the shirt of his pajamas.

"Dammit, Lady Bird, I just don't understand why in God's name we can't..."

"Lyndon, you're working yourself up for no good reason. Dawn's still a few hours away. You have a full day ahead of you."

"Those scrawny pissant sonzabitches."

"Lyndon, would you please relax?"

"I am relaxed, dammit. I'm still gettin' up. Those communist bastards. They've..."

"Lyndon! Stop it!"

The President, distraught, his cheeks red, looked around the room.

"I gotta do something."

"But, what can you do, Lyndon, so late at night?"

"I'm gonna go down and read the incoming cables while I look at that terrain model."

"Oh, Lyndon, honestly. You and that silly model."

Lyndon Johnson, disheveled, struggled with his trousers. He cinched up his belt. He put on a white shirt he had left lying across the back of a chair. His fingers fidgeted with the buttons. To hell with a necktie. The President stumbled a little as he tried to put his shoes on. He didn't bother with the laces.

"Lady Bird, I can't just lie here in this damn bed."

Luci heard the commotion from her bedroom. She left Lyn asleep in her bed and walked down the hall. She entered the Presidential suite.

"What's wrong, Mom? What's happened to Daddy?"

The First Lady, standing in her nightgown, pushed her hair from her face.

"It's all right, Luci. Go back to bed. Everything's fine. Don't wake Lyn."

Lady Bird turned back to her husband.

"OK, Lyndon, OK. Is there anything I can do to help?"

"Call down to the kitchen and have them send me some coffee—black."

Luci walked to her father and touched his shoulder.

"Daddy, what's wrong?"

"I can't take anymore crap from that pissant Ho Chi Minh. I need for that bearded communist and that damned Foe Wen Jap, or whatever the hell his name is, to get their North Viet-nese silly butts the hell out of Quang Tri Province, away from Khe Sanh!"

The President began to leave the Presidential bedroom. "Where's John Wayne when I need him?"

CHAPTER EIGHTY-TWO

HOURS TO COME

Life at the Ponderosa, as some Marines called parts of the Khe Sanh Combat Base, was not exactly pleasurable. Days came and went. No two days were the same, but in many ways each day was like the day before; and anticipated the next. Existence on the base matched the weather: miserable. Since the onslaught of heavy enemy artillery many weeks before, in late January, running, ducking and crouching were facts of life.

The latest round of shelling began just after sunset on the evening of the twenty-second of March. Enemy artillery, easily sweeping the treeless Khe Sanh Combat Base, preparing the battlefield, wreaked havoc among its inhabitants.

The concentration of North Vietnam's big guns, following the theory of artillery—dispersion and disruption—might well suffocate the Americans. This was not Gettysburg a century before where so many Confederate shells exploded harmlessly behind the Union line on Cemetery Ridge prior to Pickett's charge. No. The shells from the NVA artillery were spot on.

At the American base, the receiving end of the NVA's artillery actions, chaos reigned amid the explosions. Marines scurried to find protection, frantically searching or diving for cover.

The loud explosions subsumed everything, even time. Intervals between explosions seemed to last forever, but then, multiple explosions would occur concurrently, eliminating any interval. Time slipped from an infinite history, and simultaneously raced forward into eternal oblivion. Yet, existence for the Marines was distilled into this day, this hour, this minute. Yesterday, forgotten; tomorrow, an impossible thought.

The world had shrunk to Khe Sanh and, to those at Khe Sanh, to filthy fox holes, bunkers and trenches.

On they came, projectile after projectile; on and on, detonation upon detonation—more projectiles, more shells, more explosions. Endless. Shell upon shell, by the hundreds. The universe was filled with man-made meteors that could erase life or render it to inconsequence.

NVA 122mm rockets added to the anarchy. The devastation resulting from the rockets' explosions was equal to that of the big guns of Co Roc. North Vietnamese rockets and mortar and artillery shells exploded in such quantity, the entire base was vulnerable to deadly shrapnel, flying splintered wood, other debris; and red dirt. Multiple fires and secondary explosions erupted. The entire base was awash with dense, repugnant, acid-tasting smoke that irritated eyes, throats and lungs.

The ground shook and moved in undulating waves as the artillery shells smashed into the earth, exploding with terrifying ferocity. Shock waves crisscrossed the combat base and buffeted the sky above it. Explosions sucked out life-giving air. Desolation was matched by human wretchedness.

American 105mm and 155mm guns at Khe Sanh returned fire at supposed targets over many kilometers in breadth.

The enemy bombardment of the base continued.

Fear, crystallizing into reality, reflecting in the eyes of every American inhabitant of the base, had to be put aside. There was no time for it.

Colonel Lownds, deep in the COC, was reminded of the artillery bombardment on the twenty-third of February and the attack six days later at the east end of the base.

He thought of the briefing given to him and his staff by Mirza Baig, the eccentric captain from South Asia. Immediately after the heavy artillery, rocket and mortar bombardment, the NVA would attack the Khe Sanh Combat Base. Surely North Vietnamese infantry were now massing for the attack.

The bunker shook violently. The COC, its air stagnant, filled with red dust from the concussion of explosions above ground. The shuffle of so many boots and the chaos of moving bodies and the bustle of equipment caused even more choking dust. The lights blinked on and off, and back on. Radios were a jumbled conglomeration of multiple voices and static.

Colonel Lownds issued orders to his subordinates and relayed information to Dong Ha, IIIMAF headquarters at Da Nang and PROV CORPS in Phu Bai.

Lownds released the cartridge magazine from his M-16, checked it and re-inserted it into his weapon. The safety on, he slung his M-16 over his back. He checked his .45 pistol and re-holstered it.

The teletype, housed in a large shipping container, placed in its own nearby bunker below ground just west of the COC, chattered continuously. Burdened with incoming code, the teletype could not keep up with the demand of urgent communications.

While some radios, their antennae destroyed, could not communicate with the COC, the constant squawking was still bewildering.

The base needed to be resupplied with all essentials, the wounded evacuated. But, while the intense bombardment portended apocalypse, and the hours to come seemed more than bleak, Lownds' most pressing need at that exact moment was coffee.

CHAPTER EIGHTY-THREE

OCELOT CELL: THE B-52s RISE UP

"celot Cell Lead, revetment five five for active runway."

Captain Bill Cemanski waited for a response from ground control.

"Ocelot Cell Lead, cleared to taxi. Runway one eight."

"Roger."

Giant United States Air Force B-52s of the Strategic Air Command were lining up for take-off from U-Tapao Royal Thai Airbase south of Bangkok. Assigned to the 4258th Strategic Wing, the B-52s had been stationed at U-Tapao since mid-April 1967 to conduct bombing missions against the North Vietnamese Army operating in South Vietnam and Laos.

Loaded to the maximum in its bomb bays and beneath the wings, each of the three Boeing B-52s of Ocelot Cell carried one hundred 500 and 750 pound bombs—a typical Alpha-Bravo bomb-load configuration. The three aircraft would drop, in the aggregate, three hundred bombs totaling eighty-five tons of high explosive destruction.

A hand signal from a ground crewman who stood in front of each B-52 motioned the planes forward.

With pre-flight checks complete, instrumentation and scopes functioning, all doors and hatches secured, and with all eight engines on each plane operating, the goliath B-52s eased out of their sheltered revetments.

Like prehistoric monsters, the Stratofortress bombers lumbered slowly across the tarmac in single file. They taxied toward the threshold of runway one eight, the north-south runway; in fact, the only runway at U-Tapao.

Ocelot Cell was part of the larger Operation Niagara bombing campaign. A specific raid, as part of the campaign, was more informally referred to as an Arclight. B-52s from Thailand were embarking on an urgent assignment to northern South Vietnam. Flying time to the target would be about an hour.

The gargantuan jet-propelled machines, casting enormous shadows across the grass boundary strip, dwarfed a pickup truck containing armed security personnel sitting on the side of the taxiway.

America's largest winged war machines, heavily laden with bombs and fuel and ten thousand gallons of water that would be injected into the engines during takeoff, were poised for combat.

Captain Cemanski, sitting in the left seat of the cockpit of the lead B-52, tapped the brakes near the end of the taxiway. The plane shuddered to a stop. Cemanski pulled all eight throttles back to idle. His co-pilot, Lieutenant Ralph Bento, flipping sheets in a ringed binder book, worked through the checklist.

Elsewhere in the vibrating fuselage, the other five crew members, including Lieutenant Isaac Darnell, the navigator and Lieutenant Joe Crawley, the radar-navigator, all securely strapped in, worked through their lists, too

"U-Tapao Ground, Ocelot Lead. Holding to confirm checklist."

"Roger, Ocelot Lead."

The crew made its last check of all items pertaining to the aircraft and the flight. Cemanski keyed the mic and spoke to his co-pilot using his last name.

"Bento, this could be the main event. Intel's received reports of massive infantry movements in Eye Corps. Giap's goin' for it this time."

Bento spoke into his microphone.

"We thought that last month, back on February twenty-third, but the real ground action happened six days later."

"There's lots of heightened air activity, more than the usual bombing runs.

The movement sensors dropped in western Eye Corps must be overloaded with data and outgoing signals. A major artillery exchange has been underway. Other Arclights are being diverted."

"Yeah, I saw the board. Scheduled missions are scrubbed and replaced by new ones. Eight cells from U-Tapao alone. Twenty-four sorties. Criminy."

"Jesus Christ, Bento, this is the shoot-out at the OK Corral. There's gonna be a lot of people get hurt."

Ralph Bento keyed his mic.

"I'll contact Bomber Charlie?"

The codename given to a mobile control facility, Bomber Charlie provided contact between the plane's crew and ground personnel if an emergency occurred.

Bento switched channels.

"Bomber Charlie, Ocelot Cell Lead."

The response was aloof.

"What can I do for you, cowboy?"

"Bomber Charlie, Ocelot Cell oscar kilo. About to roll."

"Roger that, Ocelot Lead. You're the third Arclight today. Enjoy the rodeo. Safe mission, hear? Come back real soon."

Ralph Bento looked at Cemanski to his left. "Has to be a Texan."

"Probably an Okie."

Captain Cemanski and Lieutenant Bento received affirmative indications from all crew members.

The three American bombers that formed Ocelot Cell, painted in a dark shade on the sides and tops of the surfaces and black on their undersides, were ready for the bombing mission in Eye Corps.

"U-Tapao Ground, Ocelot Lead. Checklist complete."

"Roger, Ocelot Lead. Contact tower. Channel 1."

Bill Cemanski changed channels on his radio. He immediately heard the controller talking to another pilot.

"Tripoli Two Niner, cleared for landing, runway one eight."

Cemanski spoke.

"U-Tapao Tower, Ocelot Lead. On taxiway for runway one eight. Ready for takeoff."

"Roger Ocelot Lead, we have you. Hold short, runway one eight. Inbound traffic C-130 one mile final. Altimeter two niner three niner, winds one six niner at eight."

Cemanski looked past his co-pilot out the right side of the cockpit and saw a four-engine Hercules on its final approach.

"Roger, holding short, tally traffic, Ocelot Lead."

The high wing, turboprop plane drew nearer and nearer and finally crossed the threshold of the runway. It flew several hundred yards down its length and landed with a slight flare. Bluish-white smoke swirled as the tires hit the pavement.

"Ocelot Lead, taxi onto runway and hold."

"Roger."

Bill Cemanski released the brakes and pushed the eight throttles gently forward. The lead B-52 eased onto the runway from the taxiway and turned left. The bomber aligned with the centerline of the runway looking south to the sea. Cemanski pulled the throttles back to idle and set the brakes. Each pilot took one final look at the engine instruments: tachometer, exhaust gas temperature and fuel flow. The needles in each instrument indicated all systems were operating normally.

Ocelot Two and Three followed in the queue on the taxiway toward the runway.

Cemanski and Bento heard the pilot of the C-130.

"Tower, Tripoli Two Niner clear of the active. Switching to ground control."

In the distance, the C-130 turned off runway one eight and began to taxi to the ramp.

"Ocelot Lead, U-Tapao Tower, cleared for take-off. Winds now one seven zero at ten."

"Roger."

Bill Cemanski placed his hand on the throttles again and pushed them slightly forward. He paused briefly. The B-52, rumbling, sat still for about ten seconds. Satisfied all engines were working properly, Cemanski keyed his mic.

"Ocelot lead rolling."

Cemanski released the brakes and pushed the throttles to eighty percent.

The eight throttles sent signals to an equal number of powerful engines. They spooled up, coming fully alive with a thunderous sound that deafened the area.

Atomized water, injected into each engine, turned immediately into expanding steam due to the excessive heat. Since the volume of the combustion compartment remained constant, the pressure increased. This natural phenomenon, associated with the properties of steam, quantified centuries ago by an Italian named Bernoulli, was put to work for the benefit of man. The steam and burning fuel mixture, creating more power, added thrust to the engines of the B-52.

The turbines screamed. The long fuselage shook and vibrated as the B-52 rolled along the centerline with ever increasing velocity. The magnetic and gyro compasses showed a south heading equal to that of the runway. The familiar buildings of the U-Tapao base quickly passed to each side. The white paint stripes slid beneath the giant plane faster and faster. Ahead, beyond the runway, azure waters loomed.

While Cemanski guided the B-52, Ralph Bento monitored all engine instruments and the airspeed indicator.

"V1," the co-pilot said into the mouthpiece of his headset. The plane's velocity had reached a point where there was no chance for an abort.

A few seconds later, the airspeed indicator read one hundred fifty-five knots.

"V2."

Bill Cemanski waited a split second more, then pulled steadily back on the yoke. Ralph Bento kept forward pressure on the throttles. The wings bent upward. The blunt nose of the plane lifted and within another six seconds the monstrous B-52 was flying. Ocelot Lead, making a horrendous noise, on the start of yet another bombing mission in Vietnam, flew less than five hundred feet above the startled people gazing up from the beach.

Cemanski ordered his co-pilot to raise the in-line landing gears. The wheels rotated and swiveled up into the cavernous guts of the plane. The doors of the bays swung shut and locked.

The other two aircraft in the cell repeated the entire process moments later.

Soon, all three B-52s of Ocelot Cell were in the air. They left in their wake suffocating black exhaust that spoiled the cerulean skies over the Gulf of Siam.

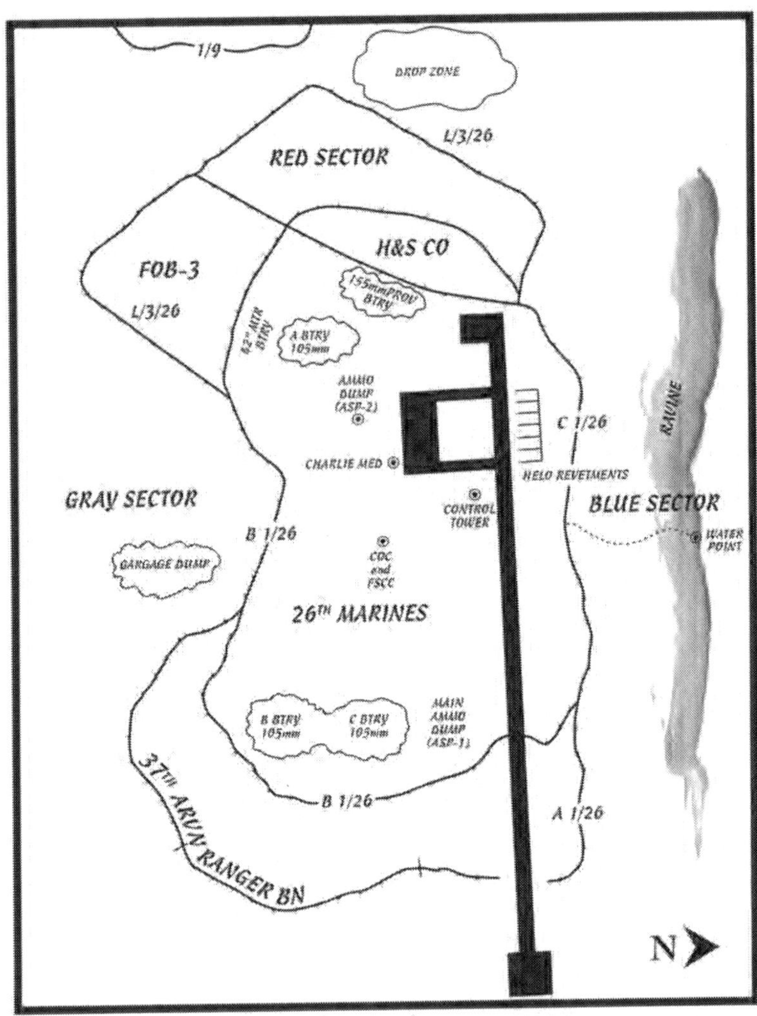

KHE SANH COMBAT BASE

CHAPTER EIGHTY-FOUR

COME AND TAKE IT

Not long before two a.m. on the twenty-third of March in Washington D.C., Lyndon Johnson left the company of a concerned Lady Bird and Luci in the Presidential suite. He was wide awake, but consumed with worry. Casually dressed, a hulking figure, Johnson stood now among his aides and high level military personnel in the Situation Room. Deep in thought, his mind didn't register the presence of anyone. At almost sixty years old and now in the fifth year of his presidency, Lyndon Baines Johnson may as well have been alone.

President Johnson could not stop thinking about the fate of the U.S. Marines. The increasingly intense circumstances at Khe Sanh gnawed at the President, exacerbating his anxiety. The massive flow of forwarded cables fueled his fears.

SUSTAINED ENEMY ARTILLERY BARRAGE. STOP.
MULTIPLE CASUALTIES. STOP. —LOWNDS

More cables with special abbreviations arrived from Saigon.

KS MARINES UNDER HVY ARTLRY ATTCK. STOP.
XPCT FLL GRND ASLT SN. STOP—COMUSMACV

THE PRESIDENT'S SANDBOX

"My God, it's happening. Khe Sanh's being attacked."

An anguished President Johnson sought relief. He faced his nemesis the only way he could. In the darkest, pre-dawn hours, he hunched over the Khe Sanh Terrain Model. He glared down at the imitation geographic features of the Khe Sanh plateau, reduced in scale, neatly contained and sanitized within the flat, wood box.

The terrain model presented some semblance of the area—at least the President had an idea of the geography. But, the immobile model didn't reveal any solutions for him or allay his fears.

Lyndon Johnson looked at the multiple shades of green, the white-thread grid lines, Hills 861 and 881 South and NVA positions represented by the red flags. But, it was the words—Khe Sanh Area—that haunted him, and would do so for the rest of his life.

The President tried to imagine the horde of North Vietnamese attacking the base perimeter, to witness the action in miniature scale. He could do no more. The model laid bare a flat representation of a chilling predicament, but the horror of the reality, thousands of miles away, was infinitely more terrifying.

The President spoke softly as if he could communicate with the North Vietnamese.

"You bastards may think you have us cornered, you little pissants, but it's gonna be our show now."

Flown in Gonzalez in 1835, the first flag of Texas taunted the Mexicans to try to seize the Texans' bronze cannon. The flag's slogan, written in black ink on a field of white, couldn't have been clearer. The President repeated those words out loud.

"Come and take it."

Lyndon Johnson removed his glasses and massaged the bridge of his nose. He remembered a passage by Yeats he had memorized many years before: "And what rough beast, its hour come round at last, slouches towards Bethlehem to be born?"

This is what the war in Vietnam has come to. This is where the Twenty-sixth Marines and the First Battalion each of the Ninth and the Thirteenth Marines are surrounded by the enemy.

"You want our flag, Giap? Go ahead, try taking it."

CHAPTER EIGHTY-FIVE

WE DID SOME DAMAGE TODAY

"Ocelot Lead, climb and maintain zero five thousand feet, heading one eight zero. Contact U-Tapao departure control on three two three point five."

Captain Bill Cemanski responded.

"Roger U-Tapao Tower, three two three point five, maintain zero five thousand."

The needle on the altimeter of the lead B-52 rotated slowly as the heavily-loaded plane, maintaining its southern heading, struggled to gain altitude. The engines labored hard. The B-52 rose up through one thousand, two thousand, three thousand feet.

Cemanski switched channels again.

"U-Tapao Departure, Ocelot Lead. Heading one eight zero, six miles out, at zero five thousand."

"Roger Ocelot Lead, maintain current heading for zero one minute and turn left to heading zero niner zero. At the one three five radial, turn left to heading zero five seven. Make contact. Two and Three to follow. Copy?"

"Ocelot Lead. Roger."

Cemanski retracted the huge flaps, each the size of a house roof. They slid slowly but effortlessly back into the main wing.

The water injection supply for the engines had been exhausted—indicated by the decrease in propulsion. Cemanski pushed the eight throttles to full military power and restored thrust.

Buffeted by tropical air currents, the plane's massive wings, like those of an albatross, moved noticeably up and down. The plane bounced through the air as it gained altitude and airspeed. The crew members felt the sensation of weightlessness when the plane moved down; and contrasting heaviness when the plane rebounded in the opposite direction.

At exactly one minute after his last contact with departure control, Cemanski began a shallow left turn to an east heading. He confirmed the intersection with the designated TACAN radial.

"U-Tapao Departure, Ocelot Cell at radial one three five, turning to heading zero five seven, Ocelot Lead."

The B-52s formed up into a triangle and climbed to thirty thousand feet. Ocelot Two was five hundred feet above and to the left rear of Lead; while on the other side of Lead, Ocelot Three was stepped up another five hundred feet. The three B-52s, now arranged in their bombing cell, made their way northeast through the clear skies of Thailand.

Sometimes, departure control vectored the B-52s more north to Korat Royal Thai Airbase or, farther to the east, over Ubon, before entering Laotian and Vietnamese airspace. But, for today's mission, the B-52s would fly in between the two airbases straight toward Savannakhet.

Lieutenant Isaac Darnell took over the navigation. He followed the flight on his instruments. There would be no need for further vectoring through the airspace controlled by the four Thai airbases from which the American Air Force operated.

The B-52s achieved their cruise speed of 0.77 Mach.

Darnell spoke.

"Pilot, maintain heading zero five seven. Korat TACAN radial one two five in one niner minutes. ETA Savannakhet in four one minutes."

"Roger. ETA four one minutes."

The flight progressed to the northeast. Cemanski intersected the radial.

"Navigator, confirming Korat TACAN radial one two five, Correcting left two degrees."

"Roger, Pilot. Correction two degrees left."

"Bento, look at your three o'clock. Must be Buffalo Cell way out there. They sure got airborne quickly."

Both pilots looked to the right. In the distance they saw the unmistakable profile of three B-52s.

Cemanski turned back to his left and strained to look toward the left wing. "Nothing on the port side."

He turned back to look at Bento. "Rhino Cell's out there somewhere. Man, we're gonna drop some bombs today."

Lieutenant Darnell, sitting behind the two pilots, continued to provide route updates to the aircraft commander. He used the TACAN radials as convenient checks.

"Pilot, Ubon radial two eight five in one zero minutes. Continue to Udorn TACAN radial one five zero."

"Roger."

The B-52s passed through the Ubon radial as predicted.

Cemanski switched to channel thirty-one to pick up Udorn's TACAN, located way to the northwest of Ubon. The signal came up. The B-52s proceeded through the Udorn radial.

"Pilot, maintain heading. ETA Savannakhet in zero niner minutes."

And then correlating with another electronic signal from Ubon to confirm the destination. "Ubon TACAN three five five in zero niner."

Cemanski changed channels again back to Ubon TACAN and continued to track the interception with the three five five radial from Ubon. The flight, on course, on schedule, was routine, a normal mission.

The B-52s' northeast flight path intersected the Ubon TACAN signal. Ocelot cell flew directly over the town of Savannakhet on the Mekong River.

"Pilot, turn right to heading zero eight six for IP and MisQu Bravo Five Two. Estimate target in one five minutes."

"Zero eight six to IP and MisQu, ETA target one five. Roger."

Ocelot Cell proceeded east.

"Pilot, maintain heading. IP in zero five minutes. Will advise."

"Roger, IP in zero five."

The B-52s of Ocelot Cell, maintaining the altitude separation, tightened up their formation. The cell made its way to the IP, the Initial Point.

"Pilot, IP in three zero seconds, on my mark."

The radio became suspensefully quiet. The constant drone of the aircraft's engines filled the silence. Isaac Darnell, the navigator, then made a crisp announcement.

"Mark!"

Suddenly, the communication between the lead B-52 and ground came alive. Joe Crawley, a radar-navigator with exceptional experience, would control the bombing mission until the bombs were released. He spoke with professional confidence.

"MisQu Bravo Five Two, Ocelot Lead at IP, inbound your position."

"Roger Ocelot Lead, we have you. Maintain heading and altitude, MisQu."

"Roger, Flight level three zero zero, Ocelot Lead."

"Pilot, center the PDI," Crawley said to Captain Cemanski, indicating he was taking over control of the flight.

Crawley, monitoring the crosshairs on his scope, worked closely with the ground controller.

"MisQu, Ocelot Cell lined up."

"Ocelot Lead, adjust heading to zero eight niner."

"Roger, zero eight niner," Crawley responded.

Then to Cemanski, "Pilot, give me second station."

The aircraft would automatically adjust its heading as the crosshairs on Joe Crawley's scope changed.

The crews of Ocelot Lead and the other two B-52s in the cell, now in the experienced hands of Joe Crawley, were on their final heading for the bomb run.

"Ocelot Lead, correct right zero three degrees. Maintain flight level three zero zero."

"Roger, zero three degrees right. Flight level three zero zero."

A few minutes passed. MisQu spoke again.

"Correction. One degree left. Wait target instructions."

"Roger, MisQu, one degree left."

The B-52s, glued to the mission, continued to bore through the sky to the target. Ralph Bento looked at some charts to confirm the flight path.

"Pilot, they're vectoring us almost to the Khe Sanh base, Sir. We'll be dropping bombs near the Marine perimeter."

"Ocelot Lead, open bomb bay doors. Target in one minute."

Farther back in the fuselage of each B-52, behind the pilot and co-pilot, the radar-navigator transformed into bombardier. Joe Crawley's concentration became intense. Accurate bombing was the only reason for the existence of the B-52. Lieutenant Joe Crawley was the best.

Sitting in a windowless compartment, Crawley activated a switch. The giant rectangular bomb bay doors beneath the B-52 opened, causing a hurricane of air inside the bomb bay. Now fully open, the truth of each plane's being was revealed.

Precisely arrayed and suspended on racks in the cavernous bowels of each B-52, row after row, stack after stack of dark green tapered cylinders with fins attached at the backs, awaited the moment of release.

"Ocelot Lead, Target in four zero seconds. Tango Golf in four zero."

"Roger, Tango Golf, four zero seconds."

Silence, then the mysterious voice of MisQu spoke again.

"Five...four...three...two...one. Release bombs."

Lieutenant Joe Crawley responded.

"Ocelot Lead, bombs away."

The bombs, rippling one by one off their racks in rapid succession, spilled out of the three planes and off their wings. Like a vertical train of dominoes, the cascade of bombs descended through the atmosphere to the ground in the near proximity of the Khe Sanh Combat Base. The planes, now relieved of their heavy burden, suddenly lurched higher.

Less than a minute later, and with the B-52 back under control of Captain Bill Cemanski, a line of staccato lights, sharp as a welding torch, erupted on the ground. If Niagara was used to describe the deluge of bombs, Arclight came by its name as honestly.

The bomb bay doors beneath the three American warplanes, now empty of their destructive cargo, swung up on their hinges, closed and locked shut.

Subsequent cells of B-52s, each with its unique call sign, would be in the air this day, and probably for several days. MisQu Bravo Five Two would vector them to other targets in the same area.

The bombing run complete, Captain Bill Cemanski maintained his preplanned heading toward the Vietnam coast. He and Bento, looking level through the cockpit windows at thirty thousand feet, could see the coastline and the South China Sea beyond and the white clouds that characterized the Southeast Asian weather.

While Ocelot Two, now a lone B-52 that had been part of Ocelot Cell, turned to the northeast to fly to Guam on its scheduled rotation, the other two aircraft made a long sweeping turn to the south over the Vietnam coast to begin their return to U-Tapao from the skies over Vietnam's jungles. The mission fulfilled, and with a sense of relief, Cemanski spoke to the navigator in a casual manner.

"Darnell, take us home, amigo."

The B-52s would fly unfettered as if flying across the plains of the American Midwest. Each B-52, benefitting from the elimination of so many heavy bombs, along with the reduction of fuel, were that much lighter.

Cemanski spoke to his flight companion.

"We did some damage today, Bento. Joe Crawley did a number on 'em this time."

The trip back to U-Tapao would take a little less than sixty minutes. Captain Bill Cemanski and Lieutenant Ralph Bento, their mission accomplished, would be in contact with the tower at U-Tapao. They would soon see the welcome threshold of runway one eight.

"Captain, I know there's a scotch with my name on it waiting for me."

That evening, the aviators of Ocelot Cell would consume alcohol in the officers' club, maybe to an extent more than they should. Early the next day, they would fly another mission, most likely over Khe Sanh.

Captain Cemanski looked to the right at his young co-pilot.

"Bento, you still drinkin' that Red Label shit?"

CHAPTER EIGHTY-SIX

TRUE SOUND OF WAR

"Men of CT43, get up! We must move now to Attack Point One before the artillery barrage ends."

The North Vietnamese had been pounding the Americans for hours with heavy artillery and rockets. The American howitzers fired back; not at the guns of Co Roc, but at areas the Americans thought the NVA might be preparing for attack. Though causing some casualties, American guns did not thwart the enemy.

"CT42 and the Leopards will attack soon. We will follow as soon as we see the flare."

Bui Van Que didn't hear the words. He was shocked out of his sleep by something more dreadful than he had ever experienced. Bright flashes and an overwhelming crashing roar began one thousand meters to his left—the true sound of war.

Uninterrupted, the horrendous booming noise swept the length of the broad valley faster than Que's mind could comprehend. Shrapnel, spreading out radially from concurrent explosions, sliced through the trees.

The ground shook from the overpowering detonations. Shock waves rolled throughout the valley. The resulting pressure waves condensed the hot, moist air. The entire earth was under attack.

Then, in the moment between heartbeats, the thunderous explosions and violent flashes were on top of Que and the others. The assembled soldiers had no time to react. There was nowhere to go.

Like a mighty ocean wave that rose and crashed onto the length of the shore, gathering its unbounded energy from the infinite sea, a turbulent wall of dark soil, a rippling curtain of primeval earth, green trees and foliage torn from the ground, along with shredded human bodies, everywhere, lifted a hundred meters into the sky. Torsos, some without legs, flew up the side of the hill through the thick dust and smoke.

Shoulder-fired B-40 rockets ignited and flew crazily into the sky. Hand grenades and mortar rounds exploded. Stultifying smoke and dense dust covered the area. The running destruction continued down the valley to the right of where Que had been sitting. It abruptly stopped.

Knocked unconscious, Bui Van Que was blown thirty meters backward along with the tree against which he had been leaning. Human meat mixed with dirt, tree limbs and vegetation fell on Que, almost burying him.

Que regained consciousness after several minutes had passed. He fought to dig himself out from beneath the rubble, Gasping and choking, Que could not inhale and exhale properly. His lungs had been compressed by the concussion. Confused and laboring hard to breathe, Que, his body covered in dirt, trembled spasmodically. Que's ear drums had been destroyed. Blood was flowing profusely out of both ears. It ran freely out his nostrils and from the swollen, infected gums of his mouth. A sticky deep lavender covered his dark green uniform, what was left of it, as the blood flowed freely down his neck and cheeks. His forehead, just at the hairline, suffered a deep gash. His neck and both arms and shoulders were deeply cut. His left collar bone was fractured.

Que tried to rise on one elbow, but his balance was off. He looked around at what had been jungle. Pockmarked by large, smoking craters, denuded and turned into a raw brown-red, the earth had been instantly transformed into a world of colossal desolation.

In a state of delirium, on the verge of shock, Que was unable to restore his balance. He coughed and vomited, spitting up thick blood and bile. His heart raced. His swollen tongue and seared throat were dry, yet sweat poured off his skin. Que's left eye closed. He could not open it. Blood flowed continuously from the socket.

Disoriented, Que frantically tried to restore his breathing.

Half of a human head and an arm torn from a body at the shoulder lay to his right. A mutilated torso lay hideously to his left with bloody intestines strewn about. Below him, ruck sacks, equipment and pieces of guns—like so many toys—and human body parts lay motionless in the steaming mud and smoking dirt of the valley. Fires smoldered.

The area was drenched in the smell of a stagnant, toxic swamp. The air, thick with dust, was fouled with bitter, noxious fumes from expended explosives and the horrific odor of eviscerated remains.

A dismembered body, blown into a splintered tree, fell to the ground with an inert thud next to Que.

Bui Van Que could not move his left arm. His organs shattered, Que's broken body was hemorrhaging inside. His relatively undamaged eye bulged almost out of its socket.

Que wiped the blood from his eye. He looked skyward.

High overhead, thin-white vapor trails, like the elegant filaments of a spider's web, streaked silently through the blue sky straight east toward the Vietnam coast. The silvery gossamer threads were remnants of man-made flying machines that had passed many miles up directly over Que. The contrast of the beauty of the vapor trails and the complete repulsiveness of the total destruction that had occurred on the ground beneath them only moments before could not have been more striking.

In a second, the world of Bui Van Que and his strike group, already austere, had been literally turned upside down. The soldiers of CT43 who, like Que, had left their families and walked many hundreds of kilometers south, who had been consolidated into a tight compact of humanity, were not to be seen. Que surveyed the destruction, the eradication of existence that surrounded him. The soldiers with whom he had marched would never fight at Khe Sanh. They were extinct, expelled from the living forever. Bodies had been ground into small bits and pieces and blended into the soil to be consumed by the ancient earth.

Que could not avail himself of life-giving oxygen. He could not take in air. Que's lungs, torn to shreds due to high-pressure waves from the explosions, convulsed.

Not able to stand, Bui Van Que sat in the mud. He thought of his grandfather and his girlfriend Hang, whose soft kiss and beautiful eyes he cherished so much. He remembered her tender words beneath Harmony Tower in Hanoi.

Que's eighteenth birthday was only three months away in June. He managed a small smile. Hang would celebrate her sixteenth birthday, exactly three months before his, today, the twenty-third of March 1968.

A wounded, wretched soul, Bui Van Que, the teenage soldier from Hanoi, had come south to serve his country, to fight the American Marines at Khe Sanh. He faced the unimaginable at Vinh, Dong Loc, along the Ho Chi Minh trail, in the rugged Truong Son Mountains of eastern Laos, at binh tram hai muoi and now, in the valleys of Attack Sector N3.

Que slumped forward. The life in his body diminished to darkness.

Bui Van Que was dead.

CHAPTER EIGHTY-SEVEN

INTRIGUE SIX

The NVA artillery bombardment suddenly ended. Explosions no longer echoed across the Khe Sanh Plateau. The Marines could only hear ringing in their ears as they massaged the numbness from their faces. Although they took measures to minimize harm, casualties were plentiful.

Helmets slowly emerged from the trenches and earth bunkers. Bloodshot eyes looked warily around. Each Marine pondered what would happen next.

Below ground, in the operations room of the Combat Operations Center, dust continued to settle. Scratchy chatter and static from the radios in the cramped communications room and the Fire Support Coordination Center filled the void.

Colonel Lownds smoothed out his moustache with his thumb and forefinger. The silence, punctuated only by sounds from the comm gear, was now strange to him. He tilted his head and moved it slightly from side to side, listening.

"They've stopped shelling us."

In his usual composed manner, Lownds looked at each of his officers. "We can't discount the intel Captain Baig gave us. We're gonna see a whole lotta short people with guns within a matter of minutes."

The big battle which Westmoreland had sought surely was about to occur. Lownds felt the bunker vibrate. He heard a muted thundering sound of distant explosions. His eyes widened.

"B-52s."

The rumbling continued.

Colonel Lownds and his Executive Officer Louis Rann, armed with loaded M-16s and pistols on their belts, walked quickly the length of the long corridor to the stairs of the COC. The intelligence and operations officers followed.

Lownds passed the chessboard in the alcove area. He had been playing a new game with an unknown person. Lownds had lost two pawns, a knight and his queen which now sat to the side of the chessboard. His opponent hadn't fared much better, but was in a superior position. In a quick, precautionary move, Lownds castled.

Lownds turned to his XO.

"Louis, stick with me. "I need an immediate status report for each unit on the base. The radios may not be working. I can't wait. I need a visual now."

The regimental CO and his executive officer climbed up the concrete steps and disappeared into the sunlight. Behind them, someone bumped their head into the low concrete overhang. The sound of a metal helmet against the concrete lintel rang out.

Colonel Lownds stopped suddenly at the top of the steps ringed by demolished sandbags. He was shocked into words.

"Oh, man, the NVA's guns sure tore things up."

A private ran up to the COC.

"Sir, your jeep is damaged."

"We're on foot then. Let's go."

Lownds didn't want to be too far from the COC, but he needed to assess the damage first hand. He made a sweeping gesture with his right hand to the south. He turned to the nearest person.

"Make a visual sweep of the area between First Battalion headquarters and B and C Batteries, the 105s. Be sure to check with Captain Gunn and the Thirty-seventh ARVN. Be quick."

Lownds turned in the opposite direction and walked purposefully past Charlie Med, past ASP number two. Craters and debris were prolific. He crossed the road and continued to the south side manned by Bravo Company.

"Captain Baig is right. They're gonna come from the south this time, right through the garbage dump. The last attack at the east end last month was too costly."

Below Lownds' feet, in the trenches and fighting holes, Bravo Company Marines were standing alert and ready. Their loaded guns were pointed out. Belts of brass shells lay in the breeches of their machine guns. Mortar rounds were stacked next to the mortars on the edge of the pits.

Lownds heard a voice.

"Colonel, the radios are coming up."

"Thank you, Lieutenant."

Lownds stopped toward the west end at Alpha Battery.

"Captain Bryant, today's the day."

"We're loaded, Sir. Took it hard, but no serious damage. We're zeroed-in six clicks south."

"Captain, the NVA are in closer, more to the southwest. Got fléchettes, like the 106s?"

"Beehives ready, Sir."

"Make sure the claymores have a clear field of fire."

"All good, Sir, they'll never get this far. We got plenty of support from the fifty cals. They'll kill the bastards like prairie dogs, Sir."

"Captain, stay alert. They're coming."

"We'll nail 'em, Sir. *Semper Fi.*"

The captain's last comment caught Colonel Lownds by surprise. He could not actually remember the last time he'd heard the Marine Corps motto, shortened from semper fidelis. Although he lived by the code, he seldom expressed it verbally. It could come across as presumptive, even contrived. Civilians would never understand. But coming from this young captain from Maine, the two Latin words rang with true sincerity. His heart and courage were in the right place.

"Thank you, Captain Bryant. After all this, son, you can see your wife and go camping in the north woods of Maine, even go to law school. From here on out, everything in life will be easy."

Another wave of B-52s had unloaded their bombs. The earth vibrated.

Colonel Lownds crossed back to the runway and hurriedly made his way down the planking, past the motor pool, onto the aircraft apron, past graves registration and Charlie Med. The influx of wounded was a staggering sight. The water tower was long gone as was the base PX. Torn up, the air control tower was rendered useless.

The colonel, carrying his rifle by the handle, reached the COC, and stood at the steps. Sweat poured down his face. He breathed heavily. Lownds shouldered his M-16 and grabbed a cigar from his vest. He unwrapped the cigar as he spoke to his XO.

"Louis..." Lownds bit off the tip and spit it out. "The NVA may be coming, but no one—I don't care who they are—is gonna stop me from smoking this cigar."

Lownds lit it while he continued to talk. "Maybe the last one."

"Enjoy it, Sir."

Status reports began to flow in from Lownds' staff.

"Colonel, First Battalion Ninth Marines at the quarry. In complete readiness."

"Thanks. One Nine's to move east, if needed. Deliver that message to the CO from me, with my regards."

Colonel Lownds turned to his S3 who had been at his side since having left the COC.

"Castagna, issue instructions to Lima in the Red Sector. Be ready to wheel left."

A small crowd gathered around the colonel. A lieutenant emerged from the teletype bunker. He cupped his hands to his mouth.

"Colonel! TTY for you, Sir."

Lownds turned. He recalled a ribbing the lieutenant received once from his mates about his New York accent.

"Read it to me."

"Sir, supporting artillery from Rockpile and Carroll are lined up with pre-planned fires, Sir."

A captain approached Colonel Lownds.

"Sir, Lima Company reporting. West end is secure."

"Captain, the enemy artillery attack wasn't random. They pinpointed their targets. The ground attack will come from the south and sweep toward the east and west ends of the runway. Guard your backside."

"Got it, Sir."

A messenger approached.

"Colonel, I was sent to report to you, Sir. The land line's cut and the antenna's destroyed. They don't want to use the PRC25, Sir. The NVA can hear us."

"Your report, Corporal."

"Sir, Alpha Company is ready at the north side."

"Corporal, the NVA won't attack Blue or Red Sector in force. Any attack will be a feint. Pass the word to the COs. Be prepared to bring half their men to the south side to reinforce Bravo Company."

"Sir, we have only a few casualties, but all can fight. We're investigating the trail to the water point, Sir."

"Son, this battle won't last an hour. By the time anyone climbs back up from the water point, the shooting'll be over. All guns need to be manned."

Lownds pointed in a sweeping gesture. "You tell your skipper he needs to be ready to reinforce Bravo Company. Now, go."

"Yes, Sir."

Lownds caught sight of a dirty brown-red lump on the ground. He thought it was a dead rat until he looked closer. It was a remnant of a human hand, a partial palm and two fingers.

"My God, bombs blew this guy apart. Pieces of his body rained down on the base."

Another messenger, a second lieutenant, arrived.

"Colonel, lots of hits on Charlie Company, but the men are ready. Our weapons have not been damaged, Sir."

"How's your ammo?"

"All good, Sir."

"The NVA will be aiming straight for the COC from the south. The fighting will be very bad. Prepare to maneuver your men for maximum effectiveness. We will need every hand grenade, every rifle, pistol, machine gun and mortar…and every Marine."

The Khe Sanh Combat Base became a hornets' nest of armed activity.

Canteens were emptied into dry mouths, fighting knives and bayonets were drawn, helmets were adjusted and guns were pointed out of the wire. Lownds heard the distinctive sound of gunners manning fifty caliber and M-60 machine guns. The American encampment bristled like a scorpion.

Another voice: "Colonel, radios are up. Hill 861 and Dabney on 881 are reporting sporadic firing but no assault. Sir, 558 is reporting the same, 950 is scanning the countryside. Will report movement of NVA."

Lownds thought: can they really see that far, in such detail?

"Stay in contact and inform of any change."

A corpsman approached Colonel Lownds.

"Colonel, Plasma is low. Medevac is needed, Sir."

"Cannot evacuate WIAs now. Go back to Charlie Med, get ready to defend yourselves. Make sure every wounded Marine who can fight has a weapon."

The lieutenant who had come from the teletype bunker re-emerged from its steps.

"Colonel! Two messages for you, Sir, one from MACV Saigon."

"Read it, quick."

"COLONEL LOWNDS, YOU WILL HOLD."

Lownds thought. This was the same message Christian de Castries received at Dien Bien Phu.

"And the second message?"

"Sir, from Prov Corps Sir.

"Air strikes on way, B-52 cells diverted, A-4s and A-6s inbound from Tico, Sir."

The A-4s could stay on station for only short periods of time. The A-6s could drop enormous loads of ordnance and remain on target longer.

Four fighter jets laden with bombs screamed overhead just beneath some low clouds. Their exhaust left long black streaks in the sky.

Lownds looked up.

"Hey, those are Air Force F-4s! Where'd they come from?"

The colonel yelled back at the lieutenant still not far away.

"Send this message back: All units ready. Will hold. Lownds."

"Got it, Colonel."

The Marine started back down the steps. Lownds yelled after him.

"Grab your rifle, you're not gonna be on that teletype much longer. And Marine, put your helmet on."

"Sir."

The gravity of the moment was palpable. It's at unique moments like these, that the bond between comrades, regardless of rank, is solidified. A show of camaraderie between junior and senior officers is not typical. But, Lownds was genuine and spontaneous at times, and besides, everyone, at this particular moment, was in the same boat. They were about to kill and some would be killed. A grin crossed the colonel's face.

"Hey, New York..."

Lownds held the stub of his smoking cigar in between his thumb and index finger at face level. Smoke swirled around his head. "Next time I'm in the city, martinis are on me."

The junior officer was caught off-guard. How should he respond to the CO? To hell with it.

"I'll have to learn to smoke cigars, Sir."

Movement on the base, paralyzed moments before during the latest artillery barrage, but now urgent, came to an abrupt halt. The Marines stood ready.

The NVA guns remained silent. Outside the south wire, what would be the killing ground was eerily still.

Lownds looked at his wristwatch. They should have attacked by now. He spoke to his Executive Officer.

"Louis, I have no idea what's happening. Pass instructions to all units to remain at their positions and keep alert. Guns up!"

The Marine 105 and 155 howitzers continued fire with three rounds each at preplanned box locations to disrupt enemy movement.

Overhead, the F-4s returned and flew south. All ordnance had been dropped from beneath their wings. Navy A-6s arrived. The faint, pounding drum-sound of the props of A-1s could be heard in the distance. The Navy jets departed the area to the east as the A-1s stayed on station circling above the base or attacking specific targets. Then, they turned east, too. The skies above Khe Sanh were suddenly clear of low-flying aircraft. Air support had disappeared. For a brief moment, all was quiet.

"Come on, Giap. Show us what you got."

Then, the familiar dull thunder, this time very near, came from nowhere, and yet was everywhere. There was no visual scene, just a constant shaking roar. More B-52s were dropping their heavy ordnance.

"Colonel, MACV Actual on the radio, Sir."

"Lownds descended the steps into the COC. He ducked beneath the concrete overhang and passed the alcove without looking at the chessboard. He grabbed the handset.

"Intrigue Six."

The response at the other end was curt.

"Colonel Lownds, we are confident the Twenty-sixth Marines will come through this battle with honor and victory."

Lownds, recognizing the voice at the other end of the line, responded.

"Thank you, General. The NVA will be cut down, Sir."

"Good luck to you and your Marines. MACV out."

The three Battalions of the Twenty-sixth Marines and the First battalions of the Ninth and Thirteenth Marines, who for weeks had been tasked with the unfamiliar, if not detestable role of landlord, were now about to transform into something more deadly. The siege of Khe Sanh would now be played out. Steeped in the tradition of the Corps, the U.S. Marines at Khe Sanh would honor their forefathers. They would fight. And die, if they must.

The American defenders were hovering on the edge of a cataclysmic confrontation with the same enemy who were victorious at Dien Bien Phu fourteen years before—the same enemy who had encircled the Khe Sanh Combat Base and pummeled it daily with their artillery from Co Roc, the same enemy who ambushed and assassinated Marine patrols, killed friends and comrades, hurled hand grenades and fired mortars and rockets, who left the area outside the wire strewn with their putrefying dead, and who, through indecipherable invective, vowed to kill the Marines—all of this… the final battle was about to be joined.

Or was it?

CHAPTER EIGHTY-EIGHT

THE HONORABLE WILLIAM VACANARAT SHADRACH TUBMAN

The convoy of black limousines left the embassy in Washington, D.C. at six o'clock on the evening of 27 March 1968. The official vehicles and escorting motorcycles, their red lights flashing, turned left from Colorado Street and motored south on Sixteenth Street, across the bridge over the Piney Branch Parkway and, farther on, past the Russian Embassy. The limousines negotiated the chicane around Lafayette Park with its low statue of Andrew Jackson on his horse in the middle. The gable of the White House entrance, brilliantly lit, stood out in majestic, yet solemn display.

The first three limousines proceeded through the gate of the White House grounds and up the sweeping driveway. They stopped just beyond the main entrance to the Executive Mansion. The fourth limousine stopped directly beneath the heavy chandelier that hung from the atrium ceiling of the North Portico. A gold trimmed flag, featuring red and white stripes and a single white star, stood up from each front fender of the vehicle.

Two men dressed in special uniforms and white gloves opened the door to the limousine. A smiling woman stepped out of the car. A man, smartly dressed in a tuxedo, followed her.

Lyndon Johnson, wearing formal evening attire, with an elegantly dressed Lady Bird on his arm, emerged from the front portal of the White House and stood at the top of the low landing. Bothered by events of the day, the President, allowing his mind to drift, couldn't help but reflect about Khe Sanh.

Another man accompanying the visiting dignitaries, also dressed in a tuxedo, stepped forward.

"Mr. President, I have the pleasure to introduce the Honorable William Vacanarat Shadrach Tubman, President of the Republic of Liberia, and his wife, Mrs. Tubman."

An aide to the American President responded equally formally.

"Honorable President and Mrs. Tubman, the President of the United States and the First Lady are honored to receive you in the nation's capital."

President Johnson spoke directly to his Liberian counterpart.

"President Tubman, and Mrs. Tubman, the First Lady of Liberia, it is our pleasure and that of the American people to welcome you to the United States. You are special guests."

State dinners at the White House could be tedious affairs, especially if the guests did not speak English or if, for some quirky reason, they didn't find the food or the company appealing. Dinners had, in some instances, proved boring when the conversations were less than lively.

But, not this night, not with the highest ranked government official from Liberia. There would be no language barrier. Genuine laughter would be abundant.

The meal of duck went off without a hitch. At about eleven p.m., guests began saying their formal goodbyes.

Even though the hours were slipping toward the next day, Mrs. Tubman followed Lady Bird Johnson for a tour of the White House and then to the residential quarters for coffee. President Johnson and President Tubman escaped to the Oval Office.

"Mr. President," Johnson smiled, "would you care for an after-dinner drink, a cognac perhaps?"

"To be very honest, maintaining my image of a convivial African, I'd prefer a cold beer."

"By God," the U.S. President exclaimed as he slapped his knee. He turned to the smartly-dressed butler. "I'll join the convivial African. Make that two cold beers."

Lyndon Johnson never stopped laughing at Mr. Tubman's stories.

A driver named Moses once drove a car into a service station in Monrovia to buy gasoline, but abruptly left.

Johnson raised his eyebrows.

"Why'd he do that?"

Tubman was smiling.

"Mr. President, the fuel inlet was on the side of the vehicle opposite the pump."

President Tubman gulped a taste of beer. "Moses said he was going to find a service station that fit the car."

Both Presidents burst out laughing. President Tubman continued. "He could just as easily have turned the car around in the parking lot."

On the road back to Monrovia from Buchanan, another driver from Guinea named Adama slumped to his right. The passenger in the back seat asked him what he was doing. Adama responded, "Sleeping boss."

Now, on a roll, Tubman followed up amidst the laughter. The same driver ran over a big snake. His only comment was, "The snake's gonna feel the pain."

But, the one account that made the U.S. President laugh the most took place in someone's home. To frustrate thieves, the homeowner, a man nicknamed Bo, who had a shop and a small bar on Roberts Street just around the corner from the Episcopal Church in Monrovia, kept his portable generator hidden away when not in use. President Johnson nearly fell off the couch when he heard that the generator was stashed in a wardrobe under lock and key.

"You mean he had a generator in the damn closet?"

The two presidents talked about affairs in the Congo and how Liberia's infrastructure was developing. Education and health and the development of hydro-power on the St. Paul River were top priorities. Tubman requested continued support of the American people.

"President Tubman, Liberia serves as a model for all Africa. But right now, there is not much we can offer beyond what we are currently doing. I'll be candid. The conflict in Vietnam has us, well, let's just say, by the financial short-hairs."

President Johnson paused for a moment. "You've heard of Khe Sanh, right? It's in the news a lot these days. Tell me, I would imagine the terrain in Liberia is much the same as what our Marines are experiencing around Khe Sanh. Tropical, right? Rugged mountains, lots of rain?"

"Oh, man," the President of Liberia responded. "During a downpour, the streets of Monrovia become rivers."

President Johnson raised his beer glass to his mouth.

"Damn, this tastes good. They won't let me have a beer very often because of my diet."

Tubman finished his beer and placed his glass on a coaster bearing the seal of the President of the United States that sat on the coffee table.

"Mr. President, I know you are busy with issues in Vietnam—with Khe Sanh, as you told me—but please allow me to personally thank you for tonight on behalf of my wife and the Liberian people."

The two Presidents shook hands.

"President Tubman, you are always welcome in the United States."

CHAPTER EIGHTY-NINE

RESCUE...OR RELIEF?

President Johnson, keeping his own counsel, reeled from the public's reaction to the unsubstantiated news that his administration was about to authorize a mobilization of two hundred thousand men, ostensibly for Vietnam. Cognizant of suggestions not to embrace escalation, understanding warnings that he was on a dangerous course that held no chance of success; and finally realizing the USA could not win the war in an acceptable timeframe, the President took solace that the Twenty-sixth Marines were going to be given a badly needed break.

General Earle G. Wheeler, Chairman of the Joint Chiefs of Staff, and General Leonard F. Chapman Jr., Commandant of the Marines Corps, two of the highest ranking officers in the U.S. military, stood before President Johnson in the Situation Room. They made quick preparations for their presentation. General Wheeler unfolded a large map he had retrieved from his briefcase.

"Major Jarell, please lift the model over here, thank you."

The major placed the Khe Sanh Terrain Model on the conference table in front of the President with Wheeler and Chapman standing on the opposite side.

General Wheeler turned his head to the side and coughed.

"Excuse me, Sir. I'm just getting over a sore throat."

"Had a sore throat myself last month, Earle. A stiff scotch would help."

"Perhaps later tonight, Mr. President."

General Wheeler began. "Mr. President, we're about to embark on a large-scale mission to rescue the Twenty-sixth Marines and lift the siege at Khe Sanh."

"Yes, General, I'm aware. Please go on."

"On 1 April, at exactly 7:00 a.m., Vietnam time, Operation Scotland, the defense of Khe Sanh, will end and Operation Pegasus will begin. In a combined operation, the U.S. Marines and the U.S. Army will launch a coordinated assault westward along Highway Nine from a settlement named Ca Lu."

A subtle nod from the President indicated his appreciation of the opening statement and perhaps the general's choice not to use Zulu time.

"Ca Lu is located just where Highway Nine dips south for a few kilometers, then turns west again. We've looked at constructing new roads and bridges up the Ba Long valley, but we are going to re-open Highway Nine, instead. From Dong Ha toward the west, Highway Nine passes through wet terrain. Then it cuts south toward the Quang Tri River, west again and…"

"Go on Earle, no need for the preamble."

"The Marine Eleventh Engineers, Naval Mobile Construction Battalion Five and the Eighth Engineering Battalion First Air Cavalry Division, or First ACD, constructed a staging area and jumping off point just north of Ca Lu called Landing Zone Stud."

The general pointed at the location on the enlarged map. "Right about here, at this corner. Ca Lu and LZ Stud are only about twenty kilometers by road from Khe Sanh, sixteen by air, Sir. They built a short runway for helicopters and fixed-wing aircraft the size of the C-123 Caribou."

"Got it."

Wheeler traced the road from Ca Lu as it parallels the Quang Tri River to the Khe Sanh Plateau.

"The road diverges from the Quang Tri River at the confluence with the Rao Quan River and continues up the Rao Quan valley for a ways. Then, after crossing the Rao Quan River at a switchback, it climbs more steeply before it reaches the plateau. A number of gullies have to be crossed along the way."

"I understand the road isn't even suitable for a fence road in Texas."

"Correct, Mr. President. In some places, it's nothing more than a dirt path. In spots, it passes beneath sheer cliffs."

Wheeler paused. Maybe he should be more detailed. Or, perhaps he was already too detailed.

"Mr. President, please let me know if I'm explaining this too fast. An operation of this size is very complicated with lots of moving parts. It's necessary to introduce the main players and describe their mission. I know there's a lot to digest. I want to be sure what I say is clear, Sir."

"Let's have it, Earle. I'm with you."

"I'll try to make this as simple as I can, Sir."

"Continue on, General."

"Mr. President, to back up for a second, General Westmoreland created MACV Forward headquarters just south of Hue at Phu Bai. General Creighton Abrams was placed in charge there. On about the tenth of March, the structure changed and MACV Forward became Provisional Corps, Vietnam, or PCV, Sir.

"I might add, at that time, General Westmoreland was briefed and agreed to the concept for the rescue of Khe Sanh. He has additional plans, Sir."

"So I understand. We can talk about those later."

"Sir, two offensive initiatives were evaluated. One, the Marines were to invest the A-Shau Valley. And second, re-opening Highway Nine and rescuing the Twenty-sixth Marines at Khe Sanh. The Khe Sanh operation took precedence.

"Planning for Operation Pegasus has been underway since the middle of January, but was interrupted by the Tet Offensive. It resumed on the eleventh of March, Sir. Major General John Tolson, commander, First Air Cavalry Division, prepared detailed plans for the operation in coordination with the Third Marine Division. The duration for Pegasus was debated, but Westmoreland feels the operation should take its own course as a result of the evolving situation. He has emphasized that operations must inflict the maximum amount of damage on enemy forces.

"Prior to the start of Pegasus, First Squadron Ninth Cavalry...the Headhunters,

Sir, will initiate reconnaissance activities in widening circles to facilitate air operations. They will destroy any anti-aircraft capabilities and try to find hard intelligence.

"Second Battalion Fourth Marines and Army Third Squadron Fifth Cavalry and two ARVN battalions, all combined into Task Force Kilo, will push toward Gio Linh, east of Con Thien…near the DMZ. These diversionary operations, way to the east of Khe Sanh, along the coastal plains, will be short lived."

General Wheeler raised his hand to cover his mouth while he cleared his throat.

"Mr. President, on the first day of the operation toward Khe Sanh, First Battalion Seventh Cavalry will open the air assault into Landing Zone Mike. First ACD will attack by helicopter along Highway Nine. They will occupy LZs Robin and Cates north of Highway Nine and LZ Thor, just south of the highway. First Air Cavalry Division will attack with a combination of air and ground assaults to clear the road. They are to seize the high ground through successive helicopter assaults. Large bombs called daisy cutters will clear wide areas of jungle to make LZs."

The President adjusted his glasses.

"Very interesting, General Wheeler."

"The rescue operation will receive intense close air support prior to and during the assault. To support the westward advance, we have brought in additional artillery batteries and large caliber mortars and Marine eight-inch howitzers. We have assembled the largest array of artillery in the war to date.

"Air Force, Navy and Marine attack jets will saturate the area and support the troops as they move forward.

"Second Battalion First Marines will advance westward on the north side of Highway Nine while Second Battalion Third Marines will advance on the south side of the road. Marine Eleventh Engineering Battalion will repair Highway Nine and restore the bridges.

"About a day or two later, Second Brigade, First ACD will swarm into LZs Tom and Wharton. We expect to emplace three batteries of 105s there."

Wheeler stopped to point to the area of the combat base denoted on the model by the words Xom Cham. "Elements of the Twenty-sixth Marines will egress the Khe Sanh Combat Base. They'll link up with the advancing Marines coming from Ca Lu. In a combined maneuver, they will attack Hill 471, just southwest of the base.

"We are investing about thirty thousand troops into the area. We have more held in reserve. The siege will be terminated. Khe Sanh will be rescued."

The general moved his hand over the Khe Sanh Terrain Model westward and northward to indicate the supposed retreat of the North Vietnamese Army.

"We will place the enemy on the run, Mr. President."

Wheeler tapped the edge of the terrain model and continued. "Sir, we expect to be in Khe Sanh within ten days, maybe sooner. Once the area is secure, we will airlift the U.S. Army Third Brigade into the combat base."

Brigades, Regiments, Battalions, Engineers, airlifting men and artillery. The operation was indeed complicated.

"General...this Pegasus operation...wasn't that the code name for some operation during World War Two?"

"Sir, Pegasus is the name of the mythological winged horse, but I guess you could say we borrowed the name. Operation Pegasus was a mission on the lower Rhine to rescue Allied troops trapped behind enemy lines after the battle of Arnhem."

"Well, " the President said, "I don't know much about that, except for the movie ...what was it? *A Bridge Too Far*?

"Earle, what about the Marines on Hills 881 South and 861, and the other hills? What's gonna happen to them?"

"Mr. President, the NVA will not have time to get into any scraps with the Marines on the hills."

"You've told me how rugged the area is and the narrowness of Highway Nine. Won't our boys coming from Ca Lu get pinned down somewhere?"

"Mr. President, with thirty thousand U.S. troops converging on Khe Sanh, the mobility provided by our helicopters and the superior support of our artillery and air power, we have taken sufficient precautions against this scenario. The concentration of American firepower will be so great, the NVA cannot survive."

"General Wheeler, I admire your thoroughness. My congratulations to you and Generals Tolson, Rosson, Cushman and your immediate staff."

"Thank you, Mr. President. I believe..."

The President held up his hand.

"But now, Earle, I want to hear from the Marine Corps Commandant since the vanguard of the ground assault along Highway Nine appears to be with the Marines and it's the Marines at Khe Sanh who will benefit the most."

The President turned his eyes to the Marine officer. "General Chapman, your thoughts, Sir."

Leonard Fielding Chapman, Jr., Commandant of the Marine Corps since 1 January 1968, a native of Key West, Florida, served in the Pacific during World War Two. He was decorated for his actions at Peleliu and Okinawa. Chapman, wearing four silver stars on each shoulder, didn't hesitate to respond.

"Mr. President, the U.S. Marines are a small but elite fighting force when compared to the might of the U.S. Army. We are a tight-knit family. Ever since our founding at Tun Tavern in 1775, the integrity of our military traditions remain very strong. We take pride in who we are. We're called leathernecks. We bear the name proudly. We turn out the most capable officers at Quantico, not more the fifty miles south of here. We've been in some of the toughest fights in military history and have always prevailed. I believe you know the code by which we live. We are loyal to our own and to the United States.

"We are not burdened with massive stockpiles and overwhelming logistics. We react quickly to any situation and adapt to overcome adversity. We embody the can-do spirit.

"Marines are not accustomed to long term siege warfare where we are static. We are not caretakers for some piece of real estate in a remote part of the world. We are given an objective, we achieve that objective and we move to the next one. We like to hit the beach, Sir, if I may use that expression, and keep going. From boot camp to the day he leaves the service, a Marine trains for only one mission: assault."

The Marine general, a straight shooter, continued in a plain-spoken, but polite manner. "I mean no disrespect to my Army colleagues. They also have a prestigious history and they, too, can be justifiably proud. We are all Americans fighting under the same flag.

"Khe Sanh was not of the Marines' choosing, Mr. President, but we have once again adapted to the task and triumphed through the worst of it. I don't mind mentioning that my son Walter is a platoon commander with First Battalion Twenty-sixth Marines at Khe Sanh. I'm proud of him, Sir."

"I can understand, General, as well you should be."

A quizzical look crossed the President's face. "General, there is more to what you are saying. No need to beat around the bush. We're all in this situation together..."

The President smirked. "That's why they call this the Situation Room."

"Mr. President, everyone talks about the siege of Khe Sanh. Those Marines at Khe Sanh have performed remarkably. They have gone above what has been required. They have successfully executed an unfamiliar role imposed upon them.

"Mr. President, Operation Pegasus is a bold military plan. The Marines, the Army, the Air Force and the Navy are working together in this coordinated mission. I'm confident we'll succeed.

"But, I also want to say that I, for one, feel strongly, and there can be no doubt..."

The general paused briefly. "The Marines would never have been defeated at Khe Sanh. The three battalions of the Twenty-sixth Marines and First Battalions of the Ninth and Thirteenth Marines are professionals who have faced down adversity. I believe the country should be indebted to them for their commitment and for what they have accomplished under the most dangerous conditions.

"Implications are that we're being rescued by the U.S. Army. Pegasus is a relief mission, a relief, not a rescue. While re-opening Highway Nine is a relief to all of us, I must say, the Twenty-sixth Marines can defend or, if need be, fight their way out of Khe Sanh. Any insinuation of rescuing the Marines...well, Sir, please. It's laughable. These are the best."

General Chapman stopped talking.

The President removed his glasses and rubbed the bridge of his nose without speaking. A moment of suspense ensued.

His glasses back on, Lyndon Johnson focused his gaze on the Marine Corps Commandant. The President's reddening face was expressionless, almost sullen, that of a judge about to pass sentence; the dourness of an executioner prior to performing his grim duty.

General Chapman looked at the seated Johnson. Had he annoyed, even insulted the President of the United States?

The President's face lightened up with a big grin. Then, with an abrupt laugh, his Hill Country candidness surfacing:

"Leonard..."

Lyndon Baines Johnson slapped the palm of his right hand down hard on his desk. "You're Goddamn right!"

The room fell completely quiet.

"I am proud of those Khe Sanh Marines. This is what America's made of."

General Chapman showed no reaction except for a slight smile that turned the corners of his mouth up.

"General Wheeler and General Chapman, I'm looking forward to good news."

The President rose to shake hands. "Good luck, gentlemen."

The two generals excused themselves.

Now alone in the Situation Room, the President's countenance changed. Tormented for months about something he knew he had to do, the speech he would soon give would declare an important milestone in his administration. Perhaps he had waited too long, but since he made the decision, he was going to stick by it.

CHAPTER NINETY

A VIGILANT AMERICA

The world, the nation and the United States Marines in their isolated outpost at Khe Sanh learned the news almost simultaneously. People were shocked and disbelieving, relieved, even elated. Others felt sympathy, while some harbored disdain.

At nine o'clock at night in Washington, D.C., on the thirty-first of March 1968, the President started a lengthy televised nation-wide speech. Lyndon Johnson, wearing a dark blue suit, a light blue shirt and a red tie, spoke from the Oval Office directly into the television camera.

"Tonight, I want to speak to you of peace in Vietnam and Southeast Asia."

The President's speech addressed many issues. Johnson talked at length about economics, congress, national security and divisions in America. But, the primary focus concerned the conflict in Vietnam. President Johnson declared in a surprising twist, a reversal of his policies.

"I have ordered our aircraft and our naval vessels to make no attacks on North Vietnam."

President Johnson had been seeking a way to begin substantive discussions with the North Vietnamese. Maybe an earnest offer of a bombing halt would compel negotiations. Henceforth, the bombing campaign over North Vietnam was suspended.

But, there was more. Much more.

Saturday, the day before the speech, the weather had been sunny with the promise of a warm spring. However, overnight the temperatures turned bitingly cold and harkened a return of winter.

Sunday morning, the last day of March, began on a drab note. The President rose early. He wanted to be with Lady Bird to welcome Lynda who arrived from the West Coast where she had kissed her Marine husband Charles Robb good bye. Captain Robb was on his way to Vietnam. Lynda was hounded by reporters to the point she was distraught. Her plane trip to Washington lasted all night. Once she arrived at the White House, she went straight to bed, exhausted.

The speech the President was now giving had been in development for days. He spent all of Sunday, virtually to the last minute, revising it: a change here, a different word there, adjustment of a paragraph or two, some re-wording and re-phrasing. One word in the very opening sentence required modification. War was replaced with peace.

It was the ending of the speech, however, that consumed the President's thoughts.

While Lynda recovered from her long trip, the President attended an early service at St. Dominic church in southwest Washington with Luci and her husband Pat.

The President was surrounded for the rest of the day by Arthur Krim, Walt Rostow, Marvin Watson, George Christian, Juanita Roberts and Lady Bird. The phone rang off the hook constantly.

The President asked Ambassador Anatoly Dobrynin to transmit to the Hanoi government his sincerity to end the war. Johnson conferred with Texas Governor John Connally and Hubert Humphrey who was, at that moment, in Mexico City.

At eight that evening, Lady Bird ordered up refreshments. Thirty minutes later, people began to gather in the Oval Office, behind the bright lights.

CBS positioned a camera five feet directly in front of the President's desk. A microphone on the desktop captured his words. A man sitting on the floor in front of the camera, amid a byzantine tangle of electric cables, tended to a spool of yellow paper that was fed into the teleprompter. Words were displayed on the long sheet of paper with holes at each edge for the spindle gear to move it. Long dashes indicated pauses. Some misspelled words were corrected in ink.

The President stared at the camera. His face, ashen and drawn, was suffused with a look of deepening fatigue, of interminable sadness. The furrows in his forehead and his sunken cheeks revealed a lassitude that had been accumulating in the President for months. His hands hung to his sides.

Just a few minutes prior to nine o'clock, Lady Bird walked quietly to her husband's desk.

"Remember, Lyndon, pacing and drama."

Nearing the end of his speech, the last of the words from a despondent-looking President echoed everywhere as the spindle rolled the most important part of the speech up in front of him.

"With America's sons in the fields far away...with America's future under challenge right here at home...with our hopes and the world's hopes for peace in the balance, every day, I do not believe that I should devote an hour or a day of my time to any personal partisan causes or to any duties other than the awesome duties of this office...the presidency...of your country.

"Accordingly, I shall not seek and I will not accept the nomination of my party for another term as your President."

There it was. The thirty-sixth President of the United States was stepping down.

The President, in a solemn voice, continued.

"But let men everywhere know, however, that a strong, a confident, and a vigilant America stands ready tonight to seek an honorable peace..."

The cameramen, photographers and reporters in the Oval Office were stunned, as were those around the country who had not turned off their television sets.

The President's forty-five minute speech ended. The camera stopped rolling, the bright lights were extinguished. The President stood up immediately and turned to his right. Lady Bird, a prideful smile on her face, hugged him.

"Well done, dear. Very noble."

The camera crews began to dissemble and pack their equipment. Noise rose in the Oval Office as everyone bustled about. Lady Bird reached out and touched her husband's shoulder. Her words anticipated what she knew would transpire.

"Oh, Lyndon, I know how difficult this is for you. No one can ask for more than what you have given."

While a follow-up press conference was being held, the Johnsons retired to the living quarters of the White House.

Lynda and Luci gave their father big hugs.

Luci was deeply disappointed. Soon to turn twenty-one, she would have been able to vote for her father in the November elections, an honor now denied. The President put his arms around her.

"Luci, everything will be OK. No need for tears."

"Dad, you're the best president this country's ever had."

"Luci, please..."

"Daddy, you've done so darned much for the United States."

"It's OK, pumpkin. I can't be here forever."

"Daddy," Lynda spoke up. "Luci's right. You passed more legislation, including the Civil Rights Act, than any other President. You created the Departments of Transportation and Education. You provided research funds for disease prevention and Medicare and Medicaid, farm programs, child nutrition and clean air. You've fought poverty, joblessness and discrimination. The list goes on. You helped Mom with her highway beautification program. You set up the National Endowment for Humanity and the Arts and got the Public Broadcasting Act passed. No one could have accomplished what you have. You've been involved with so many worthy causes your entire career."

"Lynda," the President began, "one day, you'll think back to what happened tonight. You'll never forget that America is the greatest country in the world, but right now, it's in turmoil. I may not be able to rid the disharmony and unite our country. I have tried my best, but, well, I think I've failed."

"Daddy, you didn't fail."

"Lynda, I hate to leave public service, but I've made the right decision to step down. I'm going to focus all my energies on ending the war in Vietnam."

The President's daughters stayed with him awhile longer, then retired to their rooms.

Lady Bird looked at her husband. The President was putting up a good front, but she wasn't fooled.

"Lyndon, I know this has been nerve-wracking. You're exhausted. I can see it."

"Lady Bird, Claudia Alta Taylor of Karnack, Texas, my wonderful wife. You've been at my side all of my political career. You've been my foundation through so many crises. You've been the cornerstone of raising our daughters. I wouldn't have known what to do without you."

The President smiled slightly. "This isn't a tragedy. I've finally made the announcement I thought about making during the state of the union address and didn't. It's the decision, about which I conferred with General Westmoreland last November, but didn't follow up.

"Lady Bird, you and I have talked about this for so long. The election will be a fight. I'm not sure I have the energy. The way things are going, chances are I would lose. My health may not allow me to complete another term in office. I'm not going to be like Woodrow Wilson after some stroke."

"Lyndon, I know we've talked about you not running for re-election—I even helped you with some of the speech. I accepted what you were going to say, but I was still not prepared to hear the actual words."

"Do you think less of me, Lady Bird?"

"Oh, Lyndon, don't be silly. You've thought long and hard about this. Both girls are very proud of you, Lyndon, and so am I.

"We'll go back to the ranch and have the biggest barbecue ever. Luci, Patrick, little Lyn and Lynda and Chuck will be there, even Yuki. We'll have a great band. Remember the dance steps Luci taught you?"

"You're right, Lady Bird. A big weight has been lifted from my shoulders."

The President smiled after hearing himself say those words. "You know what is more important to me than anything, darling?"

The President didn't give his wife a chance to answer. "You and Lynda and

Luci are the most important part of me. I would be a very empty man without all of you in my life."

Lady Bird took his hand.

"Lyndon, Texas is your home."

In Vietnam, the news reverberated like a wildfire. Marines were perplexed.

Wait a minute. We're here because the President wants us here. Now, the Prez is copping out? What kind of bullshit is this?

CHAPTER NINETY-ONE

FPO SAN FRANCISCO

Sarah Reickert sat in contemplation at the breakfast table in Westwood. Her soft skin, high cheek bones and the radiance of her eyes, enhanced by the exquisite symmetry of her face, could fool anyone into thinking she was a Hollywood starlet. Her blond hair pulled into a spritely ponytail, Sarah peered through the window of her apartment.

Kids were playing on the dichondra near the swing sets in the shade of willow trees that grew abundantly in the park across the street. The night's rain had stopped. The air, fresh with the smell of orange blossoms and eucalyptus, was invigorating. The palm trees towered above the verdant gardens that blended shades of green into a vivid tapestry. The rose blossoms lining the sidewalks were at their most vibrant red. The sun shone brilliantly, allowing southern California to live up to its claim of paradise on earth.

Sarah picked up the smudged aerogram, the letter from Khe Sanh, mailed from Mobile, Alabama. She read for the tenth time certain passages that Ben Bradford, her old boyfriend, had written. Sarah shuffled her delicate feet under the table, then slid them beneath her chair as she rose up on her elbows. She stared at the crucifix hanging on the wall.

Sarah had made plans for her and her husband to drive to the San Gabriel Mountains for the weekend. She needed to call the cabin owners to confirm their arrival time, well after nightfall, and to make sure the cabin was warm when they arrived. But that task, one of many on her list, was just another distraction.

Sarah, finding any reason she could, kept postponing writing to Ben about the news of her marriage. She thought about not writing at all, in fact. Succumbing to guilty feelings, she finally started a note.

Dear Ben,
I was thrilled to receive your letter.

Sarah stopped. She tore the page from the tablet, scrunched it up and tossed it at the trash can. She twirled the pen in her slender fingers then wrote the date, April 2, which she had forgotten to do before, on a clean sheet. She started her second attempt at the letter beginning simply with:

Ben,

And continuing…

I received your letter of early February that you gave to your friend to mail to me when he returned to the U.S.

This was sounding better; not too personal—a little more distant and cordial.

Sarah pondered how to tell Ben their relationship had changed. "By the time he receives this, it will have been many weeks since he wrote to me," she thought. "The impact may be lessened."

I received it when I visited Mom and Dad in West Covina. I was shocked when you told me you were wounded, but relieved to learn you're OK. News about Khe Sanh is on TV every night.

Sarah thought, "This all sounds trivial."

Ben, I'm very sorry, but your friend Howard died of his wounds. His mother forwarded your letter to me.

Now, the bombshell. "May as well get it over with," she said to herself.

Ben, please try to understand. I met a man at UCLA. We had a few dates together, mostly over beer; nothing complicated. We bumped into each other at a party before Thanksgiving and had a late night pizza. We came to enjoy each other's company. His name is Donovan. He's a doctor; or rather will be in June. He proposed to me. We got married and had a wonderful honeymoon in Hawaii. We're supposed to be moving to San Francisco after graduation.

Ben, I won't ever forget our time together—the football games were the best. UCLA forever! Yea! Beat USC! But, I would never make you happy. One day, you'll find someone; maybe in Timbuktu. After you see the world, you'll know so much more than me. Take care of yourself.

Sarah signed her name and laid the letter on the table. She addressed an envelope, but didn't bother with a return address. Sarah couldn't remember whether she needed to place a stamp on an FPO letter to San Francisco, but she licked one and stuck it on the envelope.

Sarah walked to the corner not far away. She dropped the letter to Ben in a large red and blue U.S. mailbox.

Similar mailboxes on campus had been defaced with a yellow star painted on the horizontal line separating the red from the blue near the top. Sarah paid little attention to this at first until she learned that the star stenciled on the line mimicked the flag of the Viet Cong; a sign of protest against the war in Vietnam.

The letter door closed with a sound of finality. Her letter could not now be retrieved. It was on its way to Khe Sanh, to Ben Bradford.

But, as she walked back, the words she'd written lingered in her mind. Sarah reached the apartment. The telephone was ringing.

"Hello."

"Hi, Sarah."

"Oh, hi Mom. How are you?"

"I'm fine, honey. Whatcha up to, sweetie?"

"Donovan and I are getting ready to go to Lake Arrowhead."

"Oh…I'm sure you'll have fun."

Sarah detected a tone in her mother's voice she had never heard before.

"Hey, Mom, we're really looking forward to seeing you and Dad at Easter."

There was a brief silence at the other end of the line, a certain distance.

Somewhat uneasy, Sarah continued. "Donovan performed a laminectomy last night. I have no idea what that means."

"Sarah…"

"Mom, I just responded to Ben's letter."

"Sarah…Honey..."

"What is it, Mom? Is it Dad? Is Dad alright?"

"Honey, Dad and I are fine."

"Mom, something's wrong."

"Ben's mother asked me to call you. She said she couldn't bear to talk to you just now"

"Mom, you're scaring me. What is it?"

"Sarah, Ben was…Honey, it happened last week."

Sarah's mother hesitated, then, "Sarah, Ben was killed at Khe Sanh."

Sarah gasped.

"Oh, my God! What are you saying, Mom? He sent me a letter that he had been wounded, but that he was all right. I just wrote to him. I mailed the letter…just now."

"Sarah, I'm so terribly sorry. I know how much fun you two had together. Sweetie, if there is anything I can do, just let me…"

"Mom, this must be a mistake."

Sarah tried to form her words. "I…I can't believe..."

"Sarah, darling…"

"Mom, please tell me it's not Ben. This can't be right."

Sarah dropped the phone receiver. It bounced off the table and banged on the floor. Sarah rummaged through the letter caddy on the counter filled with envelopes and notes. She retrieved a black and white snapshot of Ben he had sent to her many months earlier. He was standing alone in front of sandbags and some sort of tent with his rifle in his left hand. Dressed in his utilities with an open collar, Ben's dog tags hung around his neck. He was unshaven and wore a soft Marine cap. He looked healthy, just like she remembered him when they'd dated.

Ben's penetrating eyes and that million-dollar Irish smile reminded her of the many times they spent together at Redondo Beach. Sarah, now crying uncontrollably, threw herself on the bed.

"Please God. Not Ben!"

CHAPTER NINETY-TWO

WE'VE GOT SOME DIFFICULT DAYS AHEAD

Lyndon Johnson entered the Situation Room. Everyone stood to acknowledge the formally-dressed President.

"Gentlemen, please be seated. I regret the agenda change and that it comes so close to the fund raising dinner but…well, that's the White House schedule for you. We need to keep this short."

Johnson looked at his watch: 6:50 p.m. Not late on the East Coast, but near dinner time. He took his seat. "Hanoi has made overtures to us to initiate peace talks. I will leave for Hawaii late tonight for internal strategic sessions. That in mind, we'll hear only from General Wheeler about Operation Pegasus. General, please, Sir."

"Mr. President, the weather precluded helicopter operations in the early morning hours of the first of April, the jumping off date…D-Day, Sir. Nevertheless, First and Third Marines initiated their ground assault along Highway Nine. Part of the highway west of Ca Lu is secure. Vehicles are making their way cautiously. Seventh Cavalry ran into opposition almost immediately.

"The battle for the old French Fort east of Khe Sanh Ville, has begun. A Lieutenant Colonel Robert Runkle was killed, Sir. He and his First Battalion Fifth Cavalry Regiment were airlifted in from LZ Wharton and bumped into a battalion of NVA.

"Elsewhere, our attack helicopters are keeping the NVA at bay, weather permitting. The concern at the moment is the road leading to the Rao Quan River. The vehicles must descend to the valley slowly, then make a tight left turn at a switchback to cross the river."

General Wheeler stood in front of a large map and pointed to the alignment of Highway Nine. He moved to the terrain model. "The Rao Quan crossing, an important objective, will be the last natural obstacle, other than a winding grade uphill to the Khe Sanh plateau."

The President sat back and looked at the terrain model, then over the top of his glasses, to those around him.

"Slow going, huh, General?"

"Yes, Sir. We're not setting land speed records. All the bridges have been blown up or severely damaged. The Eleventh Engineers are improvising crossings. Fighting has been intense at times."

"I see. I can imagine the NVA are not very happy to see the Marines and Army advancing to reinforce Khe Sanh."

"Sir, we will be in Khe Sanh within a few days."

"Khe Sanh or bust, right, Earle?"

"No bust, Sir"

President Johnson saw the door to the Situation Room open slightly. George Christian entered and motioned to Walt Rostow to join him in the hallway. Rostow, also dressed in formal dinner attire, rose and walked outside.

Johnson remembered the passionate discussion with General Leonard Chapman days before.

"I'll just bet those Marines will be pleased as punch to see the U.S. Army. I can just see their faces now."

The President spoke candidly, the tongue-in-cheek irony apparent. "They'll just shit."

Laughter ensued around the conference table. The rivalry between the U.S. Marines and the U.S. Army was well known.

"Thank you, General Wheeler, for the bright news."

Johnson removed his glasses. "Gentlemen, it's 7:20. I'm sorry to rush, but I want to wrap this meeting up before eight. Dinner guests are arriving now. Let's take a break for five minutes before we continue. Coffee is on the table over there."

The pressure of a command appearance and the unpredictable reaction of the President, unpleasant at times, could be nerve wracking. General Wheeler, his presentation complete, was now a spectator for the rest of the meeting.

There was a sudden bustle in the room as chairs were pushed back from the conference table. A calm mood prevailed. Other topics about Vietnam would be covered quickly.

Khe Sanh had vexed the President for weeks. At times, stress would show clearly on his face and color his words and expressions, if not his temperament. But now, the United States was reversing the predicament. Furthermore, Hanoi was interested to start peace talks. The President was making progress.

Richard Helms, forever the organization man, looked at a brown plastic desk calendar sitting on the conference table. The square date sheets had not been turned on the dual spindle since the tenth of March as evidenced by the date staring up from the sheet.

Compulsively, Helms flipped the sheets over, right to left, to show the correct date: April 4, in large letters, and beneath the date, the digits that marked the year: 1968.

Some people were looking at maps of Eye Corps. Each province was clearly denoted: Quang Tri, Thua Thien, Quang Nam, Quang Tin and Quang Ngai. Two people sipping coffee were pointing to the red flags and the route of Highway Nine on the Khe Sanh Terrain Model.

Walt Rostow re-entered the Situation Room and approached the President directly. He spoke softly into his ear.

"Mr. President, may I see you outside, Sir…just for a moment."

The President, coffee cup in hand, stepped into the corridor.

"Mr. President," Rostow said in a low voice. "A few minutes ago..."

Rostow stopped.

"Come on, Walt, I have to wrap up this meeting. The dinner guests are waiting."

"Sir, at one minute past six this evening, Central Time, just past seven o'clock here, Sir, Martin Luther King Junior was shot."

President Johnson's face turned ash white. His mouth fell open in disbelief; his eyes widened behind his glasses.

"Shot? You mean killed? Please don't tell me that."

"Yes, Sir. Assassinated. A single rifle shot, apparently."

The images of the dreadful event in Dallas in November 1963 spilled forth from the recesses of the President's mind like an avalanche.—the hollow sound of multiple gunshots, the triple overpass, John F. Kennedy slumped in his limousine, his shattered head resting on Jackie's lap, Parkland Hospital, the bouquet of flowers lying on the back seat; and the oath of office hours later on Air Force One.

The President stood motionless, his head bowed.

Like so many Americans, he had heard what turned out to be Reverend King's last speech given the day before in Memphis, Tennessee.

> *We've got some difficult days ahead. But it doesn't matter with me now. Because I've been to the mountaintop...He's allowed me to go up to the mountain...And I've seen the Promised Land.*

But, it was the very next sentence of the Reverend's speech that jolted the President. The words hit hard.

> *I may not get there with you.*

The President spoke to Rostow in a slight whisper.

"You're telling me Reverend Martin Luther King Junior is dead."

"George Christian just informed me, Sir. I wanted to tell you a few minutes ago, but you were in the midst of your Vietnam briefing."

The President raised his right hand to his bowed forehead, Rostow continued.

"Lynda informed Lady Bird. She's with your daughters now, Sir."

The President's shoulders slumped.

"Sir..."

"Cancel all plans for Hawaii. Lady Bird and I have to talk with Coretta as soon as possible. I need to read a statement of sorrow and condolence to the Reverend's family from the White House."

"I understand, Mr. President. Is there anything I can do, Sir?"

"Rostow, this is a terrible tragedy. My God, I can't believe what you just told me."

Now more angry than distraught, the President shoved his cup at his security advisor and, out of clear frustration, added, "This coffee is rotting my gut."

CHAPTER NINETY-THREE

GET THE HECK OUT OF DODGE

On the eighth of April, lead elements of Operation Pegasus entered the Khe Sanh Combat Base. The relief operation in Quang Tri Province, spearheaded by the U.S. Marines, supported by the might of the U.S. Army, succeeded.

The Marines re-opened Highway Nine from Ca Lu to Khe Sanh. Army helicopters, flying into the base in droves, brought water, supplies and fresh troops.

The air was filled with a continuous drone of chopper noise. Officers emerged from the dust and commotion, some wearing new uniforms, a few with polished brass.

Colonel David E. Lownds, a veteran of the U.S. Marine Corps for so many years, could hardly believe his eyes. The unfamiliar influx of helicopters, new military personnel and the sudden rush of activity taking place around him were bizarre. The Khe Sanh Combat Base came alive from a hellish, battened-down dormancy.

A few days later, Lownds took particular interest in a conversation he overheard near the COC between two junior Marine officers. One of them was Captain James Bryant.

Captain Bryant removed his helmet.

"Jesus, now the Army is here. This place'll never be the same. I'd rather see the NVA. At least we can shoot at 'em."

Lownds smiled at the statement, the pride of an honorable warrior evident on the Marine's face.

Captain Bryant continued.

"The Army misses the entire battle and now they prance in here in their shiny rotor wing chariots, thinking they're the victors. They'll have everyone believing they saved the Marines, as if we Marines couldn't defend ourselves. 'We friggin' saved 'em.' That's what they'll say. Makes me wanna vomit."

With men like this in the Corps, how can the Marines be less than the best?

Captain Bryant flipped the cigarette butt from between his fingers.

The other officer spoke.

"Bryant, we no longer have to do the Khe Sanh shuffle. We're going back to the world on the freedom bird. Hot showers, hot food, hot women."

Both men laughed.

"You're right. I've got fifty-nine days left, then I'm done with the Marines. I'm gonna grab my wife back in Maine, never let her go, and enroll in law school."

Colonel Lownds remembered the captain liked to brew coffee on an open fire while camping in the woods. He recalled with slight embarrassment the good-natured lecture he had given him about having children.

Bryant's forehead was bandaged. Blood seeped through the gauze.

"Captain Bryant, stand to for a minute, son."

Lownds turned to the other Marines.

"Gentlemen, please allow me to have a word with the captain?"

Then back to Bryant. "Captain, I overheard you're going home to your wife in Maine and you're going to law school."

"Yes, Sir. I've made up my mind."

"Son, tell you what. I can make arrangements for you to leave the base today on a chopper. I think I can get you home sooner than you think, maybe within forty-eight hours."

Bryant smiled immediately.

"Really, Colonel?"

"But you must promise me one thing, Captain."

"Sir?"

Colonel Lownds looked at the young, wounded warrior.

"Captain, you should consider a career in the Marines Corps. The Corps needs good officers, men like you…uh, even if you do become a lawyer."

Colonel Lownds smiled. "You've paid with your blood. You've honored the United States and the Marine Corps. Now, let the Marines honor you with more than a purple heart. I'll write a flattering recommendation for you. It won't get you a medal, but it may get you accepted into law school. The Corps can fund your education."

Bryant's face lit up at hearing such complimentary and motivational words from Colonel Lownds.

"Captain, you've been with me throughout this entire fight. You stood with me, as did others, on the twenty-third of March when we thought the NVA would attack. You've proven yourself an outstanding combat leader. You have what it takes to become an exceptional field grade officer. With a degree in law, you'll be set."

"Colonel, I'll take you up on the letter of reference, but I'm staying with my unit until it's time for me to rotate home. It wouldn't be right for me to leave so easily when the other men cannot. We'll be gone from this place soon enough."

Lownds nodded his head.

"A great career in the Marines is within your grasp."

"Sir, I think you would like to go into business. I'm sure you'll be a success, Sir. Just don't forget that grandfather clock you've always wanted to make. Your son will appreciate it, your grandchildren more so."

Lownds slapped Bryant on the shoulder.

"If you'll excuse me, Captain, a ceremony is about to start and I think I should be there."

Lownds. a Marine whose utilities were filthy, torn and slightly bloodstained; wreaking of sweat and grime; and Colonel Bruce F. Meyers, another Marine whose utilities showed the effects of hardened battle, worn with equal pride, also stained, grungy and dirty, faced each other at attention. Two colonels who had served together as battalion commanders in the Second Marine Division at Camp Lejeune recited words and made gestures as the colors were held high.

Bruce Meyers, from Seattle, Washington, on the west coast of the United States, briskly read his orders directly to David Lownds, from Holyoke, Massachusetts, on the east coast.

"Colonel Lownds, Sir, I relieve you of command of the Twenty-sixth Marines and the Khe Sanh Combat Base."

Lownds responded.

"Thank you, Colonel Meyers. I stand relieved, Sir."

After two hundred forty-five continuous days at Khe Sanh and almost three months of constant bombardment and enemy threats, after so much destruction within and around the Khe Sanh Combat Base, David E. Lownds was going home.

On the twelfth of April 1968. Lownds relinquished the regimental colors to Colonel Meyers.

The siege of Khe Sanh was over.

The change of command formalities, not overly conspicuous, were complete within twenty minutes.

A despondency swept across David Lownds' face. He was no longer needed. But, the emotions were quickly assuaged by the pride he garnished from what the Marines under his command had accomplished.

To round out events, just days before the change of command, Bravo Company First Battalion Twenty-sixth Marines settled an old score. They attacked an NVA complex where a previous patrol, dubbed the Ghost Patrol, had been ambushed on the twenty-fifth of February, more than a month earlier. The Marines would not forget their fallen comrades. In other actions, between the fourth and ninth of April, the Marines assaulted Hill 471 and later, secured Hills 700, 552 and 689.

The assembly of regimental officers made its way quickly to the underground COC. NVA shells began pounding the base in the near vicinity where the ceremony was held. Below ground, Colonel Lownds spoke candidly to the new commanding officer.

"It's time for Lownds to pack up and get the heck out of Dodge."

"Colonel Lownds..."

Bruce Meyers reached for his pack. "I nearly forgot. I was asked to give this to you."

David Lownds opened the package to find a box of Cohiba Panatela cigars and an envelope addressed to him attached with tape to the lid. The note read,

> *Colonel Lownds,*
>
> *Please accept this gift as an expression of my sincere appreciation of your dedication to duty. I and the citizens of the United States are indebted to your service in times of grave danger. I thank you and the Twenty-sixth Marines (Reinforced) for your courageous defense of Khe Sanh.*

At the top of the note, what would be considered a return address, words simply read *The White House*. The signature at the bottom was that of Lyndon Baines Johnson.

CHAPTER NINETY-FOUR

RESURRECTION AND RETALIATION; REDEMPTION AND RECONCILIATION

Easter Sunday, the day of resurrection, was also a day of retaliation. The siege had been lifted, but for companies of the Third Battalion Twenty-sixth Marines who occupied Hills 861 and 881South, their fight was not yet over.

Kilo Company had arrived from Hill 861 and assembled on Hills 881 South and 800 a couple of days before. Together with India and Mike Companies, they intended to do some bad business on the enemy who fired rockets and mortars from Hill 881 North. The time for justice was at hand.

The Marines attacked at dawn on the fourteenth of April. They put on a magnificent show of force. They descended from Hill 881 South into the saddle and, following a wall of U.S. artillery and 106mm recoilless rifle fire, advanced up the slopes of Hill 881 North. The Marines reached the top of the hill and completely destroyed the North Vietnamese units. By nightfall, the Easter egg hunt was over.

Three days later, a wounded Mick Farnsworth, who had returned with his unit to Hill 881 South, contemplated the sorrowful landscape. Still stunned into silence, he surveyed the distant smoking hilltop from its southern sister.

Off the hill's slopes, the tendrils of fog were like those Farnsworth had experienced sweeping through the broad swales in his native Montana during late summers.

India Company had been ordered to depart Hill 881 South. Farnsworth didn't pay much attention to the noise as members of his company prepared to leave their mountain redoubt.

The makeshift gate in the concertina wire, with two uprights and a cross beam, the concertina wire itself where so many NVA had perished, some at Farnsworth's own hands, the trodden pathways, trenches and all the debris of war were being left to history, handed over to archaeology.

As had often happened in the four years since his enlistment, with the recent assault on Hill 881 North being at once the culmination of violence and a catalyst for personal remembrances, Farnsworth slipped into sadness as memories surfaced.

On three separate occasions, Mick Farnsworth had argued with his mother and father to such a hateful degree that in the middle of a winter's night, he opened the door of his parents' house in Hardin and walked into the darkness. Vowing never to see his family again, he abandoned his parents and his siblings. Mick Farnsworth joined the Marines.

But, the shouting arguments and the horrible insults never left his mind. Four years later, after the last bitter fight on 881 North, Farnsworth came to understand how much he regretted his past actions with his family.

Smoke rose from the crest of Hill 881 North and drifted west. As if from a mural of a forbidding landscape, the distant serenity belied the horrors that occurred there.

Farnsworth's boots, their soles torn and all but missing, were about to fall off his feet. His vest, ripped by so many pieces of flying metal, was barely recognizable. Mick's neck was bandaged, as were both his arms. His teeth were filthy, his gums infected. His deeply bloodshot eyes had receded inside his skull only to peer out from their dark hollows. Mick had lost twenty pounds. His face was gaunt.

Mick packed deliberately: helmet, M-16, forty-five, pack and webbing. He lit a cigarette and inhaled, but he was numb to the smoke and the taste of tobacco. The cigarette was balanced between his brown-stained teeth which acted as a vice to hold the slender white paper cylinder in place.

Mick looked at Lenny Clarke who sat immobile next to him.

"The friggin' NVA didn't win, they didn't push us around."

He pointed to Hill 881 North. "We beat the shit out of them over there, the bastards."

Lenny Clarke slid his helmet back.

"I've only been in-country six months. I never want to go through that shit again."

Farnsworth inhaled.

"Lenny, when I came here in sixty-six, Khe Sanh was a bunch of dirty hamlets. I've been in all of them. Khe Sanh town was a little dump of a place. It always smelled like pig urine, cow dung and chicken shit. The terrain here was the same then as it is now. Bad-ass steep, covered in jungle and brush."

Mick lit another cigarette and handed it to his comrade while he continued.

"I heard a Colonel Stent, some Marine, was here in 1937 hunting for tigers. Many years later in 1962, MACV opened a CIDG camp at the base. Civilian Irregular Defense Group. Four words that could be summed up in one word: mercenary.

"In February of sixty seven, the big boys came. Khe Sanh was reinforced. It became a resort. Later that April, all hell broke loose in the hills. The Hill Fights were the worst, man. We worked with the Montagnards, little bastards chewing that beetle nut all the time. They hate the north gooks, but I was never sure if they liked us.

"Out in the open, the grass was always over my head. We fought in every stream, on every side slope…everywhere. The place was crawlin' with NVA. Ambushes, fights, machine guns, screaming gooks all over the place shootin' their RPGs, flying lead, explosions everywhere, the whoosh of napalm. My God.

"We killed about a thousand of 'em. Never saw so many bodies. But, we lost a lotta good Marines.

"I left for Da Nang. Then, I found myself right back here again while they made Khe Sanh look real homey just like Hardin. We built a runway at the base with gravel and planking.

"Six thousand Marines are here. Where're we gonna go now? Khe Sanh's the only home I got."

"Farnsworth, you got a home, man. It's back in Montana..."

"Shit, I ain't got no home. I get stuck up here on this hill for four months, the same damned hill where we killed a lotta gooks a year before. We had 881 North, gave it up, then we friggin' attacked it again. Firefights everywhere.

"I seen skeletons that were dead gooks last year. Bones will lay out there in the dirt forever."

"Who gives a damn, Mick? They're not our bones. Got shot twice. Got the scars to prove it. Got all bandaged up, the promise of a Bronze Star... never got it. But, I'm alive."

"Yeah, Lenny. I know, man. I got shot, too. Hurt like hell."

Mick pointed toward the Khe Sanh Combat Base. "Man, that's Fifth Avenue down there. I don't know who thought this Khe Sanh crap up but whoever it was, he sure as hell ain't here now, just like that Stent guy.

The helo-evacuation slowly depleted the American population of the hill.

Nothing moved beyond the perimeter except burned palm fronds that blew in the breeze. The side of the hill overlooking the Khe Sanh Combat Base was barren and brown. The vegetation on the slopes had been destroyed by bombs, rockets and artillery shells. The denuded soil, so churned up, was lifeless. North Vietnamese bodies lay rotting on the slopes. Military equipment littered the hillside. The hills and valleys, usually lush green throughout the year, had morphed into a dark inertness. However, nature's resilience, revealed by small tufts of seedling grass, promised redemption.

High in the sky, vultures, riding updrafts, circled hungrily above the hill's crest to pounce on the stinking corpses of the North Vietnamese soldiers.

THE PRESIDENT'S SANDBOX

Swirls of brown dust swept across the denuded hilltop and disappeared down the far slope of the mountain.

The area around Hill 881 South had become a graveyard for helicopters. The metal carcasses sat rusting away, to be consumed by the hills.

Mick's nostrils flared at the smell of the dust, the wetness of the lower lands, the carnage, the stench of cremated flesh, the guts, and his own sweat.

Mick Farnsworth felt a spike of panic as horrible images, caught in the evanescent, garish light of the nightly parachute flares, flashed in front of his mind. Immediate death was all too real. The body bunker wasn't too far away. Is it over? Has hell gone away? Did he really live?

Mick hated the hill but had become one with it. The nauseating odor of decaying bodies and the ripe smell of the latrine that made him gag months before now blended perfectly with the pitiable terrain.

The scars on the hill matched his own. The hill was ugly. He was just as ugly. The hill had survived thousands of years. He had survived the last three years. The hill would survive the next thousand years. He would survive his entire life.

Farnsworth wanted to return home in the worst way, but the thought terrified him. He would have to reconcile that from which he ran four years before. It was a burden to pretend loathing against those who did not deserve such treatment. He wanted to see his brother and sister and his parents again, but he couldn't give up the façade.

Without saying anything, Mick stood up. He tossed his cigarette pack to Lenny Clarke, picked up his gear, shouldered his M-16, and walked steadily to the CH-46 that had just landed.

Mick saw the squadron designation HMM364 on the fuselage. He noticed a large number, 12 7/8, above a yellow sign next to the door in the shape of an arrow that read RESCUE.

"Really?"

Mick Farnsworth turned around. He raised his hand to wave to his friend. "Good luck, Lenny."

Once on board, he gazed with detachment out the chopper's back ramp at where he had spent four months of his life—each day a day of possible extinction.

As the helicopter slowly lifted off the mountain, Mick took one last look at a place suspended in time, a place to which he would never return. He said "so long" to the hill.

The CH-46 began its flight. The blades of its giant tandem rotors chopped through the sky. Lenny Clarke decreasing in size, faded away.

Drafts of cooler air swirled throughout the chopper. Mick removed his helmet, laid his head back and took a deep breath.

Farnsworth paid scant attention to the spiritual side of life, but as the big blades thrashed the air above him and the vibrations shuddered through the chopper, Mick realized one thing. By whoever's hand, by whatever measure, he was being given a second chance to do something meaningful. Mick had accomplished absolutely nothing in his life except cause hurt among those who didn't deserve it. He had succeeded at Khe Sanh by keeping his life, a reckless, aimless life he thought was worthless.

Mick Farnsworth would flourish now as a human being. He would make amends with those he hurt. He would seek a new understanding of the family he deserted a long time ago.

Like an eagle in the full grace of flight, the helicopter, flying through wisps of clouds, left the hill and the surrounding carnage far behind. The chopper slid into the valley, an eternal chasm, and disappeared beyond the lip of the plateau.

And just like that, Khe Sanh no longer existed. The chopper, gaining altitude, flew high above the Rao Quan River and turned left. It entered the abyss where the Quang Tri River met the horizon.

The helicopter flew into the void and was swallowed.

CHAPTER NINETY-FIVE

HANGING GARDENS

"Giap," Prime Minister Pham Van Dong said as he looked around Vo Nguyen Giap's home. "You know how much I enjoy visiting your family. Your terrace is always peaceful. I've brought your children some Fauchon chocolate from France."

Even though Pham Van Dong and Vo Nguyen Giap had disagreements, each showed considerable respect for the other.

"Mr. Prime Minister, you're always welcome."

"Giap, we're in the early stages of talks with the Americans."

"So I understand."

"But, the Americans are intent on supporting South Vietnam. Johnson's entreaties do not extend to the unconditional withdrawal of troops."

"Dong, an American withdrawal seems unlikely, America could resume bombing. But, I agree, we can open a dialogue nevertheless."

"Once we rid ourselves of the American imperialists, discipline needs to be instilled in the southern populace through re-education camps. The southerners must learn their old ways are no longer acceptable. The transition will be brutal, but there is no alternative. Opposition will be crushed throughout South Vietnam. We must eradicate those individuals who opposed us. Re-education in communist dogma is a must."

"I appreciate what you say, Dong, but the population of Saigon is many times larger than that of Hanoi. Installing a new government and administering all of South Vietnam will be a heavy burden. The NLF may be good fighters, but they're hopeless administrators."

Giap sipped his tea. "We need to think beyond the war now. We must rebuild our country and pay back our debts."

"Giap, the Russians have offered to build a new bridge across the Red River, but they may have a questionable agenda. And China has extended its hand. The Chinese have been an enemy for so many hundreds of years… can we have confidence in them?"

Giap raised his eyebrows.

"Dong, my dear friend, you surprise me. You have so many friends in China. You are better equipped to answer that question yourself."

Pham Van Dong addressed something more current.

"The Americans' interest in Khe Sanh is waning. The American base will eventually be ours, right, Giap? Khe Sanh may become as famous as Dien Bien Phu."

"Dong, I'm tired of hearing the comparisons over and over. Dien Bien Phu was a national initiative. Khe Sanh was something less. If we lost at Dien Bien Phu, we would have lost our bid for nationalization. With the Americans, we will have to wait a little longer for reunification.

"Early on, I was sure we could defeat the Americans at Khe Sanh. We had the firepower and we had the position. We knew everything about that base and the surrounding hills. We knew when the Marines sent out patrols and when and where to ambush them. We knew when planes were landing at Ta Con. Our big guns controlled the Khe Sanh air strip. There was no way in and no way out."

"Giap, you say all that, but you didn't attack, not in full strength, not like at Dien Bien Phu."

"Dong, there is more to the story. Khe Sanh was a very fluid problem. We could have defeated what was within the American base, just like at Dien Bien Phu, but we could not defeat what was outside the base. We could not compromise America's air power."

Dong changed topics. "The general offensive-general insurrection in the provincial capitals—the Tet Offensive—was a strategic victory…of sorts.

Even though it didn't incite insurrection, it showed our resolve against the interventions of an imperialistic country with a much stronger military force."

Giap tapped the table.

"But, let's not fool ourselves, Dong. The Tet Offensive was also a demonstrative failure. We acted brashly. We didn't prepare for it sufficiently.

"I opposed the big-area warfare strategy the politburo adopted. It was too early to abandon our protracted guerilla war strategy. Our forces did not yet have the logistics that large area warfare requires. Nor did it have the tactical mobility, firepower and command and control systems. I warned that our forces would suffer enormous losses of men and material if we moved to a broad strategy prematurely. Events proved I was correct regarding our losses on the battlefield.

"After the Battle of Hue, the Americans were sure that Khe Sanh was the next target. They positioned reserves which were unmolested. Our reserves were being chopped up. The Americans resupplied from Dong Ha and Da Nang, from relatively short distances, by air. We had to resupply all the way from Hanoi by ground, many times farther, by comparison. Had we attacked in full force, the Americans would have struck back overwhelmingly within twenty-four hours.

"I must admit, however, I did not foresee the benefit that accrued to us on the diplomatic front as a result of the country-wide attacks. The world took note."

Pham Van Dong reached for the teapot.

"Giap, I'm curious. The efforts against Khe Sanh about the third week in March that you approved..."

Giap remembered something he had to do. He turned over his right shoulder and motioned to a guard to tell an aide to come to the garden quickly. Back to Pham Van Dong, he responded in carefully couched words.

"Yes. About that. I chose another tact, a reasonable strategy that was designed to inflict acute damage on the Americans. The initiative revolved around a novel formulation of what we termed Chien Thang strike groups. We thought we had an opportunity, without risking the divisions. I approved the attack of the twenty-third of March knowing the forces were insufficient to make the Americans capitulate, but sizeable enough to cause disruption to their command. A slap in the face.

"But, we failed. We could not overcome the airpower the Americans had. The American B-52s bombed us relentlessly. The most telling incident was the overwhelming destruction of the Chien Thang strike groups."

Vo Nguyen Giap looked at the fish nudging each other in the pond. They were expecting to be fed. "Mr. Prime Minister, a strike group and a special sapper unit were wiped out. And, in less than a minute, a bigger strike group code named CT43 was completely destroyed. Not one soldier made it into combat. We could not continue to incur such losses at Khe Sanh."

Pham Van Dong looked across the garden toward the bomb shelter. A flower fluttered down from the overhead trellis and fell on his shirt. He brushed it off.

"Well, Giap, we have not compelled the American imperialists to leave Vietnam. We must assume a strong stand against them at the negotiating table. We are not going to give in to their false premise that the puppet government in South Vietnam deserves its right to exist."

"Mr. Prime Minister, there will be more battles. I have to choose them carefully. We must continue to build our military and civilian support forces and prepare for many more years of engagements...protracted warfare. We must develop new tactics and acquire more effective weapons. But, the Americans are developing new tactics, too."

"And Khe Sanh, Giap?"

"Khe Sanh? Dong, please. We should stop with the analysis."

"Giap, I'm not sure who will replace President Johnson in the November elections. The war is becoming more unpopular in the U.S., but I don't think we can expect a change in America's militancy."

An aide rounded the side of the house and appeared at the garden settee.

"Mr. Prime Minister, Mr. Minister, I am told you need something."

Giap spoke solemnly without smiling.

"I've read the report from the 675th Artillery Regiment. I want to add the name Lieutenant Nguyen Van Canh on the list of commendation recipients for his leadership at Co Roc."

"Yes, Sir."

"Also, I need for you to make immediate contact with Miss Ngan, my clerk, and deliver an important message directly from me."

"Yes, Sir. And the message, Sir."

"You will tell her that the units in B5T8 have experienced bitter fighting. We have lost many soldiers at Khe Sanh."

Giap paused but quickly continued. "Please relay to her that I personally inquired as to the whereabouts of her husband and…"

To spare the general any inadvertent show of emotion, the aide followed what he thought was Giap's line of thought for his benefit.

"Yes, Sir. I will inform her of the sad news."

Giap caught the verbal nuance.

"No, Major. Please inform Miss Ngan that her husband is safe. His anti-aircraft unit will be deployed back to Hanoi. However, I regret to say he cannot return home for at least a month, maybe two. Tell her I have personally approved his thirty-day leave upon his return at that time."

CHAPTER NINETY-SIX

AMERICA'S FINEST

The daily White House schedule was always grueling. The days were filled with one meeting after another until late at night. The twenty-third of May promised to be long, but it was a special day for the President of the United States.

Lyndon Johnson slept until 8:15 a.m. He ate a hearty breakfast served to his bedside on a silver tray. He washed his meal down with a big glass of orange juice.

George Christian, his hand still on the brass door knob, stepped inside the President's suite,

"Morning. Mr. President, I came by for the night reading."

"Over there on the table."

"Sorry to bother you, Sir."

"No bother, George. I'll be down in about thirty minutes."

After a hot shower, the President dressed in a light gray suit, white shirt and handkerchief, gold cufflinks and dark tie.

Lynda entered the room with a cup of coffee.

"Oh, Dad, you look great."

"Your mother is always telling me I need to wear clothes that make me look, uh…"

"Younger, Dad?"

The President chuckled at Lynda's rhetorical response as he wagged his right index finger at her.

"Well, yeah, I suppose."

"Dad, I brought you the letter from Chuck."

"Oh, yeah. Thank you, sweetheart. When I meet with those French-speaking people today…can't remember from which country…I want to read what your husband wrote about Vietnam."

"I know it's a big day for you today, Daddy."

"I have to meet Congressman Rostenkowski about the tax reduction bill. The awards are immediately after that. You'll be there, right?"

Lynda leaned up and kissed her father on the cheek.

"Of course, Daddy.

"How's my tie look?"

"Very nice, Dad. Relax now."

Lyndon Johnson hugged his daughter as she stood on her tiptoes and laid her head against his chest.

"Daddy, you've got to slow down."

"Oh damn, Lynda, you know I can't."

The President pointed. "Give those folders to me, please, sweetheart. I need to look at Barefoot Sander's memo and I want to read the speech I'll give today."

"Daddy, you're always reading this stuff."

"You're a dear. If I didn't know better, I'd say you're fond of your old pappy."

The hours passed quickly, but not fast enough for Lyndon Johnson. Immediately after his meeting with the congressman, close to noon, the President entered the Cabinet Room. Conversations abruptly ended. Attendees who were seated stood immediately.

"Ladies and gentlemen: The President."

Lyndon Johnson was smiling from ear to ear.

"Thank you, everyone. I'm pleased you could come today."

The President made his way around the large table shaking the hands of General Leonard Chapman, the Commandant of the Marine Corps.

"Hi Leonard, damn good to see you. This is a great day for the United States of America."

"Indeed, Sir."

The President moved on a couple of steps.

"General Jones, good of you to come."

"Thank you, Mr. President. Wouldn't miss this in the least."

"Congressman Brooks, welcome."

Turning back to the left, the President said, "General Walt, thank you for being here."

"My pleasure, Mr. President."

"And Secretary Ignatius,"

"It's a privilege, Sir."

The President thanked the Marines who were invited to attend. One of them sat in a wheel chair. The President shook the young man's hand.

"Son, I'm mighty proud of you."

The young Marine, smiling with unabashed pride, was awestruck.

"Thank you, Mr. President."

The President turned finally to the person who, in his mind, was the most important person in the room. He stared unblinking at the man who was wearing the uniform of the United States Marine Corps. He walked up to him with a purposeful stride. The President stared at the Marine's medals and the silver eagle on each shoulder.

"I want to personally welcome this Marine officer. Damn right, I do."

The President looked straight into the officer's eyes, smiled and extended his big right hand to greet this special guest who was standing rail-straight.

"Finally, I get to meet the famous Colonel David Edward Lownds, the Commander of the Twenty-sixth Marines at Khe Sanh."

"I am honored to be here, Mr. President. And, thank you, Sir, for the box of cigars you sent me."

The President laughed out loud.

"Hope you enjoyed them, Colonel."

"Sure did. Thank you, Sir."

The President gestured to Lownds' face.

"But, what the hell happened to your mustache?"

"I promised my wife I'd shave it off before I came home. She's the top boss."

"Yup, with three women in my home, I certainly understand that, Colonel."

President Johnson's smile broadened. "Too bad, though. It was very distinguished."

"Mr. President, if permitted, may I ask something of you, Sir?"

"Yes, of course, Colonel Lownds. Anything."

"After the ceremony, if it's not inconvenient, would it be possible to see the Khe Sanh Terrain Model for a moment, Sir?"

"Absolutely, Colonel. I'll arrange that for you. Believe me, it's in a safe place."

The President walked to a microphone, hesitated, then spoke.

"It was twenty-three years ago that the Twenty-sixth Marines took part in a mission that some people believed to be impossible—the capture of Iwo Jima, the most heavily fortified island in the world. That mission was accomplished, and the Twenty-sixth—after being awarded a Presidential Unit Citation for its part in that battle—passed from the active rolls of the Marine Corps on into history."

The President talked about how the Twenty-sixth Marines carried the colors into battle in Southeast Asia and how, with six thousand men, they heroically defended the Khe Sanh Combat Base against an enemy with a superior number of troops.

The President went on to make favorable comments about General Westmoreland, saying, "The judgment of this battlefield general differed considerably from that of some here at home who then predicted that Khe Sanh would be another Dien Bien Phu…the base should and could and would be held. For more than seventy days and nights they held despite massive and merciless attacks by the enemy."

The President made other comparisons with Dien Bien Phu and how American tactics at Khe Sanh defeated the enemy. "Unable to conquer," he said, "the enemy withdrew."

The President's speech continued: "Some have asked what the gallantry of these Marines and airmen accomplished. Why did we choose to pay the price to defend those dreary hills?

"All of us in America hope that the road to peace will lead through to the talks in Paris. But it is still not clear that Hanoi is ready for an early or an honorable peace. For our part, we shall seriously and soberly pursue negotiations toward an honorable and peaceful settlement of this war. But this should also be clear: We shall not be defeated on the battlefield while the talks go on. We shall not permit the enemy's mortars and rockets to go unanswered and to permit him to achieve a victory that would make a mockery of the negotiations.

"We have faith that an honorable peace can be achieved in Vietnam. But if there must be more fighting before it comes, then we shall not be found wanting. Brave men such as the Twenty-sixth Marines will carry on the fight for freedom in Vietnam. Soon, God willing, they will come home...But until they do, we shall express—at moments such as these—on behalf of all our American people our great gratitude for the protection they have given us and our great appreciation for their selfless bravery."

The President, ending his speech, turned to the Secretary of the Navy.

"Secretary Ignatius, please read the citation as the streamer is presented to Colonel Lownds and the Sergeant Major."

The President of the United States awarded the highly coveted Presidential Unit Citation to the Twenty-sixth Marines symbolized by a streamer on the flag of the United States Marine Corps.

Although he would not pin them on the uniforms of the recipients—that honor would be left to Secretary of the Navy Paul Ignatius—the Navy Cross was awarded to Colonel David Edward Lownds and the Bronze Star to Sergeant Major Agrippa W. Smith.

The President smiled broadly.

"These Marines are America's finest."

CHAPTER NINETY-SEVEN

DEWEY BEACH

Walt Rostow, holding file folders in his hand, stood at the entrance to the Oval Office. A calm expression on his face, he tapped lightly on the doorframe.

The President stared over the top of his glasses.

"Come in, Walt. I was just reviewing this memo on national parks."

The President pointed to his right. "I've got a stack of papers to look at, but nothing exciting. What's on your mind?"

Walt Rostow continued to stand at the Oval Office entrance.

"Sir, I wanted to remind you of the Hemisphere Festival opening in San Antonio this week. Also, it seems the East Germans have adopted their constitution by a majority vote. Nothing urgent, Sir. Perhaps you don't want to be disturbed."

"Nonsense. Come in, Walt. Like I say, nothing exciting. The Hemisphere sounds terrific."

The President placed the memo to his right. He pointed at it. "The Black Hills and that Mount Rushmore are incredible. I have no idea who carved the presidents."

"Gutzon Borglum was the designer, or rather the artist, I guess you would say, Sir."

"Rostow, now I know why I chose you to be a senior person on my staff. You know every damn thing."

The two men laughed.

"Was Borglum Jewish, Walt?"

"A Mormon, I believe, Sir."

"See, what did I just tell you?"

Walt Rostow was reminded of the time the President made a contrary statement.

"I don't know everything, Mr. President."

"Walt...nothing to be done about the East Germans."

"Sir, also, just so you know. Plans are being developed for Operation Charlie, the dismantlement of the Khe Sanh Combat Base."

Walt Rostow approached the President's desk as he continued talking. "Fighting around Khe Sanh is still intense; lots of gunfire and small arms. No major artillery barrages like before."

"I don't get it, Walt. After all that's happened there over the last several months...and now we're abandoning Khe Sanh?"

"Seems so, Sir. But, on a practical level, with the army and its helicopters, our forces will be more mobile."

The President stared out the window.

"Walt, know what I don't like about the Oval Office?

"What's that, Sir?"

"I never see a sunrise or a sunset. I stand outside and look to the east and all I see is the monstrosity of the Treasury Department building. There's more sunlight in the Texas White House than in the real White House."

The President motioned to the front of his desk. "Sit down, Walt."

"Mr. President, I mentioned a few weeks ago, that I...well, Sir, I'm planning to take a few days off, if you don't mind, a long weekend with my family. We're going to the Delaware coast before the summer crowds—just a four day vacation at Rehoboth. Actually, we've taken a short-term rental in Dewey Beach."

"Of course, Walt, Take five days. The White House can be awfully damn stressful, can't it?"

"I never think about it, Mr. President."

"Things are relatively quiet here now, Walt. The weather is supposed to be nice. Don't get a traffic ticket. The Delaware State Police are tough on speeders…or, so I hear."

Rostow took a seat. Johnson stood from behind his desk. He walked over to the three doors that looked out at the Rose Garden.

"Walt, I'm glad you stopped by, actually. I want to pick your brain about something."

Long evening shadows sliced across the south lawn. Flower buds, their diverse colors portending a bright spring, had come to life after the long, bleak winter. There was more than a hint of green as the President looked toward the Ellipse. His gaze focused farther south.

Beyond the Jefferson Memorial and across the Potomac River, a new person sat at the helm of the Pentagon. Clark Clifford had replaced Robert McNamara and, with that change, came a new scrutiny of America's involvement in Vietnam. Westmoreland did not receive the troops he wanted. His plans to invade Laos were dashed.

"Rostow, we had a horrible mess on our hands at Khe Sanh, didn't we?"

"We certainly did, Sir."

"I don't understand how Giap could have thought that a win at Khe Sanh would have been more beneficial to him than a victory would have been for us. I almost hesitate to ask questions that have been on my mind for weeks."

"Questions about what, Mr. President?"

"Was our strategy in I Corps correct? Were our tactics at Khe Sanh sound?"

"Mr. President, I believe our military actions were perfectly logical and appropriate, given what we knew, Sir."

"Yeah, I understand that, Walt. Maybe I didn't ask the question right, or I didn't ask the right question."

"How so, Sir?"

"Walt, Giap moves sixty thousand men down the Ho Chi Minh Trail. Shit, he probably had more than a hundred thousand men, right?"

Walt Rostow nodded.

"Our intelligence says Giap prepares for a big battle at Khe Sanh. Then, out of the blue, the NVA and VC attack the provincial cities throughout South Vietnam. All hell breaks loose from the sea to the highlands. Hue is just about destroyed. Our embassy is overrun. In the meantime, our Marines are locked up at Khe Sanh under threat of imminent attack, right?"

"Sir, there may be many theories as to the NVA's strategies. We never had deep penetration into Hanoi's military decision-making."

"But, Walt, surely there was widespread disillusionment within the Hanoi government after Tet. The popular uprising didn't happen. The enemy seemed to abandon his strategy of a prolonged conflict in favor of higher stakes in a short period of time, but he got beat up pretty bad. I guess the thing that completely baffles me has more to do with Giap's ego."

"Sir, I'm not following you. Sorry, Sir."

The President looked at the painting of Roosevelt hanging on the wall above the fireplace.

"Why did Giap not attack the Marines at Khe Sanh in full strength?

"Sir, it seems..."

"Walt, if I were to ask that question of the Joint Chiefs of Staff or the CIA, I'd get academic answers based on social indicators, attrition, geo-strategy, economic duress, asymmetric planning and...I dunno what. A lot of closely-couched rhetoric and hypotheses. I'd be drowned in a lot of Harvard hooey, quite frankly—no insult intended personally, Walt."

"No insult to me, Sir. You know I went to Yale."

"Rostow, I know the battle would have been bloody, but I'm confident we would have won. Giap is a confident person, too, however. What kept Giap from attacking full out?"

"Mr. President, I'm not sure I can answer the question to your satisfaction. He did try some sort of attack on the twenty-ninth of February. Then, a month later, in March, his forces never got close."

"Tell me honestly, Walt, what you think."

"Well, Mr. President, Ho Chi Minh, Pham Van Dong and Vo Nguyen Giap relied on their past experience with the French.

"The French would argue they lost Dien Bien Phu because the USA did not support them, when they, in fact, could not support themselves. Giap just whittled them down. No country has come to our aid either at Khe Sanh, but we have the capacity to fight back in a sustained manner. Giap knew that too well.

"Vo Nguyen Giap is not above making big sacrifices to gain a victory, but he is also a very calculating person. He attacks and retreats quickly. His forces can fade into the jungle. However, to make such a big investment with an all-out attack at Khe Sanh, the jungle would not provide any sanctuary from our air power.

"Khe Sanh wasn't the American Dien Bien Phu. If an NVA divisional attack had happened, we would have lost a lot of lives, but Giap would have paid as dearly, even more so. His sacrifice would have been too great with no guarantee of success. That's what I think, Mr. President."

"I don't know, Walt. I don't have any answers myself."

"Mr. President, the Tet Offensive, however poorly planned and executed, was a decisive move on Hanoi's part. It's safe to say the Tet Offensive disrupted our thinking, corrupted our confidence and distorted reality.

"There is a polarization of views about Tet: the enemy lost, and the enemy won. The illusion of urban security was shattered and the offensive undermined popular confidence in South Vietnam's government. But, Tet proved to be an ill-conceived side show. Their country-wide uprising never happened.

"Giap was brought up short at Khe Sanh. He could not afford that kind of loss for a victory that was not assured, at a place he could not have held. Hanoi must have realized the losses were out of proportion to the gains. I recall from an interview with a Polish visitor, Giap described his forces at Dien Bien Phu as being on the verge of exhaustion. I think the same applied in Eye Corps. Khe Sanh was not the battle Giap thought he could win with an all-out assault.

"Looking deeper, the North Vietnamese appear to be resilient and patient, Sir. They see the war in an on-going sense. They are more on a war footing than we are. The Vietnamese have nowhere to go. They don't have great society programs like you've been able to legislate. They are focused on one thing, Sir. After the campaigns in Quang Tri Province, I believe they will reinstate their theory of protracted war."

"Walt, Twenty years from now, I'll still be wondering why Giap didn't attack, It'll be a riddle for the rest of my life—the riddle of Khe Sanh."

"We may never know, Mr. President."

"Enjoy Dewey Beach, Walt."

CHAPTER NINETY-EIGHT

THE PRESIDENT'S SANDBOX

Washington, D.C. was sometimes described as being too far north and too far south. For such a southern city, it could be harshly cold in winter. At the same time, for a city far north of Atlanta, Washington could be uncomfortable in the sweltering heat and humidity of summer. Regardless, four months after the state of the union address, Washington finally emerged into the warm sunshine of late spring 1968.

Lyndon Baines Johnson, the most powerful person in the world, had declined, many weeks before, to run for office again. The Oval Office would be occupied by a new president—maybe a Democrat, perhaps a Republican. The candidates were lining up.

Although Lyndon Johnson was not fond of the White House as a structure, he liked the special attention that came with it. He didn't enjoy all the security and formalities or the food, but he treasured the power associated with the office.

Secretly, however, or perhaps not so secretly, the President found the responsibilities of the highest office in the land to be overwhelming. His popularity continued to slip.

The President sat in his favorite chair in the residential quarters and read the *Washington Post.* He picked up a Leon Uris novel, but laid it back down. *Mila 18* wasn't nearly as interesting as *Exodus.* He reached for his shoes.

Lady Bird, working on some correspondence nearby, turned to look at the President.

"Lyndon, are you OK?"

"Lady Bird, order some vanilla ice cream with chocolate syrup for me in thirty minutes. See if they have any of Lynda's pecan pie in the kitchen."

Johnson left the Presidential quarters and strolled to the Situation Room. He scanned some papers and paced the floor. The quietude bothered the President. What was missing?

He walked over to the Khe Sanh Terrain Model.

The door to the Situation Room suddenly opened.

"Oh, I'm sorry, Mr. President."

Startled, the President turned his head to see a familiar person entering the room.

"So late at night, Major Jarell?"

Garnet Jarell, who had been in the room many times as a senior officer's aide, pointed at the papers and documents.

"I came for the DOD material. Surely there will be other crises and you won't need all these things lying about."

"No problem, Garnet. It's strange without all the craziness of the last many weeks. I just wanted to be here for a few minutes, to take a last look around. I guess I'm somewhat…I dunno…nostalgic—not sure that's the right word—at the sudden halt of all the activity. Damn, a lot went on since January. Khe Sanh, the Tet Offensive, the embassy in Saigon, Hue, Pueblo, Martin Luther King Jr., the B-52 crash—H-bombs on board—the Israelis, the Congo, Berlin. What craziness, huh?"

"Yes, Sir. At times, we didn't know what the outcome would be at Khe Sanh, or with Tet."

The President looked at some maps hanging on the wall.

"Khe Sanh. Major, I never heard those two words before, to any real extent. I have said them so many times lately, that my mind automatically says them internally. Khe Sanh, Khe Sanh…My God, the siege of Khe Sanh."

The President cast his eyes down and touched the edge of the box. "This model has assumed special meaning to me, it became an immutable friend. The Presidential Unit Citation for the Twenty-sixth Marines was well earned."

"I agree completely, Mr. President."

The major placed the lid on the box.

"Wait a minute son. Where are you taking the model?"

"Those guys at NPIC will want it back, Sir. I thought I'd drop it off tonight at Building 213."

The President thought for a moment.

"Tell you what, Major. Bring it to the Oval Office. I may need it later for presentations...who knows, maybe at some Rotary Club function."

Ten minutes later, Major Jarell passed the Secret Service agent in the hallway. He carried the large flat box on its edge by one of its leather handles—like a giant briefcase.

"Mr. President, where shall I put it, Sir?"

"Just place it on the table there, between the couches."

"Have a good evening, Mr. President."

President Lyndon Baines Johnson stood alone and looked at the gray-blue box.

A floor lamp and candle-like light fixtures on the Oval Office wall provided soft illumination that matched the solemnity inside the historic room.

The President removed the lid. He stared at the replication of a foreign terrain in a forgotten corner of the world.

U.S. Marines occupied the very ground that he looked at, in a virtual sense, everyday; the ground on which so much American blood from the sons of so many parents, from so many towns, communities and villages across the breadth of America, had been spilled.

The President thought of the storms that swept across the plains of Texas. He remembered his father and the strength of his mother Rebekah and how she endured rural hardships. He recalled the old iron pump on the back porch of his first childhood home in Hye from which she drew water every day. He thought of the lonesome Hill-country highways and the fox he tried to catch.

Lyndon Johnson's memories swept back to his courtship with Lady Bird and how she enjoyed the bright, Texas wildflowers. He cherished, with sweet fondness, when each of his daughters was born. He could even remember the license plate number on the Corvette he had bought for Luci: BJJ74…or was it 75?

The President smiled at how Juanita Roberts snapped back at him just before a rally for his first senate race: "Dammit, Lyndon, do it yourself."

Lyndon Johnson had started a tradition of having visitors sign what he called friendship stones at the ranch. Johnson never tired of watching sunsets or the Perd'naliss River flowing over the dam in front of his ranch.

He recollected launching his political career in the 1930s from the porch of his childhood home in Johnson City.

After five years of living on Pennsylvania Avenue, the President and his wife would soon leave the White House. *How lonely sits the city that was full of people.*

Johnson thought back to the day the Khe Sanh Terrain Model arrived at the White House and Juanita's reaction to something so ghastly.

The staff, making light-hearted fun of the President, talked behind his back, sometimes with veiled laughter. They soon became more brazen and started commenting openly about the flat square box, giving it a sarcastic name.

Call it what they may, make fun of him all they want, Lyndon Baines Johnson wasn't going to give up the President's Sandbox.

AFTERWORD

The Khe Sanh Terrain Model resides on display in the Lyndon Baines Johnson Library and Museum in Austin, Texas. The model was built from art-construction material common to the day. The wood box within which the model is contained measures forty inches long, by thirty-three inches wide, by three inches high.

On a very hot, cloudless day—16 July 2010—Veterans and a few civilians—twenty-five people in all—made a pilgrimage to Austin from San Antonio where the Khe Sanh Veterans Association held its 2010 annual reunion. They were allowed to see the solution conceived in 1968 to help the President understand the siege of Khe Sanh. Unaltered, the Khe Sanh Terrain Model had never been shown to the public.

Forty-two years before, to the month, on 9 July 1968, Hanoi's preeminent daily newspaper, *Quan Doi Nhan Dan*, published a surprising front page story. Printed in dramatic effect, atypically in bright red ink, the flamboyant headline read:

Tập đoàn cứ điểm của giặc Mỹ ở Khe Sanh đã thất thủ

The attendant story presented outlandish statistics. The newspaper claimed the "People's Army" killed seventeen thousand enemy soldiers including thirteen thousand Americans while capturing another several hundred at Khe Sanh. They shot down four hundred eighty American aircraft and seized several hundred tons of food rations and military equipment. The paper announced the American Highway Nine defense line had been completely shattered. The Khe Sanh front, commanded by General Tran Quy Hai, had been victorious. Khe Sanh was exactly the Dien Bien Phu the North Vietnamese said it would be.

From another perspective, had they understood the meaning of the headline, American defenders would have been incredulous.

Translated into English, the headline read:

The Aggressors' Entire Network of Strong Points at Khe Sanh has Fallen

After the war, the Vietnamese—no longer distinguished as North or South—constructed a crude museum on the combat base. One entry in the guest book made by a U.S. Marine veteran in 2000, provided a brutal truth. Unambiguous, and with clear rebuttal to the headline in *Quan Doi Nhan Dan*, thirty three years before, the personal testimony read.

> *Let me set the facts straight. We (the Marines) left because we were through kicking ass in this area. I have much respect for the 15,000 plus NVA soldiers who died here, they were terrific brave men. But they lost. Sorry. But that's the way it was…*
>
> *—Dennis Mannion, Kilo 3/26 on Hill 861.*
> *Wounded twice. Now a teacher/coach in Cheshire, CT*

The United States Marines were never defeated at Khe Sanh. No Marine garrison fell to the North Vietnamese. Actual loss of American lives was grossly exaggerated by the communist newspaper.

Today, Khe Sanh town is flourishing. Highway Nine, complete with a sweeping bridge over the Rao Quan River, has been reconstructed. The vestige of the Khe Sanh Combat Base is open to all visitors.

For some Marine Veterans who visited the Lyndon Baines Johnson Library and Museum in the summer of 2010, the Khe Sanh Terrain Model may have resurrected images they would prefer to forget. For others, the model may have brought their Khe Sanh saga to closure.

In either case, welcome home.

APPENDIX A

Honored and privileged, the following individuals viewed the Khe Sanh Terrain Model at the Lyndon Baines Johnson Library and Museum, Austin, Texas, 16 July 2010:

Veterans of the Siege of Khe Sanh

Michael Archer	HQ COMM 26th Marines
Chuck Chamberlin	C/1/26th Marines
Bill Foster	HQ COMM 26th Marines
Floyd J. Graham	HQ COMM 26th Marine
Joe Haggard	HQ COMM 26th Marines
David E. Harper	50 TAS USAF
Jim Kaylor	E /2/26th Marines
Dennis Mannion*	K/3/26th Marines
John Mattern	C/1/26th Marines
Bill Maves	E /2/26th Marines
Larry McCartney	E /2/26th Marines

Merle Moritz	E/2/26th Marines
Raul "Oz" Orozco	HQ COMM 26th Marines
Steve Orr	HQ COMM 26th Marines
Michael Reath	HQ COMM 26th Marines
Lee Rimkus	C/1/26th Marines
Nick Romanetz	C/1/26th Marines
Dave Smith	HQ 1/13th Marines
Leland Upshaw	B/3rd Recon
Richard Vaughn	H & S COMM 26th Marines
Steve Wiese	B/1/26th Marines
John Wolfe	3/26/9 MAB

Civilians Also in Attendance

Joan Mannion
Rita Moritz
Gary Foster

Professional Representatives of the Lyndon Baines Johnson Library and Museum.

John Wilson, Archivist
Renee Bair, Assistant Registrar
Ruth Goerger, Museum Technician
Lara Hall, Museum Technician
Michael MacDonald, Registrar

---

*Thanks to Dennis Mannion for arranging the visit to the LBJ Library and Museum, for the group photo of visiting veterans and for compiling their names; and who wrote the poignant entry in the Khe Sanh Museum guest book (see Afterword) in Quang Tri Province, Vietnam on 10 July 2000.

APPENDIX B

PRESIDENTIAL UNIT CITATION TO THE TWENTY SIXTH MARINES (REINFORCED) THIRD MARINE DIVISION (REINFORCED) AT KHE SANH:

For extraordinary heroism in action against North Vietnamese Army forces during the battle for Khe Sanh in the Republic of Vietnam from 20 January to 1 April 1968. Throughout this period, the 26th Marines (Reinforced) was assigned the mission of holding the vital Khe Sanh Combat Base and positions on Hills 881, 861-A, 558 and 950, which dominated strategic enemy approach routes into Northern I Corps. The 26th Marines was opposed by numerically superior forces--two North Vietnamese Army divisions, strongly reinforced with artillery, tank, anti-aircraft artillery and rocket units. The enemy, deployed to take advantage of short lines of communications, rugged mountainous terrain, jungle, and adverse weather conditions, was determined to destroy the Khe Sanh Combat Base in conjunction with large scale offensive operations in the two northern provinces of the Republic of Vietnam. The 26th Marines, occupying a small but critical area, was daily subjected to hundreds of rounds of intensive artillery, mortar and rocket fire. In addition, fierce ground attacks were conducted by the enemy in an effort to penetrate the friendly positions. Despite overwhelming odds, the 26th Marines remained resolute and determined, maintaining the integrity of its positions and inflicting heavy losses on the enemy. When monsoon weather greatly reduced air support and compounded the problems of aerial resupply, the men of the 26th Marines stood defiantly firm, sustained by their own professional esprit and high sense of duty. Through their indomitable will, staunch endurance, and resolute courage, the 26th Marines and supporting units held the Khe Sanh Combat Base. The actions of the 26th Marines contributed substantially to the failure of the Viet Cong and North Vietnamese Army winter/spring offensive. The enemy forces were denied the military and psychological victory they so desperately sought. By their gallant fighting spirit and their countless individual acts of heroism, the men of the 26th Marines (Reinforced) established a record of illustrious courage and determination in keeping with the highest traditions of the Marine Corps and the United States Naval Service.

—LYNDON B. JOHNSON
23 May 1968

ACKNOWLEDGMENTS

Historical mistakes which may occur belong to the author. Characters other than the historical personages, are contrived. Any resemblance to real individuals is a coincidence.

To facilitate approximate English pronunciations, diacritic marks, common in the Vietnamese language, have been omitted from Vietnamese words.

Thanks to CBS for permission to reprint the transcript of Walter Cronkite's statement of February 27, 1968.

Recognition must be given to the following individuals who provided valuable advice and background information:

Annette Amerman
Michael Archer
Kathy Bankhead
Tom Bankhead
Carol Bolton
Tom Bolton
Stacey Bonnacci
Maurice Bourne
Dino Brugioni
Sherry Christmas
Laurie Clayton
Robert Dallek
Robin Davis
Betty Jo DeBusschere
Gary DeBusschere
Robert Destatte
Silas Dreher
Hoang Tran Dung
Tommy Eichler
Donna Elliott
Roger Ferguson
Joey Filosa
Tom Ford
Gilda Freitas
Rick Hoar
Lee Humiston
Dan Jenkins
Wayne Johnson
William D. (Willie) Jones
John Keay
Paul Knight
Sophia Kornacki

Le Van Lan
Simon Letts
Sandy Lownds
Steve Lownds
Ly Tran Ngoc
Mike MacDonald
Tailen Mak
Ben Malmberg
Dennis Mannion
Paul Mather
Bruce F. Meyers
Alex Myers
Mike Najim
Aniko Olah
Nguyen Thuy Ngan
John Pessoni
Glenn Prentice
Merle L. Pribbenow II
Jim Reed
Jack Rollins
Raymonde Rossi
Lori Schoening
Mary Sobrevilla-Gonzalez
Dick Soderberg
Ray Stubbe
Mark Swearengen
Nguyen Tien Thanh
Keith Thomas
Craig Tourte
Nguyen Ngoc Tran
Cathy Tuhey
Marcy Vannoy
Vo Dien Bien
Vu Ha
Nicola Walton
Mike Webb
Craig Willoughby (*no relation to Captain Frank Willoughby*)
Gene Wilkie
John Wilson
Denny Wisely
John Yuill
Chuck Zaloudek
Jane Zaloudek

LIST OF HISTORICAL CHARACTERS

Lyndon Baines Johnson (1908-1975)
Lady Bird Johnson (1912-2007)
Lynda Bird Johnson (b.1944)
Luci Baines Johnson (b.1947)
Hubert H. Humphrey (1911-1978)
Robert S. McNamara (1916-2009)
Earle G. Wheeler (1908-1975)
William Marvin Watson (b.1924)
George E. Christian (1927-2002)
Arthur C. Lundahl (1915-1992)
Ellsworth F. Bunker (1894-1984)
Richard M. Helms (1913-2002)
Robert J. Arrotta (1945-2009)
William C. Westmoreland (1914-2005)
David E. Lownds (1920-2011)
Leonard F. Chapman (1913-2000)
Dwight D. Eisenhower (1890-1969)
Connie Kreski (1946-1995)
Joe DiMaggio (1914-1999)
Rev. Martin Luther King, Jr. (1929-1968)
Maxwell D. Taylor (1901-1987)
John G. Tower (1925-1991)
Walter Cronkite (1916-2009)
Bruce F. Meyers (b.1921)
Arthur B. Krim (1910-1994)
Walt W. Rostow (1916-2003)
Mirza Munir Harry Baig (1932-1971)
Juanita Roberts (1913-1983)
Robert Ellison (1945-1968)
Walter Jetton (1906-1968)
Francois Sully (1927-1971)
Ho Chi Minh (1890-1969)
Vo Nguyen Giap (1911-2013)
Le Duc Tho (1911-1990)
Le Duan (1907-1986)
Van Tien Dung (1917-2002)
Chu Huy Man (1913-2006)
Nguyen Chi Thanh (1914-1967)
Pham Van Dong (1906-2000)
Tran Quy Hai (1913-1985)
Le Quang Dao (1921-1999)
Dong Sy Nguyen (b.1923)
Frank C. Willoughby (1939-2000)
Christian de Castries (1902-1991)

ABOUT THE AUTHOR

Gary Wayne Foster has spent a number of years living abroad. A graduate of University of California at Davis, and holding graduate degrees from University of Alaska and The George Washington University, he first visited Vietnam in 1972. He has traveled there continuously since 1994. He is the author of *Phantom in the River: The Flight of Linfield Two Zero One*, about the 1967 downing of an F-4 Phantom near the Ham Rong Bridge and capture of the aircrew, and *Launching Motor*, a humorous recollection of an early-life event.

The President's Sandbox is his first novel.

46071422R00316

Made in the USA
San Bernardino, CA
25 February 2017